THE DIAMOND DEEP

THE DIAMOND DEEP

||| BOOK TWO *of* RUBY'S SONG |||

BRENDA COOPER

an imprint of **Prometheus Books**
Amherst, NY

Published 2013 by Pyr®, an imprint of Prometheus Books

Cover illustration © 2012 John Picacio
Cover design by Nicole Sommer-Lecht

Inquiries should be addressed to

Pyr
59 John Glenn Drive
Amherst, New York 14228–2119
VOICE: 716–691–0133
FAX: 716–691–0137
WWW.PYRSF.COM

17 16 15 14 13   5 4 3 2 1

Library of Congress Cataloging-in-Publication Data

Cooper, Brenda, 1960–
    The diamond deep / Brenda Cooper.
        pages cm. — (Ruby's song ; bk. 2)
    ISBN 978-1-61614-855-3 (pbk.) — ISBN 978-1-61614-856-0 (ebook)
    1. Teenage girls—Fiction. 2. Revolutions—Fiction. 3. Social classes—Fiction.
4. Space ships—Fiction. I. Title.

PS3603.O5825D53 2013
813´.6—dc23

                                                2013022361

Printed in the United States of America

AUTHOR'S NOTE

This story was inspired by *Evita*, the musical about Eva Peron. It is not an account of a life exactly like Eva's although I watched documentaries about her and read books about her and by her as I prepared this novel.

This is simply the story that Evita's legend teased out of me. Since I am a science fiction writer, I placed this story of love and revolution in the future. In this novel, the culture is a mix of old and new. I am grateful in advance to all of the modern women who will forgive me for the way this story is told. I could set the story far into the future, but I could not remove the patriarchy or the story would not have felt possible. But after all, the patriarchy remains in many places on Earth today.

To women everywhere who have fought for rights and freedoms.
And to Katie Cramer, who still has all of her choices before her.

PART ONE

INTO ADIAMO

CHAPTER ONE

Ruby sat on the edge of the bed, as silent and still as possible. Now, more than ever before, she felt all of the generations that had been born and died in *The Creative Fire*. Their work, their hope, their dreams, and their pain seemed to float around Ruby like a fog of intent.

Joel's quiet breath filled the room, punctuated with the creaks and groans of the great ship around her, the sigh of machinery that filled the space inside with air and delivered water to grow food, to drink, and to clean. Living so near the center not only sounded different, but it felt different; as if the entire mass of *The Creative Fire* centered here on Joel's room.

On their room. It was their room, and she would stay in it. She would share his power, and she would do it well. She had earned it. She would find a way to fit here.

Beside her, Joel rolled over and stretched. She put a hand on his shoulder, kneading softly to work at his stiff muscles. As her fingers worked, Joel's breath lost the even rhythm of sleep.

He pushed himself up on his elbow. "You might as well be pacing."

"I can feel the ship around me. At home," she gestured outward, toward the working habitats, "at home there would be robots going by and children laughing and bells for shift change."

"Isn't your home here now?"

"Of course." The tone of her whisper was a caress to match the hand that trailed along his back. "You worked out hard yesterday."

"Winning has given me more enemies." He touched her hair, stroking it. "You have them, too. You should start working with KJ again. It's been five weeks since the last actual fighting. Get back into routines. I'll send two guards with you."

Ruby laughed. "No guards."

He turned her face toward his. "It's not a request. You don't know who hates you yet. It's a risk of being with me."

"I'll take friends. Like Ani and Dayn."

"Good thing there isn't a stubborn bone in your body."

"Or yours." She fell back onto the bed against him. "Ix!"

"Yes, Ruby." The ship's AI chose a soft female voice.

"Bring up the Adiamo system." She loved having a display in the bedroom. A luxurious manifestation of Joel's power as captain of *The Creative Fire*. The screen sprang to life, presenting a view of a single brilliant sun with two gas giants, and cradled between, two inhabited planets. Tiny lights blinked for the orbiting space stations. "Is that real yet?" she asked Ix.

"It's still the game view. I can see the sun, Adiamo, but we aren't close enough for the cameras to pick up planets or stations."

She frowned and whispered into Joel's ear. "What are we going to find there?"

One hand roamed her torso. "Our home."

"Our destiny."

She closed her eyes. Change. She loved change, she had made change, created it with all of her being.

So why did she feel so unprepared?

CHAPTER TWO

Onor had to work around small crowds in the park on B-pod as he searched for Marcelle. He finally spotted her walking so fast it was nearly a jog, her dark curly hair bouncing against the shoulders of her blue uniform shirt. Onor's face broke into a grin he wasn't really expecting. After all, it had only been a few weeks since they'd last been on a patrol together. She sped up and reached him, smelling like sweat and stim, and punched him in the arm. "Long time."

"Not so long."

"Long if you're me."

He shook his head at her. "Joel wants a report about how dangerous it is out here."

"And you?"

"Wanted to say hi to you."

"That's better."

He felt awkward around her even though she was his next-to-oldest friend. The fighting had changed everything. The different places they'd all ended up had changed them more. The three of them had been inseparable once, but now he was standing next to Marcelle for the first time in weeks. "You could live near us. Ruby's offered to find you work in command."

"She needs me out here more. Someone has to remind people Ruby cares about them."

"She'll be doing that herself today or tomorrow. I overheard her and Joel talking about it."

"Good." Marcelle plucked at his sleeve. "Let's go."

Something above them groaned and the floor gave a slight shudder. Marcelle stopped and turned to look at him. "The *Fire* knows she's going home," she whispered. "Only I don't think she wants to get there."

Onor laughed louder than he meant to.

"Well," Marcelle started walking again. "She seems to be falling apart a little more every day."

"We'll make it."

"Too bad I'm almost the only gray who believes you."

"There are no grays."

"Being able to wear blue and red doesn't make people forget who they really are."

"Do you really believe that?" he asked her. "Isn't it better now?"

"You are so naïve, Onor Hall."

They hit the end of a corridor and Marcelle consulted her journal, sending them left. She stopped and he ran up against her, her back and shoulder suddenly tucked into his body. Warm. She whispered, "How long until we get there? You should know."

"I don't." He forced himself to step slightly back.

"Doesn't Joel tell you anything? Or Ruby?" A slight edge in her voice made him wince.

"No one knows," he replied. "We know how far away Adiamo is, and Ix is working on calculating the other orbits now that it's found one of the gas giants."

"We're close enough for Ix to see the planets?"

"Just Mammot so far. Not Lym."

"So we'll get home this year?"

"Ix will tell us when it knows. I'm as anxious as you are to see a sky."

"I can't imagine it. Nothing above you. What does nothing look like?"

He laughed. "I have no idea."

"You're infuriating."

"If I knew when we'd get home, I'd tell you."

She stopped right in front of him, blocking his way. "Really?"

"Yes."

"Good."

"Be quiet. We're getting near the danger zone."

For the next hour, they patrolled as silently as they could. They noted a pile of debris and Onor pulled out his journal and called a cleaning bot for it, but nothing more eventful happened until they slid out of the maintenance corridors and into the B-pod maintenance galley.

Ruby sat in a chair, a half-full cup of water in her hand. "There you are."

She'd been waiting for them. She wore a flowing green shirt over gray pants and low-heeled gray boots. Her red hair had been pulled back from her face and braided on top of her head, the back left flowing over her shoulders. She looked so beautiful that he felt awkward, his cheeks hot and his tongue tied. The worst of it was that he felt sure she knew what her simple presence did to him.

Ruby rose and gave Marcelle a long hug.

He and Marcelle both waiting for Ruby to speak.

"I've got a few hours before I promised to be in common."

"Joel said you wouldn't be here for a few days."

Ruby ignored his comment. "Ix told me where you two were, and I thought we could be together for a bit." She looked from Onor to Marcelle and back. "I miss how it used to be. Can you tell me how things are out here?"

Marcelle started talking so he sat back to listen.

"It's fractured. The Jackman and Conroy rousted a whole cell of true reds yesterday—I think there were seven of them. They're in lockup. But we didn't see any trouble today. The living areas feel more normal. Most of the repair and maintenance shops are back up."

Ruby looked pleased. "Does it feel better? You know—safer?"

Marcelle got up and poured two cups of water. "We lock the reds up now. That's better than them locking us up." She set the two glasses of water down, making a little show of taking care of Onor. "But it's hard to tell who to trust."

Ruby leaned in and whispered, "Will you keep it secret that I'm here?"

Before they could answer, the door opened. The boy Haric led a much older man in behind him. Ben. Ben looked older than Onor remembered. His eyes were almost buried in shadowed cracks, his face framed with wispy gray hair. He moved stiffly. This man wouldn't be able to chase recalcitrant children through corridors and force them to go home. He still dressed in red, though. Ben's only concession to the new order was that he wore the multi-colored necklace Ruby had beaded him right on top of his shirt where everybody could see it. He stood for a bit, looking at Ruby curiously. "Good to see you're safe."

Ruby took his hand, and kissed it. "You kept me that way for years." Her voice sounded thick, almost choked.

Haric pulled a chair out for Ben and waited until the old man sat down before he looked at Ruby.

"Thank you," she told him. "See you in common in an hour."

Haric looked disappointed at the dismissal, but he obeyed.

After the door shut behind him, Ruby leaned over Ben, giving him a hug. "Can I get you anything?"

"No." Ben looked pleased and awkward in Ruby's arms. "I'm glad you got my message."

She poured him water anyway. "I wasn't sure Haric could find you."

"He found me yesterday. I was overseeing a group of teenagers in E-pod, and it took a while to get here on the train."

"I'm sorry. We haven't got them all repaired yet," Ruby said. "What do you need to tell me?"

Ben gave a her a long, hard look that reminded her of how he used to look at her when she was a child. Like she was being reckless. "You should have more bodyguards with you."

"I've got Onor."

Not true. She'd gotten here by herself.

"You never did listen." Ben shook his head, his eyes unfocused in remembrance. "Not one day. But you've got to be more careful than you used to be."

"Surely I'm safe *here*," Ruby said.

Ben leaned in toward her. "That short blue, Ellis, he's trying to make trouble for you for sure. He's stayed true."

"Sylva's stayed true, too. She's as red as my hair, and a bitch besides."

"So you know this? You're watching for it?" Ben asked. "That some of us might be out to hurt you?"

"Grays? My own people?"

Ben dropped his eyes, like he didn't want to tell her any more. "Lya. She's recruiting women and getting them to hate you. And Ellis and Sylva have a few, at least."

Ruby worried her lower lip. "I didn't know they were recruiting grays."

"I don't know how many," Ben said. "Or exactly who."

Ruby's eyes widened and she spat out, "Joel. What about Joel? Do they intend to hurt him?"

"I expect so."

"Do you know about any plans?"

"Nothing specific. I'll watch for you, let you know. I want you to tell Joel, too. I couldn't get a message to him."

"Did you try?"

"He's surrounded by keepers these days."

Ruby gave a soft smile. "I've not taken good care of you. I'll see that Joel meets you and knows all you did."

"Oh, I know Joel well."

That made Onor curious, but he didn't want to interrupt. Besides, this was their lunch break, and he was hungry. He turned to open the refrigerator, half listening as Ruby chattered with Ben and Marcelle about less critical things like her songs (yes, she was writing new ones) and her mother Siri (who loved Ruby's power and tried to take credit for it). Onor found two orbfruit a bit past their prime, and some stale bread. He peeled the fruit and put the bright yellow-orange slices right on the bread to soften it, then rummaged in the cupboard for stim. The whole conversation felt surreal. If the world were the old way, Ben would be chasing them instead of bringing warnings.

How had Ruby gotten away by herself anyway? Clearly she'd come here to meet Ben.

As they finished, Ruby said, "I've got to go. Either of you coming to hear me?"

"I am," Onor said.

"Me, too," Marcelle added.

Good. She'd have both of them for protection.

Ruby cocked her head at Ben. "Will you come, too?"

"No." Ben pushed himself up from the table. "I've got to start back. I'm on patrol tomorrow."

"All right. Stay safe."

"It's not me I'm worried about."

Ruby gave him yet another hug, as if she were starved for it. They fell silent until the door closed.

"I bet he's lonely," Marcelle said. "It must be tough to be an old red and have to patrol for groups of true reds or true blues."

At least he and Marcelle hunted old enemies and not old friends.

CHAPTER THREE

Even though she'd only leaked her impending visit an hour ago, common was nearly full of people, and someone had found multi-colored ribbons to decorate the doorways with. Ruby remembered many of the faces in the crowded room from training or battles or concerts, or from the victory party.

A plump woman put a hand out to touch Ruby's shoulder, her eyes puffy and red with tears.

"What happened?" Ruby asked her.

"My . . . my brother died. In the fighting. Seeing you reminds me of what he died for."

"For all of us." Ruby leaned in and held her, appreciating her solid form. "He was brave. I'm sorry."

A nod.

"And your name?"

"Louisa."

The woman lifted up a hand, and held out a necklace with blue and red and gray beads on it. Ruby slid the necklace over her head, on top of three others. As she said, "Thank you," she focused on Louisa's face, tried to memorize the way her eyes were set wide over a full mouth. Her right incisor was missing.

She would try to remember them all. These were her supporters, and the backbone of *The Creative Fire*. The people who planted and fixed and fed and cleaned.

The next person who stopped her was a dark haired girl as thin as Marcelle but with straighter hair and a wide scar across her nose, the edges still puckered and slightly pink. Her name came to Ruby from some deep haze of memory. "Hello Min. How did you get that?" She pointed to the scar, which marred a natural beauty.

"I fought for you. This is from a knife." Min's voice held pride and determination, and her chin was high and her shoulders squared off. "They tried to cut my throat."

"I'm glad they missed," Ruby said, trying to keep it light.

Min responded with a laugh. "Me, too." She looked hungry for something, but Ruby couldn't tell what.

"Can I help you?" Ruby asked.

Min hesitated. "I don't know."

"Will you tell me if you think of anything?"

"Yes."

Then a man Ruby knew from logistics, Harold, took her hand and she turned away from Min. He grinned at her like an old friend. Not that she had ever seen him without his smile—it was part of him. He gave her a thumbs-up, dropped another necklace over her head, and faded aside to let her through.

As she climbed up onto the stage, she spotted her aunt Daria watching the crowd. Daria gave Ruby a brief hug and pushed her to the edge of the stage.

Ruby raised her hands above her head and stood still, waiting. "My friends. My family."

They began to call out the names of songs.

"Thank you," she yelled over the noise. "Thank you all."

She stood with her hands clasped in front of her until the crowd quieted.

"Thank you," she repeated. "You helped win this fight. You gave us all more freedom. You supported Joel and you supported me."

More clapping came at her like a wave.

She stayed silent until they quieted, a slow process that seemed to ripple outward from her to the back of the room. "I'm glad to see you."

People kept calling out the names of her songs.

A small disturbance at the back of the room caught her attention, and she noticed Onor escorting someone out the door. She couldn't see the face of the person, or even tell if it was a man or a woman.

Onor had become efficient.

Marcelle stalked the opposite side of the room from Onor, effective, driven, and bouncy as ever. If it hadn't been the wrong moment to do it, Ruby would have burst out in happy laughter. They were all together again.

She had been going to say she needed to talk more than sing, but clearly the crowd wanted song. She closed her eyes and imagined her voice, strong and loud. "Homecoming" bubbled up in her and she started the first verse with no musical accompaniment.

> *Long and dark is our night flight*
> *No stars shine inside Fire's skin, only*
> *Me and you. And love. We're going home*

By the time the last bits of the song faded away, the crowd looked calmer. Children perched on their parents' hips and people had moved closer, like just the one song had driven them together. They needed this, needed unity. It was the best gift she could give Joel, the best reward for his love. The support of her people.

"We are all one," she said. "Everyone on the *Fire* is going home. We will get there soon. A week, a month, a year. Two years. We don't know. We can use the time between now and then to heal and to learn about each other.

"We're not separate anymore. If Joel can love me, if Joel can work to liberate you, then we are one ship." If everyone believed this, it would be so. She took a single step back, lifting her arms.

The crowd cheered.

"We are one."

They cheered again.

Onor and Daria and Haric and Marcelle paced the edges, clapping and watching, and from time to time stopping to have brief conversations.

It felt like a dance.

Someone in the crowd called out, "Sing the Owl's Song."

She shook her head, pleased even though she refused. "This is not a time for a funeral song. It is a time for happiness." She sang two traditionals, one about working and another about the stars. During the second one, she realized it must be from before the journey, a song from home. After all, there was no way to see stars inside the Fire. She lowered her voice so far that the sound of others singing rose above it, so the experience became a group bonding more than a concert.

Two hours passed before the crowd began to fidget between songs and the mothers of toddlers started to sneak away with unruly children. She ended the session the way she had opened it, with the chorus of "Homecoming." She stood on the end of the stage, looking out, wishing she could hold the moment longer. "Thank you."

They began clapping.

She stepped back, and then back again, and only then did the noise begin to dim and shift to the sounds of feet moving and whispered conversations between friends and family.

A small group of admirers caught Ruby at the end of the stage and held her there to answer questions while the rest of the room emptied. Haric stuck by her side, watching her, trying so hard to be like Onor that it made her smile.

A mother with five-year-old twin girls stayed behind to ask Ruby, "How safe will it be at . . . Adiamo. Home? What kind of welcome will we get?"

"I'm sure they're looking forward to seeing us, just like we're looking forward to getting home. Ix says the Adiamo system is a lot like the game."

"I want to live on Lym," one of the girls said.

Ruby smiled. "Perhaps we will. In the meantime, it can't hurt for you to play Adiamo a little more. Learn more details."

The child gave a sweet, solemn nod. "I want to be like you," she added.

"Well, you can sing anywhere."

The woman pulled her offspring closer to her. There was a touch of fear in her eyes, even if none of it came through in her voice. "I want a better life for my girls."

"I know," Ruby told her. "At least we're all equal now."

The woman licked her lips. "Maybe." She took each girl's hand and turned, the children looking back to wave at Ruby.

Marcelle and Onor finished sweeping the room and stopped by her. "Haric and I need to get back," Ruby said.

"Before Ani and Joel go crazy," Haric added.

Marcelle narrowed her eyes. "You snuck out?"

Ruby grinned. "There wasn't anyone to tell me not to come. Joel was meeting with his advisors, and Ani had gone to get Dayn from somewhere. I left them a note."

Marcelle gave her a high sign while Onor looked away. He was so sensitive. His features fit him—high cheekbones in an oval face, dark hair and eyes, eyelashes too long for a man. Sensitive features, the face of someone who spent his time worrying and daydreaming. Ruby had to admit, he was getting good at being a bodyguard. He'd grown strong and wiry with work, and he was even a bit handsome.

"Walk with me?" she asked him.

Onor's answer was to start off while she and Marcelle followed. She loved him. She truly did. They'd grown up together. But she couldn't give up Joel, or what he was doing. Nor did she want to. Joel challenged her in ways Onor never could.

Onor led them into a side corridor and then through a doorway into one of the maintenance corridors. They dodged two cleaning bots and came back out into a bigger hallway surrounded by habs.

"Where are you taking us?" Ruby asked as he twisted into another empty corridor.

"It's a shortcut."

Onor stopped suddenly, flinging a hand up to get attention. "Wait," he hissed.

Marcelle stepped toward him.

Ruby wanted to giggle. Marcelle had never listened to Onor. But she sobered up immediately when his hand leapt for the stunner tucked into his belt. He turned and glanced at Ruby, catching her eyes and looking at the weapon in his hand. Before she had time to understand, the heavy weapon arced through the air toward her.

She caught the gun and pointed it down, her heart racing.

Onor pulled out a second stunner and kept it. Beside her, Marcelle had her own stunner out and was turning to look behind them.

Ruby crouched, making herself small, staying ready to run in either direction, to help either friend.

Onor's breathing sounded loud. Marcelle turned and bumped into her, almost knocking her off her feet. The corridors looked empty behind and ahead.

"It's okay," Onor whispered, his voice quivery.

Ruby stood up and touched his back.

"No," he said. "It's not okay. But it's safe. I think."

What could have made him stutter so?

She stepped around him. A red in full uniform stretched across the floor. His head had been bashed in from behind. One of the rogues? Then some instinct made her empty stomach sour and she leaned over and rolled the body so that she could see his face. Ben's face.

Ruby crumpled in on herself, her knees hitting the hard floor. A thin wail of grief rose around her, filling the corridor, and at first she didn't recognize it as coming from her own heart.

CHAPTER FOUR

Ruby periodically wiped angry tears from her face as she, Onor, Marcelle, and Haric walked warily through the back corridors of the ship. She kept seeing the pool of blood below Ben's head in the corridor. Blood stained the necklace she'd made him, stained her hands, and her hands had stained her new shirt and then her gray pants when she shoved the necklace into her pocket. Blood everywhere.

Ben's death cut deeper than any death from the days of fighting, even deeper than Hugh's. It was like Nona's death, all those years ago.

It would haunt her. It would haunt her a long time.

She would fight harder now. That was how she'd handled Nona dying in her arms, and it was how she'd handle Ben dying in an empty corridor.

From time to time she swiped at tears.

It took well over two hours to get home. At least Onor herded them at a good clip, his worry keeping her tense until they neared the barrier between command and the rest of the ship. Once there, she turned to Onor and said, "Will you do me a favor?"

"What?"

"Check on Ben's body. See that he's treated right, prepared for a full funeral."

"After I take you to Joel."

She cast a meaningful glance toward the door-symbols which showed they were just on the other side of command. "If I'm not safe in there, I might as well give myself up now."

Onor looked like he wanted to refuse, but Marcelle tugged on his arm and said, "You can come back here later. But I have to go home, and I don't want to be alone."

That made Onor go, although he looked pained about it. Bless Marcelle.

Ruby and Haric headed for the map room.

"I wish I hadn't found Ben for you." Haric sounded miserable.

"It's not your fault."

Haric looked up at Ruby. "Ben said nice things about you. He liked you a lot. And he was nice to me."

Not everyone was. Haric tended to place himself in the middle of everything. He was one of those older boys who wanted to be a man so bad it hurt him. Ruby responded, "He was sweet to everyone, and I'm glad you're with me."

"You do need someone to keep you safe."

She smiled for the first time since they'd found Ben's remains, but hid her smile underneath a cough. "Perhaps we'll see something in the map room that will tell us something."

"Can I go in?"

"If you're with me." Not that she knew that, but she didn't really care. When they got to the door, she swiped her wrist in front of the lock and pulled Haric in after her. He stopped stiff beside her, his mouth agape.

The awe on his face reminded her of the first time she'd seen the command table. Command was the only place on the *Fire* with interactive and detailed maps. Sure, Ix could display bits and pieces anywhere for anyone he wanted, but there were no other display screens big enough to show the whole ship in detail.

The map room was roughly half the size of the common room she'd just been singing to hundreds of people in. Unlike common, which had odd corners, this was an exact square with seats neatly fastened to the walls. The square table dominated the center of the room.

Haric raced to the table and stared at the shifting images that showed on its surface.

On the right side, Ani and Dayn sat beside each other on a couch. Ani's dark skin stood out from the white walls. Her hair trailed down her side in a thick, unruly braid. Beside Ani, Dayn was gesturing in the air about something, looking quite convinced about some point or another.

Ruby didn't see Joel anywhere.

Movement from the far side of the room caught her eye. A man she'd seen in Joel's cabinet meetings started straight for Haric. Laird? Yes. He'd led some of the fighters from command, which was more an act of giving orders than of firing a stunner. He'd never shown any appreciation for all her people had done, never welcomed her or Onor or anyone new. She moved to intercept him.

"What happened to you?" he asked. "There's blood everywhere."

"A friend died."

Laird nodded curtly.

She wasn't at all sure he was sorry. It was possible he was wishing *she* had died.

"Why is that boy here?" he demanded.

"I let him in."

"He's not cleared."

Haric had turned to watch them, his back to the table and his eyes wide. His longish brown hair curled over a dirty blue shirt. The knees of his pants were stained by Ben's blood. Not exactly the neat look that permeated command. "Haric is my personal runner."

"Really?"

Surely she could convince Joel she needed one. And Haric knew the ship. "Really. He'll keep our secrets."

The glare on Laird's face told her he had trouble believing either what she said or that she was saying it to him. Maybe both. "You are accountable for him."

"Very well."

Haric's shoulders relaxed a little and he seemed to stand taller, but otherwise he didn't acknowledge that he had been the subject of the conversation. He'd grown up in the cargo bars, so he was used to tense situations. Hopefully he considered this a promotion. "Haric, this is Laird. He is one of Joel's trusted men."

Haric held out a hand. "Pleased to meet you."

Laird gave Haric's hand a very short shake, his facial expression suggesting that touching Haric was about as attractive as a headache. Well, she was getting used to that. Not everyone on this level was charmed by her, either.

Dayn and Ani had noticed the confrontation and flanked her. "What happened?"

The blood.

She nodded at Laird, an attempt at dismissal. He only took a step back and turned, standing with his back to them and contemplating the table but close enough to hear anything she said. "A friend was killed."

"In gray?" Ani asked.

"On the outer level," Ruby automatically corrected her. "He was a peacer. He used to patrol our area. You saw him. On the vid, the day I sang for Owl Paulie. Ben. The big bulky one who stood beside me, the one I gave a necklace to."

"Is that why he was killed?" Haric asked.

Out of the mouth of a child. "I don't know." Ben had been one of the first reds to openly support her, to wear the multiple colors of the revolutionary sign. The idea that he might have died because of that raised a lump in her throat all over again. "We'll find out." She didn't want to talk more with Laird there, so she addressed Ani. "Do you know where Joel is?"

"Right here." His rich, strong voice came from behind her, softening her before she even saw him. She had no idea how he'd slid into the room unnoticed.

Relief filled her.

He looked down at Ruby, his greenish-blue eyes hard. "I heard there was a murder out there."

She felt the tug of him. His presence always warmed and attracted her. Even when he was angry. "I found him. Or, Onor and I did."

"I'm sorry."

"It was brutal. Whoever did it bashed his head in with something heavy." She looked down, her throat thick with new, unshed tears. "I'd just talked to him, just before." She hesitated again, remembering the hug she'd given Ben. "He came to warn me that Ellis and Sylva are still planning a coup. Ben said they want me, but I bet they want you, too." She took in a trembling breath and waited for Joel's reaction.

He looked even angrier, his jaw set tight. She couldn't tell if it was because Ben had died, or she had gone out, or on account of Ellis and Sylva.

In spite of the anger she could feel, he looked neat. That was a signature thing about him; everything in its place. As always. Joel was a little like Ben, she realized. He stuck to his old personae, wore his old uniform. The only visible concession to the new order was a belt her aunt Daria had given him, one Daria'd made herself from braided and dyed tree bark. He took her hand and his face softened a little. "You need to clean up."

Yes. And to be alone with him. "Ani, Dayn. Will you show Haric how the table works and then get him a room near ours?"

Ani nodded, but Dayn mocked her good-naturedly. "Yes, Ma'am. At your pleasure."

They had once both been her keepers, almost jailers, and Dayn had ranked Ani. In the last few months, power had reversed. They still worked well together, but since Joel took command, Dayn had grown ever more sarcastic. She liked that about him. "Thank you, Dayn."

He grunted. A small laugh escaped Ruby's lips in spite of her tired, burning anger.

Ruby worked on the blood in her shirt, periodically double-tapping the water button to demand more than her allotment. It didn't matter, not right now. All that mattered was getting the damned blood out of everything. That, and not crying. She couldn't cry. Joel hated weakness.

When the water finally ran clear, she hung her dripping shirt to dry in the tiny shower. She ran a comb through her hair, then pinched her cheeks to color them. Clad in damp underwear, she walked from the privy to the bedroom. Joel sat on the bad, fully dressed, a serious look on his face. "You shouldn't have been out there."

"Of course I should have."

"I don't intend to scrub your blood from my hands."

She opened a drawer. "Good. I don't want you to. Ever." She faced him and gave him her best smile. "I have to go out there." Her voice still shook a little. She took a deep breath. "It's for you, too."

He pulled her back on the bed, turned so he held her down ever so gently. "Having you safe is good for me."

She stayed still under his arm, thinking about how to handle him in this moment. "We need my people. They won't respect just talking to them through speakers. They need to see us." She took a deep breath. "Besides, that's what we fought for. So I could be here." She wriggled, rolled to a face him. "I fought to be free to go anywhere on the ship. That meant to go home to my people, and to come home to you."

He smothered her mouth with his, and she returned the kiss. Hard. As soon as he lifted some of his weight from her, she pushed him further away and sat up on the bed, crossing her legs in front of her as if she were in a dress instead of nearly naked, and leaning back on her hands. "I will not give up my freedom."

He stared at her, his incredibly colored eyes looking directly at her, blue and green and flecked with gold, and so strong. She loved those eyes, could fall into them. "We have to work together," she whispered.

"We can work together here."

"You could come with me," she countered.

"No." He shook his head and reached a hand out, setting it warm and firm on her calf. His voice was soft. "I've been there before, you know. It's where I met Onor. But right now there is no time. You have no idea how many people need a piece of me, or how many enemies we have."

She did have an idea of the enemies. "I'm among friends out there. I'll be sure Onor or Marcelle or someone is with me." And before he could argue further, "Oh . . . and I told Haric he could help me—be a runner. Can you fix up his security?"

Joel blinked at her, as if barely following the change, then she saw his first smile since she'd come out of the privy. It quirked up one side of his mouth a little more than the other, taking a few years off. He was still older than she was by double, but when she could get him to play, it relaxed him. She uncrossed her ankles and bent slightly at the waist to take his hand from her calf and cup it in both of her hands. "Thank you."

"I didn't say yes."

"Please?"

"Yes."

She would take that as a yes for permission to travel and for Haric.

He let her pull him up beside her and then they were kissing again, her fingers undoing the buttons on his uniform shirt as his hand slid between her thighs.

CHAPTER FIVE

"**S**he's never going to leave him for you," Marcelle muttered.

"I never thought she was." Onor sipped his stim, savoring the bitter taste. The big shared galley was noisy with traffic as people waited for Ben's funeral to start.

"Are you going to be alone your whole life?"

He swallowed. "I don't know."

"I can picture it now. You can sit and watch her sing every day. You can collect a hug every night as she goes to some other man's bed." Marcelle pushed away from their shared table. "I'll be right back." She left too quickly for him to make out the nuances of her expression. She hadn't sounded bitter or mad. Maybe frustrated. He sighed.

This was the first time he'd seen Marcelle since they found Ben's body three days ago, and here she was teasing him about Ruby already. He couldn't remember a time when he didn't know Marcelle. Maybe there was a downside to being known too well.

He sighed and sipped more stim, feeling it crawl along his nerves and wake him up from the inside out. Joel probably knew exactly how he felt, but surely he also knew that Onor respected him. Ruby alone would not have freed the ship, could not have. She'd needed Joel's contacts in command, and his tactical skills. His ruthlessness. He'd needed her support in gray. A relationship built around mutual power.

"Hey." Marcelle slid back into her seat. "Quit thinking so hard. We have work to do. Whoever killed Ben might show up at his funeral."

"You know," Onor mused, "I thought that when we won, we won. That everything would be better. But it's almost as bad."

"It's not as bad." Marcelle gave her cup down to a passing kitchen bot. "Before we won, we knew who was on our side, and it was almost no one. It's harder to see our enemies when they don't show themselves by the color of their clothes. At least there are fewer of them."

"There's more. We used to only see the ones who came to us. Now there's a ship full."

"And a ship full of friends."

"The dangers are a little harder to smell out."

She laughed. It was true, though. Before the day the ship's walls opened between the outer habs where the grays lived and worked and rest of the ship, they hadn't been sure of the *Fire*'s size. There were four levels, each level a ring inward from the outermost skin of the *Fire*. He liked to think of the setup as keeping gray closest to space, to the planets and suns and other worlds that were surely just on the other side of the insulating cargo ring. He imagined that he and Ruby and Marcelle grew up as near to the stars as they could get. When they were kids, Ben had chased them out of all kinds of trouble. Onor swallowed, his throat hot with memory. "I miss Ben already."

"Me, too."

Onor set his own cup on another bot, and stood up. "I'm tired of people dying. Let's go make sure no one else dies today."

When they arrived in common, the big room was already crowded.

"I didn't expect so many people," Marcelle said.

"Ruby wanted everyone on the ship to watch. So orders went everywhere."

Marcelle let out a long, slow whistle. "Wow."

"I bet a lot of people are here just to hear her sing."

"Well they certainly didn't all know Ben," Marcelle muttered.

Sure enough, there were hand-lettered signs with Ruby's name on them, and he saw three shirts with her name worked into them as well: dyed, and in one case, embroidered in multi-colored thread.

Onor touched the pin he and Marcelle wore. The flattened-oval pin was the same shape as the *Fire*, and the only way to tell he and Marcelle were on patrol.

Screens around them hummed alive, still blank but ready. Ix's most commanding voice played from all of the speakers at once. "Please take a seat. We are gathered to honor the life of Ben Lubuck, a member of the peacekeeping force of *The Creative Fire*."

There weren't enough places to sit. Children got pulled fussing into laps and some adults chose to simply lean against any available wall space.

There was no way for this ceremony to avoid echoing Owl Paulie's funeral, where Ben had stood beside Ruby as she sang "The Owl's Song," which—in a way—had started all of this.

Ruby chose to play up the parallel. Everyone in the cramped room with her had dressed in a mishmash of uniform colors. She'd even gotten Joel to change his usual green dress shirt for a gray one. Onor smiled, wishing he'd had a surveillance bot on the wall for that conversation. Instead of the usual two blue attendants, Ani stood at Ruby's side, and beside Joel, Chitt, who had been a red—a peacekeeper—like Ben. Also like Ben, Chitt had supported Ruby's bid for equality early. It also meant there was a green, a blue, a red, and a gray on the stage, all of them wearing mixed up colors now. Onor admired Ruby's choices.

Joel spoke first, his voice booming through the speakers. "Thank you, thank you. Thank you for the honor of your attendance. I don't know how many of you knew Ben, but when we are done with his story, all of you will know him, and will know how much he meant to this ship."

An interesting opening.

On-screen, Joel continued. "Ben started his career as a peacekeeper in command. He was my bodyguard when I was in school. He escorted me to and from school, to and from play sessions, and kept me safe. He stopped a plot to steal Garth's daughter, Alinia. He was hurt in the process, but highly decorated for saving the young woman's life. After he recovered, he was offered a job with fewer physical requirements, but he refused. He asked to go out to gray and help there."

Wow. A whole backstory Onor hadn't known at all. Interesting.

"And now, I'll pass the storytelling onto Ruby Martin." Joel gave a little flourish.

A smattering of clapping started.

She put her hands up, palms out, to request quiet. After it came, she said, "I hope that clapping was for Ben. Without him, I wouldn't be wearing these colors. I wouldn't have sung for Owl Paulie all those months ago. Ben watched over me and my friends when we were children. He failed to report us when we snuck into workshops and onto roofs, although he chased us back home. He gave us grief for bad choices, but he didn't let them ruin us."

Onor felt his eyes sting and his jaw tighten. He had the same memories, the same love for the old man whose body lay wrapped in red cloth at Ruby's feet.

Marcelle's arm slid around Onor's waist and he leaned into her a little, forgetting to watch the crowd.

"Because of Ben, we learned enough fear to be careful. Most importantly, Ben taught us that reds were not all evil. Oh, he could be tough. I saw him turn in a thief once, and catch a man who drank and beat his wife and children. But he didn't overplay his hand on the simple transgressions of childhood. He acted like a father to us. That was something none of the three of us had.

"I met other reds who used their power for evil, who raped, who killed, who tormented."

She paused, and Onor remembered uncountable nights alone. Reds had killed his parents.

Ruby spoke into the silence of his remembering. "Ben was never like that. He never betrayed or hurt anyone. He disciplined, he lectured." Her voice had grown thick but it only made the quiet in common deeper as people strained to make out her words. "He loved."

He held Marcelle's small hand tight while Ruby said, "Ben was a traditional man. He would have wanted me to sing the traditional song. So join with me while I do that. When we're done, I have a special song that I wrote just for you all tonight. But first . . ."

She launched into the funeral song, her voice coming from all around them. She left out all of the frills and trills that had crept into some of her more recent work; she sang as true and traditional as he'd ever heard.

Tears ran down Marcelle's face. He gave her hand a fresh squeeze and leaned over to whisper in her ear. "I'll be back. Save my seat."

"No, I'll come," she said, wiping at her cheeks.

They walked slowly around the room, scanning the crowd. Most people seemed affected by the funeral, quiet or even tearful. There were people he knew. Fingers to touch and shoulders to put a hand on briefly.

He watched for The Jackman, but didn't see him.

Two boys pelted along a wall with makeshift guns and almost knocked him down, but he managed to avoid them.

The song trailed off. Ruby held the last note for a long time, her voice strong. She fed from these people, from being watched.

She spoke. "Thank you for joining me. We wish Ben good travels."

Then the ritual started—the picking up of the body, the careful slide of corpse and board down the chute and out to become space debris among the stars. Maybe there was something good for Ben to see out there. Maybe, like the song suggested, the dead among the *Fire*'s crew would meet Ben in space. He snorted. A child's hope.

The world had lost someone good.

Ruby turned back toward them, a faint trail of tears visible on her cheeks. "Ben was a symbol—he was red through and through. He held the highest ideals of a peacekeeper. He should be an example to all of you who once wore red.

"We, the crew of the *Fire*, must be one people, for we will be home soon and we must speak with one voice." She took Joel's hand. He stepped forward, the move a little scripted.

"We are facing the unknown," Joel said, "and we must face it together."

That was the perfect opening for "Homecoming," but Ruby moved directly into a song Onor had never heard. He was still walking and watching, so he didn't catch all of the words. The chorus repeated three times:

> *Together we are a seed*
> *Preparing to open in the light*
> *Of Adiamo. To flower.*

"Now," Ruby said, "Now we must all be together. We must forgive the past and we must stop killing. Now is the time to whisper your own small last goodbyes to Ben if you haven't done so yet, to do a last honor. Tomorrow, we will have a festival. A new festival."

She hadn't told him about that.

He found Marcelle. "What do you think?"

"I think it was brilliant that she didn't mention Ben was murdered. Everyone knows it, and they all know she knows it, but she's taking us higher."

Onor recalled the way he'd imagined the death song being sung for Ruby herself. "I hope she doesn't get herself murdered."

Marcelle frowned. "I bet she's planning on attending as many of the festival spots as possible."

"I'll stay with her," Onor said.

Marcelle gave him a long look, and he wasn't quite sure what he saw in her eyes. She was as almost as tall as he was, so it was easy for her to lean over and kiss him right on the lips. "Good."

CHAPTER SIX

Ruby paced the command room, threading through people dressed in finery, careful not to meet their eyes or stop to talk, She needed to think.

It was time for another celebration. Past time. Bright banners streamed digitally across all of the screens in the *Fire*, proclaiming tonight the Festival of Hope. She imagined people all over the ship getting ready, finding their best clothes, doing each other's hair.

Joel was elsewhere with his commanders.

Jaliet had helped her choose a purple dress belted in gray. It swung loosely around her hips, the color shifting and changing with her movements. She felt pleased; Jaliet had driven her staff to create a color that Ruby had never seen rendered in fabric.

She paced the room slowly, full of pent up energy. Ix had told her it could still be months before they got close enough to home to make voice contact, especially now that the *Fire* only moved at about a tenth of the speed it used between systems.

Just yesterday she'd heard the rumor again—that Adiamo would be abandoned. To believe that would be to accept death aboard the struggling *Fire*. So, assuming there *were* people, what would they be like now? Although she didn't understand why, Ix and Joel and others had told her more time passed in the Adiamo system than on the ship.

"Ix?" She spoke to the air. In this room, that was enough.

"Yes, Ruby?"

"Could we start schools? To learn what we knew when we left home?"

There was a slightly longer silence than usual. "What do you want to know?"

She shook her head. Customs would have changed. Joel had helped her see that one of the great weaknesses of the *Fire* was that knowledge didn't change fast or go deep. She had learned to repair bots, but she would never have been able to build one.

Her hands fisted, and she took a deep breath and forced them to relax. "Can you make a list of what we used to know and don't know anymore?"

"Knowledge slip is a matter of degree. You have all been taught the skills you need for your jobs."

Damned AI. "Will you or won't you?"

"I will try."

She came up beside Haric, Ani, and Onor, who were leaning over the map table. Four pods blinked orange. The others were yellow or green. Ruby touched Ani's shoulder. "What did you ask it?"

"Where you can go safely tonight."

Ruby squinted at the colors, memorizing the red ones. "How did you decide?"

Haric answered. "Onor asked Ix where people are saying bad things about you."

Ruby frowned. "Then that's where I should go."

Onor looked exasperated. "Some days I swear you have a death wish."

Ani interrupted the potential argument. "We're classifying your enemies. There's Lya and her crowd. Not too dangerous, although Lya's still mad enough to slap you."

Ruby laughed. "I can take her. And there's Ellis and Sylva. Do you know where they are?" That was a group she might just avoid.

Haric answered. "Not in the outer levels. Not on command. So that leaves them in between." He glanced at her. "You could stay away from there."

Hardly. "What about cargo?"

"Colin keeps that. It's safe."

She smiled at Haric's defense of his old boss.

Joel came up behind her. "Are you almost ready?"

"Yes, sweetheart." She loved the way she smiled at the sound of his voice. "Can we start in cargo?"

"I'll order the train to take us there."

The cargo bar hummed with activity. Most of Colin's strength seemed to be on display: men and women with well-muscled limbs, stunners, and the periodic scar or disfigurement that went with hard work. These were the people who lived in the shadows of the ship, trading on goods, information, and services that the formal power structure needed but couldn't perform itself.

Colin came up to greet them, clad all in black. His clothes matched his graying black hair and intense dark eyes, and the tiniest bit of black beard. "The beard's new," Ruby commented.

He laughed. "With you rogues in charge, I needed to look more dangerous."

"So you're not going to obey us either?" Joel smiled as he said it.

"And lose my reputation like you've lost yours?"

"Someone has to lead," Joel said.

"Better you than me." Colin took Ruby's arm. "Can I get you a drink?"

"We want to talk to people."

"Later. Let me get you a drink."

"Wine," she said.

Joel leaned down and gave her a hug. "I'll catch up to you."

She watched him walk away. Even from the back, even from a distance, he made her feel short of breath.

When she focused back on Colin, he was looking at her quizzically. "You really do love him, don't you?"

"Don't you?" she shot back. "No matter what you want to believe, he is your captain. He's very good at his job."

Colin laughed. "He's a better captain than the old one." The gentle pressure of his hand on her arm steered her toward the bar, where she hopped up on a seat and crossed her legs, being careful not to muss her dress. Colin brought her wine and poured a glass of still for himself. As he handed her the glass, he said, "How is it? Being close to the top?"

"Harder than I thought."

He gestured expansively around the room. "It's been ten times as hard to keep this place going as it was to compete for the top spot."

He meant more than the bars. Colin controlled a whole population of strongmen and misfits that he glued together with a combination of power, promises, and a sense of home. "How different is it now that Garth's out of power?"

He laughed. "We never cared much who ran things. Going home is a bigger deal. There's far more people coming here for drinks or dances or songs. Change makes people crave ways to forget it."

She sipped at her wine. "Your drinks here are always too sweet."

He ignored her comment. "Is Joel going to let you come sing for us again?"

"Of course."

He looked skeptical.

"Well," Ruby said, "There's still a few strays to round up. We won, but there's people who won't accept that. Surely you hear stories."

"In a bar? Never." He tilted his head back and poured the entirety of his glass of clear still down his throat, barely reacting.

"I'd fall over if I did that."

He laughed.

"We need to focus on what happens when we get home." She set her glass down. It wouldn't do to get tipsy so early in the evening.

"Can you tell people when that might be?"

"No. If I knew, I'd tell."

"Then what good are you?"

She missed everything about the outer level. As she moved from the inner circles to the outside, the *Fire* seemed to go from clean to gritty, from back-stabbing to brutally honest. "Will you show me more about the cargo holds? Take me through them? I'm trained for null-g."

He narrowed his eyes. "Why?"

"That might be our wealth when we get home. And I have no idea what's in them."

"I'll talk to Joel."

"I can make my own decisions."

He gave her a long thoughtful look. "You should stop that. It's dangerous." He ran a finger across her cheek, sending heat into her belly.

He'd always been attractive, and she'd always resisted. She leaned away from his touch. "I need to lead from in front. That's why people respect me."

"That's a dangerous way to do it."

"You should try it sometime."

"You know nothing," he said. He looked away, but not fast enough to hide the hurt she hadn't meant to cause him.

CHAPTER SEVEN

Ruby's feet throbbed even though she wasn't standing on them. They'd spent an hour visiting two parks out in the working levels of the ship, and now they were headed one level inward by train. Ani and Dayn and a few others had caught up with them, and sat talking softly near the back of the train car. Ruby let her head rest on Joel's shoulder, lulled into dozing dreams by the low conversations around them, the soothing whoosh of the train, and the warmth of Joel's arm against her back.

The whine of metal on metal snapped Ruby's eyes open, and Joel's arm tightened around her. His other arm shot out and braced them as the train car jerked and jerked again.

They inched forward and came to a complete stop. Dim light showed the outside walls, just a touch more gray than the black of the deep tunnel.

Ruby stood and peered through the window.

Joel stood beside her, close but not touching. "What do you see?"

"Nothing yet. Doors and darkness."

Behind them, Onor started yelling at people. "Up. Be ready."

The train jerked forward, rocked, and jerked forward again. Ruby barely managed to keep her feet under her.

The station and train doors aligned. Actually, one door, and with only a small window in it. Nothing more than a maintenance stop.

Perhaps the *Fire* had another damned problem. But if so, she hadn't felt it or seen it, and surely Ix would have used the train car's speakers to tell them about it.

The station door opened.

Joel shoved Ruby behind him. His stunner appeared in his hand as if it sprang there by his will alone. Onor stood beside him, fumbling with his own gun. Haric was a step behind Onor and next to Ruby, his face ashen with fright.

The train doors slid open.

Ruby didn't have a weapon. She peered around Joel's back. The room was full of men and women wearing pure red and blue, a protest in color. They pointed stunners at the train doors, aimed, shot.

The bodyguard closest to Joel fell, fast but loose, the boneless crumple of the stunned.

Joel fired once, twice, his shoulders moving against her as he aimed again.

He stood completely exposed, as exposed as their attackers' front line. The groups were maybe twenty steps apart.

A scream from inside the station drove their enemies toward the train car.

Ani tugged on Ruby's arm, pulling her back as the orderly group outside turned into a mob and rushed the train doors.

Joel twisted oddly and leaned toward her. She leaned back into him for a moment to hold him up, then stumbled.

He fell on top of her, face to face. He caught some of his weight on his arm, crying out. At least Joel wasn't the dead-weight of the completely stunned, although he must have taken a partial hit. His eyes were wide, like the idea that he could be hurt had startled him.

Ruby hissed for Ani.

People fought hand to hand, clogging the train's doorway.

Onor and Haric were in the front.

Ruby spotted Ani's dark skin through the legs of a tall guard who leaned over her and Joel.

From behind her, a barked command. "Down!"

Onor ducked, pulling Haric down with him. The guards fired over them.

Ani scuttled up and she and Ruby each took one of Joel's arms and tugged him back. He struggled and then found his feet, standing up near the back of the train car. His left arm hung loosely at his side and a grimace of pain marred his features. He turned toward the door but Ruby held him back. "Wait until you're steady."

He grimaced but obeyed. He climbed up on one of the train seats and looked over the heads of their defenders.

Ruby stood beside Ani, trying to make sense of the chaotic movement. Screams and grunts came from inside and outside the car. The stunners were too quiet to hear over the chaos of commands and counter-commands.

One of their guards fell backward into the train, hitting his head on a seat and gashing his scalp. He had been stunned, and didn't react at all to the blood pouring down the side of his face from the fresh gash. Ruby cursed, and told Ani, "Keep the blood out of his eyes and put pressure on the wound."

She reached across the man's inert body and picked up his stunner, which had fallen on the other side of him. She checked it for charge. It was good, barely used at all.

She stood up behind the other guards. There were at least twenty or twenty-five attackers standing close outside the train door. None had gained entrance. A few sprawled on the ground, as stunned as the guard who now lay bleeding behind her.

She looked for a face she knew among the attackers, found it. Sylva. Right there in front, her small pinched features pulled tight by her high gray ponytail. She wore a full red uniform and held a stunner in each hand. She seemed to be searching the train car.

Looking for Ruby.

Ruby took a half-step forward.

Sylva's eyes met Ruby's.

Ruby screamed, "Hope." She raised her arm and aimed. "It's about hope, you bitch!" She fired.

Sylva sneered at her and raised her right hand, sighting down the stunner.

Ruby ducked. It was clear now that she'd missed.

The man closest to Ruby fell.

A door in the back of the train station sprang open.

Two of the reds fell forward.

Three of Joel's people pushed in through the door. One of them was built like Chitt, although Ruby couldn't see her face to be sure. It looked like there were more behind them. Some of the attackers turned and fired at the new threat.

The fight looked surreal. Part dance, part struggle.

The train beeped and someone pulled her backwards. The station doors and the train doors shut in concert, and all she could see through the porthole window in the door was a blur of activity.

Ruby checked to be sure that everyone was okay. The stunned man had stopped bleeding and there were two more stretched out on the floor. Ani moved among them, making sure they were in natural positions; they couldn't move themselves until their nervous systems woke up. Onor saw to Joel's arm. The remaining guards wandered about the train car, talking in low tones and watching the dull and featureless tunnel go by.

She leaned against the wall of the train behind the door, muttering, "It's about hope."

CHAPTER EIGHT

Onor didn't relax until the train doors slid open to reveal the muted greens and golds of a command station. Four of Joel's staff stood waiting for them: Laird, SueAnne, Bruce, and Michael. Three old men and an old woman, all of them gray-haired and severe.

Onor turned to help Joel and Ruby off the train. Ruby looked shocked and Joel's arm still hung limply at his side. The effect of the partial hit should wear off soon. The three men who had been more thoroughly stunned were all awake now, although they needed help getting out of the train. Joel ignored Onor's offered hand and helped Ruby down himself, but he did give Onor an approving nod. "You were good back there. Thank you."

Onor fought a rising blush in his cheeks. "I want to know how they made the train stop."

"Not as much as I do."

Joel's lieutenants surrounded them. SueAnne put a gnarled hand on Joel's arm, and whispered just loud enough for Onor to hear. "Ix has news. It's waiting for you."

A brief pout crossed Ruby's face, quickly replaced by curiosity. As they moved down the corridor toward the map room, SueAnne shuffled and hitched in an odd gait, her face screwed into a look that suggested moving this fast required a true effort.

Maybe the battle they'd just been in was one of many. Maybe there was a bigger organized resistance than he or Joel had thought possible. After all, no one had expected the opposition to be able to stop a train. It implied a lot of people helping Sylva and Ellis.

He'd been fascinated with power for a long time, with the way it changed people's actions. And since they'd won, he'd learned something else about power: the loss of power drove people crazy. Some losers reacted well to the changes, even embraced them. Some of these did their old jobs while wearing different clothing. A few had chosen to trade peacekeeping for gardening or repairing or nursing.

But some who lost real power rebelled. Ellis and Sylva had just tried to kill Ruby for her power.

They should be punished for it. He would see to that, find them and lock them up.

First he needed to find out what SueAnne was so upset about. She had always been the only woman in Joel's power structure, unless you counted Ruby. And now she looked really worried. Almost shocked.

They nearly tumbled into the map room. Everyone with any formal power in command must have also been called. Onor spotted three or four other lieutenants, his own ex-boss Conroy, KJ and three of his special trainees—the dancers who fought with no weapons and won.

Inside the map room, people ranged shoulder to shoulder almost all the way around the map table, which displayed its default map of the *Fire*, the edges of the ship touching the edges of the table.

"Ix!" Joel proclaimed. "I'm here. How did they stop the train?"

"I have something more important to discuss." Ix's command voice, the clipped one.

Joel simply stood, waiting. His face was a mask of patience, but Onor now knew him well enough to be sure he was sorting through ideas faster than anyone else in the room.

Ruby must have been thinking like Onor, since she asked, "Were there any other attacks?"

Ix answered in pictures. The image of *The Creative Fire* in the table shrank in front of them, becoming no bigger than a fist, visible over on the side of the table near Ani and Dayn. The background morphed from black to a night sky full of stars, nebulae, and wheeling galaxies.

Onor leaned over the table. He whispered, "Adiamo. We've heard from Adiamo." He hadn't known the table could show the stars they flew through—he would have stood here entranced for days.

The whole room had quieted.

A structure appeared on the far side of the table. It was bigger than the *Fire*, maybe twice as big. Now Ix spoke. "Onor is almost right. The *Fire*'s velocity is being matched by a ship, which must be from the Adiamo system. It has not attempted to contact us, nor has it responded when I have tried to contact its AI. It is violating protocols."

Joel spoke. "Do you have any idea why?"

KJ said, "Perhaps so much time has changed that the computers speak different languages."

"That is possible," Ix replied. "I cannot tell if it is an official delegation or a semi-random encounter."

"Which is the most likely?" Joel asked.

KJ wanted to know, "Will it get physically close to us?"

Ix answered them both. "We cannot turn the *Fire* at this speed and we have no long-range weapons. The only option is to watch, listen, and prepare. It may be quite close by this time tomorrow."

"If we don't have long-range weapons, what do we have?" Ruby asked.

"There are objects we might turn into weapons. I am testing."

Joel's voice was calm. "Can you tell how big the ship is?"

Perspective shifted so the image of the strange ship flew in the exact middle. Ix zoomed in.

Onor leaned close, holding his breath. Home. Something from home. Change. He bit his lip, the pain telling him this was real.

Where the *Fire* was a flattened oval, just barely too thick to look like a disk, this ship was a cylinder. The *Fire*'s sleek skin was smooth outside. This one bristled with things Onor didn't recognize. Smaller ships stuck to it, ovals and long poles stuck out from it. Pits marred its surface.

Onor disliked the ship on sight.

Ruby voiced it better than Onor could, her voice full of dismay. "It's ugly."

KJ raised his voice. "We should withhold judgment."

Joel snapped, "Acknowledged."

Ruby pushed herself away from the table. "We have to tell everyone."

"No." Joel gave her a glance full of warning. "Not yet."

Ruby tensed. "Of course we do. What if it's dangerous?"

Laird spoke over her, his steady gaze a clear challenge. "What can they possibly do to help?"

Joel looked at Laird for a long, contemplative moment. "It's decent to tell them. But we need a plan first."

Laird dropped his eyes and his lips twisted into a bitter half-smile.

SueAnne spoke up. "They are possible fighters."

Ruby grimaced, but offered a compromise, "Perhaps we need to plan both a welcome and a defense."

Joel grimaced. "Defense first."

Ruby had achieved a partial victory; Onor and Haric were ordered to take the train to the cargo bars and tell Colin about the ship. This time, there were no unscheduled stops. For the most part, the train was returning tired festival-goers to their homes. A peacekeeper rode quietly in each car.

Onor had believed Ruby when she told him they were going home. He had felt the journey when she sang "Homecoming." But never before had there been physical evidence that anything except the *Fire* existed.

He wanted to see a planet and a sky. Animals. The *Fire* held no live animals except humans.

Now, after staring at all of the mysteries on the outside of the ugly ship and contemplating the mysteries inside, he wondered if he had been naïve.

Maybe he should be afraid instead of excited.

The train stopped, and he and Haric got off and jogged to the cargo bars. It felt good to move, and even better to turn up the steps and take them quickly.

The watchers at the door waved Onor and Haric past without hesitating. Inside, the room hummed with the extra-loud laughter of drinkers.

Haric led Onor to Colin, seated over a game of Planazate with a man Onor had seen but didn't really know. He struggled for the man's name. Allen. He'd led a group of Colin's fighters, and Onor recalled that he had been successful. There wasn't a mark on him.

Although Colin was the same age as Joel, and also had graying hair and a slight but strong build, the resemblance ended there. Colin had a wildness about him that Onor loved and feared. He smiled at Haric as they walked up. "How's my little turncoat doing?"

"Miss you too," Haric shot back. He pulled himself up and looked serious. "Ruby and Joel sent us with news."

"What is it?"

Haric shifted his weight from foot to foot. "We need to talk in private."

Colin looked across the game board. "This is Allen. You can talk in front of him. He's trusted."

"It's not about last night's attacks."

Colin merely raised an eyebrow.

Onor spoke as softly as he could. "There's a ship. Another ship. Ix saw it. We could see it on the map."

Colin stood up and gestured for Allen to do the same. "Come with me."

He led the four of them to a small office and shut the door. A table and four chairs filled one side, a long couch on the other. A dark vid screen hugged a third wall. They sat around the table and Colin leaned forward, his features tense and curious. "Tell me."

They told him, Haric filling in details after Onor told the main story.

When Colin ran out of questions, he sat back, his face as stony as Joel's had been at the news. Maybe that was a lesson about leading: don't give your emotions away.

Allen wasn't nearly as hard to read. His dark eyes had narrowed and he brushed a lock of dark hair from his face, tucking it behind his ear and shaking his head. He looked both determined and scared. He blurted out, "We need to get everyone ready for a fight. Just in case."

Colin unclipped his journal from his belt and fiddled with it for a few seconds. His voice was as cold as the dark parts of the ship. "Ix."

"Yes, Colin?"

"Why did I have to learn this from couriers?"

"I can only relay threats to the *Fire* to those in formal command."

"I thought you would say something like that, you damned hellion of a machine."

"I cannot override my command structures."

"Unless you want to." Colin's laughter sounded bitter. "You are also charged with protecting the ship. I hardly imagine that if there was no command structure left you would ignore the dangers."

Ix didn't reply.

After a few breaths of silence, Colin asked the machine, "How dangerous do you think this is?"

"If I can find a way to communicate with the strange ship, I may be able to answer that question."

"Can you show them what it looks like?" Haric asked.

Ix normally didn't obey people who were still underage, but the image of the ugly ship showed up on the face of Colin's journal. Colin stared at it for a long moment, handed it over to Allen to give him a good look, and then took his journal back. "You told me we wouldn't make contact this soon."

Ix did not respond to statements.

Colin shifted his attention from the journal to Onor. "What do they want us to do?"

"Deploy fighters. There will be a ship-wide announcement in two hours. Joel asked that you keep the people in the cargo bars and the working cargo bays all in line and calm."

"At least Joel plans to tell people," Allen said. "Garth would have kept it secret."

Haric added, "Ruby made him. She says it will make everyone pull together to have an outside force."

Colin laughed. "I doubt Ruby actually made Joel do anything he truly didn't want to do. But trust her to see hope everywhere."

Onor remembered the way her face had been screwed up in anger when she fired on Sylva. "Hope can be good, even in a fight."

"Especially then," Colin said. He looked at Allen. "Call up your fighters. Split them between two shifts. Tell them there will be news, but not yet what the news is."

"Will do." Allen rose and left.

Colin addressed Ix again. "Tell your new captain that if he will give you permission to tell me anything I ask, I'll do what he wants."

"He is everyone's captain."

"Really?" Colin looked lost in thought for a moment, and then he said, "Let me reword my *command* to you. Tell Joel that if he will give you permission to tell me everything that you tell him, I will do what he asks and we will guard the cargo. Remind him that this is the outer part of the *Fire*, and thus the most vulnerable." He hesitated a moment. "In fact, you might suggest that he send extra troops." Colin flicked his journal off, which effectively ended the conversation.

Onor remembered the other threats. "Colin? What do you know about the attack on the train?"

"Sylva and Ellis have enough logistics people with them to hack the train's central command system."

"What happened? After the train got underway again?"

Colin looked disgusted. "We caught three of them. Everyone who matters got away. Sylva and Ellis both, and most of the people they had with them."

"I thought you had them. The doors looked like they were blocked off."

Colin narrowed his eyes, and Onor realized he'd just challenged him. Colin's voice was clipped. "They went through the train tunnel."

"Wow." Gutsy. The tunnel was so thin in spots Onor liked to close his eyes when they passed through it in a train.

"At least you all got away before Ruby or Joel got themselves killed. Stupid girl, I saw her standing right in front screaming." Colin sounded proud of her.

"She's brave."

"I know." Colin said. "We were lucky it didn't take Ix long to notice they'd hacked in. It closed the holes and kicked them out. That's why you had a ten-minute fight and not a longer one."

Haric looked confused. "I didn't think Ix took sides."

"Ix is on the side of stability. Always. Don't ever make the mistake of assuming the machine has an ounce of loyalty."

Onor wasn't sure about that. In Onor's experience, Ix understood a lot that it wasn't willing to share. It might be Ruby's most aggravating supporter, but as far as Onor could tell, it *was* a supporter.

Colin got up and held the door open for them. "There's food at the bar if you want some before you go back."

"We've been assigned to you for now," Onor said.

Colin smiled. "So Joel understands me more than Ix does."

"What do you mean?" Haric asked.

"Joel knew I would need you more than he does. And Haric, you'll be a runner back if I need one. After all, that's what you left me to do, isn't it? Run for Ruby?"

Haric stood up a little straighter. "Yes."

Colin smiled at them both, although he looked deep in thought and determined. "Take time to rest and eat. I presume you'll want to be on the shift that greets the strangers?"

"I'm not hungry," Haric proclaimed.

"Of course you are," Onor said. "You're just excited. Come on and eat. We won't have to work for a few hours and we haven't rested all day."

"I won't sleep."

"Of course you won't."

CHAPTER NINE

As Ruby closed the hab door behind Joel it felt like she was closing a thousand worries inside with them and a thousand more outside. "How is your arm?"

"It's fine. It was just a brush from the edge of a beam."

"It knocked you down."

"I get back up well enough."

"I don't know what I'd do without you."

He laughed. "You'd bounce."

She collapsed on the couch, unable to keep up any pretense of strength. Ben's funeral, the festival, the attack, and dwarfing it all, the news of the strange ship. She felt stripped clean and beset with change and danger.

They'd spent hours in the map room, staring and asking questions, going round on the new ship and on Adiamo and on the reds' attack. At the end they'd been asking the same questions over and over with no new answers.

Their living room was big, the wall opposite them dominated by a vid system which was blessedly off at the moment. Joel stood in the middle of the room, awkward, as if unsure how to rest in the middle of a slow-motion encounter with a strange spaceship.

Ruby reached up and stroked his cheek. "Turn around, I'll work on your back."

"Can we lie down for that?"

He wasn't teasing, he was exhausted. "Maybe you should eat something before you pass out?"

He shook his head. "We only have a few hours."

She wasn't hungry either.

In the weeks he'd been in charge, his hair had grayed even more. But then, he almost never slept. In spite of that he often had time to think of her, to touch her and appreciate her and walk through her thinking.

If anyone ever hurt him, she would kill them.

If whoever was on this ship killed him, she would kill them.

The ugly ship scared her. She couldn't have told anyone why, but something felt deeply wrong.

In the bedroom, Joel pulled off his shirt but left his pants and socks on.

He stretched out over the bed diagonally so Ruby had room to work.

She rubbed his head, her fingers moving in slow circles across his scalp. "What do you think they want?"

His reply sounded muffled by the bedclothes. "Maybe they want to make us all slaves."

She leaned down and kissed him, then went back to her ministrations. "No, really?"

"I didn't expect our first contact to be with a ship that looks like a child's put-together robot toy."

"It does look like that."

He shifted under her hands. "Lower, right in the middle of my back."

She found the place he wanted. He moaned softly as she worked knots out of the long muscles beside his spine.

"Maybe it's more like a home than a ship. Like a space station?" There was a space station in the game of Adiamo. Players had no access to it until they got one of the last two levels, and then they didn't get to spend much time there. But she'd won the game over and over, and she remembered. It had looked much neater than this, though, and bigger.

"Maybe."

"If they're friendly, I want to plan the welcoming party. I've always imagined we'd sail into Adiamo and be escorted home by friendly ships that would tell us what to do. That we'd be like lost children coming home or something."

He pushed up onto his elbows. "Maybe it will be just like that."

She let out a long sigh. "I don't think so."

"Maybe Ix will learn something soon."

"If it does, you should sleep through it for now. We put SueAnne and Laird in charge so we can rest."

He pulled her down beside him. "You could rest, too."

A brief heat flared in her at his closeness, but she forced herself to ignore it and keep working on his muscles. In no more than a few breaths, he was sound asleep, the wrinkles in his face relaxing as he fell away from the world.

Ruby kept her fingers moving lightly over his skin. The *Fire* sounded quiet all around her as if it, too, waited.

CHAPTER TEN

The metal of the corridor felt cold against Onor's back. They'd done nothing but wait for hours. Haric's dark eyes stood out against pale skin turned paler by the bright white light in the corridor. "When's the ship going to do something?" Haric asked.

Onor spoke as soothingly as he could. "You know as much as me."

"Which is nothing."

"That's right." Onor shifted to find a more comfortable spot.

"Will they look the same as us?"

"Of course they will. Ix says the ship's from Adiamo, and we came from here." Onor's head turned at the sound of familiar footsteps. Claire, from the cargo bar. She handed them each a wrapped-up snack that smelled fabulous. Fresh orbfuit and peppery flat crackers and a dollop of protein cake for each of them.

"Thank you," Onor said.

Claire had never much liked him, since he came from gray. Right now, she looked both nervous and like maybe he was her best friend.

"I needed something to do," Claire muttered, as if the confession embarrassed her.

He understood. "Thanks." He smiled at her. "Food helps."

"I hope so." She continued down the corridor.

"I'm glad we're close to the bar," Haric said as he spread his protein cake over his crackers with a dirty finger.

"Me, too." Onor figured the easy assignment was because Colin had a soft spot for Haric and wanted him safe. Or maybe because Colin knew the kind of trouble Haric could get into and wanted to be able to see him.

Ix's voice came crackling from just above them, a modulated, calm, and factual recounting Onor had grown used to after hours sitting under the speaker. "The unidentified ship has now almost completely matched our trajectory and speed. It is not likely that it can come any closer to us without risk of disturbance between the drives. It has not hailed us in any way we understand."

The speaker went silent again.

Great. More non-information. Onor and Haric continued eating until all of the food was gone.

A maintenance bot whirred past them, followed by a stocky older woman with a limp. Penny. She stopped in front of them, a hand-signal stopping the bot as well. Onor leapt up, folding her in his arms, breathing in the smells of robot grease and cleaner.

She stiffened. She always stiffened when he held her. Damned old woman, independent as hell. "You look great," he told her.

She stepped back, rubbing a spot on her head. "Got a few new scars."

"A lot of people do."

"You went up in the world," she said. She stood still, looking awkward. "I knew you would."

He had missed her. He should have visited her, but he hadn't. He took her hand. "This isn't your territory. Is everything all right?"

"I came to tell you something."

"What?"

"There's an attack being planned. Other people want to be in charge when the ship contacts us. They think they're running out of time."

"Ellis and Sylva?"

"And more. I hear there's even some grays, although I never can tell. Hardly knew anyone before anyway, me living down low like I do. Now they're all wearing whatever."

He laughed. She had that right. "You're wearing a few colors yourself." In fact, she had on everything but gray, and even a bit of green wrapped around one of her arms like a bandage.

"Yeah."

"Do you know what they're planning?"

"I overheard a conversation about getting right into command. Like now, while we're standing here talking. But I don't know how they plan to do that. They sounded tense and angry."

He couldn't leave his post. "Is there anything else I should know? Or that I can do for you?"

"Well, one thing. Can you tell me how scared I should be? About the ship?"

As if responding to Penny's question, Ix's voice began its calm recounting from the speaker again. "Three ships have detached from the Adiamo system ship. They are approaching *The Creative Fire*. It appears that they will arrive in less than two hours."

Penny's eyes widened, and Haric stood straighter. Onor fought back the lump of fear trying to creep up his throat. "It could be okay. One theory is they want to talk to us."

"Do you believe that?" Penny's voice shook. "Really?"

"I don't," Haric said unhelpfully.

"I hope so," Onor leaned down close to Penny. "Remember the first day I met you. The day you led me to get my beating?"

"Hazing," she said, a short smile playing around the edges of her lips, and then gone back to worry.

"You didn't tell me what was going to happen then, but you did tell me this time. I'm grateful for that."

"You're my friend," she said.

"And you're mine." He pointed at the now-silent speaker. "Are you getting the same news we are?"

"Yes."

"All right."

Colin and some of his fighters were coming their way from the cargo bar. They looked determined, and they were moving fast. Onor only recognized one, Colin's second in command, Par. Two were women. "Look Penny, go back under. See if you can figure out how to turn the robots into weapons. We might need everything we've got."

She reached in and gave him a little swat on the arm. "I'll do my best."

"And stay safe."

"Probably not."

"Do it," Onor told her.

Colin's hand fell on his shoulder. "Come on. Both of you. There's nothing landing here."

They snaked past Penny, leaving her and her bot pressed against the wall to make room. She'd be okay. She was tough.

They started into a slow, sustainable jog. The sound of maybe twenty pairs of feet reminded Onor of training below the park, running and running for hours just to get in shape to run when it mattered. Like now.

Onor spoke to Colin. "Where are they landing?"

"Outside of C."

Onor laughed. "Something breaks our way?"

"Is that good?" Colin asked. "I'm not sure. There's no one to greet them there."

"But at least no one lives there," Onor said.

"So are we going to greet them?" Haric asked.

"We're heading that way. We might just suit up." Colin looked at Haric. "You need to go back."

"Back where?"

"To the cargo bar. You can help watch over it. I need Onor—he helped with the salvage operation on C-pod."

"I want to stay with you." Haric's breathing was more labored than Onor's or Colin's, almost ragged.

"It's dangerous."

"I'll be safer with you."

Colin snapped at the boy this time. "It's not safe anywhere. Go."

"Can I stay," pause, "until there's some kind of information," Haric breathed hard, "to take back?"

The desperation in Haric's voice tugged at Onor, but there was another job to do. He matched his pace to Haric's, the run clipping his sentences, too. "Colin's right. Go back now. Stop in the cargo bar. Tell Ix what Penny told us. That there's going to be fighting inside. Then go home. To Ruby and Colin."

Haric looked betrayed, but he turned and ran back the way they'd come. His footsteps echoed, loud and angry.

Colin didn't slow down, but he said, "Thanks. What did Penny tell you?"

"That there's people mad at Ruby and Joel."

"That's news?"

"Are we taking a train?" Onor asked.

"They've all been shut off until the fight's over."

It was a long way to C-pod. Onor settled in for the run.

They stopped about halfway, ducking out of the maintenance corridors into a row of habs. The first one they found was miraculously unlocked. Or maybe a gift from Ix. They liberated some water and relieved themselves.

"Ix?" Colin spoke. "Any news?"

"The ships are closer now. They haven't contacted anyone. Joel wants Onor and Colin to suit up outside of C pod and wait to see if anything develops. More will join them. I received Haric's warning, and it is a threat."

"What warning?" Colin asked.

"Reds, moving in on command," Onor said.

"Why didn't you tell me?"

"I did. Sort of. We can't do anything about it anyway."

Colin frowned at him.

"Besides, it's hard to talk when you're running."

"Later. Ready to run again now?"

"You bet."

Then they were off again. Onor started thinking details through. "How are we going to get into C without the train?"

"We'll take a maintenance cart."

He'd done that. A long time ago, He'd even learned to drive one. "Should work."

"Tell me about C," Colin commanded.

"It's mostly intact. Life support is off. Water's all been moved, everything else worth keeping. I grew up there, but it's like a ghost town now."

"Ship fell apart there? Was it really that simple? That's what I heard."

"It was scary. Not sure it was that simple. Rumors said sabotage."

"I don't think so."

Onor agreed. "Me either. I think the *Fire*'s wearing out. Marcelle thinks it knows it's going home."

"Is Marcelle your girlfriend?"

"No." It came out more forceful than Onor intended.

"Someday you'll outgrow your crush on Ruby."

"I don't have one."

Colin laughed as he led them to the carts.

Colin and Onor climbed onto a cart with two of the other fighters Colin had brought. It barely lurched forward. One of the people climbed off, and the cart moved much better. There was only one more cart. Colin appointed two more people to come with them, and sent the rest to do random patrols.

There were suits near the garage the carts were kept in. "Should we put these on now?" Onor asked.

Colin hesitated, holding up the suit he'd chosen. "I could leave the helmet off."

"Ix can talk through the speakers in the suits."

Colin nodded. "We'll do it your way." He still held the suit awkwardly. "I haven't done this since I was twenty."

"So why are you going in? You usually send people."

Colin grinned. "Call it a little challenge between me and Ruby."

Onor helped him, and then put his own suit on. It was kind of endearing that there was anything Colin needed help with. It wasn't like him at all.

CHAPTER ELEVEN

Ruby paced around the map table, nervous energy keeping her from stopping at all. She should be writing a song about this, a composition driven by the awfulness of waiting. Except she was sure they were almost out of time. For everything.

Ix had locked up command, but Ellis and Sylva and their small avenging army was almost there. Even if they couldn't get in, she didn't like her worst enemies this close.

The approaching ships were a far bigger worry, but Ruby couldn't shake the feeling that Ellis and Sylva might burst through the door any time.

As she came around to Joel, he reached an arm out and snagged her. "Stop. You're driving me crazy."

SueAnne wrung her hands and kept her eyes on the table, where the image of the small ships that had detached from the larger one grew inexorably closer to the skin of the *Fire*.

Ix's voice. "They're turning."

They were. They changed orientation, a series of tiny shifts that looked a little jerky. Something even smaller left the small ships. Ruby tried to adjust her thinking. The *Fire* was huge, the ugly ship almost as big. "Ix? How many people can those smaller ships hold?"

"Probably a hundred each."

Joel asked, "Do we have a closer view?"

The table switched from what was essentially an illustration of all of the ships—*Fire*, ugly ship, three smaller ships and three even smaller ships—to a camera view of the smallest ships coming in to land on the surface of the *Fire*. They were rounded vessels with small eyes all over them—portholes perhaps. Kind of like the small, strong windows in the train cars.

SueAnne gasped. "I didn't know you had cameras on the outside."

Ix replied, "They are not as clear as my star cameras, and some are broken. They were meant for use while orbiting a planet."

Something that looked like metal claws began to descend from the round ships. "Where exactly are they—what part of the hull?" Laird demanded.

"On the outside of the cargo pod in C."

"Why there?" Ruby asked.

Other questions piled on hers. KJ asking, "Can they get in?" and Laird wanting to know, "Do you see anything that looks like weapons?"

Ix didn't answer any of them. "Ellis and Sylva are outside the door to command. They are discussing how to get in, in spite of the fact that I've locked them out."

Laird glanced at Joel. "Can we just take them? I have some force on hold."

Joel frowned. "Keep them ready." He glanced at the table, and the approaching ships. "They're neutralized right now. I trust Ix's locks. Ix—tell me if they seem to develop any plans that might work."

"I will."

Ruby looked back down at the table. From this angle it looked like one of the clawed feet was going to step right into the center of the table.

Then the view went dark.

CHAPTER TWELVE

The suit stank of both Onor's own fear and the stale sweat of generations. He grumbled at having to push the legs to move; if it didn't smell so bad he would have sworn the suit had hung stiffening in the closet for generations. He panted. "Sorry Colin, I'm trying to keep up. This thing's not responding the way it's supposed to."

"Want to change it out?"

He didn't. It would cost time. "It'll be okay. It's not like it's leaking. Maybe it will loosen up."

Two others had suited up, Par and one of the women. Most people in Colin's employ had experience in the shifting gravity of the cargo bays. The four in suits would go in; the others would stay near the airlock and guard.

Colin spoke to Ix. "Open the outer door."

Onor's gloved hand was on the latch, so he felt the release even though he couldn't hear the metallic click or the warning bell through his helmet. He pushed the door open and waved Colin in. Two was a tight fit. Ten minutes of cycling later, they were on the far side, waiting for the other two to join them.

The C bays were completely null-g, and had been null-g since C-pod was closed down.

Onor had been in them, of course. He'd practiced null-g maneuvers using the myriad traverse lines that criss-crossed the wide open spaces in the center of the bay. It had been a long time though, and for now he clung to the handholds on the ledge and tucked one foot under another handhold, trying to control his slight nausea with slow breaths of awful-smelling suit air.

Lights had been turned on. A few of them didn't work, so there were spears of light that went all the way through the cavernous space, and dark places that the light barely touched. The bay held many of the biggest cargo containers: Five times the height of a typical man and longer than they were high. They lined the outer wall, the one closest to space. "What's in those?" Onor whispered.

Ix answered. "Ballast and shielding in some, minerals and dried samples of biology in others, trash in one."

"Trash?"

"Medical waste. Had to go somewhere."

Ix had sent them in after one of the strange ships landed on the outside of the cargo bay and began giving instructions to the outer locks. Onor couldn't tell from Ix's calm voice, but he felt certain that this was not supposed to happen. Random ships should not be able to breach the *Fire*, and shouldn't do it even if they could. This was no welcoming delegation of visitors, it was an attack force.

It pissed him off. No one had invited them to touch the *Fire*.

The lock behind them opened and the other two climbed out.

Can you hear anything from the ships?" Onor asked Ix. His own ability to hear was muffled to near-zero by the helmet and the whirring processors and servos in the suit itself.

"Not exactly. When you're ready, traverse the pod. Other people will meet you."

Onor clung for a few more minutes, waiting for Colin to get his own null-g sense about him. Colin breathed out, "Ready," and pushed off, arms stretched toward the nearest traverse line.

As soon as Colin got a good grip on the cable and fumbled his safety hook onto it, he looked back to check on the others. Onor was right behind him, and the line vibrated as each of the other two landed and attached their hooks.

Colin led the four of them across the bay, pulling in and out of beams of light. New lights kicked on near one of the entrances on the far side when they were about half-way along. They stopped, clinging. "Ix? Is that who we're supposed to meet?"

"Yes. Can you go faster?"

"I can." Colin sped up and Onor worked harder, pulling hand over hand. He went so fast he fumbled once, floating away from the line, the hook holding him on. Colin gripped tightly with one hand and used his free hand to pull Onor back. Onor gritted his teeth and worked on precision as he tried to be even faster to make up for the short delay. Every pull felt like work. A spot on the inside of his arm felt seared as it chafed against a seam in the suit that should have been soft but felt like a dull knife.

He glanced toward the other door. Three suited figures. He had no sense of whether there should or could be more of them, but it felt there should be more.

As they reached the far side, hands pulled him in and helped him unhook then handed him along the wall. At the far end, he passed the third person, who gripped his hand as tightly as possible, glove to glove.

Marcelle.

He chilled, seeing her here. Whatever was about to happen was going to be bad. He felt that, felt it deep.

Her features were distorted by the scratched helmet glass, but he could make out a welcoming smile below eyes wide with wonder and fear. He held onto the wall with his left hand, a slight push setting him to floating 90 degrees from the wall. She did the same, using the other hand. It set them floating belly to belly. They touched free hands. A null-g hug they'd learned as youngsters when they were first taught how to suit up.

They exchanged looks of pleasure at the success of the small joint maneuver.

Ix. "Watch the far side."

The skin of the *Fire*. Onor braced, made sure Marcelle was braced. Everyone looked ready, and awkward. They bulked against the wall of the cargo bay. Onor felt naked without a weapon, but they had nothing that would work well in the awkward gloves.

The outer locks were designed to allow the biggest cargo containers in and out the ship.

Lights showed through one of those locks.

CHAPTER THIRTEEN

Ruby chewed at her lip as the invading ship that had stepped on the camera attached itself to the outside of the *Fire* with a wobbling movement, as if it were testing its stickiness. The camera angle Ix had found was fairly clear, but even zoomed in, details were tough to see. A second ship did the same thing. "They are landing over airlocks," Ix said.

The third ship failed to get a grip on the *Fire*'s silvery skin and ripped away so fast it seemed as if the ship vanished in an eyeblink. Ix replayed the bit of grainy footage. It was impossible to tell why this ship's feet didn't stick to the *Fire*, but in slow motion it looked more spectacular that it had when it happened. One of the legs ripped off and tumbled away. The other three feet held on, flexing, and then lost their holds fast, like a zipper, and the ship disappeared from between frames.

Ani put a hand over her mouth and no sound came out, although her shoulders heaved.

"Is it going to try again?" Ruby asked.

"I'm sure it's gone. It did not appear to have enough power to catch us."

She stared at the place it had been. "Were there people inside?"

"I don't know."

The invaders—that's how she thought of them now—*the invaders* looked small against the big generation ship's outer skin.

The sheer surprise of them clung to Ruby. "Those are the ones over C?"

"Yes," Ix replied.

Onor and Marcelle were there. Ruby wanted to be with them. "Can they know?" Ruby asked. "That the habitation section on C is empty?"

"I do not believe it is possible."

Ani had dropped her hand from her mouth and it joined her other hand at about waist level, fingers twisting tight.

"I've never seen you so nervous," Ruby told her. "It'll be okay."

"Really?"

"It has to be." Ruby spoke to Ix. "No one from the Fire could have sent them information?" she asked.

"I would know."

Ruby believed. "So it must just be dumb luck."

Joel stood just far enough away that Ruby couldn't hear the details of his whispered conversations. She slid over by him and curled her hand around his arm, wanting to be close when something happened.

"Look!" KJ commanded their attention.

An even smaller pod had detached from one of the bigger ones, or maybe been let loose. It looked like it came through a door, although between the graininess of the picture and the angle, it was hard to tell. Whatever it was that came out, it had emerged from the invading ship's belly. It grasped the ship's landing legs.

"How many are there?" Joel asked.

"At least two," Ix said. "I cannot tell yet."

The smallest of the ships bent down—that was the only way Ruby could describe it—and clutched the feet of its mother ship. The center of the cluster of legs moved down and attached itself to the outside of the *Fire*, just above one of the locks.

No one spoke until Ix said, "It looks like it will be able to get in without hurting us. Like they have the right codes. This should not be possible."

KJ spoke the worst conclusion. "If they know how to open the locks on our ship, then they could have found a way to talk to us."

CHAPTER FOURTEEN

The light that shone from the hatch illuminated nothing. It had been designed for people *in* the airlock. All that Onor and Marcelle and the others clinging to the insides of the cargo bay could see was the light surrounding the door, limning it, making the door itself look even blacker than the surrounding metal.

It seemed to take forever for the lock to cycle. Onor's breath rattled inside of his helmet, full of fear and stomach acid.

He braced for the people coming through the door, for unfamiliar weapons.

The inner door of the lock opened, pushed out by . . . he squinted, drew in a breath: Pushed out my metal claws. Behind the claws, metal arms. Behind the metal arms, small metal bodies with thick legs attached. Four? No, six legs plus the two front ones with the claws. The thighs were thicker than a man, maybe much thicker.

Strength and flexibility. He quickly saw that he should add speed to the words that the robots brought to his mind. That's what they had to be. Bots. There didn't seem to be room anywhere for a human unless there were humans in each leg, and that made no sense. They were all leg and claw. All machine.

The first one *jumped*, moving impossibly to latch itself to the wall at least twenty meters from the airlock door.

Onor pressed closer to the wall.

Ix spoke into his helmet. "Don't move. Yet. They don't know you are there."

Onor tried not to move his lips much as he asked Ix, "What are they?"

"They are not in my library. The claws are sharp. They appear to be strong."

"Understatement." Onor hissed.

The first of the robots scuttled along the wall, using the hand-holds and the traverse lines to move quickly down to the cargo pods. It seemed to know exactly where it was, to belong in the deep holds of the Fire. This alone—the familiarity—was enough to give Onor shivers.

Three more came through. One waited by the hatch. Two of them followed the first robot and fanned out. All four moved in different directions.

The first one that had come through snapped the straps on a cargo pod and lifted the entire structure of the bin away from the wall.

"What should we do?" Onor whispered.

Ix didn't answer.

The fourth clawed robot started moving along the wall toward them.

"What do we do?" Onor repeated. In just two jumps it had come a quarter of the distance.

When Ix remained silent, Onor bit his lip to make himself think. Pain drove his fear deeper inside, opening up his airway and giving him more ability to talk.

They were attacking his home.

"Ix. How do I hurt it? That one's almost here. How do I hurt it?"

"Don't move yet."

"It's coming."

"You have no weapon."

It took one more hop toward them, stopped. With no visible eye, he couldn't tell how it saw. Yet he felt sure it watched them, knew they were there.

"Can you jam the airlock closed? Block them in?"

No answer.

They were all linked to Ix and not to each other. By design. So there would be one set of orders, and so Ix could control the conversation. It was a price they often paid for talking to the machine.

Ix would protect stability and not individuals. Onor heard Colin's earlier words inside his head, a truth he'd resisted. *But it was true in this case.* The machine would sell them for the *Fire*'s future if it had to.

"Stay quiet," Ix told him.

Ix must be telling them all to be quiet. He needed a human. Colin. "Patch me through to the others."

To his surprise, Ix did so. He could immediately hear Colin swearing, and the hard, fast breath of five other people full of fear.

"Stay calm!" Onor commanded. "Ix is going to lock them in if it can. Get out. Then we can plan."

Colin immediately backed him up. "Joe, Lisle, use the lock closest to you."

That was the lock closest to all seven of them. It would only hold two at a time, and the two Colin had named were the closest to it. They were also the closest to the robot.

"Marcelle," Onor hissed.

"We could go across to the other lock." Her voice was shaky and high, but brave.

It was a better idea than waiting. Only one machine was focused on them. Splitting up felt right. "Now," he urged.

Marcelle pushed off, a stiff humanoid form with a bubble head and nothing like the powerful legs of the machines that had entered their space. Even though he knew her as a warrior, in this moment Marcelle looked vulnerable. Prey.

Onor bent down, crouching sideways against the wall, and followed her through nothing.

She didn't stop to attach her hook but just grabbed the line and started pulling along it.

"Hook in," he urged her.

"No. It might follow us."

Colin's voice. "She's right. You might need to float free. Good luck."

One mistake could leave them untethered.

Onor's arm hurt all over again, heating as it chafed. He drove forward with it anyway, the whole motion like swimming. His helmet bumped Marcelle's boot. "Sorry."

"It's okay."

Heavy breathing sounded in their helmets, fear breathing from the four who hadn't followed them. A scream stopped all other sound, strangled, then stopped abruptly. Ix had cut the voice off.

Onor's fear grew.

It was almost impossible to look backward in the bulky suit. It would slow him down. "What's happening?" he whispered through his teeth as he pulled along frantically after Marcelle. "What just happened?"

Colin's voice sounded high. "It ripped . . . ripped—"

Onor took another long pull along the line, felt blood running slowly into the arm of his suit, hot and wet.

Silence went by for so long Onor was afraid whatever happened to the screamer had also happened to Colin. Onor pictured a suit cut in pieces, pulled harder. Colin's voice vibrated in his ear again. "It . . . we lost two. Just go. Don't look back."

Oh my. This was so much worse than fighting humans through the *Fire*. So much scarier. Colin again, his voice choppy. "Good luck."

"I'll try." Colin. Colin afraid. There was no way to know what he faced, no way Onor could slow down.

"Can you follow us?" he asked.

"I am."

Ix, very brief. "Go to the airlock. Get out."

Now Onor could only hear his own breathing. Marcelle's had silenced as much as Colin's. The machine had cut them all off from each other again. He cussed.

His breath came fast and uneven. He knew better. He took two deep breaths, tried to recenter.

Looking ahead wasn't too hard. The lock was further away than it should be. He took even more control of his breath, paid more attention to the way the line slid between his gloved fingers.

He couldn't tell if he was faster or not.

It seemed surreal, the two of them moving along the line, Colin catching up. Every once in a while he could feel the pull of Colin's arms, a tightness in the line that disappeared and reformed. He only heard his own sounds, the way he moved in his suit, the small grunts of pain he couldn't help any more when his arm scraped across whatever was cutting him.

He glanced below. There were two holes where spider bots had taken cargo containers.

The line in his hand jerked.

The claws on the spider bots were strong enough to cut the straps on cargo containers; they were strong enough to cut the traverse lines.

"Ix?" he queried.

"Yes?"

"If we tie on, will gravity stop them? Should you turn on the gravgens?"

"I have been running calculations. You might be harmed more than them by sudden gravity."

Marcelle's boots receded and he chased them.

"It might be bad for the ship as well. Nothing in this bay is used to real gravity. The gens should be ramped up slowly with handlers available."

Stupid machine could talk through anything.

Time dragged. Focus shrank to the feel of the line across his gloves, to the way his suit didn't move as fluidly as it should, to the cut on his arm, to keeping the same distance between his helmet and Marcelle's boots.

Marcelle grabbed the far wall, one hand on a handhold, then the other, then she was vertical to his horizontal, helping him.

He wanted to cling to the wall beside the airlock with his belly but he had to turn.

Colin was more than half-way to them.

Onor's biggest fear wasn't true; no spider robot swarmed up the line behind them. Perhaps they were too bulky to balance.

Two of the robots were by the airlock they'd come in through, one of them on the wall opposite them, and another down by the cargo containers. At this moment they all seemed to be stopped.

Onor looked for the other crew-members. There should be two other humans even if two got out.

He didn't see them.

He was back to only being able to talk to the machine. "Where are the others?"

"Two have died."

"And?"

"Two escaped."

So five of them and four robots, and Ix.

Beside him, Marcelle inched toward the airlock and pushed the button to release the door.

Opposite them, on the far wall, Onor glimpsed a robot's claw slide over the line and close.

The traverse line—complete with Colin on it, slackened.

Onor braced himself, tucking his feet into two of the handholds. He pulled. The spider that had cut the line started to jump. It stuck to the walls, avoiding the open spaces. Coming for them.

Spiders had been a hazard to avoid in the game of Adiamo. In the game, they had been the size of his thumb.

Onor kept pulling.

Something moved down below and Onor risked a glimpse, saw a bot headed toward them from there. Closer than the one that had cut the line.

He pulled harder. He couldn't leave Colin and he needed to get Marcelle out.

Breathing hurt, his shoulders hurt.

Ix's voice in his head. "You can make it. Keep going. The airlock is open, behind you. Up and to the right."

The bot was half-way to them. It must be doing the same calculation, and it must think it could get to them.

He gave a last hard tug and extended his hand, letting Colin float into it. He grasped Colin's arm with his glove and twisted, pushing Colin toward the open door.

His feet should have stayed locked into place, but when he twisted one of them came free. The stiff suit hadn't let him move the way it should have.

He still had Colin's hand, and he couldn't turn back.

Colin flexed his arm, trying to pull himself into the wall. The movement pulled Onor all the way free, the two of them floating near the airlock, just out of reach of anything. The momentum they had went the wrong direction.

Something bumped him from below, startling him. He expected to feel the edges of a claw, but it was a gloved hand, holding him.

Marcelle had kicked off the wall with the line in one hand. She'd grabbed him with the other.

Now she had no free hand. Onor held onto Colin's boot with his right hand.

Marcelle tugged him toward her, clasped his waist with her thick, suited legs.

The fingers of his right hand slipped, the movement changing the angle of his head so he could see how close the other bot was, the one that had been below him. The claw loomed large as it came toward him.

He flinched, even though it was too far away—barely—to actually touch him.

Marcelle started pulling.

Onor reached toward Colin, trying to get a two-handed grip on him.

Just as his hand came around, Colin kicked free.

The movement pushed Onor and Marcelle toward the wall.

Ix whispered to him. "Colin knows that three won't fit in the lock."

He felt the hard stop as they reached the door, Marcelle twisting to get purchase and grab a handhold, her other hand coming around under his shoulder and lifting him up and in.

Ix's voice said, "Get out. Now."

With Marcelle in the lock behind him, he turned to grasp the door and close them in, looking for a last minute way to grasp Colin and jam him into the tiny spaces left between him and Marcelle and the walls of the lock.

He would need to grasp pieces.

CHAPTER FIFTEEN

Ruby had stayed glued to the shifting pictures Ix displayed on the table during Onor and Marcelle's long pull down the traverse line.

She watched when the robot dismembered Colin.

Now, not long afterward, her stomach still felt flipped and her mouth tasted dry and metallic.

There wasn't much to see. The spider-like robots moved silently around the bay, and from time to time they stopped by a container as if pondering, but went on.

Marcelle and Onor were out and safe. That was the only good thing. That, and the strange robots hadn't been able to get the cargo out—Ix had found a way to jam the electronics on the outer locks and trap them inside.

Thieves.

All of her illusions of a grand welcome to the world of the video game Adiamo felt like a child's daydreams.

Thieves and murderers.

Colin.

Damned machines.

Colin.

The robots gave her pause.

Maybe the ugly ship would talk to them now. They had captives.

She hadn't seen Joel since shortly after they got their first good look at the robots. Laird and SueAnne and KJ and Dayn were also gone. And others. Surely it was a grand meeting somewhere. Without her.

Not that she'd have missed seeing what just happened, no matter how awful it was. Surely Joel had seen it too. He'd know how violated and empty she felt. Even though the room was still full of people, the simple fact of Joel's absence made it feel empty.

Ani stood beside her, stiff and still. From time to time she gasped or pointed at a particular scene on the table, even though there was nothing to see but the robots moving around, and occasionally a piece of a person or a suit.

Haric brought Ruby a cup of stim. His face had gone completely white and he looked awful. He had just seen Colin killed. His old boss. A man he had loved deeply, had looked up to. A man who had taken care of him. And yet he was thinking of her. Doing his duty.

Ruby couldn't force herself away from the table, but she took the stim from Haric and spoke softly to him. "I'm sorry."

"Why did he go?" Haric asked. "The last thing he said to me was to run away and stay safe, but he wasn't safe at all."

Ruby whispered, "I challenged him to lead from the front."

Ani shook her head. "Colin never delegated the really hard stuff. I've known him all my life, and while he had minions for almost everything, he handled the real deals, the tough negotiations."

Haric pointed at the map. "Something's happening."

A view of the outside of the ship had appeared, showing one of the locks. There were no strange ships attached to it, so it was somewhere else.

"Ix," Ruby said. "What are you showing us?"

"The best answer to aggression."

Damned machine. She watched. "It's not a cargo lock," she said.

"No," Haric sounded more alive. Interested, at least. "It's where we keep the landers."

"How do you know?" Ruby asked. She hadn't know that.

"Colin made us tour the whole inside of *Fire*'s skin and learn everything inside it. I've been in every cargo bay, and every ship's bay. There are three ship's bays. Three ships in every bay. One is too broken to ever use again."

"A ship, or a bay?"

"One of the ships. How did you think we got down to planets and brought up cargo?"

Haric's voice had taken the tone of a lecture. Ruby laughed softly. "I don't know everything. Perhaps you can tour me around some day."

"I'd like that."

The lock opened. There was no shot with an angle that allowed her to see what was inside. Light brightened and then three ships floated out of the opening in the *Fire*'s skin. They were almost the same shape as the biggest of the ships that had come off of the ugly ship: cylinders.

The *Fire*'s landers floated long enough for Ruby to finish her stim, put away the cup, wash her face, and come back to watch.

"Ix? What is in those?"

"Explosives. Things meant to blow holes in the surface of planets or moons to see what's there."

She crossed her arms and thought. "You want to blow up the ugly ship?"

"If possible."

Haric almost squeaked. "It could blow us up, then, couldn't it?"

As always, Ix did not sound worried. "It can probably blow us up now."

The landers drifted backward alongside the *Fire*.

"Ix. Are there people on those?"

"No. We have no trained pilots at the moment."

Ruby only had the vaguest idea of what they carried in the *Fire*'s holds. Dead animals and chipped rocks and minerals. None of the places they'd been to had been civilized. Still, whatever they carried, it was the reason the *Fire* existed.

"Maybe we're going to have to fight for our cargo," she said.

"Well," Ani said, "that's what we're doing now."

"I mean all the way. After this. Even when we get home. I thought we'd be heroes."

"You are a hero," Haric said.

The machine contradicted the boy. "You are naïve."

Joel and the others rushed in and went directly to the side of the table closest to the door. They focused immediately on the landers, and since they asked no questions they must know of Ix's plans. As if they had been waiting for Joel and the others to come in, the three ships stopped floating and *moved*. Ruby gasped at the quickness of the change. Clapping erupted all around the table.

She stood beside Joel. He looked haggard. It had been hours now since they slept and she wanted to take him someplace private and help him rest. But that wouldn't be possible. And here, among all of his people, only the slightest and most occasional of touches was allowed.

"What are our chances?" she asked him.

"Ix says they are good. The explosives probably have to reach inside of the ship to do enough damage—they cannot simply get close."

"What do you believe will happen?"

"It's out of my hands. Only one of them has to succeed."

"How long until we know?"

He frowned. "I think we could fail any time. Lose the ships. It depends on what kind of weapons they have, and what they think we can do. They know more about us than they should; they may have anticipated this attack."

"But if we don't fail? When will we know that?"

"It will be a few hours, I think. There are choices the machines will have to make."

"Don't you mean Ix?"

Joel shook his head. "Maybe you could think of the ship's computers as pieces of Ix. But Ix won't be making the decisions."

"What about the Ellis and Sylva? What are we going to do about them?"

"I already did something," he said. He looked away from her.

"Are they in jail?"

"They're dead."

She went still. "What did you do? And what happened to their followers?"

"They tried to kill you." His spoke firmly, but she knew him well enough to hear the insecurity behind the strength. That didn't stop her from being afraid of what she'd hear.

"What did you do?"

"I turned off the life support where they were."

Ruby felt gut-punched. "How many?"

"Twenty-two."

"Ix allowed that?" It hadn't allowed them to kill during the insurrection unless it was self-defense.

"Even Ix knew that we couldn't fight two battles. It picked the one that matters the most."

It was a hard death. When she was a child, she'd had nightmares about losing air and heat. They'd all been drilled in the creche about life support failure, told there were only moments to leave anyplace the air was rushing away from. The warnings from the drills ran in her head. *Get out, get to a door, do it immediately. There's ten or fifteen seconds before your heart stops.*

Ix must have actually done it. At Joel's command. *But Ix had turned off the air.*

Ellis and Sylva had tried to kill Joel. Had damaged his arm, if only for a while. Inches closer, and he might have been stunned completely, maybe killed. Surely that was what they meant to do if they got here. To kill everyone in the room.

She remembered locking eyes with Sylva. Ruby's shot had been wild, but she would have killed Sylva then. Even so, this felt different.

She stared into Joel's eyes, searching them. Was he sorry?

Was this just part of leading?

Even though it hurt inside, what she said to him was, "I love you."

Laird came up and clapped Joel's arm. "Good to see the ships are away. What's next, Captain?"

Joel kept looking at Ruby in spite of Laird's clear request for a conversation. He hadn't yet responded to her whispered declaration that she could accept the horrible thing he'd done in spite of her own feelings about it.

Her teeth worried her lower lip as she kept watching him, hoping for his face to soften. She thought she saw concern slip across his eyes, relax his mouth, give him warmth.

But of course, now that Laird was here, he wouldn't say it out loud. He did nod at her and give her a slight, secret smile before he turned and smiled—more broadly but not half as deeply—at Laird. "We need to decide what to do about the invaders. Make sure KJ rejoins us."

"I will." Laird turned and walked off, and Ruby put a hand on Joel's arm.

He twitched it off. "Not now."

SueAnne and Bruce came up. SueAnne looked exhausted, while Bruce seemed excited about the danger, almost like an adult version of Haric. "Ready?"

Joel started for the door

Ruby took a deep breath, and followed. She could help.

Joel held the door open for Bruce and SueAnne. The old woman hobbled through even more slowly than usual, her footsteps showing the strain of being part of command during the attack on the *Fire*.

Ruby stepped up to take her arm, prepared to help her get to wherever they were going.

Joel's hand on her shoulder stopped her. He shook his head.

"I can help. I know how everyone on our level thinks. I've been in the cargo bays."

She saw regret on his face, but it wasn't audible in his sharp words. "Stay. You can see what's happening here, and you'll be safe."

"I don't care about safe."

SueAnne turned. She looked almost apologetic, or at least empathetic. Her words, however, were clipped and iron. "Officers only."

Ruby glanced from her to Joel. Both looked resolute.

Laird and KJ came up behind her. She was going to have to step through the door and defy Joel or step back for them to get in.

She took another deep breath, used it to control her anger. Even though every part of her rebelled, she stepped back, and watched Laird and KJ and two others go through. The door shut. She stood and stared at it, furious and bereft all at once.

CHAPTER SIXTEEN

Onor jerked so hard on the lever that secured the airlock door that he nearly lost his balance. His breath came in great foul gasps that stank of fear and his hurt arm screamed pain at him, but what mattered was that there were two sets of metal doors between him and Marcelle and the robot spiders.

"I never want to see those things again," he whispered. "Never." Never an enemy like that, never the rending of a friend into parts. He'd seen death, but this was death covered in horror.

Colin. Onor felt dizzy remembering. He peered back through the lock, but all he could see was light. "Ix?"

"Yes, Onor?"

"Where is it? Are we safe?"

"The spider bots cannot open the lock if it's dogged shut."

Onor protested. "They opened the outside door of the *Fire*. The *outside*."

"I can keep them out of the rest of the ship."

"Could you have kept them out of ship at all?"

"I don't know."

"Damned machine." He wanted to say worse things, but knew it for the heat of adrenaline. He took three deep breaths, his lungs seared by the pain in his arm, which seemed to go to the bone. As soon as his hands stopped shaking too hard to undo the clasps, he stripped his helmet off. Marcelle did the same, and then he had her in his arms, both of them bulky in their suits, not really touching. There was no way to reach her face to kiss her. He ripped his glove free and stroked her hair awkwardly. "I'm so glad you're safe."

Her face had gone white as bone except for pink spots on her cheeks from the exertion of pulling along the line. Her breath came in fast little gasps like his. Tears hung in her eyes.

He closed his eyes, searching for something to focus her on, to get her back into control. The pain in his arm throbbed, demanding attention. It would do. "I need help. A medikit."

"Back. Right outside the airlock." She was already turning. "Are you hurt?"

"A cut. It's bleeding." He could still feel it, warm and sticky inside his suit.

"I'll get the kit."

He slithered out of the bulky suit, standing mostly-naked in the corridor until Marcelle returned with a fistful of medical supplies held in a bare hand and one suit-glove clutched in her gloved hand. She stared at his arm, which dripped red blood. "You should have left your suit on until we got all the way back to a working hab."

"You sound like The Jackman."

"Someone needs to protect you," she shot back at him. "What if they space the air in here?"

He grimaced. "If the damned suit had worked, I could have saved Colin."

Her face screwed up into an expression that looked like rage and sorrow blended. As she wrapped the bandage around his arm, the look softened, replaced with calm and concern everywhere except her dark eyes. *They* were steeled and angry. "Hold that," she whispered, "use pressure." She helped him onto the cart and found a way for him to hook his elbow around a rail to hold on with the bleeding arm so he could keep pressure on the cut with his good arm.

Ix gave them directions.

Marcelle turned out to be quite deft at flying the cart.

If his arm didn't hurt so much he would have felt silly being out between levels in his underwear. As it was, it just meant he had to hang on tighter since his sweat-slicked bare skin wanted to slide off the smooth surface as Marcelle cornered faster than he would have. Not that he blamed her. Every turn left the robots further behind.

They rushed through the open space between cargo and the living pods, an eerie thin corridor full of supports and pipes and catwalks and storage.

The images in his head were all bad. The worst was Colin. He could see Colin whole and then not-whole. Over and over, like the picture wouldn't leave his mind. He barely felt the jerk as the cart stopped. Marcelle had a hand on his arm, and was helping him off before he understood they'd returned to the suit locker. His clothes were there, but of course hers weren't. She put on Colin's clothes, and did a second quick wrap of his arm before she let him put on his shirt.

As he followed Marcelle up the ladder into B-pod, he had to stop and hold on with both hands to keep from falling. She leaned down into the hatch Ix told them to go up, a worried look on her face. "Are you okay?"

"Dizzy."

"Come on, then. We'll find a place to rest." She braced herself on the rim and held her hand down to him. It took him three tries to grasp it with his good hand.

She had taken his hand a lot today.

She pulled, and he came up the ladder, slowly, step by step. He crawled out of the hole and fell onto his side, breathing hard.

Marcelle picked up his arm. "It's bled through." She supported him into a nearby hab. They had no trouble getting in—probably once more a gift from Ix. The hab was empty, and smelled stale.

She closed the door hard and double-checked with Ix to make sure it was locked.

He had to lean on her to get into the bed.

His shirt was caked to the bandage. He barely managed not to scream when she pulled it free. "That's deep," she murmured. "Good thing I brought something to close that with." She wrinkled her nose. "Let's get clean first. You've got blood everywhere."

She stripped him the rest of the way without blushing or teasing. Her calm strength let him relax as he stood under the water and she sponged blood and sweat from him. Then they were both naked and in the shower. They didn't talk, which he was grateful for. It wasn't very much like Marcelle to be quiet, and it was what he needed. To just stand and feel the water.

The shower stayed on longer than usual, recognizing the two users or perhaps helped by Ix. The water seemed to pick the fear up from his skin and wash it away one thin layer at a time. He left the shower before she did and dried himself off as best he could. His cut still bled, and he stained the towel.

By the time Marcelle emerged, wrapped in a towel herself, he had stretched out on the bed with his arm flung up by his ear and the other hand trying to put on enough pressure to stop the blood.

She pulled on her underwear and Colin's T-shirt and came to him. She wiped the cut clean with an astringent pad and filled it with a sharp-smelling paste. "This will keep it from getting infected."

"You were good back there," he murmured. "Fast. Might have saved our lives."

She bound the edges of his cut with thick, clear tape, then wiped the excess medicine and blood off his arm. Her fingers felt warm, gentle. "That was the most awful thing I ever saw. Colin. I can't . . . I can't believe it."

"I know."

"Do you know it's not your fault?"

He didn't have an answer. If he'd gone back to trade suits, if he had been stronger, if he had been more graceful . . .

She gave him one of her looks, the one that said *no nonsense and listen up*, the one that made him feel like a recalcitrant child. Then she said, "You did your best. We all did. You saved us both by sending me over the traverse line. Otherwise, I'd be dead, too. And you. Colin . . . Colin hesitated when you didn't. You can't blame yourself for that."

She was so damned earnest. "I'll try not to." It felt like a faint promise, but not quite a lie. Colin's death seemed so big, and so awful.

She checked the work she'd done on his arm, left her fingers on his shoulder. "I get it that they wanted to steal the cargo. I guess we learned a lesson there. But why hurt people?" Her voice sounded thin and high, like she might break. "Why kill Colin? What did they get out of that?"

Her fingers had tightened on his shoulder, and the human contact felt good. "I have no idea."

"We almost died," she said.

"We might die yet. Who knows what other surprises that ship has for us?"

"I want to live." She bent over him and kissed him on the lips. He didn't have the strength to turn away, and before he knew it he was returning her kiss as enthusiastically as she was delivering it. She smelled like stale sweat and fear and concern, but it was also the scent of life. He could feel it in her pulse, in her lips, in the way she put weight on him carefully, avoiding his arm.

He was already naked under the towel.

The heat of her erased the pain in his arm and the robot spiders and everything else he should be thinking about. It almost erased the pain of the last sight he had of Colin.

CHAPTER SEVENTEEN

The mood in the map room felt thick and dark.

Ruby sat on one of the benches along the wall, still fuming even though the command staff had been gone for at least twenty minutes. Haric had fallen asleep near her. His head and arms were pillowed on the bench and she could just hear his soft snores.

She stared at her journal as she struggled with words for speeches. All of her phrases came out awkward, but it was better than staring at the map table and waiting for news. Even though she was shut out of the real discussions, Ix did occasionally provide updates. The last had been unhelpful; a reminder that while they were trying to blow up the invader, it might be trying to blow them up, too.

Any moment could be her last. Their last.

As if sensing her thoughts, Haric moaned in his sleep.

There were a lot of people on the ship who knew less than she did. They would know enough to be frightened; rumors were social blood through every level of the ship.

She shouldn't be writing about speeches, she should be giving one.

"Ix?" She whispered so she wouldn't wake up Haric.

"Yes, Ruby?"

"Can you broadcast throughout the ship from here?"

"Yes Ruby. But I will not. Only command staff are allowed to broadcast from here."

Of course. The anger fisted even tighter in her, like a screw being turned slowly. "Where can I broadcast to everyone?"

"From any common."

"Will you also run a feed for me? So I can see what happens in the cargo bay with the robots?"

"I can run it to your journal."

It could do more, but she could live with this much. "Run the feed to Haric's journal, too. And Ani's. And make an announcement that I'll be talking. Tell everyone."

"Yes, Ruby."

The AI couldn't feel, but she was almost certain it understood sarcasm, at least on some level.

Ruby stood up quietly so she wouldn't wake Haric. She went home and took a shower and put on the best clothes she had: a pair of neat red pants and a deep green shirt with a blue vest the exact pale shade of her eyes. She circled her neck with multi-colored beads and pinned her hair up. Remembering the unexpected hike through the below corridors the evening of the festival, she slipped on comfortable boots that she could run in. She stopped back by the map room and shook Haric's shoulder softly. "Wake up. We're leaving."

Ani lay stretched out on a bench, her tall form folded and one foot hanging off. Ruby shook her shoulder. "Come with me?"

Ani opened her eyes and blinked at Ruby. "What's happened? Did the bombs work?"

"They're not there yet. We may have hours. I'm going to my people."

"All the way to gray again?"

"Ix says it will turn on a train to get us most of the way."

Ani ran her fingers through her hair. "The AI is spinning up a train for you?"

"The AI is doing a lot of things it doesn't usually do." Like killing. But she couldn't make herself tell Ani about that.

After they disembarked from the train, they jogged through a nearly-empty corridor.

A woman stepped out right in front of them, forcing Ani and Ruby and Haric to a stop. Women surrounded them, at least ten or maybe twelve. Directly in from of Ruby, Lya stood with her feet braced wide and her hands on her hips. "You should go back."

She had been beautiful once. She was only a year or two older than Ruby, maybe three. Her blonde hair hung in uneven strings and her shirt had two big holes in it that showed bones lifting skin across a thin frame. Ruby smiled as softly as she could in the face of Lya's continued deterioration. "I can't. I have to go tell the people something."

"Only what you want them to know."

Ruby signaled to Haric and Ani to stay quiet, and let out a breath as slowly as she could. "Isn't that always what any of us tell people? What we want them to know? In this case, I'm telling them that we are being attacked, and that we are counter-attacking. Don't you think they would like to know that?"

"You never told us you were going to abandon us."

Even though she knew there was no point in arguing with a broken mind, perhaps some of Lya's silent followers could be swayed. "If I were going to abandon you, I would not be standing here. There are dangers I need to tell people about."

"There's always danger near you," Lya said. "But that's not the biggest problem. You've changed." She made a gesture that encompassed Ruby's neatly clipped hair, her dress uniform, and her multicolored beads all at once. "Too fancy now. You've lost touch. Go away."

"And if I go away, who'll tell you what's happening?" She waited a moment. "Move. I need to pass, Lya. I don't want to hurt you."

Lya's cheeks were stained with dark circles and she stank of sour still. But she was still stubborn. If only Ruby could get her to be stubborn about things that either Lya or Ruby could change. At the moment, she looked like she wanted to spit on Ruby. "Hugh wouldn't have wanted to see you like this. All high and mighty. It would have hurt him."

"And he wouldn't have wanted to see you addicted to still."

That moved Lya far enough for Ruby to press harder and pass. "I'm sorry," Lya said as Ruby pulled Haric and Ani through the crack of corridor that Lya and her followers didn't fill. "I'm sorry."

Ruby wasn't sure what Lya was sorry for, but she couldn't think about that now. They were so close to common she heard the buzz of conversations.

The big room was full, but people immediately made a path for her. Fear and anxiety echoed in tones of voice and on faces, and in the way parents clutched children's hands. Each familiar face made all of the things that could go wrong seem both worse and more likely.

They could all die.

She pushed toward the podium. The crowd included people she knew. Her aunt Daria. Kyle, the man who'd taken her and Onor and Marcelle in long ago, balancing plates of cookies. He must have been cooking long before the announcement. Maybe he did more for people with his food than she did with her songs. The idea made her laugh a little, released some of the anger she still felt toward Joel and toward the ugly ship.

She liked the idea that Onor and Joel would be furious that she was here with no guards except Ani and Haric. It gave her extra energy to feel like she was breaking rules. But that didn't mean she should be stupid. She leaned down and spoke softly to Haric. "Wander through the crowd and guard. Let me know if you hear or see anything. Make a circle, and check in with Ani on each circle. Try not to let people know you're watching them."

"Okay."

"There's a man with cookies—Kyle. Bring me one. And have one yourself—they're fabulous. Tell Kyle I said thank you for being here."

Haric looked very solemn. "Kyle. Cookies."

"Thank you."

He'd be discounted since so many people only saw or knew the child in him, and he'd feel big for being asked. Ruby set Ani to watching her journal, and kept her close so she could signal Ruby if there was any news.

Ruby stood at the end of the stage and waited until they quieted. "You deserve to know what's happening."

She told them about the ship and had Ix broadcast a picture on the screens in the room. She thought about leaving out the explosives or the worry that the other ship could attack them. She took a deep breath and kept talking. They deserved to know they were in danger. She talked for so long that Haric passed through twice, giving her the high sign in both cases.

By the time she finished, the crowd was very, very quiet. People sat close together in family or friend groups.

She wanted to stop and talk to Ix, to find out about the robots, and to know Joel was okay. But she could see from the faces looking at her that they needed something more. "I'll sing now. Just one song." She sang "Song of the Seed," the one she'd sung after Ben's funeral. It was the most hopeful song she'd ever written. When she finished, she let a beat go by, then another before she addressed her audience everywhere on the ship. "Wait with me. If you're just listening, and you want to be here, come if you aren't on shift. If you are on shift, thank you for your service.

"We're going to wait for success or failure. Now, I'm going to take a break and see if there is anything new to learn."

Ruby stood at the edge of the stage for a few minutes and looked quietly out over the room. About a quarter of the people left amid whispered conversations and brief kisses.

She sat down by Ani, speaking softly. "What's happening?"

CHAPTER EIGHTEEN

When Onor woke, it felt as if he were coming up from someplace as deep as his past and as far away as the world when he and Ruby and Marcelle were children dodging reds like Ben through the corridors between workshops and habs.

Marcelle's even breathing drew him back to the present. He felt . . . not regret. There was no way to regret becoming lost in Marcelle, being one with her if only for a moment. The comfort of it. The way it had felt right and inevitable in spite of how it felt wrong . . .

Marcelle snored. He remembered that from lying on the bottom bunk under her at Kyle's. Her snoring had amused him then. It sounded better beside him than it had above him, even though it wasn't muffled by a mattress. He opened his eyes and watched her take little snorting breaths, shaking a tiny bit from time to time as if she were dreaming. She was beautiful—her hair messy from lovemaking, the hollows in her cheeks filled in by sleep, as if they were caused by worry when she was awake. She was so thin the ridge of her spine and the low mountains of muscle beside it were clear and distinct.

He had participated in an act that would change their relationship forever. If they lived.

"Ix," he whispered. "What's happening?"

In answer, a small screen on the wall at the base of the bed snapped on, glowing brightly.

Marcelle groaned at the light and covered her eyes, not quite waking. She had rejected all of the pillows, so Onor stacked three up and watched as Ix showed him a view of one of the common rooms. Ruby stood on a stage, holding a microphone close to her lips as if she wanted to swallow it. The volume was down, so he couldn't hear her words, but her feet were planted slightly apart, her back straight, her head up. She moved fluidly, crossing the stage and recrossing it, her eyes meeting the camera from time to time as they scanned the room. She couldn't know he was watching, but she knew she was being broadcast.

There had been a time when Marcelle was better with a crowd than Ruby. But Jaliet and Fox and necessity had made Ruby stronger. Now, in times like this when she wanted to make a difference, she not only changed a room, she commanded it.

Marcelle groaned and rolled over, her hand bumping up against him. She startled awaked, propping herself up on one elbow. "I didn't dream."

"Maybe you were too tired."

"No. I didn't dream . . . you and me."

He reached over and touched her cheek. "No."

She got up out of bed and visited the privy. When she came back, she sat beside him, watching the silent Ruby. "She looks good." Marcelle mused. "But she has to be as scared as we are."

"Maybe." He remembered being chased, which prompted him to put a grateful arm around Marcelle's shoulders and to ask Ix to turn on the volume.

"What else is happening?" he asked.

"We're attacking the other ship."

"Wow. Can we win?" Onor asked.

Marcelle snuggled in closer to him, skin to skin. She smelled of sex and soap and sweat.

"It is possible."

Onor kissed Marcelle's cheek. "What about Ellis and Sylva? They were going after Ruby. Did you stop them?"

"I did not."

A fresh resentment of the machine jarred him more alert. "But Ruby's okay?"

"Ruby is fine. You were just watching her."

Oh. Right. "So what happened to Ellis and Sylva?"

"They died."

"How?" Marcelle asked. "Who killed them?"

"They died of lack of oxygen. That's all the information I have for you."

CHAPTER NINETEEN

Ani sat on the back of the stage, leaning against the wall with her journal in her lap. She was so focused on her journal—propped against her knees—that Ruby had to repeat her question. "What's happening?"

"They're just now going into the cargo bay."

"Really? I was sure I'd missed it all."

"KJ made them practice."

Ruby laughed in spite of the tension, maybe because of it. "The hammer of an enemy hangs above us, and KJ demands a perfect, practiced pose."

Haric had left one of Kyle's cookies each for Ruby and Ani. Ruby bit into hers. It tasted like warmth and friendship, and smelled of the fresh herbs Kyle grew in his tiny galley. "Have you ever kissed KJ?" she asked.

"No. Get your journal. They've climbed into the airlocks."

"How many?"

"There's ten going in. From five directions."

Ruby peeled her journal off her belt and opened it out. "KJ will beat them. He has to. I can't imagine flying home with rogue robots in one of the bays."

Ani's entire body tensed, her face a mask of resolution.

It must be torture to love someone who barely noticed you. Ruby was furious with Joel, but had no doubt that they would be together tonight. He needed her, and he would remember that.

The small screen was much harder to watch than the map table. She took another bite of the cookie.

All four robots had gathered on the ground floor of the cargo bay, or what passed for a ground floor in null-g. They huddled close together almost as if they were talking.

KJ and his people cycled in through the airlocks.

Ruby expected the robots to attack them as they came in, but instead they scuttled into four separate positions.

The humans were less than a quarter of the size of the robots.

KJ spread his people in two groups of four and one group of two, keeping as much distance between the people and the bots as possible.

"It'll be okay," Ruby whispered back, even though Ani hadn't been talking to her. "It has to be."

"Be careful," Ani whispered to her screen. "They're fast."

Ruby glanced away from the image. People were coming in with blankets and pillows and snacks. Parents had children by the hand, some looking like they never intended to let go. A few stood by the stage, watching her and Ani gravely.

Haric came by and spoke softly to her. "They're frightened but they're all okay. No one seems mad at you right now."

"No. This is bigger than me. Do you need a break?"

"No."

"Thank you."

Haric disappeared back into the crowd.

"Ix, what about the ships? Are they there yet?"

"No."

Ruby returned her attention to her journal. Something had happened—the configuration was different. There were lines and chains wrapped around one of the bots. Two people were tying the chains tighter. One of the bot's forelegs got a good grip on a line and snapped it and then waved it very close to one of the humans. Another human sailed by and dropped a thicker line over the freed limb. KJ's people were far more fluid in null-g than Colin's had been, than Onor or Marcelle or even Colin himself. They must practice.

One of the figures approached the bound robot. She would be willing to bet it was KJ, even though she couldn't have said what subtle clues she was getting from the way one figure moved differently than another when they were all in bulky environment suits. He held something out in his hand and fired it at the bot.

It convulsed once and then all of the legs relaxed as much as they could inside of the chains and lines that bound it. That was it—a touch and the thing had stilled.

"Ix. What is that. What did KJ do?"

"It's called electromagnetic pulse. EMP. It destroys circuitry."

"A robot stunner?"

"Worse. A tight-beam EMP gun."

"It won't wake back up?" she asked.

"No."

Good. The camera shifted. A second bot had already been tightly bound. She watched it struggle and then go completely limp, shift from alive to dead.

She'd never thought of robots as something that could be alive before.

The other two bots had moved as far away from humans as they could get. One inched toward the lock to the outside, perhaps trying to escape what was beginning to look like a sure fate.

She watched the next capture. The humans met together in a group of six, some distance away from the target. They separated, five of them moving in five directions, making what looked like a net of chain and lines. They pulled the bonds out from a large bag held by a single suited figure.

One bot was under them and one was over them. The one "above" them clung very near the door to open space. They moved the chain in the "up" direction. The bot tried to cut the net of chain that was surrounding it in slow motion. It managed to sever one line, but all of the chain and all of the other lines held.

It looked like it was trying to stay alive.

Ruby had grown up expecting to be a robot repair person. She'd apprenticed. She'd spent hours breaking fingernails on parts and getting grease in the cracks of her elbow. None of the robots she'd worked on had ever complained if she stopped them, parted them out, or put them away. Not one of them had thanked her for fixing a broken part. Come to think of it, none of them had ever killed anyone either, except one big cleaning robot that killed a child by accident when Ruby was five. And that was the fault of the creche worker, not the robot.

"Ix."

"Yes, Ruby."

"Ix. Stop them. Stop them now."

"I cannot do that."

As she spoke, the next to last bot that they had tied up was stilled.

She almost screamed, as if volume could make Ix understand. "Leave the last one alive."

"Why?"

"I can learn from it. Tell them, now. It's important."

"Now? You want to study it now?"

"No. Have KJ tie it up and leave it. I'll study after we beat the ugly ship." Or not. It didn't need to be said.

Ix stayed silent for so long it must have been conversing with humans. She was pretty sure it was talking to KJ and Joel and maybe also to Conroy, who was surely one of the suited figures in there.

These were not the robots she knew how to repair, not the robots Onor had learned to run when he was working down below with Penny. These were more like Ix. Maybe the ugly ship was actually a ship full of sentient robots.

That didn't make sense.

But still, she felt certain these robots had not only demonstrated thought, but also feeling. They might be clues about what else they'd find at Adiamo.

Her journal screen showed that the fourth robot had been tied up. It twitched in its bonds, as if trying to stretch them so it could free itself.

It hadn't been killed yet. The humans were still in the cargo bay, still waiting. Her best hope was that Ix had really understood what she meant. That perhaps Ix had seen what she'd seen. Surely it would be curious about other machines that could think.

Ani looked at her. "I hope it's sorry the other robots died. When I think about Colin and the other two, I hope it knows that we're three for three now. Is that right?"

"Revenge can't replace Colin," Ruby replied.

"Of course not," Ani said. "That's not what I meant. But I agree with you. Those things don't look like people, and they don't entirely act like people, but in some ways they reminded me of people. They *chose* like people."

"I'm glad I'm not the only one who noticed," Ruby told Ani. She stood and stretched, looking out over the crowd. Some of the children and old people had dozed off. Soon, she'd stand up and have Ix display pictures of the dead robot spiders.

She wanted the verdict on the life of the last one first.

CHAPTER TWENTY

Kyle walked around the crowded common room, bending down to let people choose food from trays. A few children followed him around.

Ruby stood beside the stage, watching. She had sung two rounds of songs, taken two long down times, and even managed to close her eyes and doze—but not sleep—for ten minutes. Some in the crowd had come and gone with the last shift change. The room felt thick with stale apprehension. Children played in the bare spots.

Haric stood beside Ruby. He looked tired. Of course he was—she had interrupted his sleep in the map room after all, and brought him down here and given him a job. "Did you see anything?"

"Maybe. Not see. Hear. I heard a little fight in a corner of the room. Loud whispers. Your name was in it. One of the people sounded angry."

"Thanks. Which corner?"

"The far left if you stand in the doorway we came in."

Ruby glanced at Ani, who stood up. "I'll do a round. It's time for you to eat, Haric."

"We're out of cookies."

"People have been bringing us food. I saved you some." She handed Haric a fruit, a piece of candy and a small stack of crackers.

"Any news?" he asked.

"I think it will be soon."

"I hope so."

Ix spoke through the tinny speakers on her journal. "Ruby?"

"Yes."

"KJ will leave the robot bound and functioning."

It hadn't said alive. "Ix, are you alive?"

"In what sense?"

"Never mind." Haric looked puzzled but she didn't take time to explain the robots or the questionable life of AI's to him. "Any news about the explosives?"

"One of them was intercepted. It went off, and destroyed the part of the enemy ship that found it."

Ruby grimaced. "Now it knows to watch for bombs."

"It probably does."

"Why don't you ever just say yes, you dumb machine?"

"I say 'yes' when I am certain of the answer. The answer is likely in this case, but it is not certain."

She sighed.

"You might consider standing on stage."

To tell them about the robots? "I might. Is it *certain* that I should?"

"Yes."

She wondered if it knew she was teasing it. She obeyed, though, and stood on the end of the stage. There were at least a hundred people spread across the benches and floor, maybe more. Probably more. Some slept.

She took the microphone and started to sing, letting her voice rise from low tones to slightly louder on each chorus of a popular Heaven Andrews working song.

People stirred. Whispered conversations happened. Onor and Marcelle came in and stood in the back of the room.

Good. A part of her released worry she hadn't even realized she had been holding onto.

The speakers in the room popped, alerting her just a few moments before Ix's voice came on. "Watch." Screens came alive, displaying a picture of the ugly ship.

The AI wasn't above creating drama.

For most of the people in the room, it was the first view they had of the enemy. Ix fell silent, and Ruby waited a few beats before she raised her voice. "This is what we sent three ships to destroy. It is almost as big as the *Fire*."

Many people stood, as if that would give them a better view. Others stood to see around the people who had stood in front of them. She asked, "Please sit down, so everyone can see."

Most people sat, although a few in the back ignored her request.

Ix's voice. "I will show you the trajectories of all three flying bombs that we sent to destroy this ship."

Three orange dots showed up. They flew fairly far apart. One almost immediately connected with a similar-sized dot far outside of the enemy ship, and then disappeared. That must be the one she knew about.

The other two made it half of the distance between the place the first ship blew up and their target before one of them, too, winked out of existence. Ix. "It will be success if the orange dot touches the ship."

By now, she knew it would. She had come to understand Ix that much. Even so, she held her breath, waiting.

The orange dot impacted the ugly ship, moved into it—barely, but into it. Penetrated it.

It seemed like a small thing, but a few people clapped. Ruby clapped. More clapped and then more.

The orange flashed red and gold, a simulation taken from one of the games people played.

A piece broke off of the strange ship and floated free. Some of the smaller ships that had hugged its outside tumbled away from it, as if pushed by a force that wasn't visible on the screen.

Everyone who wasn't standing moved like one to their feet, whooping. People jumped up and down. Children screeched and found their parents, showed up on people's shoulders, clapping.

Ruby wished Ix were human so she could thank it properly. She did whisper, "Thank you. Thank you. Thank you."

If Ix replied to her, the room was too noisy for Ruby to hear what it said.

During the long time that it took for the room to quiet, Ruby wondered if humans had been hurt on the ship, or if instead they had simply damaged robots. Maybe Adiamo was populated by machines, and they were coming home to become the soft slaves of robots.

Nothing else happened on the screen. The ship continued to hang in space, and no more pieces broke off. "Can it hurt us?" she whispered.

No response.

She spoke into the microphone. "Ix! Can it hurt us?"

"I'm calculating."

Onor and Marcelle had come closer to her. Ani was with them.

The screens went dark, as if to signal that the show was over. Ix spoke. "I believe we have damaged the other ship enough that we will be able to pass it and continue on our way. It may or may not be able to repair itself. For now, we are safe."

CHAPTER TWENTY-ONE

Ruby sat at the head of the bed, naked, her legs curled up close to her, her body a ball she held together with her interlocked arms. Exhaustion and relief warred in her nerves. They could have died. Winning felt like exhilaration and abomination all at once, like victory tinged with a feeling she couldn't quite put a name too, but which was like the way she felt about what Joel had done to her enemies. Power used because there was no other easy or comprehensible way to survive.

Joel moved around the room, putting things away, organizing. His jaw was tight and stiff, his face unreadable. Usually he relaxed in here, with her. Even though he had refused her entry to his councils, it seemed like so much had happened since then that they were already different people than the ones who had started the argument that still lay between them.

She forced herself to stretch, used breathing techniques KJ had taught her to let go of the fears and exhaustion gnawing at her. She spoke quietly. "I could add value to your councils."

He stopped and stared at her, his face softening a tiny bit. "You will not add any value if I am not able to hold onto my power. I may have disposed of one enemy, but there are more."

Ruby winced but kept her voice as soft as she could. "You need representation from my people."

"It wasn't possible, not today. Save this fight for a time when it won't distract us from more important things."

Ruby bit her tongue.

"Besides," he continued, "If you didn't press in public, I wouldn't have needed to turn you down in public."

Damn him. She held her temper and her hurt as far away from her heart as possible. "My people have good strong voices. They're brave and they know how to work together."

"Are they your people?"

Joel's words made Ruby flinch.

"Even now when you're here, with me?" he added. "How long can that hold true?"

The implications of his thought made her angry. "Of course they are. I grew up with them. I went to them when you wouldn't let me join you. I sat with them in the common room and we waited for the ships to win, sure they might not. I sat with them, waiting to die."

His voice rose a touch and got more commanding. "If I had let you into our council, you wouldn't have gone to *your people*. Maybe that was the right decision. For you to be there."

That stopped her for a moment. "Maybe so. But everyone needs a voice in your councils. If Ix had failed to blow up that ship, we would *all* have died."

He raised an eyebrow at her, still standing in one place, one hand on an open drawer. "What would have changed about the decision if you had been there? Or if more people had been part of it? A crowd makes a decision impossible."

She turned her head to hide the frustration that must be visible in her eyes. Not to acquiesce, never to acquiesce. "It was a good decision. Almost all of your choices are good. But decisions made in the dark aren't always fair. You and I—we can be a symbol. We can be the mother and father of our people, united. We can stand side by side and represent the balance of work and command, the joining of man and woman, the beauty of song and the strength of a ready warrior."

He laughed and she realized how exaggerated her words were—something meant for lyrics instead of to heal an argument. But they were true. She didn't try to take them back.

He pushed the drawer shut and continued stripping, standing there long and lean, marked with old scars from years spent training and fighting, but nonetheless whole and vibrant. Even when she was angry with him, he drew her. Maybe even more then. She opened an arm toward him.

He came to lie beside her.

She let her fingers play through his short, graying hair. He had not acknowledged what she asked for. "I love you," she said. "Remember before? The first time we met? I told you that I needed to matter, that I needed to be more than a lover."

"You do. You are."

She ran her hands over his shoulders, her touch light.

"The best lover," he murmured. "So strong, so perfect."

For a few moments touch was the only conversation between them. Then he whispered, "You have more power than you know. But there are places others are not ready for me to allow you to go."

"But they will be. You can help them to be ready for me."

He reached a hand up and caressed her cheek. "In the meantime, I am happy to listen to you."

"I'm valuable for more than bedroom advice." She took his hand in two of hers and began massaging his palm, using her thumb to draw strong circles in it. Perhaps she had pushed far enough for this moment. He would think about it. He was like that often, listening to her with no reaction and then evaluating what she said. "Ask me a question."

He smiled, his blue-green eyes bright in a face paled with exhaustion and slightly reddened by arousal. Such a hard life he led, so much pressure. She wasn't sure he was going to answer, but he finally asked, "What do you think it means that the only greeting from home so far is an attempt to steal from us?"

"That we must be very, very careful."

He sighed. "Yes. There may be no need for any of us at all now that the ship is back. Perhaps we were always slaves."

She drew in a sharp little breath, and then let it out slowly. "It cannot be like that. We are too brilliant, too creative, too strong to waste."

"But we were wasting you, even inside this small ship."

She put a finger over his lips. "At least you know that now."

Yet he had wasted the people who followed Ellis and Sylva. She slid to her knees and straddled him, her naked body touching his in as many places as she could manage without dropping all of her weight onto him. "Perhaps we should make sure not to waste this night. Tomorrow is getting even more uncertain."

In answer he pulled her down, kissing her so hard that she felt her lips bruise. It felt good.

PART TWO
CHOICES

CHAPTER TWENTY-TWO

Onor finally found Ruby in the cargo bar, chatting with Allen. Colin's fight leader had become one of a handful of heirs-apparent after Colin and Par's deaths, but in the three days between then and now, no decisions had been made. Ruby smiled up at the man, her head cocked, her face fully attentive.

Onor hesitated: Ruby twirled a glass of wine in her hand and a hint of red flush stained her cheeks. She turned her head as Onor approached, and it became too late to back away.

Besides, he didn't want to.

Clearly she was able to read his mood. She stood up, her face instantly gone from soft and teasing to tense. "What happened?"

"I need to talk to you in private."

She looked torn, but this wasn't a conversation he was willing to share with Allen. "This won't take long," he added.

Ruby whispered something to Allen, kept her glass, and followed Onor as he turned and led her out of the room, and into the same private space where he and Haric had told Colin and Allen about the approaching ship. Unsurprisingly, Ruby ignored the table and sat on the worn blue couch. She gestured for him to sit beside her.

"I prefer to stand." Now that he had her in a private place, he didn't know how to begin. Angry sentences piled up behind his lips, unwilling to emerge.

She waited him out, twisting her hands in her hair and pulling out clips, letting it fall.

He turned away. He tried to modulate his voice, but failed. "I know what happened to Ellis and Sylva. And the others."

She didn't say anything.

The silence dragged on until he couldn't help himself, and he turned to look at her. Her pale blue eyes showed no remorse at all. Her muscles had tensed, and her lips thinned. Some of the other sentences he'd been holding back came out, sounding disjointed. "It was murder. Turning off life support. How could you? Do you know how horribly they died?"

She nodded, controlled calm to his storm. Her words came out slow, as if she were on stage talking to a group of children. "They were trying to take over the ship's command. Right when we were being attacked by an enemy."

"That doesn't make it honorable."

"They would have killed us."

"Maybe. But you could have locked them up. They could have been killed in a fair fight. Most of their followers were just blind; we could have saved them. KJ and his people could have taken them. I doubt they *could* have gotten in to command." He realized he had moved to stand over her.

She smelled of wine and spices, and her face stayed cool and collected. She took another sip of wine, holding the glass to her lips for a second too long. When she finished, she said, "They were your enemies, too."

"I wouldn't have done that to them."

"Even to protect me?" She stood up, her gaze meeting his evenly. "Joel did it to protect me, so he didn't need to worry about me and the ship all at once."

Her words felt like punches in his chest. Not because they were wrong. Because they were wrong for her. She lived for fairness, fought for fairness, and now she was defending cold-blooded murder. He stepped back, and the wall stopped his movement too fast, the room too small to contain them both. "We did this—we fought this fight—for justice. For everybody. You can't just become like Garth, and kill people because they . . . they *inconvenience* you."

Ruby took another sip of wine. She had become so much better at controlling herself than she used to be, so much more . . . theatrical.

He slammed his fist backward into the wall, the sharp thud and the pain both good. "You're not the same anymore. You would have hated yourself."

She closed the distance between them and her hand came up and slapped his left cheek hard enough to shift his balance so that he fell against the wall and had to shuffle his feet to keep them under him.

Her cool had gone completely, her voice high and tight. "You cannot know what we have to deal with, what it's like to be responsible. Every day Joel and his people have to make decisions they hate. I do fight them, some of them. I fight more than you can possibly know."

"So tell me how you fought this one?"

She met his gaze for a moment, and he finally saw guilt and confusion on her face before she turned away. "I didn't. I didn't know about it. Not until after it was done."

He stood behind her, close enough to smell her again, and he put his hands on her shoulders. Her shirt was so thin that he felt her bone and muscle beneath his hands, even felt the warmth of her body. A single multi-colored strand of beads hung around her neck, visible from behind only because she'd tugged her hair all to one side. Her muscles tensed under his hands. He tried to shift his weight and turn her, but she shook her head, refusing to meet his eyes. "Why do you protect Joel?" he asked her.

"He's smart enough to keep us all safe, and he's willing to care." She turned, breaking his grip so his hands fell by his sides. Her eyes were damp. They'd lost the guilt, and instead she looked resolute. "You can't understand."

"Try me."

"I can't be everything, Onor. I must maintain my position or I will lose my ability to keep the fairness we *have* won. Choices have to be made." She paused, took a deep breath, and when she started again her voice was firmer but softer. "If we—if I—If I fight every fight, I will lose one day. And if I lose, then we—all of us from gray—will lose our voice."

Her look melted the anger out from under him, so he felt a bit loose in his moorings, a bit empty. "We can also lose if you—or we—give up our principles."

"Don't you think I know that? After all we've been through, I'm clear on what matters. But we have gained so much that we cannot afford to lose, and power contains compromise." She paused. "You're the one who is always talking about power, thinking about power. We used to be the ones who didn't have it. Now we do."

She did.

As if she were reading his reaction, she said, "You, too. Joel trusts you. The Jackman and Conroy trust you. Come on out with me and help me work on Allen. Once you have power, you don't keep it by fighting."

He touched her cheek.

She gazed at him for a long time, a universe of feelings in her eyes. Then she turned away.

CHAPTER TWENTY-THREE

Ruby hated pressure suits. They stank. The best one she'd been able to find had slightly short legs so she always felt like she should bend her knees, and the right elbow joint was harder to move than the left, so she expected to overcompensate in low-g and jerk herself to the left of where she wanted to go. Everything must have been perfect when the *Fire* left Adiamo, but she was willing to bet half of the damned ship would fail by the time it got home.

She didn't like the airlock a whole lot more than the stiff and stinky suit, especially since it felt crowded with two of them. KJ sat closest to the bay door. She had wanted Onor or Marcelle, but the only way Joel had allowed her to visit the robot spider was with KJ right next to her.

She held her breath while pressure equalized, relaxing only when KJ could open the inner door to the cargo bay. They sat side by side on the lip of the lock, looking down. The small amount of gravity that Ix let them impose on the bay—about twenty-five percent—allowed their legs to hang down in a fashion.

Lights illuminated most of the vast space, although there were corners where shadow still ruled.

The traverse lines had all been replaced and strengthened. A crew of KJ's carefully trained fighters, now nicknamed spider dancers, waited on the far side of the bay by the other airlock. They crouched as still as the metal ribs of the vast bay. They would only move if KJ asked them to, or if they perceived that KJ or Ruby were in life-threatening danger.

Blocky, multicolored cargo containers were strapped and bolted to the walls. The containers the robots had cut loose had been retied with bright yellow straps, so that they stood out from the others.

Two spiders sat unmoving, still trapped in ropes. They looked as dead as she had been assured they were; chains and ropes held their metal limbs in lifelike poses. A third had been reduced by half. Four legs had been taken out of the hold piece by piece to be examined by a bot repair crew.

The last living one sat where it had been captured, still trussed in rope and chain. It flexed its metal appendages against its bonds. "It sees us," Ruby whispered.

KJ's answer reminded her of a conversation they'd had getting ready for this. "They have a good sense of their surroundings, and act as if they can see in every direction at once."

"I want to get closer."

"Of course you do." If they were in a world without helmets and radios, she was certain he'd be laughing at her.

She grabbed a traverse line and hooked onto it.

"Be careful," KJ whispered. "I'll be right behind you."

The vertical traverse passed near a horizontal line, and she switched, heading toward the bot she'd saved. When she stood on the outer edge close to the bot, she stared in awe. Its mass reminded her she was small and soft.

Its front appendages ended in the claws that had cut cargo straps as if they were paper, severed traverse lines, and destroyed humans. The claws were as tall as Ruby, and each of the three long metal bones between the joints were also as tall as Ruby, and wide enough that she would fit inside them if they were hollow. Each leg could bend in three places. KJ glided down the traverse and stood beside her, both of them silent in front of the bound enemy.

Ruby took a deep breath through her mouth, doing her best to avoid the suit-smell and the almost unmanageable temptation to rip her helmet off. There was air, but the safety protocols in the cargo bays were strict.

She chewed her lower lip. "It's not completely different than our bots," she said. "I can see how the claws move."

KJ responded in his typical dry tone. "It is bigger than most of ours."

"There's transport bots that are a quarter this size." She tried for humor. "I suppose it's possible to consider the trains a bot."

"Whatever works for you. Just don't leave this anchor line and don't get too close. Let's get started."

As if in answer, the bot flexed all of its appendages at once, straining its bindings. She wondered if this one had torn Colin in half.

"Ix." Ruby called the AI up, surely unnecessarily. Protocol, like the helmets. "Ix, tell it we're here and tell it we want to know why they invaded us."

"I will translate."

The conversation should have been fast. Machines talked to each other much more quickly than humans. But it wasn't. She waited, and waited some more. She listened to her breath, and KJ's breath through the radio link between them.

There was time to wonder if Ix had—in fact—decoded enough of the speech between the bots to build a communication bridge between itself and the invader. She shifted, trying to get comfortable with the floating feeling of low-g again.

Ix chose a voice she had never heard, tinny and feminine. "What happened to the *Thief of a Thousand Stars?*"

Ix changed to its most common voice. "That must be the invader's ship."

Aptly named. Ruby regarded the huge bot, which did not react directly to her presence in any way. "We damaged it. It has been left far behind. We had no choice."

This time the answer was fast. "But it is not completely dysfunctional? Does it have life support and engines?"

Ruby managed to bite back a comment about how she hoped not. "We don't know."

Silence.

After a while, Ruby asked Ix, "Is it talking to you?"

"No. Nor is it moving."

"But it's not dead?"

"I'm not sure that question applies. It remains capable of responding as far as I can tell. There is nothing like this in my history of Adiamo."

Ruby had prepared questions in her head. "Ask it if Adiamo is full of people or robots or both."

More time. KJ shifted and moved, stretching. She followed his lead. It helped calm her. The spider dancers remained in the corner, but they too stretched and moved, as if following their leader.

At one point in Ix's long silence, the bot thrashed and flexed, although the bonds held.

"It is not answering."

"Very well."

More standing. She had asked Ix to record this, hoping it would be a good backdrop for a performance. She looked at KJ. "While we wait, can we climb around some? Maybe go look more closely at one of the dead ones?"

KJ didn't respond immediately.

"Please?"

In answer, he stepped back and pointed up the traverse line she still held in her right glove. He wanted her to go first. Very well.

The leap up worked pretty well, and she clung to the line with both legs. Her body remembered a trick she'd been taught, and she pushed out from the line, so her hands and feet were both on it, but not her belly. She walked her hands up, then her feet, then her hands, then her feet, hands, feet, her appendages hard to keep stuck to the line with no gravity. A matter of gripping with her gloves and toes.

KJ hadn't started up after her. She was a good way past him now, and the robot looked smaller.

She let go and *pulled*, which felt less awkward, but was slower.

She stopped again, and this time KJ started up after her. He moved with no extra movement, no real pull on the line, nothing. He made small movements to maintain trajectory and add speed, as if null-g made him dance.

She grimaced.

"Ix? Did it say anything yet?"

"No."

"Are you still trying?"

"What do you suggest?"

"Play it our history. One of the lessons from school. The one that starts when we leave Adiamo."

KJ spoke up. "You want to give an enemy our history?"

"I don't see what it can hurt."

"How do you think it will help?"

"Maybe if it understands us, it will be sympathetic."

KJ laughed. "Follow me." They had reached open space near the middle of the bay, all of the closest objects other traverse lines, the robots small again. KJ contorted his body, drawing completely in on himself, and then pushed, sailing for a nearby horizontal traverse line.

She tried to mimic him exactly, but wavered when it came time to let go, stealing her own momentum from herself in a brief flash of fear. She fell away from KJ and the lines.

A hand grabbed her long before she expected to be caught. "Thank you."

He helped her get both hands onto the new line. Her fall had cost them some distance.

"Thank you again. We should have sent you in with these damned things first. You'd have survived and we'd still have Colin."

"Yes."

She wished she could see his face. "So why didn't that happen?"

"I was guarding Joel." He paused, and then pointed. "Up. We're going to look at the one that's been partly taken apart."

Joel probably made the decision about who went where. "Ix? Make it tell us why it killed people if you can."

"It is not responding."

"Can you tell if it's listening to you?"

"Only if it responds."

Ruby was slower than KJ, but she didn't make any more serious mistakes on the way to the half a bot. It was scratched and dented where the spider dancers had separated its parts, but it was still big enough to be daunting. She gritted her teeth and looked away the first time she touched it.

All of the legs on one side had been removed by KJ's spider dancers. The remaining legs were still tied down. The torso was small, maybe the size of a human torso.

There were no animals or insects on the *Fire*, just plants and people and robots. But Ruby had seen pictures. In Adiamo, the game about their home system, there were four-legged mammals, myriad insects, and birds of all sizes.

She studied it. Even though it was far larger, it was simpler than the robots she'd grown up cleaning. It was a better description to say they all joined below it. The design of the robot encased the small torso in a cage that the ends of the legs could rotate around. Or at least that was the best way she could think of to describe it. This part of the design was nothing like what she knew. She crouched, holding onto one of the legs and staring. "Elegant," she whispered. "And what were you really?"

Whatever was in the cage, nothing could touch it during normal operation of the robot, at least not as far as she could tell. There was an inner structure that supported it, but no strength, no torque.

She pointed. "Why didn't you take this part?"

"We couldn't cut it free. There's a team coming back for it this afternoon."

"Okay. I want to see it. Tell me when?"

"We're keeping it pretty much out of sight for now."

She froze in place, wishing yet again that they weren't in suits. The bulk limited her ability to display body language. "KJ?"

"Yes." Flat, noncommittal.

"Last I checked, you and I were on the same side. The one that wants freedom and information and fairness and a voice for all, right?"

Silence.

"Answer me."

"I don't work for you."

"Of course you don't," she snapped. She took a deep breath. "But you and I *should* be working together. Before I came up from gray, I worked on robots. I know a few things. And there's some more things I suspect about these."

"I know."

"So don't keep secrets from me."

He said nothing. The man was harder to read than anyone she knew. Ani could have him . . . Sex with KJ would be a perfect dance, but you'd probably never know if you'd given him pleasure.

"Follow me," he said, inching up toward the claw. "Look here . . . we think it was designed to be a weapon."

So maybe he was willing to answer her in his own way. She paid careful attention while he pointed out features of the claw and the arm, and then the powerful, flexible feet. They stared at the object in the cage. It was almost featureless, as long as her calf, and almost as big around as her waist. Smooth and black. "Have we gotten a good look at this in the live bot?"

"The way it's tied we can't see it at all."

She rocked back, staring at it.

"No, we're not going to move the live one."

She laughed. "I'm not that much of an idiot. But maybe there's footage. Ix? Can you review your recordings for anything we can learn about this? It has to be the brains."

"Yes, Ruby."

"Is it talking to you yet?"

"No."

"All right. Let me try one more time." She needed a reaction, some kind of win for keeping the thing alive.

Back at the bottom of the bay and staring up at the bot, Ruby said, "Ix? Translate."

"Ready."

"We are unhappy that you invaded us. It is a fact that we damaged your ship, and it is done. It cannot be undone any more than the way that you killed our people can be undone. Now that you have our history, you know it has been a long time since we left Adiamo. We have told you our story. Will you tell us yours?"

Ix's spider-voice asked, "Is the *Thief of a Thousand Stars* following you?"

She didn't know. Ix responded. "No."

The machine remained silent.

She stood, nearly floating, holding onto the vertical traverse line. "Ix?"

"Yes, Ruby?"

"Is the air in here safe?"

"Yes."

She unclipped her helmet so the spider-thing could see her.

"Don't," KJ warned.

"It's only a rule." She drew in a breath of fresh air, full of strange lubricants and smells that must be unique to cargo. She'd had her helmet off on cargo before—always against orders—and she didn't remember the oily tang she scented now.

She didn't know what she was hoping for, just that maybe . . . maybe . . . the bot would react to her humanity. There had to be some way to touch it, and damned if any talk they'd tried had done it.

She started in on "Homecoming":

> *Long and dark is our night flight*
> *No stars shine inside Fire's skin, only*
> *Me and you. And love. We're going*
> *Home*

No reaction. She sang it all the way through, putting as much feeling as she could into it.

As her words trailed off, KJ whispered, "Bravo."

He didn't sound as ironic as she expected. She whispered back, "You're welcome."

She sang two other songs. Singing to the unresponsive metal seemed both ridiculous and right.

Ix interrupted. *"The Creative Fire* is being hailed by *Diamond Deep."*

"Another ship?" KJ asked.

"A space station."

Ruby put a gloved hand on a suited hip and spoke to the robot one more time. "We're going to go talk to *Diamond Deep*. We'll be back. We would . . . we would really appreciate information."

She waited, hopeful.

KJ interrupted her. "Time, Ruby."

"I know."

"After you. Put your helmet back on."

She had promised to obey KJ, and she'd already pushed it. Still, she hated fastening the damn thing again, losing her own senses to the overwhelming stench and dulled sight of the suit. On the way up the traverse lines, she struggled to turn her thoughts from the huge and non-responsive machine toward the space station. *Diamond Deep.*

Halfway up the traverse lines, she asked, "Do you think the station will be friendly?"

"Are you asking me or Ix?"

"You."

"I think it's best not to expect anything. That way, you'll always be surprised, but you'll never be caught napping."

"Like the robots."

"Like the robots."

"Next time you practice—with the spider dancers, in a cargo bay—can I join you?"

"How could you possibly have time?"

"I want to do everything."

He was silent until they reached the airlock. While they were inside, out of sight of the robot and maybe even of Ix, he whispered, "You can't be everything. You have to trust others."

The words stung. "I trust you."

He laughed. A light came on. KJ opened the outer door of the lock, and he and Ruby spilled out into the corridor. KJ took his helmet off after they were safe, and Ruby followed his lead.

"You did well in there," he said.

"How? It didn't respond to me at all."

"You didn't threaten it, or bully it. You were sincere. If—like you suspect—it is more than a machine, then you may have affected it."

"Do you believe me?"

"Yes."

"I hate leaving it right now."

"We'll come back."

"Hurry," Ix interrupted. "Joel wants KJ with him now. He's sending Dayn with a faster cart."

CHAPTER TWENTY-FOUR

O nor stood with his back to the wall of the map room. Sharp worries crawled up his spine at the new threat. After the spiders, he didn't trust anything from Adiamo. The core of the command level assembled, coming in by twos and threes until about twenty-five people filled the room. Ruby came in with KJ, looking sweaty, her hair a touch awry.

Back when Joel had been supporting the insurrection army Onor belonged to, he had felt nothing but admiration for the man. As he watched Joel walk over to Ruby and whisper in her ear, Onor wondered if power itself corrupted. Now that Joel stood in Garth's place, he seemed to have become more like the man he overthrew. Ruby herself had lost clarity, ripped between conflicting loyalties. Maybe that was what you got for sleeping with the enemy. He shrugged off the thought as uncharitable, but he felt a stinging kernel of truth in it.

Ellis and Sylva, and so many followers, killed so coldly.

After Joel and Ruby finished a low conversation that drew their heads together, Joel addressed the room. "We have received a message from one of the space stations that orbits Adiamo, the *Diamond Deep*. After you hear it, please keep the contents secret for now, and think about how we should respond." He glanced at Ruby, his voice firming. "Then we will play it for others."

To her credit, Ruby didn't argue in public. She wasn't happy, though; Onor could see that in the way she swiped her fingers through her hair, tugging on tangles hard enough that it had to hurt. Her power was twofold: the power of the love the outer levels still held for her, and her power to keep Joel's attention. No, threefold. Her feelings had power—they were what drove her to risk, what came out through her songs.

"Listen carefully," Joel said.

A warm voice issued from speakers near the ceiling, booming into the room with a touch too much volume. "*Creative Fire*. Welcome home. I am Headman Stevenson, the freely elected leader of the orbiting station *Diamond Deep*. We are pleased to see that you have returned. Please have your pilot set course for our station. We will open a data transfer to receive the downlink of your journey so that we can arrange a proper reception."

"Is that all?" Ruby asked.

"Yes."

Onor took a deep breath. Pilot must refer to Ix: no one in this room was navigating. If they hadn't run into the ship with the spider bots, he would have taken the announcement at face value. But they had. For a time, no one spoke.

Joel's quietly asked, "What do you think?"

Laird said, "I don't trust them."

SueAnne followed him. "We have to go somewhere. Even if this whole system is untrustworthy, we are slowing down and falling apart."

"I would not give them data," KJ mused. "Not yet. Let's find out what they want it for first, and who they are. Ix? We were sent out here by the government on Lym, right? Shouldn't we speak to them first?"

"Lym is no longer highly populated. It is not the seat of power in Adiamo anymore. Think of it as a big park."

Onor shifted, watching the backs of people's heads from his post by the wall, wishing he could see their faces. The conversation continued for five or ten more minutes, although it didn't get closer to resolution. There simply wasn't enough information.

He wasn't the only one who came to that conclusion. KJ spoke up. "We don't need to respond immediately. We do have two ways to learn more. One is for Ix to continue listening and evaluating and learning. And—since this must be our decision and not the machine's choice—we need to be shown everything Ix is learning."

Joel agreed, "Shortly."

KJ continued. "The other is that thanks to Ruby, we may have a way to learn directly from the invaders. As you know, one of the robots in our hold is still functional. Ruby is working on communicating with it. Although there is no real progress so far, it is an avenue worth pursuing."

Laird spoke up, "Then *we* should work on it!"

KJ countered, "She has started to build a rapport."

Laird looked at Joel, as if to ask him to stop being an idiot. Joel ignored the content of the look, and very calmly said, "Ruby is one of us now."

Laird narrowed his eyes.

"It was Ruby's idea," Joel continued, "and she has invested the time. Ix is working with her, and KJ. I cannot afford to spend your time there; I need you as my advisor and my weapons-master. Ruby will continue the work after she rests. After spending generations getting here, we do not need to answer *Diamond Deep* today."

Joel walked toward the door closest to Onor. He gave a hand-signal that Onor should follow him, and to his surprise, Onor found it was just he and Joel walking out of the command room.

Joel walked him through a maze of corridors. The ship creaked and groaned around them, and from time to time a maintenance bot whirred along a wall. Their footsteps almost matched, although Joel's fell slightly heavier.

Joel turned around at a door he didn't open, and led them back the way they'd come. Onor expected to feel angry with Joel for the lives he'd taken, but instead he remembered the man's strengths and then felt guilty for it. This was Ruby's dilemma, too. Being close to power and understanding the nuances, being torn by conflicted loyalties. Everything Onor could remember about who he was before they won battles and changed the ship would have condemned Joel for his choices. But right now, they needed him. No one in command would follow Ruby. Colin had been torn into bits, and SueAnne— the best other choice by temperament—was too old.

Laird would be a disaster. Onor hated the new order on the ship.

Joel broke the silence first. "I'm pleased at how well you did in the cargo bay—getting you and Marcelle away safely."

Onor felt surprised that Joel even knew Marcelle's name. "Thank you. If Marcelle hadn't been so fast, we would have been caught."

"Tell her I'm glad she's safe."

Joel gave him a look that suggested he knew what had happened between he and Marcelle.

Onor's cheeks heated as he said, "I will."

"What were they like? The spider bots?"

Surely Joel had seen them. "Big. Very big. And fast. I was surprised how fast they were. None of our robots are that fast."

"What did they make you feel like?"

"Angry." He felt it all over again, the sense of violation. "They invaded our space. They killed a man I respected."

"That's how you feel now? Angry?"

"Yes."

"But how did you feel when you first saw them? When you realized they could jump? When they got close to you and almost caught you? Were you afraid?"

"Of course." Onor hesitated, searching for the right words. "It doesn't matter what we felt. What we did matters, what they did. That they killed."

Joel smiled softly. "I would have been afraid." He paused. "But Ruby sees something else."

Onor had known she'd saved the last bot from destruction, but he hadn't known about her and KJ trying to talk to it. "What does she see?"

They arrived at the end of the corridor and the closed door again, and turned around again. "Information? A slim chance to learn something? Or maybe just the chance to get attention?"

Joel was getting to know Ruby. "She's brave," Onor said. "And she wants the best for us. She would fight anything."

Joel laughed, his laughter bigger and richer and more relaxed than Onor imagined it possible to feel at the moment. "She's not trying to fight it. She's trying to talk to it."

Onor's laugh was much more controlled. "Words are her most powerful weapon."

"She acts like she thinks it's alive. Could it be? Thinking?"

"I didn't think so at the time. The damn thing's metal." He paused, remembering it. "I don't like Ruby so near the thing, even if it's tied down."

"I have protection in there."

They walked a while longer in silence, so far that Onor grew thirsty. Once again, it was Joel who broke the silence, and once more it was with a question instead of an order. "Should we feel as afraid of Adiamo as you felt about the spider?"

Onor bit back his first instinct, which was to say of course they should. "Maybe we shouldn't trust *Diamond Deep* yet. But surely the entire system cannot be hostile."

Joel stopped and turned to look at Onor. "Why not?"

"Because we came from here."

Joel didn't respond until they had made another complete walk and turn.

"You and Ruby are two bridges I trust between us and the working people."

Onor felt surprised to be included. "Thank you."

"Are they afraid?"

"Of course they are."

"I want you to go and find Conroy and The Jackman, and tell them to start the drills again, and the practice sessions. These aren't to be secret any more. Right alongside the classes Ruby and Ix plan to offer about Adiamo, we will re-form an army of workers, just like the army that you all built before. Only this time it will be formal, and it will be trained, and it will even be armed. Even if we never need it, the act of making an army will soothe the ship. Training keeps people occupied."

Onor liked the idea. "Is there anything else you want me to tell them?"

"Yes. Tell them we need them."

"Thank you," Onor said. "They'll be glad to hear that."

CHAPTER TWENTY-FIVE

To Ruby's surprise, the robot repair shop smelled good to her. She had hated it as a child, wanted to be free of it, fought for just that. And now the clean and old oils, degreasers, and newly washed rags all smelled like home. She'd worn the worst clothes she owned—an old pair of blue pants and a gray shirt she'd asked Jali to dig up for her when she was recording a song about being in the working class.

The irony of her dress wasn't lost on her.

Four technicians surrounded the table. Two of them were from KJ's team of spider dancers, and the other two were robot mechanics. One man, one woman, both of them scarred on the hands and arms from wrestling with sharp metal tools and parts every day, both dirty. They greeted her as if they were in awe, voices hushed. The woman was Frieda and the man Allo.

She'd met Allo when she was a young apprentice, maybe twelve. He had looked big and successful to her then, like something she might become someday. "I met you once. You were teaching us about welding safely."

His eyes rounded. "I don't remember."

"I was young. You were a good teacher, Allo."

He looked so pleased at her words that she was glad she'd remembered his name.

A wall had been knocked out between two workshops to make enough space for the whole robot leg to spread across long tables.

Ruby stared at it, distaste welling in her throat.

"Pick it up," Frieda suggested.

"The leg?" It was huge.

"Yes."

Ruby braced and extended her arms, tensed, lifted.

And came fully to standing as if she had been bounced. "Wow. How can it be so strong?"

"It's material we've never seen here," Allo said.

Ruby addressed one of the robot dancers. "What about the middle of it? Were you able to go back and get that?"

"Over here."

Over here actually meant in a different, smaller room, on a normal-sized table, and with lights shining on it from all angles. It was still in its cage. Here, separated from the surrounding power of legs and great clawed arms, it was even harder to imagine that it had any structural significance. It could only be controls. "Is this made out of the same material?"

Allo said, "Just the cage. The thing inside of it is soft. Poke it."

Her arm was slender enough to fit through the protective bars, and so she reached in and touched the surface. Cool. Hard. It dented slightly under her finger, but she wouldn't have had the strength to poke a hole in the surface. It didn't feel at all vulnerable. Just . . . different. Slightly greasy and entirely unfamiliar, even creepy.

This time, she found a freshly cleaned suit outside the airlock. It fit her as if she'd been measured for it.

"Thank you," she said.

KJ smiled. "You won't be able to tell me you can't see through that glass."

"It's not as if the air isn't good. What's going to happen?"

"The sky could fall. Enemies could find a way to change the mix of oxygen. Besides, it might be harder for the robot to snip off your pretty little head if you have your helmet covering it."

She laughed at his list of fears. "I'll try and resist my natural predilection for stupidity."

"You do that." KJ was laughing, too.

When you were afraid, she thought, laughter was a good thing.

Back at the bottom of the traverse, the robot still towered over her. Ix addressed her, using a communication channel that didn't broadcast out loud. "It has been asking me questions."

"And have you answered?" Ruby asked it.

"If the question was something factual about the ship. KJ gave me permission to do that."

"So you answer to KJ but not to me," Ruby teased.

"KJ is Joel's chief strategist."

She didn't bother to ask what the damned machine thought she was.

"KJ suggested I convince the robot that we have in fact killed the ship it came from."

"And did you?"

"Yes. It wants to talk to you now."

KJ must have known. This explained the new, clean suit. She swallowed and took a deep breath, regretting the promise to leave her helmet on. "Are you recording?"

"Yes."

"Go ahead and broadcast." She stared at the robot, wishing there was a way to look into its eyes. Or that it had eyes to look at. "What should I call you? I'm Ruby."

This time the answer was immediate. "Aleesi."

She had been expecting a stream of numbers or something. "That's pretty."

"That was my human name."

It was Ruby's turn for a slight hesitation. "A human named you?"

"My mother. I was a girl once."

Ruby drew in a sharp breath and clutched the traverse line harder.

Aleesi continued. "That is why we live at the Edge of the worlds."

So the thing she had felt this morning *was* a brain. She felt good. The beast wasn't merely alive. It was human. She had been right. More than right.

KJ regathered his sense of equilibrium first. "But you do not look human now."

"I am not one thing."

Well that was clear. "Why does having been human mean you live at the edge?"

"We are . . . not allowed in human space."

"Why?" she pushed.

"I have not died. The inner worlds consider death an absolute. It can take a long time, but it must happen. Thus only full biologicals have rights, and I am an abomination."

"So you don't have to die?" KJ looked curious.

"This instance of me can die. That's likely, now. Being part of my ship was my protection."

Ruby wasn't quite ready to feel sorry for it . . . her. "You came here to kill us." She saw Colin's face again, heard his voice teasing her. Remembered a kiss, from a time before she met Joel. "You killed a man who I liked very much."

"We did what we were told by the controlling voices. We came here to survive. The way to change and grow is to gather new things, to have materials and knowledge that no one else does."

"Even if it belongs to someone else?" Ruby asked.

"Who owns *The Creative Fire*? The people who sent it away are long dead and they have no children with the power of such a long remembrance."

Ruby glanced at KJ reflexively. She couldn't see his face clearly through the helmet, but his eyes had narrowed and he looked stiff. "So how will you survive now?" he asked. "Will you adapt to us, or will you kill us if we untie you?"

"There is no reason to kill you now."

"We consider the ship ours," Ruby said.

The spider didn't offer an answer to that. After a few long moments of silence, Ruby asked, "Why are you in danger?"

"You will kill me or the people inside the system will kill me."

Aleesi sounded matter-of-fact about it. Ruby couldn't tell if the machine felt fear since Ix used a robotic voice to translate Aleesi's words.

"We will not kill you if we don't give us a reason," Ruby said. Her words earned a sharp look from KJ, so she added, "I mean that."

KJ didn't challenge Ruby, but changed the subject. "Why? Why would people inside kill you?"

"Because I am not allowed inside, and you are bringing me there. I am in five other machines on my home ship. If it lives, they live. *I* may yet live in those, but I cannot talk to any of my selves. No one answers. The first day, when I was alone here—after the deaths of the others." A pause. "The first hours after, I could hear my other selves on the *Thief of a Thousand Stars*. Now I cannot. We are too far away. I'm sure I never will. I have chosen to talk to you because to be alone is to die before my time. I don't know how to be alone."

The translated voice still showed no emotion, but this time there was no mistaking the feeling in the words. Ruby forced herself to let her hands unclench from the traverse line. She sucked at her water straw. The implications of Aleesi's story whirled through her head. There was cruelty and opportunity, and more hints that they should fear going home. "Have you always been at the Edge?"

"I started inside, but I was bought and sold and bought and sold. There is a black market in things like me."

"You were human and they sold you?"

"I was born of a human, my inner seed is human. But I am more. And anything rare has value in the inner worlds. You will see. You will be rare."

Fear crept in through Ruby's indignation. She would find a way to be sure no one on the *Fire* ever became part of a slave market. She said, "Go on. Tell the rest of it."

"Eventually a man on the *Thief of a Thousand Stars* bought me, and then, while I was still young enough to adapt, they stuck me in here. When you go back, and I get caught, they'll kill me."

Joel's voice startled her, tinny but serious as it poured through the speakers in her helmet. "Ask it about *Diamond Deep*. Or other places. See what it will tell us about where we are going."

She hadn't known he was listening. She didn't like it, but at the same time, feeling like he was there with her warmed her. She whispered back, trusting Ix to route her words correctly. "I will." She raised her voice. "Aleesi. Tell me about the inside."

"The inside hates us. They are united against any human/machine hybrid that includes a human mind. The inside hates others, too. We grow—the Edge—when people flee the inside. There is one government and many."

"What is the most powerful place inside?"

"The *Diamond Deep*. By far. We call it the station that rules the planets."

"And what is it like?"

"They hate us."

Aleesi was answering from its own narrow point of view. She exchanged another glance with KJ, noting he looked more puzzled than startled. "What is inside?" he asked.

"Humans. Planets. The enforcers who come out to hurt us come from inside. A friend on the *Thief of a Thousand Stars* told me there are a few good things on the planet Lym, and in the place called Moon's Refuge."

Ruby sipped water from the tube in her suit. Aleesi wasn't sounding as smart as any grown human she knew, and certainly not like Ix. In fact, the robot spider girl wasn't sounding very formidable at all. "Are there machines inside?"

"Like me? Human machines? Only if they are hidden. But otherwise, yes, of course. How would you run the world without machines?"

"But there are humans? The *Diamond Deep* is full of humans?"

"The *Diamond Deep* is full of many things. Humans are the most plentiful."

KJ spoke up again. "What do you know about us? How did you know a way into this ship?"

"I don't know how the controlling voices found a way to enter you. They gave codes to the ships that carried us. But I know that we found you in the library of history and that we know when you left, long before the sundering and the remaking and the blending and the Age of Explosive Creation. I know we came to you because anything so old must be a wealth of rare ideas."

CHAPTER TWENTY-SIX

Onor hesitated in the doorway to Jaliet's studio. Onor credited her with changing the way Ruby dressed and walked and even how she wore her hair and what she washed it in.

He had expected the studio to be an explosion of color and perhaps chaos, but instead it was neat and orderly. Colorful drawers lined one wall, a mirror another, and a third was all hanging closet. Jali herself sat in a single chair that rotated on a base bolted to the floor. He had seen her in public at events and occasionally beside Ruby, always perfect and maybe even otherworldly. At the moment she looked like a normal human being: she wore a soft gray shirt and simple blue pants and low shoes that looked both comfortable and homemade. Her black hair had been tamed in a neat braid that accentuated her generous mouth and dark eyes. She wore no ribbons or jewelry except a single thin rope of braided colors around her neck, the universal symbol for support of Ruby and Joel.

"Come in," she said. "It's good to see you again."

They'd only spoken in passing. He found himself a tiny bit tongue-tied. "Ruby talks well of you."

Jali smiled. "And of you. Did she tell you what we're doing?"

"She said something about developing a style."

Jali laughed. "That's right. We want to meet our makers in something coherent, beautiful, and simple. In all of our colors." She appeared to be genuinely having fun, which might explain why she was so good. "It will have to be something we can fight in if we need to, but also something we can attend a party in." She paused and cocked her head. "What do you think?"

"I think it's a scheme of Ruby's."

"Of course it is. All good things on the ship come from Ruby."

"Really?" he asked. It was hard to tell if she was teasing, although he thought he heard a touch of cynicism. "What about Joel?"

"Ruby keeps him in power."

"You can't think that." He felt slightly offended.

She laughed and rummaged in a drawer, pulling out a long measuring tape. "What do you think?"

"Ruby couldn't hold the command or logistics levels."

"Joel would never have won without her." She walked around him, as if she were noticing every detail. "You can relax here," she said. "There is nothing to guard against in my studio."

Except for maybe Jaliet herself. "I *am* relaxed," he replied.

"No," she said. "You're not. Drop your shoulders. Hold them back a little. Chin up. Relax your knees."

As he complied with each demand, he did, in fact, feel better.

She measured him and wrote notes, muttering. Then she made him move, so she could see him walk and stretch and reach into invisible pockets.

"Are you doing this for everyone?" he asked.

"I'm making the design for everyone. Daria and a small army are going to help make and fit the uniform onto as many people as possible."

Daria and Jali might be natural friends. They both worried about how everyone dressed and moved; Jali just did it at a higher and more precise level. "How are you going to get enough material?"

"We've collected old uniforms and found a way to dye them black. That's being done now. Well, almost black."

"So we're all going to be gray?" The thought made him smile.

"With touches of color. It will be one uniform for everyone, with purple and orange insignia that spans all of the old levels." She held up swatches of colored cloth. "Ruby asked me to fit all of her friends myself. The list is forty people long." She made a face. "I don't suppose you have any idea how much time I have?"

"I wish. We're actually in-system now, you know. Ix doesn't appear to know where to go, so we just have to choose."

"I know. I'm not sure that damned game described this system at all." She stepped back and stared at him again, a slight frown touching her lips. "Do you like the idea of *Diamond Deep* or the idea of circling Lym?"

"I've always wanted to go to a planet, to have a sky. But apparently there's almost no one there."

"Are we even sure we ended up in the right star system?"

She had said it with a smile, but it knocked him off-balance. "The planets and the sun are in the right place," he replied. "There's just new stuff here, too. More stations. Ix says people have built whole planets they live inside of."

"Almost like living in the *Fire*," she mused.

"Well, they're bigger," he offered. "We can't do that. Live here. The *Fire* needs repairs."

She paced. "From the classes Ix is teaching us, *we* haven't changed much. I keep thinking half of this place could be robots like the one that almost got you and Marcelle."

A familiar voice came in over his shoulder. "Did I hear my name?"

"Come on in. You're a few minutes early."

He hadn't seen Marcelle for days, except on the exercise floor, sweating to Conroy's commands again. She looked surprised to see him there, and perhaps a touch hesitant. The dark ringlets of her hair framed her face in a way he found enchanting enough to wipe away the slight regret he felt. If it weren't for the dark circles under her eyes, she would look truly beautiful.

Jaliet addressed Marcelle. "Ruby told you what we're doing, right?"

"I love it." Marcelle came up close to Onor, put a hand briefly on his arm as if it was drawn there. "Will you stay until she's done, and then share a meal?"

He felt the tiniest bit trapped, and guilty for feeling trapped. "Of course. I'm free for the next hour."

Jali measured Marcelle and moved her from pose to pose. She managed to keep up a stream of small talk that included both Marcelle and Onor, to brush out Marcelle's hair until it shone, and to pin it up in a way that made Marcelle's thin face look broader and softer.

As he walked out with Marcelle, he said, "That woman could run the ship."

Marcelle grinned. "She could. I love the uniform idea."

"I like that we'll all be gray."

Marcelle slid an arm around his waist. "You've been busy the last few days."

He swallowed. "I have duties. To Joel and Ruby."

She fell quiet; not a typical state for Marcelle. She seemed to sense his hesitation, to match it. She pulled her arm off of his waist. "Will you come down and visit us? I'd like to show you the teams working on the new uniforms. We took everyone that can't fight—young or old or hurt—and they're making the new material and uniforms while they watch Ruby's classes."

"Did you set that up?" he asked.

"Me and Daria. People in every pod are working together. Kyle brings food to the sewing lines. They're sewing off-time, so the regular shift work still gets done."

"All this in just a couple of days?" He and Marcelle were training with the old squads again, too.

"People need to be busy. They're scared."

Walking beside her felt confusing. He wanted to hold her and yet didn't, as if it would betray Ruby if he did. He was wrong, but knowing that didn't change the confusion being close to Marcelle caused him. They hadn't made love again, but he remembered what she felt like, and how she sighed and softened under his hands. Damn. "Are you scared?" he asked her.

"Of course I am. Surely you are, too."

He laughed. "I'm one of Joel's guards. I'm not allowed to admit it."

"Idiot."

She deserved better than he was giving her. "Marcelle?"

"Yes."

"I don't . . . I shouldn't . . ." Finding words that wouldn't hurt her felt impossible. "I have a lot to do. Joel's got me running messages again as well as being one of his three guards. I'm not going to be able to see you a lot."

She spun in front of him, stopped him in his tracks, made him look at her. "I don't regret sleeping with you, Onor Hall. I never will. And I want to do it again. And again." She swallowed, her chin trembling even though her voice hadn't. "You can be in love with a ghost if you want. I love her, too. I always will. I'll even follow her anywhere. But she has never chosen her partners for love, and she never will."

"I think she loves Joel." The words had escaped him before he thought about them.

Marcelle laughed. "She does. But would she love him if he had no power?"

"He wouldn't be Joel if he had no power."

Marcelle shook her head. "You are so exasperating I have no idea why I love you so much." She turned and stalked away from him.

He had been weak to sleep with her. Now there was this new awkwardness between them. He was pretty certain he was the biggest fool on the ship, but he had no idea how to change a truth that had existed forever in his heart.

Ruby.

Damn it.

CHAPTER TWENTY-SEVEN

Ruby spun in front of Joel, holding her arms up, doing her best to balance on one leg. "Do you like it?"

He sat on the couch in their living room, his journal perched on his knee, his face haggard. Every display in the room was lit up, showing one scene or another from the Adiamo system. Still, he found time to notice the new uniform she wore. "Tell Jali she succeeded beyond our wildest hopes."

Ruby felt pleased. "I will. They're almost done getting everyone of fighting age fitted out. They plan to sew the scraps together for children and old people."

"That's good." He returned to staring at his journal. She curled up close to him, tucking her bare feet up into the slightly long pant legs. The uniform would match her best boots. There had been no way to make new shoes or boots, so that part would look handed down in spite of their best efforts. But for a ship that hadn't seen new resources for generations, it was pretty damned good.

"You smell tired," she said.

"Of course I'm tired," he said quietly. "We all are."

"Maybe we should have another festival."

"We already had the festival of homecoming. What would this one be? The festival of ignorance?"

"Is there any new news?"

He sighed. He pointed at the screen opposite them. She recognized Lym: a ball of blue and green and brown with white caps of ice. "We've found a few places in Lym's orbit big enough for us. Ix is pretty sure we can park there without damaging anything. But no one on Lym seems to know anything about us, or to care."

"We're better suited for a planet than a space station: we have ships that will let us land on one," Ruby said.

He pointed to a small display that usually showed the map room or one of Joel's secret command rooms where he held his councils. "That's *Diamond Deep*. They say we can dock there safely, but the first contact we had with them was a demand that we send them everything we have of value."

"I remember. Aleesi doesn't trust *Diamond Deep*."

"Smart robot. I don't either. What does it say about Lym?"

"*She* doesn't remember much about it. Says it's some kind of nature preserve and only approved humans can live there. She also has a friend who hated Lym. Apparently she's only got what she's heard to go on. I think she's being honest with us. But I don't know how much Aleesi actually knows. Sometimes it's more like talking to a child than an adult. At least on politics."

Joel fell silent, staring at the screens.

"I'd like to keep Aleesi safe."

"It's more important to save our people than your pet robot."

"Pet girl!" That didn't sound right. Damn it. "*She* wants to live."

"Me too."

Ruby laughed and kissed him. "Of course. But if we can do it all, I want to."

"You always want it all."

She kissed him again. "What else is there to want?"

He laughed. "If Aleesi's told the truth, we have learned a few things."

"Enough. We learned that there's no one government in the system, and no one most powerful coalition or place or planet or religion or anything, although there are some universal laws and a single court to sit over just those."

"I don't like the idea of a court. Do you?" he asked her.

Ix had helped her study courts some on their way in. "We could have used a court here. Maybe fewer people would have died."

"The judges would have been corrupt."

"I suppose so." She had been hoping he would stop agonizing and put an arm around her, relax a little. But his body hadn't shifted to allow her to fit nicely along his side and his elbow was digging into her. She stood and started pacing. "We need to choose. Now. You said there are only a few days left, anyway. What are you waiting for?"

He shook his head. "More information."

"Well, we're not getting any."

"I know."

Ruby mused out loud. "Two stations and a planet right? We can't dock anywhere without permission, and once we stop, we probably can't start again. So doesn't that mean we're better off with the planet? At least we have ships that can get to the surface."

"Ix thinks there's more political power in the stations."

She sat down again, clutching her hands between her legs. "There's enough power in any of these places to crush us."

Now he put an arm around her and gathered her close.

She snuggled into him. "There was a legend at home that we can't start the *Fire* up again if we stop her. Is that true?"

"Ix thinks it would be hard. Starting is even harder than stopping, and the ship is falling apart."

"I want to see a sky, but I think we should go where the power is." She bit her lip and looked at him, watching his face for some clue about how he felt. This was big. Bigger than either of them, bigger than they had the tools for. But inaction was going to drive her nuts.

As if he heard her thoughts, he said, "We have to decide soon."

"So decide now."

He sat still, staring at nothing.

"It's not like you to hesitate," she whispered. "It's a big decision, but if we don't make it, Ix will be sure we dock somewhere. Its job is to protect the ship."

"And mine is to protect our people."

He looked so torn. She'd never seem him this way. "Do you want to sleep and make up your mind in the morning?"

He stared at her for a long time, his face so tight it was possible to imagine she could see him thinking. He whispered, "No. We will go to *Diamond Deep* and throw ourselves into the teeth of a power we don't understand. You're right about the power."

"We'll be all right," she said. "We're strong."

"Sing me a song?" he asked.

She started "Homecoming," but he shook his head. "The seed song. The one about how strong we are."

It was a good choice. She turned off all the screens and all the lights, and sat beside him in the dark and sang.

PART THREE

THE WELCOME OF CHILDREN

CHAPTER TWENTY-EIGHT

Ruby stood beside Joel in the crowded map room. The air was drenched with the taste of stale stim. People completely ringed the map table, including some who had never seen the map room before, perhaps never envisioned such a large display that a hundred people could stand side by side around it. Ruby had held an art contest to burn the month spent slowing, and one winner from each discipline stood around the table with their families. One of the women was visibly pregnant, a sign that their reversal of the decree against children mattered. It made Ruby feel warm. Even Allen had joined them from the cargo bay, and from the amazed look on his face when he came in, it was possible that he had not been here before either.

The ship's strength had scattered around the room to protect the leaders: KJ and his silent dancers, some of the fighters from the cargo bays, and Joel's bodyguards. This included Onor, who stood behind Ruby and Joel.

Ruby assessed the crew. The new uniform had turned out even better than Ruby imagined: Dark gray with a multicolored piping strip across each shoulder, and rank insignia on the top of the right arm and over the left breast. Jali and Ruby's aunt Daria and their entire army of willing hands had created a miracle. Daria was in the back, looking taller and thinner and more elegant, as if the simple act of working with Jaliet for a few weeks had given her new grace and purpose. Haric stood beside Ruby. She had put him on Jali's list of people to pay attention to, and his new uniform fit perfectly, although it made him look younger than Ruby had hoped for. It accentuated his thin shoulders and the smooth skin on his face.

If only they looked as strong and well-ordered as their uniforms. The people who had never been here before looked pale-face and wide-eyed, a little scared. Children were clutched tight to their parents' breasts.

This would be the first glimpse anyone outside of the inner circle would have of the *Diamond Deep*.

Through some magic Ruby found fascinating, Ix had removed the pinpoints of stars and even the sun, Adiamo, from the image that filled the table's flat surface. An image of the station sat in the middle of the screen, no bigger than Ruby's fist. It looked like a spill of colored beads had been spread across black, some lit from the inside in whites and yellows. Its shape looked as fractal as the edges of leaves.

People leaned in, squinting at it. They pointed and talked. "Look how many parts it has."

"A piece just moved."

"It's so complex."

One of the children said, "Pretty," and her mother stroked her hair and clutched her tighter. The girl was no older than three, trapped by her mother's fear, her little arms waving as if asking to be let free to go play.

Ix let the image of *Diamond Deep* grow to the size of a dinner plate, then double that, and then double again. It now filled a full third of the huge map table, big enough for people to begin to pick details out of chaos.

It was now possible to make out a variety of shapes. Each part was connected one to another, the outer texture and shape of the station appearing random. Darker blocks in a myriad of sizes had become visible at this resolution.

Ruby watched the wonder on people's faces as they realized each of these tiny dark blotches was a spaceship.

"Look at them all!"

"Are any as big as the *Fire?*"

"I bet that one's bigger."

"What are all the lights about?"

"It looks thin."

Ix responded to that last comment, which had come from Haric, by rotating the image. Haric had it right; the vast sprawl of ships and station was long and wild, but it was also thin, no more than two or three ships and bubbles of station deep.

"Is it that shape for light?" Conroy asked.

"Yes," Ix replied. "What I've shown you so far is a static photo at varied resolutions. Close your eyes."

Ruby ignored the machine and watched the crowd. Most people obeyed and stood with their heads bowed and their eyes closed. Here and there people held hands, including some she was sure had been near strangers.

She took the moment of quiet to reach for Joel's hand and squeeze it. His face showed no emotion, but his hand was warm and calloused in hers, and he gripped her fingers in a sharp hug before letting go.

Nothing before this—not even the ugly ship or standing below Aleesi and holding a conversation through the machine—nothing had prepared her for *The Creative Fire* seeming as small as a seed.

On the table, stars appeared and grew into bright points of light, and then faded as new brightness seeped from the corner closest to Ruby and Joel: the light of the sun, bathing the still-rotated and thin view of the station from above, setting parts of the structure to reflecting light through other parts, so that only a small bit of the station was actually dark. Light even reflected back, clearly hitting objects on the far side of the station from the sun and coming back from behind them.

"Mirrors!" Jali exclaimed.

"Almost," Ix replied.

The little girl who had called the station pretty wriggled out of her mom's arms and onto the table, standing over the space station, her face rapt. The light from the table bathed her skin in shifting colors. She didn't speak, but she reached her hands out and touched the surface of the table.

Ruby took the opening. "She sees an opportunity. That is what we must make this. Our opportunity. Our chance to grow as a people and to learn."

The mother called to the girl, who ignored her. Ruby loved it: the symbolism was beautiful.

"We will take care of each other and of our children."

Ix darkened the table for a moment and the child returned to her mother. As soon as her little bare feet left the table, it came back alive. The station rotated again, the sense of light remaining. Ix caused the image to grow. Here and there a part moved. A ship left. A ship arrived.

The bright spots that had looked like beads with lights in them still looked like beads with lights in them. Just bigger. Some were clear and others clouded with swirls or color or full of things inside. Haric pointed to one. "Tell me about those."

"I have been receiving some data from the station, and it has included a map. I don't understand it all. The bright places appear to be where the people who live on the stations instead of in the ships live, and where they grow their food and store their goods and attend school. It is like all of the rooms on the *Fire* separated and brightened and attached one to another by tubes. Some are not even attached."

"So we might think of the station like a big ship?" Allen asked.

KJ answered him. "That would be a dangerous oversimplification."

Joel cleared his throat. "*Diamond Deep* is so complex that parts of it might always be a mystery. It appears to be the most active place in Adiamo, and to have the most people. It is only one of many places people live, though. We think they trade with each other. Ix tells me we might not even recognize the things they trade. We will be strangers there. We'll need to protect what is ours: our stories, our goods. At least until we understand more about these new people."

He paused and people whispered to one another. Ruby moved closer to him, wanting to show the solidarity they had been working to build. She had not yet made it into his secret meetings, but she stood beside him here and now.

When Joel picked the conversation back up, he said, "We'll be docking there in a week. *Diamond Deep* is not still; it moves. We are still moving as well. Three tugships will attach themselves to us and move us into the trailing edge of the station. It will take time to maneuver the ship to attach to the station."

Allen asked, "Have you talked to anyone from the *Diamond Deep*?"

"No." Joel managed to sound only slightly unhappy about this, although Ruby knew he mistrusted the situation deeply. "Machines have talked."

One of the men from the outer pods, a water system worker, spoke up. "They aren't all machines, are they? Like the robots that killed some of ours?"

SueAnne answered him. "There are people there. Ix has verified that it is not a land of robot spiders."

Ruby thought of Aleesi, who still sat trussed in a cargo bay.

Joel continued. "After we dock, we'll stay aboard the *Fire*. There will be a process of meeting and of waiting, a way to be sure of our safety and theirs. We will proceed carefully. Earn each other's trust. We should stick together as one ship, one people.

"Ix will broadcast what you have seen and what the station looks like as we approach it to every display in every common room after dinner tonight, and will do so continuously so that each and every crew member can see where we are going.

"Some of you may feel afraid. But we are a strong people who have journeyed across the stars. We bring value to this place, and whatever we find here, we must remember our strength."

Ruby raised her voice and added, "We are people of the fire, and we will learn and grow here. We will create a home here. I promise you."

CHAPTER TWENTY-NINE

Onor stood outside the lock in his pressure suit, about to visit the killer robot spider. This had been Marcelle's idea. Something about facing their fears. Onor still wasn't quite sure how he had been talked into this. The last time he and Marcelle had been here they were nearly killed, and he had lost himself in her afterwards. His insides felt plagued with unsettling knots of fear and arousal that didn't go together at all.

At least this time the suit fit, worked, and smelled more of cleaner than old sweat.

"You'll like this," Ruby said, "Aleesi is a very social being. She was taken as a fairly young girl and put into her first robot body. She seems simple sometimes. I don't think of her as a child, just as someone who has been limited. She is used to having other copies of herself to talk to, and to being surrounded by others. I guess it's like a family."

"A family of killers."

Ruby already had the door to the lock open. He had offered to go through first and wait on the other side, but Ruby had decreed that Marcelle and Onor would go through first and she would follow. He suspected she knew how things stood between him and Marcelle, although she had never said anything about it.

The women probably talked.

On the far side of the lock, he and Marcelle stood on a wide beam and clutched the ribs of the bay. He had sworn he would be strong, but as soon as he saw the spiders—even trussed—fear washed over him and his hands shook. Maybe it was a good thing he was in the damned suit—it let him hide his physical reaction. "How do you feel?" he asked Marcelle. "Are you okay?"

"I'm scared. But I wanted to come."

"I know." He hadn't. "But you don't have to be tough."

"Coming in that lock was one of the hardest things I've ever done. But I can't become a scared person."

"You've always been brave."

There was silence, then Marcelle said, "I promised Ruby I'd keep up what she's been doing. Learning from the damned thing. She says she's going to be too busy when we land."

He glanced across the bay at three spider dancers, who hung on the far wall, watching them. Guards, in this case, but they spent time with Aleesi and gathered information. He'd read their summary reports. They'd learned more about the Edge than about inside, but they were also getting some language and culture. He glanced back at Marcelle. "Why you and not just the spider dancers?"

"She trusts me even more than them."

"I do, too." He told her. "I trust them with my life, but you with my secrets."

She laughed, the first time her voice hadn't sounded tense since they cycled through the lock. "They used to *be* secrets."

The sequence of lights that indicated the lock was about to open blinked white and red light across Marcelle's faceplate, and then Ruby joined them on the beam. "Let's go."

They followed Ruby down a traverse line. She had become so fast and natural in here that he and Marcelle struggled to keep up with her. They stopped at the bottom beside the trussed robot. He had been this close when they were being chased, maybe closer, but he couldn't recall details. Only fear. Rushing blood made his fingertips feel like hearts beat in them.

There were so many chains holding the robot down that he shouldn't feel this way.

"Hello, Aleesi," Ruby said. "These are my friends Marcelle and Onor. They may come back and visit you when I cannot. We'll be at *Diamond Deep* soon and I'll have other duties."

The robot spoke in Ix's voice. "Pleased to meet you."

"Talk to us about the *Diamond Deep*," Ruby said.

"I have told you everything I know."

"For my friends' sake. So they can ask questions. Just summarize the things that you've told me."

Ix's Aleesi voice went off in Onor's helmet again. "*Diamond Deep* is the oldest station here, and the biggest. It was built as a project of a long-ago government, started just before your ship left the system. Old spaceships that could no longer move, but which could be lived in, became part of it. The station survived the sundering by staying neutral and letting ships from all sides of the fighting meet here. *Diamond Deep* came out ahead in that, winning so much material and metal from fleet salvage that it was three times as big after the war. Then the nano-tech revolution changed it yet again, remade it piece by piece, built the habitat bubbles and gave it manufacturing facilities. Ships are made here for the whole system, and have been since before the Edge was created."

It sounded like a prepared speech or a memory of a lesson. "But you have never been to the *Deep*?" he asked.

"No. When I was a human child, I was on Lym."

Onor asked, "Did you miss being on a planet?"

"Yes."

It felt absurd to be having an almost normal conversation with something that had tried to kill him. "I heard you don't like it that we came here."

"My kind is not allowed to live here."

Marcelle asked, "Will they know you're here?"

"They will know everything about this ship."

Ix broke in, using its deeper voice so they knew it wasn't the robot talking. "She is very convinced that there is no way to keep secrets from anyone inside."

"Is she right?"

"Perhaps."

"How long ago were you a human child?" Marcelle asked the robot.

"At the beginning of the Age of Explosive Creation, which was many generations ago, even though it began after you left. It is when robots created their intelligence, and when humans learned to live longer and younger and where beings like me were created and rejected and fled to the Edge if we wanted to survive."

"So why are you talking to us?" Onor asked. "Why help us?"

"Because there is no one else for me to talk to. You will be like me. Cast-off and strange. I understand the math of star travel, and that you were gone from here for generations of humans. You are a small society, too small and too poor in resources to have changed much from when you left. The speed of change increases with the size of the network."

"What?" Marcelle asked.

"The more people interact with each other, the faster cultural change happens. Change is driven by volume of information."

Ruby broke in this time. "I'm still not sure I understand. If we had a ship with three times as many people on it, we would change faster?"

There was a machine's breath pause before the answer came back. "A little. But since the bigger the network grows, the faster the change happens, you would not see much of a difference. The *Fire* has thousands of people, at most, right?"

"Yes."

"Adiamo has trillions of people."

He understood the size of the number from a lesson in math class years ago, before they became adults. Numbers like that had been used to represent distances, or the number of stars in the universe. But numbers of people?

"You have been gone for years of your time, for generations. The *Fire* has travelled far and most of its journey has been at more than halfway to the speed of light. And in that time, humanity has gone beyond what you appear to understand."

"So there will not be anyone like us?" Marcelle asked.

"I have never seen anyone like you, nor talked to anyone who understands as little."

As soon as they were through the door, they all started jabbering at Ix.

"Did you know how many people were there?"

"Did you know about numbers of people and change?"

"Is it lying? Are there really that many people?" The rumor Onor had been most afraid was true had been that they were all dead, and the *Fire* was flying back to someplace empty and cold.

Ix replied. "I am learning about this system as we speak, and have been since we got close enough to get information about it. It truly is different from when we left."

Ruby's helmet was off now, her long red hair sweaty and mussed and her face white. "So our classes haven't helped anyone. They've been lies."

Ix said, "They've been history lessons."

He could see Ruby bite her tongue. No use fighting with the machine. It always had a better way to fight back.

Now all their helmets were off, and they stood in the corridor in their suits. "It was talking down to us," Marcelle said.

Ruby shook her head. "No. Aleesi is actually very simple. In many ways, she isn't as smart or as subtle as we are. But there are things she knows—like that bit about network effects—that we don't even know the questions for. That's why I keep coming back."

Marcelle asked, "Did you know how many people are there?"

"We hadn't put that number to it, but we knew it was a lot. Think about it. Remember that picture of *Diamond Deep*? It's hundreds of times bigger than the *Fire*, maybe thousands. And the *Fire* has a lot more cargo space than people-space."

Antony, another one of Joel's guards, came around the corner.

Ruby seemed to be expecting him. "Just a moment. Let me change into my uniform." She started stripping off the rest of her suit. "Whoever designed this place should have put a shower right here," she muttered.

Marcelle's laughter broke the worries that he'd left the cargo bay with, and he laughed, too. Not as good as running, but anything to release the thought of trillions of people.

After they'd all changed, Ruby left Onor and Marcelle hanging their suits up in the locker closest to the cargo bay. He watched Ruby's back as she walked away beside Antony.

Marcelle's hair was mussed from the suit and she looked worn out. "Are you okay?" he asked her.

"Walk with me to the cargo bars?" Marcelle asked him. "I was too nervous to eat before we went in there."

"Of course. Did you get what you wanted from going in there?"

She rummaged in the pack she'd left stuck in a cubby on the locker, coming up with a hairbrush and starting in on her sweat-damped hair. "I wanted to be brave. I expected to hate her, to want to kill her when I stood in front of her. Or to be scared. She would have killed us if she could, at least on that first day. So I can't—really—feel sorry for her."

"But it is a little pathetic."

"I wouldn't have chosen that word." She put her brush away and shouldered her pack. "Let's go."

"What would you call it?"

"Dangerous."

"Yes, but I like pathetic better. It's easier to think of it that way. Her that way." They started down the corridor.

"I didn't understand everything she said," Marcelle said.

"We learned how different we are from everything here."

"I knew that the minute we saw six robots bigger than habs scuttle into the cargo bay."

He walked next to her, debating whether or not to take her arm. "Have you got your assignment for docking day yet?"

"I'm on peacekeeping in common. C-pod."

"Really? Did you ask for that?" She was a good warrior; she should stand on the front lines. Hopefully, defense would be for show, but still, it was the respectful place to put someone who had been by Ruby's side so long, and who had become a squad leader in practices.

"I want to be with the people. And with the families."

"You could be with us."

"I know. I'm just feeling tender about our people. Everything is going to change, and faster than we want. What happens if we never see each other again after we dock?"

"Ruby and Joel will keep us together." He straightened. "And we'll keep us together."

She put an arm around his waist, pulled him close to her. She was his size—well, his height. It felt good to be walking beside her. He put an arm around her as well, resting his hand on her waist where he could feel the glide of her muscles as she walked. It wasn't a commitment, but the damned robot always seemed to drive him closer to Marcelle.

Marcelle fell silent as they walked through the corridors. She seemed as awkward as he felt, her gait a little stiff. She didn't look at him. "I have a reason not to be up front."

"What?"

"I'm pregnant."

CHAPTER THIRTY

R uby had done her best to turn docking day into a party while Joel's instinct was to use it as a military exercise. The result looked like an ideological fight had splashed itself across the map room. Everyone—even Ruby—wore the new uniforms. Serving robots squeaked through the few spaces between people with trays of fresh fruit from the gardens and crackers and cookies from the kitchens.

Ix played images of their approach to *Diamond Deep* on the map table. To Ruby's irritation, Ix had become unresponsive when questioned. They were close enough now that the station itself couldn't be seen in whole. It appeared as a large black structure against the black of space, edged in blinding white lights. The best thing that could be said about the image was that the station loomed. The worst was that it looked ready to consume the *Fire*.

Other people seemed to feel the same way. Some gathered in groups and watched the image in short little glimpses. SueAnne stared as if mesmerized. KJ and his dancers seemed to be everywhere.

Jaliet had managed to turn her own version of the uniform into a fashion statement by tucking it here and there and threading the multiple joined colors of the *Fire* through several tight braids in her black hair. Most of the men looked serious. Drinks abounded, all of them water or stim. Joel had ordered nothing but light food and drink, a choice Ruby had supported. She wanted the feel of a party; not the reality of one.

The moment felt full of crushing import. Ruby circulated, taking hands, murmuring encouragement, and doing her best to look brave.

The *Fire* felt wrong. Its engines had shut down two days ago, but it still creaked and popped, the noises more pronounced than before.

Ruby stopped next to SueAnne and watched beside her. The opening they were about to enter had been built for them in the week between their agreement to dock here and now. She had seen metal changed—filed or welded or heated and shaped. This had sprung from nothing, as if metal could be created out of air. "They grew that," she muttered. "They grew a cage for us."

SueAnne gave her a slightly surprised look, her dark blue eyes lost in wrinkles. "Perhaps they grew a home for us."

Ruby put an arm around SueAnne's slightly stooped shoulders. "I hope so. They have power and knowledge. I suspect they will not share those easily."

SueAnne chewed on her lower lip. Her gaze returned once again to the looming station. "I used to hate you," she told Ruby.

Ruby stiffened, but waited.

"I hated you for being young and strong, and for starting the fighting. I hated you for wanting things you weren't supposed to have." She fell silent for a moment. "I still don't approve of fighting," she fingered her new gray uniform, "but I'm glad to have Joel in charge and you beside him. We may need your courage."

"Thank you." Ruby whispered. "Thank you for saying that. It's been hard to feel accepted."

"Don't assume you are. Most of Joel's advisors believe you are evil on three accounts. You are gray, you are young, and you are a woman."

"They allow you into their councils."

"But you note I am the only woman, and that is because I helped Joel gain his following. My power rests on his acceptance of me."

Ruby chewed on her bottom lip. "They accept you because of him."

"And they are insanely jealous of him because of you."

CHAPTER THIRTY-ONE

Onor stuck close to Joel after the *Fire* ceased moving. Joel looked tired, but then they all must look that way. They had gathered hours ago, eaten lightly, and waited far longer than they expected. Ix remained silent, which made it seem like they were missing a key part of themselves, and needed to be extra vigilant.

Onor scanned faces, checking the location of everyone and looking for anything out of place. He had done this twenty times already, but he forced himself to see it as freshly as he could. Whatever was about to happen, the visitors from the *Diamond Deep* would form their first impression of the people of the *Fire* based on this meeting.

Jaliet, Ani, and Ruby had transformed the room. They'd covered the worn seating in green cloth. Hand-sewn rainbows made from old uniforms lined the bottom of bench. In a few places the decorations had begun to sag. He gestured to Haric, who was following Ruby as if he were a five-year-old after his mother. The boy started toward him, elbowing through people.

Marcelle was not here, of course. She had chosen to work in the creche. He had to think about her pregnancy, but his mind kept refusing to wrap itself around the idea. He would think about it a lot later. He had to.

Haric slid through two large men to stand in front of Onor, white-faced and pale. He stood straight and looked like he wanted to be brave. Maybe they all looked like that. Onor leaned down and asked Haric, "Can you fix up the decorations?"

Ix whispered. "It's time."

Onor had never heard Ix whisper, or heard a whisper be so amplified.

He turned. They all turned. Haric stayed beside him.

The door opened.

Allen, Conroy, and two of Allen's men that Onor recognized came in first. They were followed by a silvery being that moved like a dancer, as smooth as the finest material Onor had ever touched. He had thought the robot spiders beyond them, the materials and engineering out of reach. This was unimaginable.

Two people followed. They wore form-fitting uniforms that shimmered when light hit them. A woman in fine blues and a man in brilliant oranges.

The woman was as beautiful as Ruby, and as young. She had even darker skin than Ani, with long, white hair that hung down her back. He had never seen that color combination, and when she turned to look at him, her eyes were a deep gold. The effect chilled and attracted him.

The man was thin and no taller than the woman, brown-skinned, with black eyes and hair. But he too looked wrong, the colors of everything about him—skin and hair and eyes, while black and brown, still different than the colors Onor was used to seeing on a human.

Both people moved as smoothly as KJ's dancers, as if they didn't really have to touch the floor but chose to do so.

The robot stopped part-way into the room and flowed into a standing cylinder.

The man and woman stopped beside the robot. "Welcome to the *Diamond Deep*," the woman said. "I am Koren Nomen."

A gesture from Joel pulled Onor into a ring of six guards who walked behind Ruby and Joel as they approached the delegation. KJ and his dancers stood nearby, in casual stances that belied how lethal they could be.

Joel spoke stiffly. "Welcome aboard *The Creative Fire*. I am Captain Joel North and this is Ruby Martin, who represents our crew."

Ruby made an expansive gesture with her hands. "And these are some of the people of *The Creative Fire*. Thousands more are working or resting on other levels of the ship. We send you greetings from all of them. We have had a long journey, and we are pleased to be in our home system."

The woman—Koren—gave a soft nod. "You must be weary." She gestured to the brown man who stood beside her. "This is Naveen Tourning." Her hand swept to point at the robot. "And this is one of three assistants who will help me perform an inventory and check on your ship. We will stay with you during your quarantine. I am the *Deep*'s Chief Historian. I look forward to learning about your journey."

Joel's face had stilled, and his voice quieted in a way that Onor knew meant he was evaluating something he was very unhappy about. "We are pleased that you will stay with us. We will provide you adequate quarters on this level and we will escort you to see parts of the *Fire* that might interest you. But we cannot allow your robots to wander at will."

Koren's smile looked as insincere as Joel's. "You cannot believe that you own this ship."

Ruby stood still and quiet, her back straight. One of her fists had clenched.

Joel spoke, his words clipped with buried anger. "We are the crew and owners of the *Fire*." He looked directly at the strange golden-eyed woman.

"You have chosen to dock this ship in a place that *Diamond Deep* went to great expense to create for you, an expense which you must pay back. You cannot restart your ship from here and leave. It is in no condition to fly anywhere." Her features were unreadable, her voice like poetry edged ever so slightly with disdain. "This ship is barely good for salvage."

Ruby had stepped closer to Joel. She broke into the conversation, loudly but calmly, speaking for the whole room to hear. "We are happy to have arrived in a place where we can learn about the home that we left. We have a history of our own to share. If you are truly a student of history you will want what we offer to be given freely."

"I do. But do not assume I have control of your future. Naveen and I are emissaries of others." She paused, letting her words sink in. "We will speak of this later."

"Tell us about the quarantine," Ruby asked. "What do you mean?"

"Before you can leave the bay we have created for you, you must be scanned for anything that could harm us. This is for your good as well. You could easily be infected by germs from our world, or us by germs from yours. Your AI may only communicate with us via messaging and may not share information freely with our systems. We have disabled some of its higher functions until we can fully evaluate its logic. It is still able to run your life support and essential systems."

Ix could be controlled from outside? Ix had been silent because it was trapped? Onor hated Koren for it instantly, a hot intense hatred fueled by disbelief. Ix was *their* AI. It belonged to the *Fire*, and its job was to protect them. He was in no position to ask if Ix had consented, but he didn't think so. Ix liked its power.

Joel and Ruby stood silently, anger obvious in the tight lines of their jaws. His own body had tensed and heated, and his breath sped up. Koren spoke to them as if she were a green and everyone from *The Creative Fire* were lowly grays, or children, or both. Even Joel and Ruby.

Koren watched them all closely with her odd golden eyes. Surely she knew the effect her words were having. But she continued. "Your cargo must be examined. You have come from worlds we have never seen, and there may be dangers in your holds."

Like robot spiders from the Edge. Although the woman couldn't know about Aleesi. She must be speaking of the various treasures they had collected at far star systems long before Onor's birth, and which were protected in containers and watched over by the people who lived in the cargo bay.

After a few moments of the tensest silence Onor had ever felt, Ruby snapped at Koren. "What we have brought back from the stars is ours to share with you, not yours to take."

Joel put a hand on Ruby's arm, as if to quiet her. He smiled his not-smile again. "We are healthy. We came from here. Surely we share the same genetics."

"You know nothing of the complexities of a multi-species star system full of billions of beings. The danger of contamination is real. Diseases from the Edge can kill us if they are not caught quickly, and our germs can damage humans who inhabit the Edge. And yet only twenty generations separate us from the founders of the Edge." Koren made the word Edge sound like a curse. "We are hundreds of generations removed from you. We have evolved."

"You two came freely to us," Joel observed. "Surely if it is that dangerous, you would be speaking to us from your station and not in person."

"We volunteered. We have formidable medical resources with us. And I am willing to die to learn firsthand of your journey."

Onor didn't believe her.

Naveen spoke for the first time. "And I am here to tell of what we learn, to report out to the *Diamond Deep*. Many people inside are watching us now."

Ix was broadcasting this meeting to all of the commons. Marcelle was hearing it somewhere, probably standing among women and children, bridging warrior and mother. He wished she were here where he could see her, and that she wasn't pregnant. Not now, anyway.

Ruby nodded at Koren. "We note your interest in our welfare. We are a strong people who came from here and returned. We endured much along the way, us and our ancestors." She paused for effect, standing tall, her red hair framing her face. She was always at her most beautiful when she was angry. "We are a fair people. We will be fair and honest to those who are fair and honest toward us."

The robot flexed, as if it were reacting to Ruby's words, preparing itself in case she chose to launch herself into a physical fight with the golden-eyed woman.

But of course she did no such thing. Ruby held her ground, not looking away or down. Waiting.

Koren bowed to Ruby, looking stiff and perhaps—just perhaps—a bit uncertain. The smile on Naveen's face looked much more genuine, and Onor almost swore that he was trying hard not to laugh.

CHAPTER THIRTY-TWO

Even though only two days had passed since docking day, Jali had worked miracles yet again, helping Ruby and Ani dress for lunch with Koren. She had put Ruby in a gray dress that dimmed her pale blue eyes but offset her red hair, and given her a belt and sash made from old uniforms that contained all of the colors of the *Fire*. Jali had also braided Ruby's hair with colored ribbons. Jali and Ani both wore pale blues, with the edges in darker blues. The color highlighted Ani's dark skin and Jaliet's black braids.

Ruby surveyed the small galley they had chosen for the event. It, too, had been dressed up in color: flowers had come from the gardens to create a centerpiece and the table was set over a cloth made from braided and flattened green and blue material. Ruby hugged Jaliet close. "You are my best miracle worker."

Jali smiled briefly, accepting the compliment. "This was harder without Ix."

"I miss it," Ruby mused.

Jali laughed. "I had to find everything myself."

Ruby had never trusted Ix; its goals weren't human. Yet Ix *had* helped her directly more than once. She wanted to know what Ix thought of the *Diamond Deep*, and how would it interpret the place in light of its main directive to protect the *Fire*. Always before, protecting the *Fire* and protecting the *Fire*'s people had been intrinsically connected as goals.

They might not be, now.

"Remember your manners," Jali reminded Ruby.

"I know. Don't snarl at the nice powerful woman whose robots are scaring everyone on the ship."

"We have no way of knowing whether or not she really has to touch everyone on the ship to make sure they're safe," Jali said. "I'm angry, but I have no idea if I should be or not. It's unsettling."

"I don't trust Koren." Ruby caught herself pacing the small room and stopped.

"She might be all right," Ani said.

"Remember that you're the one who refused to believe reds were killing grays."

Ani flinched.

"Sorry," Ruby muttered. "Just be suspicious."

"Is there anything you want us to talk about?" Jali asked as she straightened a setting on the table that didn't need straightening.

Ruby glanced toward the door where Haric leaned casually against the wall. "Don't talk about Aleesi," Ruby whispered.

Don't worry," Jali teased. "We'll keep silent about your pet."

"Not," Ruby said. "She's as much as person as we are."

"You're the robot girl," Ani said sharply. "Not that thing."

Ruby kept her silence; this would be a lousy time for a fight. They were all nervous and off-balance.

Haric gave a low whistle, signaling that Koren was on her way. Ruby took a deep breath and reminded herself to stay civil.

Haric came in first. He stood against the far wall as Koren entered, trailed by her robot. This morning, it walked on two legs and looked almost human, although no features marred its smooth face. Koren set a small box down on the table in the closest place. She had dressed in black and white, which went with her black skin and white hair. Golden jewels flowed down the front of her tunic, complimenting her golden eyes.

"Please sit down," Ruby said. "We'd like to offer you food fresh from our gardens."

"Thank you. I've brought food from home." She gestured toward the box. "Until we have finished analyzing the way we react to each other's climates, we should not share each other's food." She sat, and offered a sweet smile to Ruby. "But we can certainly share a table." She sat.

Ruby sat opposite Koren. "Many hands worked on this lunch. I hope the historian in you is curious about what we eat."

"Of course. Please tell your people that I appreciate any effort spent on my behalf." Her voice was cool and controlled, formal.

"These are my advisors, Ani and Jaliet. Haric let you in."

"He will not be joining us for lunch?"

"He will keep watch," Ruby said. "Much like your robot."

Haric came around and poured water. He hesitated at Koren's glass until she nodded. She pulled a small vial from the box and dropped it in the water. Bubbles rose to the surface in a rush, almost foaming, and then subsided.

Ruby drank half of her glass.

Jaliet began small talk complimenting Koren's clothing while Haric served them salads from the garden, lettuce and small tomatoes and orange orbfruit slices. Koren pulled out a series of shaped objects that turned out to be what she ate. They looked more like the colored building blocks a child might play with than like food.

"Is that what you normally eat?" Jali asked.

"If I had brought fresh food, it might have contaminated your own food supply. After quarantine, you may be able to try our food."

"Do you have gardens?" Ani asked.

"Of course. The human body—no matter how much we have changed it—prefers to take in nutrients in raw form. But you will eat distilled food," she pointed to the colorful blocks on the table in front of her, "until you become used to our food."

Gagging might be more fun. "Surely our food gardens here will continue to work."

Koren gave her a look that suggested the idea wasn't worth considering.

Ruby changed the subject. "I'm looking forward to seeing more of the *Diamond Deep*." Perhaps they had even bigger parks. In the meantime, she had other questions. "What does it mean to be the Chief Historian?"

"I oversee the records of *Diamond Deep*. Who joins us, who does not, and why. We are the most diverse major power, and the largest economy in the system. We give succor to many ships and people who flee more restrictive environments."

"That must be a big job."

Koren's golden gaze seemed to be mocking her. "There are people and machines who help me. Much like someone else prepared this food."

"You're so young," Jali observed.

"I am far older than any of you."

"How old?"

Koren smiled. "Hundreds of years. It has been a long time since we saw aging, and death here is primarily by accident."

No wonder they had so many people in the system.

Aleesi had said differently. "Surely you cannot live forever," Ruby stated.

"We don't know yet." Koren folded her hands in her lap and added nothing more.

Ruby drank the last of her water and gestured for another glass. The differences between the *Fire* and *Diamond Deep* seemed larger with every new thing she learned. "Even though you are in charge of many people, you chose to come here yourself."

"A long life creates an interest in new things. *The Creative Fire* is the oldest ship that has ever docked here, and a miracle. Nothing else from your time—the time that *The Creative Fire* left here—exists. Everything has been remade."

"I thought we were no better than salvage," Ruby commented.

Koren didn't miss a beat. "It is possible to be many things."

"Can you tell us about your history?" Ani asked.

"We will be together for days."

"Do you know how long?" Jaliet asked. "When can we step off of this ship?"

Koren smiled. She smiled so often and so shallowly it irritated Ruby. Maybe it wasn't good to be a few hundred years old. If that was true. But if so, Ruby wanted it. To keep her energy and her looks and her abilities for decades or more? The idea shifted inside her from impossible to attractive.

Koren stopped smiling long enough to say, "You will probably be granted a new home in a week or so."

Granted? "We intend to live on the *Fire*."

Koren smiled yet again, and Ruby fisted her hands under the table but left them there. She wasn't ready to start a fight with this woman, not yet. She took a deep breath, trying to inhale politeness. "You're a historian. What would you like to know?"

Koren looked thoughtful. "Four ships of the *Fire*'s type left here. One came back, generations ago, empty. Robots and the AI had managed to get it home. There were three bodies on board. Three. Yet there are thousands of living crew here. I want to understand why you thrived and others failed."

Ani asked, "What happened to the other two ships?"

"They have not returned."

Jaliet handed her empty plate to Haric. "Surely they still could."

"We did not think any from this generation of technology would return. Travel through so much space is dangerous to human psyches. So much isolation. We send out robot ships now, and people only go afterward, if there is any place to go." Koren placed another small square of the food that she had brought into her mouth and swallowed it. "Tell me about the structure here. Your culture. How are decisions made?"

Ruby forced herself to relax her tense shoulders. There had been a formal meeting with both of the *Diamond Deep* emissaries before this, and so Koren had seen Ruby by Joel's side, and met Joel's closest advisors. "Decisions are made for the collective good."

"But it was not always this way."

She knew. Ruby could see it. "Why do you say that?"

Koren smiled. "I talked with a woman, Lya, who said that there have been wars aboard the ship. Deaths. That things have changed recently, and that you drove that change."

Of all the people on the ship, Koren had managed to find the one living person who hated Ruby the most? It couldn't be luck.

Koren's golden eyes showed nothing but curiosity. She sat with her legs crossed and her hands in her lap.

Ruby was certain the woman was trying hard not to look dangerous. She could play the same game. "We merely restored the Fire to something closer to the social structure that was true when we left here. It is, as you say, hard to fly through space for so long and not have some arguments. We are better off now."

Koren smiled an inscrutable and slightly cruel smile. "Lya said you have everything now, that you became the enemy you were fighting and left Lya with nothing."

Ruby again reminded herself to stay calm. She needed to keep Koren occupied. "If you talk to others, they will tell you that they have more freedom."

Ani chewed at her lip, looking like she wanted to talk, so Ruby nodded at her.

"There was a different social structure on the long journey home. You might think of it as a segregation of duties and a segregation of power." She glanced at Ruby. "But Ruby and others chose to change that. It would have been a shame for us to come home separated."

Jaliet spoke, "And as you see, we are unified now. All of us in this room are from different levels in the old structure."

Koren stayed silent, as if encouraging more talk.

Ruby made a gesture that told Haric to bring cracked flatbread which Kyle himself had seasoned. As he took it from the warmer, the scent filled the room. Ruby hoped it made Koren hungry. "How did you know to find Lya?"

"History is forged in conflict. A good historian knows to look for it. I am very good."

CHAPTER THIRTY-THREE

KJ had loaned Onor two of his spider dancers. They hung beside him in suits, clutching traverse lines. Aleesi's metal legs loomed just below him. Being so close made a little gibbering place in the back of Onor's mind brighter, so he felt off-balance. Maybe he'd never be able to be near one of these things without feeling sick to his stomach.

If this worked, they wouldn't have to come all the way back here to keep constant vigil with the robot spider. KJ had come up with the plan after Ruby insisted they protect the damned killer machine. KJ couldn't be spared, and Ruby had asked Onor quite nicely. The look in her eye was almost pleading, a look he rarely saw on her, and which tugged at his center so hard that he promised her even though he'd wanted to refuse.

Onor held up his journal with a recording of Ruby's voice explaining what she wanted to Aleesi. Absent Ix's participation, this was the best idea they had come up with. He wasn't sure how it was going to answer since Ix wasn't actively translating.

But shortly, the words, "I agree," scrolled across his journal.

The thing must be learning to understand human speech.

It was the answer Ruby wanted, but it wasn't the answer he wanted. His stomach threatened him yet again, but it wasn't as if he could tell anyone how much the damned machine scared him. It wasn't rational—it was all about the flight the first day and the way the machine had cut Colin into pieces. He raised his hand, which held a set of loppers. Each step toward the machine was hard, and holding up the cutters to the chains that bound the spider to the floor was even harder.

As if it sensed his fear, it didn't move at all as he and the spider dancers cut its bonds away. When all of the varied ropes and chains lay in heaps on the floor, the spider remained still.

Onor remembered how fast they moved. He forced himself to stay still and type a question onto his journal, "What do we do next?"

"Step back."

Onor was happy to oblige. The robot slowly and completely relaxed all its legs, stretching them out, so that it was as low and long as it could possibly be. In this position it did look smaller and stranger, and a little less threatening. "You will have to climb into the center of me."

Onor started in, careful not to step on limbs. The great claws were so tall that just passing through them he lost his view of the two spider dancers.

In the middle of the beast, Onor felt small. Up here, so close to the center of Aleesi, he had to stand with one foot on each of two legs near where they joined in the middle.

Looking down, he saw a cage longer than his arm and slightly thicker than his thigh. Inside the cage, a rounded blue oblong had been propped up by metal supports and protected against sudden movements. The brain.

"I will release the webling that holds my soul," the machine wrote across his journal. "You will then be able to reach in and remove the cylinder from the cage."

The mass of metal below him moved. The slight shifting of legs that occurred nearly caused him to lose his balance.

The metal cage that had been hidden at the center of the robot snapped open with a single, silky movement and the blue oblong inside darkened.

Even though his instinct was to crush it, Onor leaned down and pulled the object free. The webling. It was bigger in his hands than he had expected, and the surface felt oddly slippery.

A few moments later they were sliding up the traverse lines, the spider dancers quite close to Onor, as if they knew he was of two minds about the thing he carried. At least it was quiescent under his arm, and light in here with the low gravity.

CHAPTER THIRTY-FOUR

The lunch with Koren had become nearly unbearable. Ani, Ruby, and Jaliet finished off a small plate of Kyle's best cookies, and Koren polished off every little square bit of food that she'd brought.

Ruby felt talked out, full, and wary. She wanted to be away from Koren, and to find out if Onor had succeeded in getting Aleesi hidden.

Koren pulled a stoppered flask of something out of her box. "Do you mind if I drink?"

"Of course not," Ruby answered. "Do you mind telling us what you're having?"

"It's a mild stimulant, much like the drink that you call stim."

"We will join you and have some stim then," Jaliet said, nodding to Haric.

Koren waited while Haric prepared drinks for the other three, and left a fourth glass on the countertop. Ruby laughed and said, "Yes, Haric. You may have some."

He gave her a thumbs-up.

Koren sipped her drink. "Tell me about the trip. What were the other planets like?"

"We had not been born," Ruby said. "My grandfather's grandfather was the last one to see a planet. I could tell you what we learned in school."

"I already know that. I'm interested in stories."

"Stories?" Ani asked.

"Things that you've passed down, generation to generation. Maybe things that got recorded in poetry or songs." She looked at Ruby. "You're a singer."

"Yes." The stim must be hitting Ruby; her senses felt more alive and a slight anger crept up her spine. "But first, how do you know what we learned in school?"

"Your AI knows."

"So you know?" Ani leaned in.

"We've been mining your AI since you agreed to come here."

"So you know everything that Ix knows?" Ruby was repeating Ani, but the idea was too vast to imagine. She didn't know much of what Ix knew.

"All data that comes into the station is shared with us. Without that, we would never be secure."

Koren knew things Ix had never told Ruby. Koren knew about Aleesi. Ruby felt cold deep inside, and certain her smile was as fake as the white-haired woman's smile.

Jaliet asked the question Ruby should have thought of. "Even if you did get all of the data from Ix, how would you be able to know it all now? It's only been weeks, at most. And Ix has been running the *Fire* since we left. There's generations of information."

Ani followed it before Koren could answer. "And why is Ix part of the quarantine if you already have all the data? And for that matter, why can't Ix talk to us?"

Koren raised her little bottle and took a long, slow, sip. She seemed to like being watched.

Ruby felt like throwing something at her.

Koren put the bottle down. "I'm certain Ix is performing its life support duties." She paused. "Is there anything specific that you need?"

"Yes." Ruby leaned in so close to Koren that she could see the gold on gold edges of their captor's ancient eyes. She barely managed to keep her voice quiet. "*We need* to have as much information about you as you have stolen from us. *We need* to know how things work on the *Diamond Deep*, and how to behave. *We need* to know how to succeed there."

"We are your hosts." Koren packed her bottle and the napkin she'd used back into the box that she had brought here. "Without your engines, you cannot live without us. Our power keeps the *Fire* going and sustains everything from life support to lights. If we allow you to set foot on the *Diamond Deep*, we will teach you what you need to know to survive here." She said all of this lightly, as she weren't discussing the lives of real people at all.

Ruby tensed and bit her tongue, struggling for control.

Koren's robot slid a few inches from the wall, stopping close to Ruby as if it sensed her taut nerves.

Jaliet put a hand on Ruby's arm.

Ruby took a deep breath and smiled as broadly as she could manage. "We are pleased you joined us for lunch." The polite words nearly gagged her. "I hope that we see you again soon."

"You will." The exotic woman turned and left, her pet robot following after her.

CHAPTER THIRTY-FIVE

Onor stuck close to Joel as their group of fifteen people threaded into the nightclub that formed the center of the cargo bars. The chatter and shifting movement of hundreds of people surrounded them, a throbbing energy that drove Onor closer to Naveen.

"Where are we?" Naveen asked him.

"These are the cargo bars. Our ancestors apparently didn't need all of the space we have for stuff. This whole section has been home to cargo rats for years."

"Excuse me? Cargo rats?"

"Sorry. People who live out in the cargo bays instead of having regular jobs. I didn't know it existed when I was a kid: I found out during the fighting. It's one of the best places on the *Fire*."

Naveen looked enchanted. "I love everything about being here. Look at all the people. When I signed up for this, I thought there would only be a few, and that you'd all be starving and sad and maybe even crazy. And look, you're running dances."

Really? "Why would you think we'd be sick or crazy?"

"Being alone inside a big metal ship for generations? No growth, no new genetics, nothing new to see, ever, until now? Of course, it hasn't been as long for you as it's been for us, but still . . . I'm amazed."

"You underestimated us."

"Yes. Well. I would have gone crazy. Maybe the reason you survived is that you live such short lives?"

Onor didn't respond to that.

"The *Fire*'s return is the most interesting thing to happen on the *Deep* in years." Naveen craned his neck, squinting through the dim light. The tall walls and high ceiling were hung with bright strings of lights that illuminated symbols from the worlds they had travelled to. The painters were all long dead.

A group of drummers made it difficult to hear conversations happening just a few feet away. The room was so full that the outer guard around Joel had to work to keep even a few feet of space available. Beyond the guards, people danced, touched, bumped hips, and chattered enough to release a white noise that seemed to float the deep drum beats on top of it. Colored lights swept over the crowd, blue and green and white.

Naveen did a full 360 turn, taking in as much of the garish decoration as possible.

"Do you like it?" Onor asked him.

"Very much."

"Are there places like this on *Diamond Deep*?"

Naveen laughed. "We are far more sophisticated than this, but far less—visceral." Naveen's hand adjusted glasses that he used to scan what he saw. He recorded almost everything, and sent video out to unknown numbers of watchers aboard the stations. Naveen had said that there weren't many, but that the number was growing.

"How many people see what you see?" Onor asked.

"About twenty-five thousand."

What a thing to tell Ruby. He hadn't had a chance to talk to her since her lunch with Koren, and he had much to tell her about the questions Naveen had asked. He had also developed the idea that Naveen didn't like Koren, and didn't trust her either. Naveen had not said so directly. Rather, Onor read it in the undertones of Naveen's posture and facial expressions, the nuances of his voice.

Onor talked about the bars. "Before the fighting, this was a place where people from different levels sometimes shared secret conversations and drinks. Even now, some people live out here in the bays and never come into the rest of the ship."

"How do I get a drink?" Naveen asked.

"I thought you weren't supposed to eat or drink our food?" Onor hadn't been there during lunch since he had been saving the spider's brains, but he had heard about the afternoon, and joined Naveen, Joel, KJ, and other advisors for a tour of command.

"Didn't you just tell me this place was meant for breaking rules?"

"It does have that effect. But you won't get hurt by our stuff?"

"Koren's not here to care. And besides, I'm in quarantine right along with you. If it kills me, so be it." He smiled, his eyes still twinkling. The man was having fun. "We will all die some day, right?"

It made Onor laugh as well. He felt good, even if he was wary. "Hopefully not for a long while."

Onor glanced at Joel, who was deep in conversation with SueAnne. "Can I take Naveen to get a drink?"

"Send someone. Have them bring us all drinks."

"*You* want still?" Joel almost never drank, even in the deeper cargo bars. Certainly never with an audience.

"Of course not." He leaned down and whispered into Onor's ear. "Drink with him. He appears to like you. Maybe you'll learn more than we have so far. No still for the rest of us, though."

Sometimes Onor wondered if Joel ever relaxed, even with Ruby. Maybe that's what power did to you.

Onor sent three of the outer guards for the drinks. The room felt full of nerves and bravado. Diffuse. Undirected. People were a tad too dressed up, a bit too loud, maybe a bit more intoxicated than they should be.

The drinks Joel had ordered appeared before the drums slowed. Onor handed Naveen his, which Naveen took a picture of. Then Naveen took another picture of Onor with his drink. They clicked glasses and drank, and the still hit Onor almost immediately, sitting like fire in his empty stomach.

Naveen got a funny look on his face, then he licked his lips in an exaggerated fashion and said, "To life!"

"And finishing quarantine!" Onor said.

"Same thing."

Onor didn't know what to make of that answer. "You have bars, right?"

"Of course." Naveen took another sip. "But this is unique. You should import it." Naveen sipped at his drink some more. He'd started moving to the drums. His skin was too deep a brown for his cheeks to flush, but his eyes looked brighter.

The drums rose to a crescendo and then stopped. Scattered clapping rewarded the performance, just loud enough to hear above the constant conversation that swirled through the space.

Onor took a smaller sip of the still. "Watch," he told Naveen.

Drums sounded again. Other drums, new ones, and off-stage. They changed from a low, slow beat to a fuller and faster cadence. The stage was pitch black, the lights sweeping the back of the audience. The drums sped up again. At the crescendo, a spotlight fell onto the stage. In the center of the light, wearing a stained worker's coverall, worn black boots, and ribbons of color that matched the old uniforms from the *Fire*, Ruby stood with her head bowed. She leaned on a prop that looked like a gun a tall as she was. Her red hair flowed unbound across her shoulders.

The drums stopped.

Ruby stayed completely still for two breaths.

Naveen put a hand on Onor's arm. "Who is she?"

Onor smiled.

On stage, Ruby lifted one arm and as it came up past her shoulders, her head snapped up, and her eyes opened. The object she had been leaning on revealed itself as a microphone rather than a gun. She tilted it toward her and the familiar opening bars of "Homecoming" came through every speaker in the room.

"Oh, my," Naveen whispered.

Conversations stopped or dropped to whispers.

Ruby's voice filled the space, creating a focus completely on her. The entire bay full of people drifted toward the stage, crowding closer and closer to each other. She moved with raw sensuality, sidling up to the prop microphone as if it were a lover.

She shifted from "Homecoming" to "Song of the Seed" smoothly.

> *Together we are a seed*
> *Preparing to open in the light*
> *Of Adiamo. To flower.*

Naveen emptied his glass during the song, never once looking away from Ruby. The way he held his head still signaled Onor he was recording.

She ended "Song of the Seed" with her legs wide and straight, her hands up high holding the microphone shaped like a gun, palms open, angled backward, and her head thrown back.

The room erupted in clapping and noise.

Naveen looked at Onor. "That's really her. That's Ruby the Red."

Onor had never heard her called that. As the noise calmed some he asked, "Where did you hear that name?"

"I was interviewing people who work in the gardens. That's what they're calling her."

Ruby would love that. Her hero was Lila Red the Releaser, a woman who had led a revolution that failed. Barely. He couldn't wait to tell Ruby about the nickname.

"She's incredible," Naveen said. "The things I've heard . . . I didn't think they could be true. I didn't see how Joel's woman could be the fighter. She was so . . . politic."

"She's versatile."

"I'm jealous of Koren. She got to meet her today."

Onor sensed that hadn't gone well. Ani had merely grunted when he asked her about it. "You'll get to talk to Ruby more tonight."

"That would be . . . I hope so."

Ruby still stood on the edge of the stage, fearless, exposed.

Joel watched her protectively. Some of the crowd looked adoring, or attracted, or simply drunk. Naveen looked starstruck. Onor had seen it on other people's faces before, but never quite so blatantly. It made Onor feel warm and a bit starstruck himself, lucky all over again that he'd grown up one of her best friends.

The first swell of clapping subsided, and Ruby spoke into the microphone. "Hello!"

The crowd yelled back greetings.

"I'm glad you're here tonight! We've got a lot to talk about!"

"Talk!" they chanted. "Talk!"

"We're finally here. We're back now, back home. *Diamond Deep* is not what I expected. I bet it's not what you expected either!"

The crowd clapped a yes, catcalled.

"It is the last stop for the *Fire*, and it's in the system we came from. This moment—docking yesterday and being here now—this moment represents change such as we have never seen. Never. Not since the day our ancestors left and took on the *Fire* as our home."

Ruby adjusted her microphone, creating a moment for people to think about her words. Then she continued. "I know we're stuck right now, and I know that doesn't feel good. It wasn't our choice, but the time will pass. We'll continue to learn, to support each other, to be patient, and to be brave. "

Some muttering this time, then a clap, then another, then a swell of noise as more and more people committed.

"We must be strong. We must be proud. We must believe in ourselves. There will be strange things to encounter here. Things we can choose to fear or face. We must face them together. Can we? Can you? Can we all stay together as *People of the Fire?*"

Now that Onor was listening for it, her heard it a few times in the responses of the crowd. "Ruby the Red!" and once as "Red Ruby!"

"Now," she called. "Now I have a new song for you. One I wrote for this moment. We are pregnant with possibility here. The song honors our waiting."

She fell silent for a few breaths, and the crowd was silent now, too, waiting.

"I've called it 'A Deepness in the Stars.'"

We have arrived home to
A deepness we have never seen
Unlike anything we have seen
Unlike our souls
We came from here
We were once
Like the Diamond Deep
Once was
We should not fear

The Deep has called us home
To find a dream, a hope, a place
Where we will never be alone

The song had more hope in it than he felt, but as usual Ruby's voice—no, Ruby's being—convinced him.

The last note trailed off and the stage darkened.

In spite of the clapping and cheering of the crowd, the next time lights hit the stage a new band had set up and started tuning their instruments.

Joel signaled his security detail, and the group began moving slowly toward a set of stairs that wound up the wall of the huge bay. At the top of the stairs, a door led to a hallway that led to the deep cargo bars where Colin had ruled.

Allen greeted them there, offering Naveen a formal welcome. He led them to a booth in the back. Joel signaled for everyone except Onor, Ani, and Naveen to leave them, but to remain on guard. They ordered more drinks, Joel using hand signals to indicate that only Onor and Naveen should get actual still, and that Naveen should have some extra.

Naveen remained quiet, contemplative. He didn't stir until the drinks and a plate of fruit and crackers arrived. He blinked at the drink in his hand and then looked at Joel. "That was phenomenal."

Joel smiled. "The drink is a specialty of this bar."

"No." Naveen shook his head. "The drink is fine. But I have never heard music delivered so . . . so raw."

"You don't have concerts?" Ani asked.

"Of course we do. Maybe I can take you to some. But they are . . . huge productions. Very different. I have not heard music move that many people." He finished a third of his drink in one long swallow. "Not since I left Lym."

"You're from Lym?" Onor asked. "A real planet? I had hoped we would go there. Our ship's records say we came from there." He sipped at his own drink. Slowly. Joel may be trying to get Naveen drunk, but Onor would pay for it later if he allowed himself to get lost in alcohol. "What's it like. To have a sun? To stand with a sky above you?"

"I'm not from Lym, but I was lucky enough to live there for a year." Naveen smiled softly, his face warm. "I miss it. The openness of a world is amazing. The space and the fact that you can be completely alone."

"What do you think of the *Fire?*" Joel asked.

"It's gritty. The station is much lighter and greener." He pursed his lips and glanced at Joel. "I mean no disrespect. And of course the *Diamond Deep* will never go anywhere the gravity of Adiamo does not pull it. I'm fascinated with your history."

Joel sipped at his fake drink. "Earlier, you said you chose to come here. Why?"

"To see what we used to be like." Naveen fell silent for a moment, looking contemplative. "Koren and I were chosen partly because we're more like you."

Ani laughed. "Koren doesn't look anything like us. We've no golden eyes and no white hair that's not on the very old."

"Oh, yes, she does look like you. You'll see."

Ani frowned and leaned back. "What about the robots? Humans don't look like that, do they? Made of metal?"

Onor admired the clever way to ask about Aleesi. Ani had grown much more subtle since Ruby took power alongside Joel.

Naveen shook his head. "Humans and robots are not the same. Human minds are required to be in biological bodies, but they don't all look like we do."

That supported Aleesi's claim.

The conversation wandered across the *Fire* for a while, with Naveen asking about their history and the way they fed themselves. None of them knew the answers to some of Naveen's questions. Onor tried a few times to access Ix on his journal and failed. He settled for sipping his drink and contemplating how much power Ix had in the information it withheld, and how much they had given up by failing to learn. Ruby had been right to send them all to class. They should have been studying every free minute. "How old are you?" he asked Naveen. "I heard Koren is hundreds of years old."

Naveen cocked a head. "I'm only forty-seven. Koren is much older."

"You look twenty."

"So do you," Naveen countered, "So do you."

"That's because I am. Almost, anyway."

"How old is Ruby?"

"Like me."

"So young." Naveen set his empty glass down and leaned back against the headrest on his chair.

Joel glanced over at him and raised an eyebrow. "Are you okay?"

Naveen sat up straight again.

Onor let his drink be picked up half-full and accepted another one for Naveen. Naveen finished his in three long pulls. "I'm always okay," he said slowly.

Joel gave Onor a worried look. It was one thing to loosen Naveen's tongue, but another entirely if he got so drunk he got sick.

When Naveen reached for a piece of orbfruit, Ani leaned forward and put a hand on his arm. "You're not supposed to eat our food, are you?"

"I'm drinking your drinks."

Onor and Joel looked at each other. Joel shook his head slightly, but Naveen already had a piece of fruit in his mouth. He sat back and chewed, and nothing awful happened.

"So," Joel leaned in. "What happens next? If we pass quarantine, what happens to us?"

"I don't know." Naveen look a little dizzy. "I don't know. I don't think I could tell you if I did."

Ruby came up behind Naveen. She now wore her base uniform and hardly looked like she belonged at a party at all. Onor was pretty sure she had a plan by the way she came up quickly, but she stopped when she realized they had Naveen with them.

Naveen must have noticed Joel looking at Ruby. He tilted his head up enough to see behind him. His eyes appeared slightly crossed. "I don't want anything bad. To happen. To you."

"Why would it?" she asked.

"Nishe conchert," Naveen slurred.

"Thanks." She narrowed her eyes at Joel.

He shrugged.

Ruby shook her head and looked back at Naveen. "What bad things might happen?"

Allen appeared, as silent as Colin had been, but with none of the confidence that would have painted Colin's face in any situation. He looked quite worried. He leaned down and whispered in Joel's ear.

Joel stood up. "We'll go to her." He looked at Ruby. "Lose yourself. I'll meet you back home. Later." He looked at Ani. "Stay with Ruby."

Onor swallowed and set his drink down. Joel should have sent him. Except Ani hadn't been drinking. Damn.

Joel plucked the drink from Naveen's hand and helped him up. "Come on. Koren's here."

"Prolly read my output stats."

"Huh?"

"Implanche."

Onor shook his head. Implants? "What do you mean?"

"Our AI'sh can read our bodieshh. Can't yours?"

The idea of getting Naveen tipsy in case they could learn something suddenly seemed really dumb. Onor took his arm, and he and Naveen followed Joel and Allen toward the front of the room where the door guards kept people out who shouldn't be here. He imagined Koren in that situation, and was suddenly glad he wasn't a door guard. Of course, it might not be very good to be himself, either. Most of their guards kept a distance, although Onor had to wave one up to take Naveen's other side so he wouldn't fall down.

Joel glanced back over his shoulder. "You can leave, too," he told Onor. "Better if you did."

Joel nodded. "Thank you." But he wouldn't leave any more than Onor would. Maybe they could just hand the increasingly wobbly Naveen over to Koren and her robots and be done with it.

CHAPTER THIRTY-SIX

Ruby paced in the quiet of her and Joel's hab, back and forth the longest possible way, which led from the bedroom door down one side of the living room, past the entrance to the kitchen, and all the way to the front. The path was already worn; she often walked it when worrying about lyrics or about Joel's safety. She suspected he walked it when he worried about her, or when he was mad at her. That happened.

Right now, she worried about him. She worried about Onor, and even Naveen, who she barely knew, but liked. She could tell Onor liked him, and Onor was good at judging people. She worried about Koren, and what she had done to whom. Mostly, though, she worried about Joel. He moved from meeting to meeting without stopping, but there was nothing to actually accomplish except to wait.

She wanted Koren off their ship. She wanted their ship free from the *Diamond Deep*. Both were impossible goals.

She and Joel had bet their futures. All of their futures.

The station had a right to do what they were doing. Maybe they even did it to every ship that docked here. There was no reason for them not to have rules that Ruby didn't like. But the whole set-up felt like a threat, like she and her people were in some deep danger that she had absolutely no way to understand. She didn't even know what questions to ask, and when that was true, she was used to asking Ix.

She stopped in the kitchen, her hand hovering between stim and still, choosing water.

Next, she started running through KJ's most basic movement sequence, the one she'd learned in the big classes, way back in the days when Fox told her what to do and she listened.

She hadn't seen Fox in a long time. The last time she'd seen him, he had been promoting a band of drummers, and he'd looked away from her as she headed toward him, turned sideways into a crowd, and disappeared.

But she shouldn't be thinking of Fox right now.

She pushed all of the noise of her mind away and focused on moving her body, one flowing pose sliding into another, balance and weight and speed as exact as she could get them.

She hadn't practiced for weeks.

All of her weight rested on one foot and her back stretched out even with the floor, the free foot behind her held flat, hands extended palm-down in from of her. A line of Ruby with a single leg to hold her up, thigh tightened for strength, knee loosened for safety. When the door opened, she tipped the wrong way and had to touch her fingers to the floor to tip back so she could get her foot under her and stand properly. "Joel?"

"I'm here."

"You were gone a long time," she called to him. "What happened to poor Naveen?"

"Koren sent him to his room with an *assistant* to guard him."

That didn't sound good.

Joel came through the hall and stood in the door. His jaw was set with anger, his shoulders tight. "What happened?" she asked.

He crossed both arms over his torso and stared at the wall. "We have to leave."

"What?"

"We passed quarantine. We're being told that we have to leave the *Fire*. Not just by Koren. That's what she says, anyway."

He looked as angry as she had ever seen him, and like he could lose control at any moment. Ruby couldn't tell if he was about to explode in anger or cry. She had never felt him like this, so fragile and so angry and so frustrated. She had never sensed despair in him.

She brought him a glass of water, which he waved away. "Who?" she whispered, not wanting to set off whatever was inside him right then. "Who has to leave? You and me or all of command? What do they want?"

"They say we all have to leave. The whole ship."

"Everybody? That's thousands of people!" The mere idea of it spun her head. She'd assumed the *Fire* was their home, at least for now. That they'd move off it slowly. That people would find work or places to go. "They can't do that, can they?"

He sat on the couch and pulled her down to him. He held her so tight it hurt, his breath uneven as if he was as shocked with his news as she was, even though he'd clearly had it longer. "I think they can do whatever they want."

It felt hard to think. "Isn't there a court? Didn't you tell me that once? A system-wide court?"

"I don't see how that would stop them. They look at us like some kind of curiosity. As if we're children. Maybe they'll put us all in a play pen and watch us. I don't know."

"We need the *Fire*. The holds. The things we brought back. That's all we have."

His jaw was so tight he could barely get the next words out. "Koren says we're lucky we are being granted a place to live for six months. The contents of the holds will be payment for that."

"How does she know what they're worth?"

"We don't either."

Her brain raced. The *Fire*'s engines were off and might not be reusable at all. Certainly she didn't know how to start them. Ix could. But Ix had been silenced. The *Fire* itself had started falling apart the minute they started slowing down, as if it knew it was coming back to die. Truth be told, even earlier, if you counted how much of their equipment was scrap and parts by the time Ruby was born.

"What did you try to negotiate?"

He shook his head. "It was all presented as orders. I got them to give us another day. That's all."

He was accustomed to respect and to people following his orders. "Who knows this?" she asked.

"Ani, Allen, Onor. KJ, because I sent Onor to hunt him down and tell him. That's all. But we'll have to tell them all soon. That's why I came for you."

"How much time?"

"Koren started with two days. I turned it into three."

"That's not possible." Thousands of people. They'd all want to bring their things. They'd want to group up as families. They'd be scared. "They can't . . . what about the gardens and the parks and the water systems and the other things that have to be kept up?"

"They're turning off the water that goes to the parks and the gardens."

"That's . . . that's violating." There were other words, other things it felt like. This should not be happening to them.

"I'm not sure I can stand this."

In trade for his unusual vulnerability, she tilted her face up, stood on tiptoe, and kissed him. "We'll do this together."

He went silent for a long time. "Maybe we shouldn't. We don't know anything. We might get blamed for this."

"Some will blame us." She pulled herself out from under his arm and stood, facing him. He looked tired. But then he'd spent a whole day with Naveen, spent the evening at the cargo bars, and then had to deal with Koren. She took a deep breath, centering herself. "They need us to lead. Even the ones who blame us are going to need us. Besides, it's not like either of us could hide in the crowds anyway."

He went still and watched her, assessing. Not quite hesitating. When he spoke he sounded measured and unemotional, like he was working for all of the control that he could get. His hands were clasped tightly together, as if to keep them from shaking. "Koren offered to take those of us from command somewhere else. The others will want to go. She promised a place that was more comfortable. More privileged. That's the word she used."

"You didn't tell her yes?"

He shook his head. "I didn't tell her no yet, either."

She tried to take that in. "To buy us time?"

A slight shake of his head. "You might think about it. We could be comfortable."

"You're just tired. We can't abandon our people. And we can't trust Koren anyway. We're safer if we're all together. You heard what I told them tonight, and how they reacted. They need to know we are all a family, one family."

"I want you to be safe."

"I don't care about that. I never have. If the world were still only gray for me, if I were still a robot repair girl, I'd be maimed or dead or raped or something by now." She took his face between her hands. "Whatever happens, it's better than that already. It's better for almost everyone." She stepped back, biting her lip, giving him a moment. When he didn't reply, she said, "We can't go backwards. We have to protect them all."

He was so still. She couldn't tell what he was thinking, and he wasn't meeting her eyes.

"They need us," she whispered.

He fisted his hands and paced.

"I'll lead them myself if you won't go, but I want you beside me. You're our strength. You earned this job." *And now we need you to do it.* But she said that part in her head. It would be so hard to do this by herself.

He stopped and answered her, very quietly. "How are we going to lead them through a place we don't know anything about?"

"With our hearts."

He stood up and took her in his arms. He smelled of the cargo bars, of still and stim, of mint and talk. His heart beat against her ear.

"I will tell her we're staying with our crew."

She burrowed into his chest. "I love you."

PART FOUR

THE DIAMOND DEEP

CHAPTER THIRTY-SEVEN

Joel and Ruby stood side by side, watching the line of refugees snake through a gauntlet of uniformed *Diamond Deep* staff. As leaders, they had gone through first. Now, they waited. They'd sworn to watch as each individual left *The Creative Fire*.

SueAnne led the line, walking slowly and carefully. Her face showed pain that Ruby suspected came from having to leave home even more than it came from her painful joints. All of Joel's other advisors had taken Koren's offer of safe haven somewhere else, but SueAnne had refused. In fact, when she'd learned of it, she had slapped Laird across the face and walked away. Later, she had told Ruby she had wanted to do that for a long time.

A specific process happened for each refugee. First, a pair of uniformed women took their names and pictures. A robot injected each person with medications, using small round buttons with needles that popped out on contact with the skin. Then, everyone passed through an arch where they stood on a plate while an unseen mechanism sprayed them with a fine mist, so they emerged with drops of liquid spangling their hair and cheeks. If they had looked happy, the mist might have made them pretty. On a few faces, it combined with tears.

Ruby and Joel had done their best to message the banishment as well as they could, but without Ix to broadcast throughout the ship, the simple logistics of getting word to everyone and keeping order had required all of the three days they had been given. Koren had offered help from the *Diamond Deep* and by the end of the first day, they had grudgingly accepted a hundred people to help organize the exodus.

Her mouth tasted like ash and she was tired to her bones. It was hard to stand up straight. *Keep the rebels too busy to rebel.*

It tore at Ruby to watch how some of the people worked through the line. Some went shambling, the loss painted across features and dropping shoulders. Others walked with their heads up. Here and there, a few of the children and young adults looked excited or at least curious. Everyone carried bags of belongings, or wheeled makeshift carts.

Ruby had managed to get permission to bring some of their robots as beasts of burden, so here and there a robot squeaked by with a pile of extra gray uniform cloth, tools, first-aid supplies, bedding, or piles of food from the last harvest.

Joel stood beside her. He had chosen to wear his most formal dress uniform, and he stood still with his chin up and his jaw tight. Ruby was pretty sure she was the only person to recognize how angry he felt.

A thousand details and questions threatened to overwhelm her. Underneath of those, an anger similar to Joel's burned deep in her, eating at her belly, but she couldn't afford to let it rise to her heart. Not now. She glanced up at him. "That's a quarter of them."

"About."

Daria came through the misting arch hand in hand with The Jackman. She let go of him long enough to stop and hug Ruby.

Ruby held her close, her face tickled by flyaway bits of Daria's hair. "I sent a bot to help you with your beads. Did it get there?"

Daria nodded against her shoulder. "Thank you."

Just behind Daria, Ruby's mother, Siri, and her younger brother, Ean. Siri gave her daughter a cool hug, Ean gave her a warm one. After they left, Ruby frowned. She should find a job for Ean. She didn't mind that Siri didn't talk to her often, but she did miss Ean.

A little later, Kyle came through. He carried two plates that must have held cookies. Ruby lifted herself on tiptoe and kissed his cheek. "I bet you made a few children happier."

"I hope so."

Nearer the end, Marcelle walked amid a number of women with children in tow. She carried a girl that mustn't be much more than two or three. Marcelle had talked about being a parent since they were little girls together; she would be a good one. Ruby felt happy for her, if bittersweet. At some deep core place, she didn't expect to live long enough to raise children. She never had. She waved back when Marcelle waved, then Marcelle bent to a child walking beside her, whispering something. She and the child were soon lost in the long thin string of people.

They needed to plan for the children.

Ix had been the primary teacher. Some humans had been in the classrooms; they would have to teach. Maybe Marcelle could take charge of the schools. Hopefully they would have room for schools. All they knew was they had been promised a home big enough for all of them.

It felt as if the *Fire* was disgorging twice as many people as she had sheltered. At one point she saw Fox, who gave her a single, withering glance.

About two-thirds of the way through, a set of ex-Peacers escorted the prisoners who had been in the *Fire*'s jails. A worse problem than the schools. They should have negotiated about prisoners. Once more, she felt anger nagging at her. They had needed time! She took another deep breath and ignored it, reviewing the to-do list in her head until the anger went away.

Near the end, one of the robots going by carried a nearly-unbalanced metal box full of robot parts. Ruby bit at her lower lip and looked away as it was catalogued. When it passed by after the misting, she let out a long relieved breath.

Aleesi was safe in their possession.

Her feet were weary from standing and her cheeks sore from smiling by the time Onor and Ani came through, sweeping up the last stragglers. A few families had tried to stay aboard the *Fire*. Only the promise of failing life support systems had flushed them out of hiding. One of them had brought back a tale of two old men who had decided to stay and die anyway, but Ruby suspected that was rumor.

These last few people were the saddest looking. A few were so old that friends or family helped them walk. Others looked partly unhinged by the change that had swept across them.

Ruby leaned over to Joel and took his hand. "Let's go."

He looked back at the doorway to the hold that enclosed *The Creative Fire*.

"We'll see it again," she whispered.

"I doubt it. I believe we have been completely and totally defeated."

All she felt besides tired was a livid, burning anger. "We'll see. At least we are all together. Maybe there's some good here yet."

"Do you think so?"

"Can I think anything else?"

"No." They walked at the end of the line, following the oldest and weakest of the *Fire*'s many people to an unknown destination.

CHAPTER THIRTY-EIGHT

Onor sat alone in the small bar they'd pulled together in a corner of their new living area. A rumor of a name had started. Ash. Onor loved the irony, although he expected Ruby to change it to something more positive. Still, it had stuck for the last week.

Bar was an overstatement: ten cramped tables and a makeshift metal pouring bar with no chairs, one robotic server and one bartender. Allen. The worst part wasn't the cramped quarters, but that it was almost dry. Some of the equipment they'd used for making alcohol had come with them from the *Fire*, but Joel had refused to let them turn food to still or stim here.

Two other tables held small groups muttering amongst themselves about one or another detail of setting up a whole new life for thousands of people. They'd been here six days, enough to reduce total chaos to near-chaos.

Onor took a small sip of the half-glass of still he'd managed to talk Allen out of and stared at the device in his hand. None of their journals worked here. Instead, they'd all been given thin, flexible screens called slates they could fold up and carry around in their uniform pockets. The slates were very different than the old journals, and Onor had no idea if he was using it right. He had messaged Naveen, but he hadn't seen a reply.

At the moment, he was staring at one of Naveen's recordings of the old cargo bar, of Ruby singing the very last night they'd all been there. He'd been trying to pry secrets out of Naveen instead of paying attention to what he was about to lose, and now he could never go back.

So much for coming home in triumph.

"Onor!"

He looked up to see Naveen came through the door. Onor hadn't seen him since the day they were kicked off of *The Creative Fire*. Naveen's skin and hair and eyes were all the same inhuman shades of brown they had been on the *Fire*, but his clothes were now a myriad of blues, some of them shimmery. Onor grinned. "Glad you came."

"Glad you figured out how to get a message to me. Maybe you're not quite as dull and clueless as Koren is saying."

Onor frowned. "She could be right. I feel like an idiot here. That's why I offered you the golden chance to enlighten me."

"Wouldn't miss it. Did they really build you such a phenomenal ugliness to live in?"

"This is where they sent us."

"Well, I suppose you didn't know any better." Naveen picked up Onor's glass and sniffed at it. "Got any more?"

Allen was already on his way over with a glass. "This is almost the last I have."

"Too bad." Naveen took a small sip and let out a satisfied smile. "Your brews are—rawer—than anything we have. Maybe you all should earn your living by setting up a real bar."

"Earn our living?"

"Sure. Think air's free up here? You'll have to work."

Oh. Onor shrugged. "We all worked on the *Fire.*"

"That's good," Naveen said. He raised his glass. "To success and fame for the people from our past."

"And you." Onor sipped his drink. "What happened to you after Koren found you?"

"She locked me up and then shipped me off the *Fire.* Shouldn't have been able to do that. But she did it."

"Well," Onor swept his hand around. "We got in a bit of trouble."

"You were in that trouble from the day you chose to come here."

"And you didn't warn us?"

"Didn't know I'd like you. Speaking of liking you, how's Ruby of the golden voice?"

Taken. Off limits to you, just like to me. Beautiful and brave. "She's working her butt off, her and Joel. Setting up schools and negotiating for food and stuff. Koren has a small army in here interviewing people. Never see her anymore, though."

"Koren's heart has been replaced with ugliness and ego. I had to defend myself with the Station MPs for having this," he raised his glass, "with you on the *Fire.*"

"But you won't get in trouble here?"

"Nah."

"So will you show me around the station? We're not allowed out without escorts right now. Something about not knowing the rules yet."

Naveen laughed. "That's probably for your own good. *Diamond Deep*'s not all safety and light."

"I still want to see it."

Naveen drained his glass. "Let's go."

"Right now?" Onor hadn't expected that. "Okay." He emptied his glass, grabbed Naveen's glass, and headed for the bar. "We're going out," he told Allen with a low voice. "Pass it to Ruby and Joel."

"Lucky you. But be careful with the drunk."

"He's okay."

Onor frowned as he returned to Naveen. "I'll follow you."

Naveen immediately started to thread through the primary living quarters for the refugees. Ash was about a third the size of all of the living space on the *Fire* put together; each person's hab was half the size they were used to, or smaller. Some families were downright cramped. There were more common areas, although they were smaller than aboard the *Fire*. Nothing was broken, and water appeared to be unlimited. On balance, it seemed okay to Onor in spite of what Naveen had said, except for the crowding. People had already decorated their habs and walls with the colors from home, and Headman Stevenson had sent them a welcome gift of multiple potted plants full of bright blooms, some as tall as Onor. Even though it looked reckless to him, Onor liked the surprising bits of greenery by doors and on tables and walls. It reminded him that they weren't on a spaceship any more. "Where do you get all your water?" he asked Naveen. "I worked water reclamation, and it was hard and critical. But you have no problems."

"We make it."

"You make water?"

"We make air, too."

"But you just told me air isn't free."

"Transformation costs energy."

It was enough to make his head hurt. "I'd like to see where you live," Onor suggested. "You didn't seem very impressed with the little world the people of *Diamond Deep* decided to bestow on us."

"Cheap algorithms," Naveen snorted. "Boring stuff." He grinned. "Maybe we'll make it to my house. But there's so much to show you."

"Lead."

Two guards at the doorway out stepped back to allow Onor and Naveen through. "That was easy," Onor commented. "I've tried to get out twice."

"They know me."

"Does the whole station know you?"

"Not yet."

Onor had been in the corridor on the other side of the door on the way in, but he'd been busy herding tired people. He had spent the last part of the journey carrying two children Marcelle had handed him, one on each hip.

At the first branching hallway, Naveen led him the way Onor had never seen.

Even with gravity that was slightly lighter than Onor was used to as the daily norm, the walk felt long. "Does it take forever to get anywhere on this station?"

"Only when you let the stationmasters assign you housing on the outer edge of nowhere."

"I thought we were in the middle of this part of the station."

"But not near any decent transportation. But then, you didn't expect them to give you great real estate, did you?"

"So who decides who lives where?"

"Credit."

"Huh?"

"You don't have any. You're beggars now, and you could be close to slaves if you don't figure out how to earn credits. It's not hard. I'll show you."

Onor felt like he only partly understood anything Naveen said.

Naveen eventually led him to a train station, and they climbed aboard a train eerily like the ones on the *Fire*, only cleaner and with bigger cars. The train sped quietly along a winding track. For most of the ride there was nothing to see, although from time to time the window offered a rush of colors. Two other humans and three robots rode in the car, one of the robots so humanoid-looking that Onor had to look twice to be sure it was a machine. The other two hadn't been fashioned at all like humans. To his relief they also didn't look like robot spiders, but had arms and legs. He was so busy studying the humanoid robot he almost missed it when Naveen got up to leave. The doors nearly closed on him, which gave Naveen a laugh.

"Thanks for the warning," Onor complained.

"Any time. Do you know your station?"

"Huh?"

"Where we got on."

"No."

"Star necklace."

"Impressive." He could remember that by thinking of the bead necklaces.

"Old. It's the name of a nebula."

They went through a mechanism that Onor recognized as an oversized airlock about the time the second door started to open.

Naveen watched Onor carefully as he stood waiting. "Stop one on our tour," he whispered, sounding more serious than he had so far today.

The door slid further open.

Movement and color slammed Onor's senses, followed by the smell of growing things. Bright lights forced him to close his eyes. The voices of both humans and machines made a low buzz. Water ran.

He opened his eyes again, seeing what he had been hearing and smelling, blinking at the intensity of the light, which seemed to come directly from the walls.

They were in an open space with high ceilings. Tables surrounded by people were the primary source of all of the voices, although people walked up and down wide corridors between groupings of tables.

Naveen led him to one of the open tables. "Now you'll see why I like your still." Before Onor could protest, Naveen had ordered a drink for both of them and a plate of food, or at least that was Onor's suspicion. He shared a lot of words with the man, but there were words Naveen used that Onor had never encountered anywhere, words so strange they rendered perfectly good sentences useless.

Well, he could trust Naveen or he couldn't. His gut told him he could.

A robot deposited two drinks at their table. The orange-yellow drink tasted sweeter than Kyle's best cookies, and smooth. Like drinking a flower. He made a face at it, which Naveen captured with his ever-present camera. "Told you."

"What are you taking pictures for?"

"I'm a storyteller and a creator. It's what I do. Your people already have thousands of followers. If you want to stay hot, you need to add new footage all the time. That's one of the things I will do for you in trade for your stories. Keep you hot."

"We're already giving our stories to Koren and her people in trade for a place to live."

"That's your past. Koren can own that part—I don't care. I want the stories of how you and the *Diamond Deep* come to know each other. I want to watch you meet the people from the station."

The drink was giving his voice soft edges. "So, who are the thousands? Why are people interested in us?"

Naveen grinned again, his teeth a bright white and his smile warming his whole face. "I have made them interested in you." He shrugged. "And you are new. You will be interesting for a while. After all, even though there are over fifteen million people here, it is kind of a boring place. A hard place. At least, for most. But trust me, something else new will come here. By then you will need to have claimed your place."

A woman wearing only underwear, a tiny top, and comfortable shoes brought them a plate of breads and fruits. Her eyes were as flashy as Koren's, and her hair was purple, blue, green, and gold, shifting color as she moved her head.

Wow. She did, in fact, look more exotic than Naveen or Koren. After Onor watched her walk over to a bar, he turned to Naveen to find the camera on him again. The camera stopped him from opening his mouth to ask a question. He sipped his drink and tried to look as cool as possible while he observed the myriad strange-looking people and robots either sitting nearby or wandering about together.

Naveen waved a hand at him. "That's Lysa. She's been running this bar for a long time. She came over to get a look at you."

"She's tall."

"She's pretty, too, huh?" Naveen coaxed.

"Sure. But I like our women."

"Do you have a mate? A woman from the *Fire*?"

"Yes." He didn't want to talk about his confusions regarding Marcelle. Or Ruby. "Tell me what this food is, and if I can share pictures with my own people?"

"Do you have your slate?"

"Yes."

"Take a picture."

"How?"

Naveen showed him.

Oh. He could be recording as much as Naveen. The idea fascinated him. He took pictures of Naveen, and pictures of Lysa when she came back to check on them, and Naveen took pictures of him taking pictures.

Onor tried some of the bread, which tasted like nuts and had seeds that stuck in his teeth so he had to pick them out. The fruit tasted like orbfruit, but blander.

Hopefully the new food wouldn't make him sick.

The next stop did include a drink, a bottle full of something blue that seemed slightly less alcoholic, although somewhere in the back of his brain Onor remembered that they'd pulled the tastes-lighter-than-it-is trick on Naveen back on the *Fire*. Maybe Naveen was trying to get *him* to talk.

At least they didn't sit for long, but instead walked into a compartment full of plants, with air so damp it stuck his hair to his cheek. He took pictures of red flowers as big as his head with a thick, cloying scent that warred with the equally sweet smell of his drink. "What part of that do you eat?" he asked.

Naveen laughed. "It's for looks."

"Nothing on the *Fire* was for looks."

"Not even Ruby the Red?"

Onor laughed, bumping into Naveen on accident but managing not to spill his drink. "Don't be obsessed about something you'll never have."

"Sounds like you know about that."

Onor took another sip of the drink. "Doesn't matter. We'd have come in as slaves without her, or I'd be dead. Or she'd be dead, or both of us." He fastened his attention on a single tree that stood twice as tall as the biggest orbfruit trees they'd had in the orchard, but was not even half as wide. The leaves were thin needles in at least five shades of green. "Can you eat that one?"

"It helps make medicine."

Onor tried to capture the actual size of the tree in his next picture. "I thought you made everything you need."

"Simple things. Materials. Clothes. Some substances are better grown than made. Human bodies prefer grown food, for example. The bodies of spaceships are stronger when they're made with nanotechnology. The *Fire* wasn't, and that's part of why your return is a miracle. A medium-sized space rock could have destroyed your ship."

Onor settled for taking three pictures of the tall tree. "What is this place? If you're not eating what you grow, what is it for?"

"There are very rich people on the station. Owners of starships, nano-programming companies, miners. This was given to us, with enough resources to maintain it. It's a place where some of almost all the wild things from Lym live."

Joel's words came back to him. "Rich means having a lot of credit?"

"Yes."

"And having a lot of credit means having a lot of power."

"Yes."

"So we need to get credit."

"Isn't that what I told you on the way in? Or you need influence. Ruby can get you influence. She's already popular."

"How popular?"

Naveen grinned. "Very. I'd say she's the current wonder of the *Deep*."

Onor found his drink glass was empty. "Is there plain water somewhere?"

"Sure. There's a fountain in the next room."

Onor was pretty sure he was drunker than Naveen. At least Naveen didn't seem to be slurring his words. "Why are you helping me?"

"Because telling your story gives me influence."

And so you can get near Ruby. But she can take care of herself. "And influence gives you?"

"Power."

Damn. Things were never as easy as he needed them to be. He shouldn't have had so much to drink. "Water?"

Naveen led Onor through a door that reminded him of an airlock, with an inner and an outer door, each made of thin metal screens. Inside the set of doors, plants grew in a profusion of colors. A silver cylinder offered water as Onor walked up to it, and he savored the fresh, cool taste and splashed some on his face. He stood up, dripping. "Even after all our work in the water purification systems, your water tastes better than ours."

"That's because we make it."

"Oh, right. Water is simple." Onor looked for a towel, Nothing. He dried his face with his sleeve, feeling slightly stupid.

Naveen pushed a button and warm air puffed out of the wall.

Onor laughed. "You know how you can impress Ruby?"

"I'd like to."

"Give her classes. Knowledge. We don't understand your science." And that might be part of the path to power. Learning what the people in the *Diamond Deep* already knew.

"I can do that after Koren is finished mining you for history. Can't do it before. That would pollute you."

"And taking me drinking doesn't pollute me?" Onor realized he was having fun, that it was easy to talk to Naveen, that he liked the funny fountain and he loved the trees. He couldn't remember feeling so good. Surely he shouldn't be feeling so good. "Showing me flowers and trees doesn't pollute me?"

Naveen shrugged, grinning, looking as happy as Onor felt. "I don't really care if I pollute you, or if I make Koren mad."

"You want to, don't you? You want to make Koren mad. That's why I'm here."

"That's only a little bit of it. I like you."

"And you're recording this?"

"Some of it."

Onor couldn't quite think about whether he should worry or not. Naveen clearly had plans for them. Koren had plans for them. Ruby and Joel were too busy managing day to day stuff and dealing with Koren to make their own plans. He looked deeply into Naveen's eyes, noticing again the difference in color, the deep brown that was not natural to anyone from the *Fire*. "Can I trust you?"

"Trust me for what? I'm straightforward. I don't hide things. I'll answer any question you have. But if there's one piece of advice I have for you about the *Diamond Deep*, it's be careful who you trust." With that, Naveen opened the door and ushered Onor through.

Movement attracted him. He looked up to see a flash of bright orange darting overhead, soon lost in dark green leaves with yellow stripes on them. It had to be a bird. He'd seen pictures of birds. "I never thought I'd see one."

"A bird?"

"Yeah. Next thing you know, I'll get to see a sun."

Naveen smiled a secretive smile, and then he pointed. "Look over there."

A blue bird with a tail as long as his arm sat on a thick branch at Onor's eye level, its feathers shading to black near the end of the tail and at its wing-tips. A maroon circle of feathers marked the breast, with more maroon on the head. Three long feathers stuck out from behind its head and almost touched its back.

He had imagined what a real animal might look like. This was more . . . It was as alien to him as Aleesi the robot-spider-girl, but somehow it also felt familiar, and friendly. He found he couldn't say a thing or take a step until the bird flew away.

When it did, he discovered tears on his cheeks, and looked up to find Naveen recording them.

CHAPTER THIRTY-NINE

To Ruby, Marcelle still looked more like a fighter than a creche worker. The muscle definition in her legs and back showed through her clothes, a black pants outfit that clung to her thin frame. When she turned to respond to Ruby's greeting, she revealed a baby held close to her breast and above her barely-swelling tummy. Even the child only stripped a bit of the warrior look from her.

"How are you?" Ruby asked.

"Tired."

"That's because you're pregnant."

"No. It's because there's so much work. You look the same."

"I suppose I do. But you should be resting. There's the baby."

Marcelle stroked the infant's head. "Kids are getting sick. A lot of them."

"Adults, too." Ruby said. "The infirmary reported that ten people checked in this morning. I'm setting aside the lower level for sick, moving well people up."

"We might all get it."

"The numbers of new cases are falling." Ruby gestured one of her guards close. "Can you take the baby back to the creche?" She spoke to Marcelle. "Let's walk."

Marcelle still looked torn, but she kissed the child's cheek and handed it to the guard, which left Chitt and another woman, Samara, to guard them. Well enough.

They walked through crowded corridors. "I don't want you to work at the creche until this sickness passes."

Marcelle reacted with a tightening of her jaw, and by thinning her lips almost to nothing. Her cheekbones stuck out like shelves.

"I think it's the food here that's making us sick," Marcelle commented. "The damned squares of tasty color. Or maybe the air. Or the fact that the we're all ten pounds lighter with the gravity change. Or the way everything is different." Her voice rose into a light whine that the twelve-year-old Marcelle might have indulged in. "The walls are slick, my clothes feel slick, my hair sticks out."

Ruby laughed. "My hair does the same thing. Jali has me keep it in a braid now. The tea is from the *Fire*. I've been saving some for special occasions."

"Anything from home would be wonderful." Marcelle leaned close to Ruby and whispered, "I hate it here."

Ruby wanted to just agree so badly the words almost escaped her lips. "We have a lot to learn still."

"We have no freedom."

"I'm working on that. *We're* working on that. Joel and I are going out with Koren tomorrow."

"What about Onor? He went with that Naveen. Shouldn't he be back?"

Ruby bit her lip. "Yes. Maybe. It's too early to worry."

"But you are worried."

Marcelle always knew what she was thinking. "There's nothing for it but tea."

"Is that what we're reduced to? Tea? We used to fight things we didn't like."

"Don't you want the tea?"

"Of course I do. But I'm also going to worry about Onor."

Ruby laughed. "You used to tell me how much you hated him."

Ten minutes and one short stop in a common galley and Ruby had managed to lead Marcelle, frizzy hair and all, into a small alcove that left them nestled by slick walls on two sides. Chitt and Samara stood a respectful distance off, watching outward. "I don't think I've sat down like this for three days," she told Marcelle.

"Tell me what you've learned about the station?"

Ruby shook her head. "Not much. I'm more worried about how many people are sick. I'm also worried about what we're going to do next. Everyone here is used to working half of every day. We've had to work to get settled and organized and set up schools for children. We need schools for us. We need Ix or something like Ix back. We need something to make or fix or grow. Already there have been three fights. We have five more people in what passes for lock-up now than we brought out of the *Fire*."

Marcelle raised an eyebrow. "Is that all?"

"More room. We need more room."

Marcelle took a long slow sip of tea and said nothing for a few long minutes. It wasn't like her to be so quiet, so Ruby waited her out, finishing her own tea and wishing she'd brought food even though she hated the food squares.

"We need respect," Marcelle mused. "That's what we fought for. Now we've got nothing." She put a hand on Ruby's hand. "And sure, we need schools. That helps. But we need more than that. We need a voice."

"See? I knew I needed to talk to you."

"This place scares me."

"You've never been scared a day in your life," Ruby told her.

"I wasn't pregnant before."

"I want you away from the creche. In case whatever is making the children sick can make you sick. I need someone to manage setting up schools. Besides, I want you with me."

"You have Ani."

"Which I'm grateful for. I have Jali as well. But neither of them know what the world was like for us before. They've never had to face the kinds of things I'm beginning to think this place might do to us. We're all the equivalent of grays here. Or worse." When she looked over, she noticed a single tear hanging in the edge of Marcelle's eye, ready to fall. Ruby lowered her voice. "What's the matter?"

"I thought I'd lost you."

"Never."

After she left Marcelle, Ruby stopped by the makeshift bar. Allen stood behind the counter with a rag, cleaning things that looked clean. None of the people who had been his hangers-on and his minions from the ship seemed to be around. "Hi, Allen. Seen Onor?"

Allen shook his head. "I'm not going to see anybody. There's about eight drinks left, and then we're going to be completely out. I don't think the regulars are going to stop by for orbfruit juice." He paused for just a breath, then shrugged his shoulders. "Oh yeah, we don't have that either."

She laughed. "Why don't you find Kyle and see if he can come up with something useful out of this junk-for-food, and then you can serve that."

"Great. I can see the menu now. Square orange food. Oblong green sticks."

Ruby laughed.

"Want a drink?"

"One of the last real ones?"

"Yeah."

"No. I want two. Enough for me and Joel to share a drink tonight."

"You're hurting me." He turned. "But trade me. You can sing to us if we're not drinking, right?"

"If I have time."

"Make the time. There's more grumbling than ever. You've still got enemies, and this is a great opportunity for them."

"Have you heard anything specific?"

"A bartender never tells."

She smiled and leaned in closer to him. "Not even me?"

"Nope." He handed her a full flask. "That's sweeter than you like, but you'll have to take what you can get."

"I'll try and come tomorrow night. I'll send Chitt to tell you if I can't."

He frowned at her. "I can't advertise maybe."

She cocked her head at him. "And if you could advertise? Where would you put people? There's no place big enough for a concert here." Or a talk. Or a gathering. Or anything. She hadn't thought of it that way before. "Look, I'll come if I can."

"Will you?"

"Yes, really. But I'm not the only person on the ship who can entertain. You could have Planazate contests—the game takes hours and people will be stuck here even if you do only have water and stupid little squares of food to give them. There's other singers in the world, too. And storytellers. Get creative."

"I want my bar back."

"I want the *Fire* back. But that's all gone. We'll just have to make something better."

He gave her a long, lost look.

She took her flask and headed toward the small set of rooms she and Joel shared. She was going to spend the rest of the day figuring out what to do next instead of moving every minute. She hadn't really stopped since they got off the *Fire*, except to fall dead into awkward sleep at the end of each day. She needed a song for the people of the *Fire* that celebrated who they were, and she needed one that mourned their losses, and she needed to learn enough about the *Diamond Deep* to sing about that.

Maybe Onor had learned something.

Damn it, where was Onor anyway?

Joel wouldn't be home for hours. In an effort to get their physical conditioning up again, Joel was meeting with The Jackman, Conroy, KJ, and a few of the others to set up a training program. She'd caught KJ's dancers scaling walls for fun one morning, but there hadn't been any exercises demanded of lesser mortals since they arrived.

She climbed stairs toward the hab they shared in a corner of the top floor. On the second landing, Ruby knelt to admire a bunched group of purple flowers in a pot. Flowers made a promise: they represented at least one new aspect of life which was good here. A few plants had flowered on the *Fire*, but only to create fruit. Not just to be pretty. Something alive that existed just to be pretty was an excessive use of resource. A symbol for a song?

A hand on her shoulder startled her out of her thoughts. "Stay down," Chitt said.

"Why?" Ruby hissed.

"Lya."

Ruby stood.

Chitt glared at her with a look so furious Ruby almost flinched away from her.

Lya stood above them, at the top of the stairs, close to Ruby's door. She looked slightly cleaner than when Ruby had last seen her, but no less emaciated. Her eyes had sunk into her head. Only a year older than Ruby, but she looked ten, or more. Other women stood with her, maybe a dozen, maybe one or two more, bunched close together. They all wore white in some fashion: beads, a scarf, a shirt, a strip of material tied around a wrist.

Samara stood five steps up, mid-way between Lya and Ruby and Chitt.

"More behind you," Chitt whispered.

Ruby glanced down. Women pooled at the bottom of the stairs. Chitt drew her stunner, but Ruby put a hand on her arm, signaling for her to lower it.

"Hello Lya," she called up. "What can I do for you?"

"Listen."

The women behind Lya and below Ruby and Chitt murmured the word, whispers and just above whispers. "Listen."

Lya's face was calm, totally and completely calm. As if she had finally found her niche in life after losing Hugh.

"Listen."

"Listen."

"Listen listen listen."

Ruby let the eerie harmony die down. "Yes?"

"We demand a voice. We need to be in your councils."

Ruby held up her hands to get them to quiet for a moment. "Tell me what you need, and I will be sure you get it if I can."

"A voice."

"Voice," echoed through the crowd, creepy and irritating as much because it echoed her conversation with Marcelle as because of the strange susurration of so many whispers.

"Lya. I will do what I can for you. For all of you. What do you want?"

"You've led us to a place where we have been imprisoned."

She couldn't argue with that, so she didn't. She stood there, waiting.

"Our children are ill."

Ruby chewed on her lip to keep herself from saying anything. Yet.

"You walk around with guards and enough food. You make decisions for us without asking. You are exactly who you told us to fight."

That wasn't a new accusation. Even though there was only a grain of truth in it, it stung every time she heard it.

Lya continued. "But we are non-violent. We will not fight you. This is a time for change wrought by attention, not killing and fighting."

Good. Although Chitt remained as tense as Ruby.

"But we will follow you. We will be where you are. We will be outside your doors, outside your meetings, inside your world. We will hear what you say and what decisions you make. We will witness."

"Witness."

"Witness."

"Witness witness witness."

Lya looked down on Ruby, standing completely still. The dark circles under her eyes were a black contrast to the white shirt she wore, bookended with a stretchy white hat she'd pulled down over her forehead.

Ruby took a deep breath. "The *Diamond Deep* is not what any of us expected that coming home would feel like. I also agree that this is not a time for fighting. We would simply die. A people that can create spaces and destroy starships with machines so small we cannot see them surely has a thousand thousand ways to kill us. None of us want to find out what those are."

Lya didn't react. The women below said nothing. There were enough of them, and close enough, that their breathing was audible in the spaces between the soft creaks of the station and the footsteps of others going other places. A few people who weren't part of the conversation had fetched up against the outer edges of Lya's women, watching. One of them was SueAnne, leaning over and looking down, frowning.

Ruby spoke loud enough for all of them to hear. "If you want to help us, there are children to care for. There are stories to tell to Koren's people so that they can finish wringing us dry and let us get on with our lives. There are old people who need company."

Lya smiled. "We will witness. We will tell the people of the *Fire* of all that you do. See that you do good."

Before Ruby could respond to Lya, SueAnne said, "It is for all of us to hold all of us accountable. And if you choose to follow Ruby everywhere, she will not be able to lead, and I *will hold you accountable*. You may be setting yourselves up to choose between helping the children and the old, or sitting in jail."

Ruby winced. This is not what she would have said, or what she would have had SueAnne say. But then, SueAnne took a fierce pride in being tough, probably from being the only woman with power for so long.

Ruby looked into Lya's eyes once more. They remained full of unruffled serenity. "We must look to the future and not the past," she said. "It is my preference that you help me to do that, that we do that together."

She started up the stairs. For a moment she didn't think that Lya would move, but then she slowly stepped aside and allowed Ruby to approach her own door. Chitt and Samara stood beside her as she opened the door, and Lya and her women hissed and whispered, "Witness. Witness. Witness."

Ruby closed the door.

CHAPTER FORTY

Onor opened his eyes. They were crusty and dried. His nose and mouth were parched. His head ached. He fisted his hand and rubbed at his eyelids—slowly—until he could see blue above him. Sky? There had been birds. He remembered birds. But there couldn't be sky. He hadn't thought there could be birds, but he was certain there could not be sky.

Besides it was too close. It must be paint. Although a faint light seemed to emanate from the whole ceiling.

Moving sent pain shooting from his limbs into his head.

Naveen.

A memory of walking with Naveen, or more accurately, of being helped by Naveen.

He managed to wrestle his body to a sitting position. He wore only his underwear and a silky sheet that had tangled around his legs. A couch. That probably explained why he hadn't fallen off. Beside him, a pitcher of water, a glass and his slate. There was a note on his slate. *Drink the water and you'll feel better. Take a shower. I've laid out clothes. I'll be back. Please don't leave.*

A light blue powder filled the bottom of the glass. Onor stared at it, trying to think, which seemed particularly hard at that moment.

He'd chosen to trust Naveen.

He poured water into the glass and stirred it with his finger. The water was barely tinted blue, and smelled like water always smelled except a touch sweeter. He put his lips to the glass and found himself gulping, almost inhaling, pouring a glass of plain water and finishing that, too.

His body reacted almost immediately, membranes softening, vision clearing, the headache disappearing.

He'd have to ask about the powder. More of that would be good.

Now that he felt human, he looked around. The room had a simple taste and elegance at odds with Naveen's way of dressing. Rounded corners softened everything. Bright swatches of textiles accented the grays and off-whites that formed the basic color-palette. Here and there, plants hung in glass orbs. Naveen had been right that it looked far better than Ash. But then, if this one set of rooms belonged wholly to Naveen, the primary difference might be the amount of space.

Shower.

Except now his stomach screamed.

Onor's gait wobbled, but he managed to hit the privy and the shower and pull on the clothes: a pair of thin light-blue pants that sparkled around the waistband and the ankles and a light brown shirt that—thankfully—didn't sparkle. The outfit was so soft and light he still felt naked, and so strange and smooth he felt out of sorts and odd.

If this was Naveen's home, it was more opulent than anything on the *Fire*. Maybe not more than what he'd seen last night.

They would have expected him home.

The slates had communication capability. One of the wonders of *Diamond Deep* that hadn't been—quite—true on the *Fire*. He picked his slate up and stared at it. There were messages from Ruby, Joel, and Marcelle.

He thumbed through the pictures on the slate. He only clearly remembered seeing about two-thirds of the things he'd taken pictures of. He selected one of a bird and sent it to Ruby with the words, "I'm okay." He chose a tree for Marcelle with the same message and a picture of the whole aviary complete with trees and the tiny colored forms of birds for Joel. He smiled. That would give them pause.

He expected Naveen to show up right away, but he didn't. Onor prowled the space. He tried to send Naveen a note, but he couldn't figure out how to address one to him, nor remember the last name that Koren had given for him.

There was a door he hadn't opened. Maybe Naveen was in there. He knocked. No answer.

He pushed the door open quietly.

Inside, the walls were full of moving pictures. Videos and stills flashed on and off, all silent. Ruby featured in most of them. Some were of her standing beside Joel, some of the last concert in the cargo bar. Some were Joel, some Onor, some the *Fire* itself. A few featured Koren or her robots talking to people.

Onor stood and stared, watching.

He noticed a picture of Ruby singing at Owl Paulie's funeral.

Naveen hadn't taken that.

Onor had no access to it, nor Ruby, nor any of them.

It had to have come from Ix.

CHAPTER FORTY-ONE

R uby was dressed for their trip out with Koren, and waiting for Joel to return from a morning meeting with his councilors. She curled up on a small black couch, one hand holding a glass of what passed for stim here, far enough away from her nose that she didn't need to smell the bitter edge of it. In her other hand, she held her slate. The picture Onor had sent her was quite remarkable.

A bird.

Ever since she was young, she had been fascinated with images of birds. She had thought they only lived on planets. And here Onor had seen one, and sent her evidence.

She took a sip of the stim, glad it didn't taste as bad as it smelled. It seemed harder to wake since they had left the *Fire*, as if no matter how much she slept it wasn't enough.

Perhaps she would see a bird today.

The door opened. Joel came in and stood there, looking at her in a way she had recognized meant he felt uncomfortable. "There are women outside the door. They chanted at me."

Oh. She hadn't quite forgotten them, but she hadn't really expected them to stay. "Sorry."

"They were chanting your name, and something about betrayal."

She sighed. "They seem to think I don't care about them anymore."

He raised an eyebrow, "Maybe I should explain how many times you remind me to spend time with them."

"Maybe you should spend more time with them."

He frowned. "Will they go away?"

"I hope so. They say they're going to follow me around until I listen to them." She forced a smile and stood. "I heard from Onor. He sent me a picture of a bird."

"And he sent me a picture of a space bigger than where we live full of trees and birds. He's going to miss the tour."

Ruby frowned. "Are you bringing guards?"

"Of course. And SueAnne."

Lya was going to have fun with this one. "Is it too late to add someone else? Like The Jackman, or Conroy, or Marcelle?"

"In trade for you."

"No."

"Then no changes. Koren said up to five total. That's me, you, SueAnne, KJ, and I was going to bring Onor."

"You could trade Conroy for Onor."

"I will choose one of our personal guards."

She wondered if the women outside their door had gotten under his skin, or something else. "Is Chitt or Samara okay?"

"We'll take Dayn."

"I'd like to have someone from gray."

"Yet you keep telling me there are no more colors, no more levels. That means I can choose whoever best fits the job." The look on his face told her his mind was made up.

She forced herself to accept, the compromise acid in her stomach, especially with Lya and the other women outside her door. They were wrong, but Joel was doing everything possible to make them look right.

If she rejected Joel and her place here, she would be able to give them nothing. Not that she could bear to leave him. She stood close enough to him to smell his sweat and worry, and to touch his hand with hers. "Do you think we'll see birds?"

"I'm more interested in a way forward."

"Me, too. But a bird would be amazing."

He kissed her hair and she sighed, leaning into him.

The group of whispering women outside their door was about twenty strong, their murmurs an echo—a chorus—in her ears. Lya and her women followed behind her, a long line like a weight dragging at Ruby's feet.

Joel looked stoic but his eyes blazed.

This wasn't the moment for a confrontation, not between her and Lya, not between her and Joel. But the pressure for it was there, angry words in all of their eyes.

Near the door they had all come in, SueAnne stood waiting for them with KJ. Another level of anger, this time SueAnne looking at Ruby as if she had caused the women to choose this path.

KJ simply looked curious.

Dayn gave her a look that practically screamed *See what you've done now?* with a twinkle in eye that suggested he was laughing at the uncomfortable spot the whispering women had backed her into. If she could have stuck her tongue out and maintained any bit of dignity, she might have done just that.

Once everyone was there waiting, the women quieted. Their presence cost Ruby and Joel the moments they might have had to prepare the group, to be sure everyone was ready.

When the door opened, Koren stood behind it with four of the bright, shape-changing robots at her side.

Ruby held her breath, willing the women not to try and follow.

They didn't, perhaps because KJ stood last in line, perhaps because Koren's faceless robotic companions frightened them.

Koren offered no more than a polite greeting, leaving Ruby and the others to feel intimidated by the silence and the robots for a full twenty-minute walk. The floor under their feet was metallic and smooth, and their shoes whispered as they went, the sound reminding Ruby of Lya and the women in white. She tried to think of the people who supported her, the ones who sat and sang with her in common and joined them around the map table on docking day. They mattered more than twenty or so disaffected women led by a woman who was half crazy. They did.

Once they were all settled in a train car that held only them and the four robots, Koren stood at the front of the car. "This is a formal occasion. Until today, you have been a people who we studied, who we welcomed back into our fold and attempted to learn about our own history from. But you are not slaves. It is time for you to learn about the *Diamond Deep* and to begin to explore how you might choose to fit into our society."

The train pulled so smoothly away from the station that Ruby couldn't tell how fast it was going. Koren let the train get up to speed and then she said, "There are rules here on the *Diamond Deep*. The most fundamental are that you must own yourselves. You must harm no one. And you must add to the collective. These are the Deeping Rules, and all other rules and customs about how to live here go back to these rules.

"Society on the *Deep* is ruled by balanced forces. These are the forces of time—history and the future. As the Chief Historian, I work to see that we remember the lessons of our past. I am balanced by the Futurist, who looks to what we need to continue to grow. The Architect oversees the constant rebuilding of the station—the creation of the new and the destruction of the old. The Biologist cares for our food supply and our health. The Economist assures we remain a commercially viable society. He or she manages the Exchanges and the value of goods and services."

She paused, looking around until all of them nodded.

A slight bitterness edged Koren's voice as she continued, "Up until now, only one of your people have been allowed to leave your area."

Onor. Who had seen birds but who was still gone.

"But now you will be given leave to travel through other parts of the station and eventually you will all have travel rights everywhere. We will also allow the people of the station to come to you. Yes, you have seen my historians and my staff, but now anyone from the *Diamond Deep* can travel into your world and meet with you."

Ruby raised her hand.

"Yes, Ruby?"

"Why can't we all travel?"

Koren smiled the smile that Ruby hated. The one that seemed friendly but condescending all at once. "You have limited resources. In order to meet salvage laws, we have granted you ten percent of the value of your ship's material and cargo. That is what paid for the homes you are living in, and what pays for the food that you eat and the air that you breathe. We have chosen how to spend that for you, providing you with the simplest and least costly options at every turn. But after today, we will turn over the management of your resources to you. Travel costs credit, and you will want to maintain control over that expense."

"So we are paying for this trip?" SueAnne asked.

Koren shook her head. "This is a gift to you."

"So how much—resource—do you believe we have?" Joel asked.

She approved of Joel's careful wording. This felt like a trap.

"Credits are exchanged for everything here, and there is a base amount of credit that each being pays to exist according to the resources they use. You pay the daily tax on breathing beings, which is two credits per person per day. Every working person makes far more than that, but since none of you earn credits yet, this is a daily expense. Tomorrow you will be able to work, and tomorrow, you will have to find a way to purchase your own food."

"That does not answer my question," Joel said.

"You have credit to survive for about half a year with no one working and a low birth rate, assuming you do not use more resource than you do now. I will send someone to go over accounts with you later. In reality, there are many decisions that influence your resources. Decisions about how to add resources and how to spend them."

"And if we run out?" SueAnne asked.

"Then there are jobs that we can sign you up for in trade for the minimum required to exist here. If you are unable to work, there are places on the ship where you can live and receive minimal care."

Great. Ruby was willing to bet some of the minimal jobs were dangerous and demeaning.

CHAPTER FORTY-TWO

In spite of how disturbing they were, Onor found himself so entranced by the shifting pictures on the wall in the strange room at Naveen's that he didn't hear Naveen came through the door. "Good morning." He sounded quite cheerful for someone who could see he'd been caught out. "Or, almost good afternoon."

"I didn't plan to stay out all night," Onor said.

"I know. I'm sorry. But I have more to show you today." Not that he looked sorry.

"I was supposed to be on a tour with Koren."

Naveen gave a funny grin, like a child hiding a secret. "I know. I thought I should tour you instead. There is a lot to see that she will not show you, and there are things to learn that she will not share with you."

"Ruby doesn't like her, but why would she mean us harm?"

"It's probably not personal. There is a structure on this station, an order of things. Koren sees you very near the bottom. You have no skills we need, no unique knowledge except for your experiences, which she has already mined. I'm pretty sure Koren thinks the best thing you're bringing is your contribution to the gene pool."

"Huh?"

"You can have babies that will learn how to live here. I don't think she expects you to thrive. You know nothing."

That hurt. "And you want to help us?"

"You have assets. One of those is Ruby. Another is the rawness of your emotions—and your lives. Koren dismisses that, but it is selling on the interest webs."

"So we have value because we're stupid?" Onor kept watching the shifting pictures on the wall. Compared to the diversity of people and looks and ideas and places he'd seen so far on the station—and he'd hardly seen any of it yet—the *Fire* did look simple.

"Because you're a fresh perspective. I can make this work for you. I've already earned some credit showing Ruby off. The shots I took of the concert on the *Fire* are selling. I've saved some of the credit for you."

"Credit helps you get power?"

Naveen laughed. "More like power buys you credit."

Onor frowned.

"You'll need me to help you navigate the traps this station sets for people."

Onor still felt lost. They needed what Naveen was offering. "I'll talk to Ruby and Joel."

"Here," Naveen said, reaching down and swiping across his slate. "Here's part of the credit I've earned from your images so far. When the time is right, show it to Ruby and Joel. The rest will go directly to them after I get to meet with them. Ruby is entitled to a part of whatever I make selling her images. So are you—for your images."

"Really?"

"Look at your slate." When Onor complied, Naveen showed him how to get access to his credit balance. There was a new number there: two-hundred seventy credits. "Show that to them," Naveen said. "They'll have context for it after today."

Onor slid his slate back into his pocket.

Naveen looked quite pleased with himself, as if he had imparted some great gift to Onor.

"Thank you."

"Are you hungry?"

Onor didn't want to leave the room. "All of these pictures. I know you took some of them. But others are ours. How did you get them?"

Naveen's grin spread all the way across his face. "I hoped you would notice. I have a gift for you. You will need an AI. Most of the civilized groups like yours—the communities—have one. When you have enough credit, you can hire your own. Your ship's AI is from too old a generation to be independently employable, and you have a right to it. I grabbed a copy before Koren wiped it from the ship. I've spent the last few weeks attaching it to a communication program that will let you speak to it, and teaching it about the *Deep*."

Onor licked his lips. Ix. "How much will it be changed?"

"It should work better. It's not a very smart one, very old. I taught it what I could. You really must save for a new one; but this will be better than nothing." Naveen pulled a drawer that Onor hadn't even noticed out of the wall, and handed Onor a small round object that looked like an oversized ball-bearing from the water plants back on the ship. Silvery, but not shiny. Big enough to have weight, and for his palm to cup around.

"That's Ix?"

"That's a copy of Ix for you. You should be able to upload it to your community computer system."

"Our what?"

"Your life support computer. You must have one."

Onor shook his head. "I don't know."

Naveen sighed. "I'll come over and look. Soon."

Onor felt both grateful and confused. How much should he trust Naveen? "Thank you."

"Come on," Naveen said. "Let's eat. Time is wasting."

"How long did I sleep? I don't even remember getting here."

"Perhaps turnabout is fair play. I'm glad you enjoyed our alcoholic treats."

"As soon as we rebuild the bar stock, I'll invite you back."

Naveen laughed.

By the time they left, Onor was full of bread that melted in his mouth and smelled of herbs and flowers, strange pastes that Naveen had spread onto the breads, and three new fruits. One of the fruits had been green and smelled like sugar. He was still wearing the sparkling pants and the soft brown shirt, and felt entirely unlike himself. The ball of Ix seemed heavy because it mattered so much, even though it was actually so light and small he could barely feel it as he walked.

"Where are we going?" Onor asked.

"To scare you."

"Why?"

"This station is layered in dangers, and I'm going to show you one of them."

Onor tried to make light. "Only one?"

"Yesterday, I showed you some of our beauty. That was so you wouldn't despair after today."

How . . . theatrical. Onor didn't know quite what to say, so he followed quietly. From time to time he stopped to take a picture, or to ask a question.

They used a different train than the one they had been on the day before. It took them nearly an hour to get wherever it was that Naveen was taking them.

After they disembarked, Naveen said, "This is the worst place where normal people like you and me could end up without committing a serious crime. And more important—and you must remember this—it's not something is usually talked about. You must not tell Koren we went here. She will know you and I left together, and she will know when you return, and you now have pictures of the aviary and gardens to show for your trip. That is all you'll have, and if she asks, that is where you went."

"She won't be able to tell some other way?"

"The Deep's central systems will know—they know everything—but they're secure. Unless you commit a crime, no one can look into your every move."

Onor felt for Ix in his pocket, cupped his hand around it. "Our AI treated us about the same on the *Fire*."

"I'm not surprised. The core of our privacy laws were created long before you left. Just remember, the station won't divulge your moves, but people and robots can follow you illegally if they are willing to take the risk." He grinned. "I'm seldom followed."

"Because?"

"Because I caught some of my followers."

"And?"

"I know how to embarrass people."

Onor licked dry lips and wished he had some water. "Is this a jail?"

"Not exactly."

Naveen led Onor to a window in a wall. "This is the Brawl."

The smoky window glass distorted Onor's view, giving the scene on the other side an unreal quality, like watching the map table on the *Fire*. It showed a vast, flat place full of people. The crowding was far worse than where Onor and the rest of the refugees from the *Fire* were now. Rows and rows of cots filled the floor and served as chairs, beds, and storage. Robotic posts moved among the people. "What are the robots?" Onor asked.

"Enforcers. If you watch long enough, you'll see one of them hurt someone. Or maybe you'll see a crazy attack one and get killed on purpose. We're too far above it to really see the details, but these people live on almost nothing and a few die each day. They have air and food and water sufficient to live, but little else. Slates, I think. For entertainment."

Onor tried to notice details. They were so far above the crowd that facial expressions were impossible to see, and of course, they could not hear any sounds through the glass. But body language spoke volumes. Protective. Confrontational. Worried. Exhausted.

"There are no children."

"Children have not failed yet. You have to be at least a teenager to be sent here, but practically, it doesn't happen."

"Because there are almost no children here at all."

"Sure there are."

Not like they had on the *Fire*. They watched for at least fifteen minutes while nothing dramatic happened below them. People moved in and out of groups, and good and bad confrontations happened. Hugs and words were exchanged, and enforcers served food from a corner.

"Why robots? Why do robots watch them?"

"Because it would turn humans cruel to do that job."

Like the reds back on the *Fire*. A fight broke out below them. When it first caught his eye it was four people in a knot of arms and legs, a silent and strange dance to watch. Others surrounded the fighters, keeping some distance.

Onor had seen this, even on the *Fire*, the way people will circle a fight and then clap. Except there it had been children, maybe teenagers. These were adults.

"Watch for an enforcer," Naveen whispered, pointing. "There."

Onor squinted, looking for the enforcer through the thick window.

"And there."

"I see it."

Soon, people were stepping back from three of the cylindrical robots, tripping in haste. Something happened that Onor couldn't see and the combatants fell into a pile of unmoving flesh. A woman fell as well, but she rolled and then crawled away, struggling to reach the crowd which stepped ever further from both her and the enforcers.

One of the enforcers came close to her, and she turned on her back and was still, eyes fastened on the robot. She threw her arms out at her side, a gesture of surrender.

The crowd stopped at what must be safe distance—maybe four times Onor's height—watching.

A conversation occurred between the woman and the silver post. Even though he couldn't see her features clearly, he rooted for her, chewed his lip, held his breath. She must feel like he had when the spiders were chasing him, like a small piece of meat in the sights of a more powerful being. He let out a sigh of relief when she stood and backed into the watching crowd, disappearing in the mass of people. "The fighters." His hands were clenched on the sill, and he released them. "Were they stunned?"

Naveen's voice had none of his usual mischievous edge. "That depends on what they have done before. The enforcers are not allowed to kill in most circumstances. But life down there often does not last long."

Onor's eyes flicked over the bodies below them. He could see . . . Thousands. It had to be thousands. "How many people live on the *Deep*?"

"Millions." Naveen closed his eyes for a second, seemed to flit away. "Forty-seven million, three-hundred and twenty-one thousand, and change. It's never more exact than that with ships going in and out all of the time."

Onor stared down below. "There's more of these than this, then."

"Yes."

"And I needed to see this so I'd know how bad it can be here?"

"Your circumstances were designed to force you into the Brawl. You should know what fate awaits you if you don't accept my offer of help, or find another way to earn a *lot* of credit."

For the first time since Marcelle had told him she carried his child, Onor felt afraid for the baby. He pulled his hands away from the windowsill to hide the fact that they were shaking.

CHAPTER FORTY-THREE

Koren had stopped talking and looked forward, still and regal. Not a single white hair was out of place. Wherever they were going, they had been on the train long enough for Ruby to feel a need to stand, to walk, maybe to run. She resisted. Beside her, Joel was stiff and angry, and everyone in their group had grown quiet. Probably thinking, like Ruby, about the way things were here. They had all been born expecting to work, knowing their place. But even in the old striated society of colored uniforms where the reds like Ben used stunners and power to control the grays like Ruby, they always knew the general shape of their lives, and they knew that if they survived they would be fed and cared for. Four out of five people on the *Fire* died of old age, which did not seem to exist here. Now she felt unmoored, lost in a sea of new rules and new ideas and new demands. Her mind catalogued a flood of questions and spun across new worries.

When the power structures of the *Fire* changed, some people had died, most had adapted, some had thrived. They would have to adapt again. And some, like Lya and her whispering women, had chosen to be left behind.

In a way, Lya had refused to change as much as Sylva. Ruby would never have done what Joel did to Sylva; but she *would* have killed her in a fair fight. She put a hand on Joel's thigh, briefly, as unseen as possible, a reminder that she loved him. A reminder that he was warm and alive and vital.

The train slowed so smoothly Ruby barely realized they were stopping. Koren stepped off the train and waited for the others to disembark, watching them with her golden eyes, showing very little emotion. She looked like she was discharging an onerous duty, already bored, already about to move on. "Welcome to Exchange Five. This is where you can bargain for work.

"You will stay close to your guide. He will show you people from starships looking for crew, people from mining concerns looking for people to work for them, employers who need cargo moved or counted. Your slates have been sent directions about how to get here and how to get home."

A young man—no, Ruby corrected herself, a man of indeterminate age who looked as young as Koren—came up to them and Koren turned a dazzling smile on him. "This is Lake. He is a guide who helps newcomers to the *Diamond Deep* navigate the Exchange. We have paid him to spend a few hours with you, and to then make sure that you arrive home safely. I wish you luck on our world."

Wow. A dismissal. A complete dismissal. Koren might as well as have said, "*I have everything I need from you and you weren't, actually, that interesting. I'm going to go do more important things that fit my station.*" Well, good riddance. Ruby hadn't liked the woman from the moment she set eyes on her.

Bright colors clung to Lake's body, yellows and oranges with streaks of red. His hair was impossibly orange, a color she had never seen anywhere, and it hung down his back in a long ponytail.

Ruby felt drab next to him, and swore she would bring Jali next time she came here.

They gave Lake their names. He hesitated when SueAnne introduced herself, as if her appearance bothered him. Maybe the wrinkles and age spots and graying hair, or the shape of the old woman's body: blocky and waistless with thin shoulders.

Lake's voice was silky and easy to listen to, full of confidence. "I understand you are new to the *Diamond Deep*. Welcome to the station and to Exchange Five. The most common goods and services all flow through the exchange, as do most requests for work. This area closest to the station is where the pay-masters—the people who will be able to hire you—come every morning. It is a chaos in the early morning. An hour ago there were hundreds of people here. The best jobs go quickly."

"What kind of jobs?" SueAnne asked.

"Anything. Sorting and cataloguing incoming goods for buyers, loading and unloading cargo, working booths at food exchanges, repairs of all kinds, sometimes caring for people." He glanced at SueAnne. "Most of the work exchanged here is physical, usually a few days' worth of credits for a day of work."

Ruby frowned. The grays would do all right, or at least the young ones. "Why use people instead of robots for carrying?"

Lake smiled at her. "We use both. Robots are more expensive, and make bigger mistakes. The Economist structures a certain amount of work for humans. So it depends on the job."

Exchange Five throbbed with light and sang with a cacophony of sound. All of this mixed in a single wide-open space, a big box of a room with high metal walls and a metal ceiling, and an assault of words written on signs and in light almost everywhere. People in booths called to people outside of them. Here and there, humanoid robots played either role: seller or buyer.

Other booths sold food and drinks.

Color bloomed everywhere, although on closer examination the clothes weren't as rich as Koren's or even Naveen's. Most of the robots were less smooth or unblemished than the assistants Koren had brought with her.

KJ broke his long silence. "How many people look for work each day, and how many find it?"

Lake looked down for a moment, as if uncomfortable. "There is work for a little less than half."

Ruby wondered if a little less than half meant a quarter. "And the other half?"

"If they are lucky, they get work on a different day."

"Not all work comes through here," Joel observed. "Where would a trainer or a fighter or a singer go for work?"

"Professional work happens on the boards. You can access those via your slates. But those jobs need certificates and approvals."

SueAnne frowned. "So how do we get those?"

"With credit."

Ruby asked, "Does credit rule everyone's lives?"

Lake laughed. "You must have it. But whether or not it rules your life is up to you."

"So what can we acquire here?"

"Almost anything. Things to wear, delicacies from other lands or gardens to grace your table, medicine to help you feel better, skills to give you access to new jobs, a moment of live entertainment or a copy of a song to play over and over. You can buy a program to create new things, a larger place to live, pretty shoes for your pretty little feet."

He gave her a little bow. "You are a beautiful redheaded woman. What could you possibly need that the *Diamond Deep* cannot provide? Ask, and I will try to show you."

A short silence fell on the group from the *Fire* and they looked from one to another before Ruby looked back at Lake. "Food and sustenance for thousands."

He blinked at her, as if counting. A beat of silence passed before he said, "Easy enough to order. I'll show you."

Joel added, "Physical training."

Lake nodded. "Of course." He looked around. "Is there one more thing?"

They all looked around, and SueAnne whispered to Joel.

Lake smiled. "We should begin to tour. But you have still not told me what third thing you want to acquire today." He looked right at Ruby.

"Bits of the colored materials you used in your clothes."

"All right, then. We've talked enough. Allow me to show you the wonders of Exchange Five." They followed Lake into the swirling movement of commerce. Dayn and KJ walked side by side at the end and watched all of them. Joel let SueAnne lean on his arm so that she could keep up.

CHAPTER FORTY-FOUR

When they finally passed through the doorway to home, Ruby could barely walk and her stomach felt slightly nauseous from the assault of the new. Colors she had never seen before, scents she hadn't known existed, people with hair and skin and eyes of all colors. She'd seen a man with metal legs.

Beside her, SueAnne sat in a wheeled chair that moved by itself. Her gray hair lay flat against her face, and her lips were drawn thin with pain. Before they'd made it even half-way through Exchange Five, she had begun to falter so much that Joel's arm wasn't enough. Dayn had taken her other side, but in spite of the extra support, they had slowed so that people stepped around them. Lake had ordered up a robot chair for her and showed her how to give it basic instructions. Then he had helped them buy one. Their first purchase aboard the *Diamond Deep*.

The whispering women waited for them at the door. Lya stood in front of her, blocking the way. "Tell us what you saw."

It was all Ruby could do not to snap at her. "Tomorrow. We're tired. We'll share everything we learned tomorrow. In the meantime, can you find it in your hearts to help SueAnne get back to her place?"

Lya stopped moving as if Ruby's tone of voice had been a command to become a piece of art.

"Please?" Ruby said. "The chair probably can't do stairs. I really don't know."

Lya blinked.

One of the three women with Lya nodded and tugged on Lya's sleeve until Lya nodded as well. The five of them left, the four women and SueAnne heading silently away.

"I think you should keep them busy all the time," Joel observed.

Ruby shook her head softly, bemused. "At this point, I'll try anything except violence."

A shadowed figure sat by the door. For a moment she thought it might be Onor, but when he stood up she noticed the slighter form. "Haric, what are you doing here? Do you have a message for us?"

He shook his head. "I just wanted to know if you were all right."

The earnest look on her face touched her. She gave him a long, soft hug. "We're fine, and thank you." She smoothed back his hair. "How are you?"

"I'm scared," he said. "And I'm bored."

She'd thought she was too tired to laugh but she wasn't. "And we're very tired. We'll talk about it tomorrow. Could you pass on a message for me? Could you ask Jali to meet me in the morning? Tell her I've got work for her."

He looked pleased and left quickly, as if he had wanted something to do more than anything in the world.

As soon as they were inside, she took a long drink of water and flopped onto the bed. Joel was more disciplined about getting to the same place, and soon they were right next to each other, breathing softly.

Ruby couldn't recall being so drained since the days of fighting. Her head spun as hard as her feet throbbed. Joel lay beside her on the bed, staring at the ceiling. She reached deep inside herself for a scrap of energy and managed to roll over closer to him and touch his cheek. "I didn't see any children. Not one."

She left her fingers on his jaw so she felt him say, "I think I saw one being carried. A babe in arms. We'll ask Onor."

"Has he come home?"

"I think he would have met us," Joel said

"Or passed out from exhaustion. In the old days I could have asked Ix."

"I know."

She stretched, fighting to find a few more minutes of awareness for conversation. It had been a long day, but she still felt mystified by her exhaustion. "I didn't see anyone that looked old, either. I want to know how they do that."

"It's unsettling."

"I'm amazed we got SueAnne home." She had so much to think about now. "We need to assign someone to keep track of these credits, maybe a few people. So one can watch the other."

"The *Fire* was so much easier," he murmured. "We had to work to live, but everyone was fed."

"That's not so different than it is here."

Joel rolled to face her, stroked her hair. "But we were all always together. Even when the levels were closed off and I didn't know you existed, we were all necessary."

"We're all going to be necessary here."

He paused for a moment, and then asked, "How are we going to care for people like SueAnne? How can she earn credit?"

"People will have to pool the credit they earn, I guess."

He touched her cheek, ran a finger along her lips. "How will we make them? This is not a closed space where they must accept a leader."

"Or leaders."

"Or leaders."

Ruby had closed her eyes, but nevertheless she heard his soft laughter in his voice. She whispered, "We're going to have to be so strong, so smart. Koren is no friend, and Naveen may not be either. We may not have any friends here."

"We have each other."

CHAPTER FORTY-FIVE

By the time they made it into the meeting room they'd chosen, Joel was seething. "If you don't do something about those women, I will."

The room was still empty, although someone had already been here brewing stim, the scent of it filling the air and giving Ruby a boost. She put a hand on Joel's arm, felt the tight set of his muscles. "I will take care of this. It's only been two days since they started it. I'm thinking."

"Don't think too long."

Maybe love was always infuriating. She had learned that taking him on directly seldom worked. Not that she was happy about the women; they bothered her on a deep note. But she spoke quietly and calmly. "Lya was my friend once."

He only softened a bit. "If you allow yourself to feel guilty about Hugh forever, he will haunt you. Save your guilt for those *you* actually kill."

"What a happy thought." The door opened and Haric came in with three cups in each hand. Ruby smiled at him. "Six? Aren't we only expecting Onor and KJ?"

Haric grinned at her. "And me."

"That's still only five."

Haric simply smiled and continued to look full of a secret. He poured three cups, and the three of them sat down at the table.

"What happened here yesterday?" Joel asked.

"There's five more children that came up sick, but one of the first ones who got sick looks better. Marcelle's really worried about another one, though."

Ruby frowned. "They're all quarantined?"

"And you feel okay?" she asked Haric.

"I was sick one day. But I'm better now." He looked more closely at her. "You look tired. Are you okay?"

"I am tired. We were out a long time yesterday. I can't tell you how much there was to see."

"I wish I could have gone with you."

He was so earnest. "I know. I have a feeling we'll all get to see more of the station soon."

The door opened again, admitting Onor and Naveen.

"You're the sixth," Ruby said in greeting.

"Huh?"

"Never mind. Good to see you. Haric will pour you some stim."

They shared stories from each other's trips while they finished the first round of stim. Onor's description of the Brawl fascinated and frightened Ruby. Although it was Onor who had relayed the story of seeing the Brawl, Ruby turned to Naveen. "How do people end up in the Brawl?"

Naveen looked down at the table. "They can't support themselves, even at a basic level, and no one speaks for them."

"How can you be so cruel?" Ruby demanded.

"How can we not?" Naveen raised his head. "A space station is an enclosed system with limited resources."

"You have enough resources to feed your hungry," Ruby snapped. "No one starved on the *Fire*. No one. When we had a shortage, we all went on reduced rations." The whole idea turned her stomach. "I was there. In Exchange Five. There are enough resources there to feed thousands, clothe thousands."

Naveen looked like he was hanging on her every word. She felt like he'd baited her into feeling this way, but surely he hadn't created the Brawl. He'd just made sure she knew about it. "I see," he said, "why they call you Ruby the Red."

"Are there people here who hate the Brawl?"

"Of course. Many." Naveen shrugged. "But there is something like it on every station. It creates discipline."

Something about his tone of voice alerted her. "Are you recording this?"

"I record almost everything."

She went silent. He was helpful. Had been helpful. He had also known she would hate anything like the Brawl; like Koren, he had their history. "I want to see the Brawl for myself."

"I'll take you," Naveen said.

Onor frowned.

Joel put a protective hand on Ruby's hand. "I would like to go, too. Can you take the both of us?"

"It will cost credit."

"Did it cost credit to take me?" Onor asked.

"I paid it," Naveen said. "And if I have to, I can pay to treat Ruby." He hesitated a moment. "And Joel."

"We'll pay," Joel said.

Ruby glanced at Haric. "Can you find some kind of bread? I need to calm my stomach."

"I'm sure there's a colored square somewhere called bread."

Such irony from a child.

Onor glanced at Naveen. "Can you show him how to order some real food?"

Naveen laughed. "Spoiled you, did I? Sure. And breakfast is on me."

Haric looked downright perky as they headed for the door. "What kind of real food? I heard you saw a bird." He was still talking as the door closed behind him.

"I don't like him recording you," Joel told her.

"I'm sure he recorded you, too."

"We're being used."

Something dawned for her. "We've always been used. We were somebody's slaves on the *Fire*. Probably no one from here, although everyone will use us if we let them. Naveen. Koren. Even Lake. We will have to be careful about who we allow to use us, and be sure we get fair value in return."

Onor leaned back and bit at his lip. "That's cynical."

"Is it wrong?"

He shook his head.

"We'd better get smart, fast." She was seething, but she couldn't afford that. She had to think. "Do you trust him? You've spent time with him."

She could see Onor consider, knew how his teeth worried his top lip when he was under real pressure.

"Yes. As much as I trust anyone I didn't grow up with or fight beside. I think he can help us. If we're careful."

"Naveen taught you about credit?" Joel asked.

"He gave us some. For your songs. He's selling them and he gave us a cut."

Ruby leaned forward. "If he can sell them, can't we sell them?"

"To who? He knows everybody. We don't."

"How much credit?" Joel asked.

"Two hundred seventy credits."

Ruby leaned back in her chair. "That's life for one hundred and thirty-five people for one day." Both a lot and not a lot. "How many songs did he sell?"

"I don't know."

Ruby got up and rinsed out cups, thinking as she moved. "Was the Brawl the most awful place you've ever seen?"

"Yes. We don't, ever, any of us, want to end up there."

Ruby brooded while Joel questioned Onor about the number of people in the Brawl (more than he could count) and the number of enforcer robots (maybe one for every hundred people) and about the route Onor had taken to get there.

Haric and Naveen came back in with soft bread and fruits Ruby had never seen. "Try the green one," Onor said. "It's sweet."

"After I settle the stim a little." She reached for a piece of bread, and even that smelled sweeter than she wanted. It tasted good, and helped her back off the fight in her stomach. She needed energy. "We'll see that we don't ever end up in the Brawl. Any of us."

"That's not going to be easy," Joel said. "I did the math. We have five thousand seven hundred and thirty-five people."

Naveen's eyes widened at the number, although he didn't say anything.

"It takes two credits a day for survival. Per person. Old or young. I don't know what it takes to live a decent life, but for the sake of argument let's say we need four credits a person and a few extra, so multiply six thousand by four. That's twenty-four thousand credits a day."

"But a lot of people to earn them," Haric said. "Most of us can work."

Ruby shook her head. "Deduct the children, and the people we need to raise them. And the old. And the sick. And the people we need to care for them."

"How many children do you have?"

Joel answered. "Between what ages? How old do you need to be to work here?"

"Sixteen."

"About half of us are women," Joel mused, "and maybe one in ten women has a child, so that's about three hundred."

"Wow," Naveen said.

"I didn't see any at the Exchange," Ruby commented.

"We seldom create children on the station. They visit. The miners tend to have them."

Joel held up a hand. "Don't get sidetracked. Estimate. Four thousand can probably work."

"But they won't all be able to," Ruby pointed out. "Or at least, not everyone finds work every day. Lake said some days there is hardly any." The whole thing was beginning to sound worse than hard.

Naveen interrupted. "Not everyone can find work at manual labor. There are other ways to earn credits."

Onor looked at Naveen. "I told them about selling Ruby's songs."

Naveen sat up straight and looked serious. "I want to help you."

"Why?" Joel still sounded stiff about the idea. "What's in it for you?"

Naveen offered a small, genuine smile. "I, too, need to stay out of the Brawl, and better, to have the credit to live where I live. It's a nice place. I make credits telling people about things, and you are a unique new thing that will interest the station. Particularly Ruby."

Joel was still frowning. "We'll consider your offer. What can the rest of us do?"

Ruby had a sudden image of Joel shifting boxes of cargo from place to place. He was a fighter and a military leader.

Naveen pulled a flask of some kind from his belt and drank from it. She couldn't smell it, couldn't tell if it was still or stim or maybe even just water. "You need a structure. One set of people need to go look for work. Exchange Five is as good a place as any, and it's where Koren will expect you to be since she showed it to you. Another group needs to focus on learning.

"What should we learn?" Ruby said. "I want to see the birds. Is everything else between the Exchange and the Brawl? I mean, is that the best and the worst of it?"

Naveen paused a moment before answering her. "That's middling-bad— the Exchange—and the Brawl is the worst thing except maybe the jail. There a lot of the *Deep* that regular people don't know about, that we barely glimpse. Some is bad, but most of it is riches beyond our imagination."

Whole areas being hidden from her. Hardly a surprise. She knew there were people watching her though Naveen's camera. Right now. This very moment. She forced herself to curb her tongue.

All of her life, people had been trying to hide riches from her. Or worse, to show her the bottom of a world and claim it was the top.

CHAPTER FORTY-SIX

Onor felt uncomfortable at Joel's reticent response to Naveen's offer to sell Ruby's songs. But he had something good that had come from Naveen. He pulled the dull silver-colored ball that held Ix out of his pocket and put it on the table.

Ruby's face grew curious. She picked it up and stared at it, turning it around and around, holding it up and squinting at it.

Naveen watched Ruby. He looked expectant. "It is a copy of Ix. It still holds your history."

Ruby's eyes narrowed and she held the object up higher. "Really? This is Ix?"

Naveen said, "Ix is stored in the ball at the moment. It isn't anything physical; it does need a physical home."

"Koren gave it to you?" Joel asked.

"No."

A beat of silence passed. When Naveen offered nothing else, Joel pressed him further. "Will we get into trouble for having it?"

"By law, it is yours."

Ruby asked, "So why didn't Koren let us have it in the first place?"

Naveen grinned. "Perhaps she forgot your rights. I doubt it is in her best interest for you to succeed."

Joel's eyes narrowed. "What do you mean?"

"Nothing I can prove easily. But what was your cargo worth, and did you really get 10 percent of the salvage?"

"Why didn't we get it all?" Ruby looked irritated, but then she'd looked irritated ever since they were forced off the ship.

"Well, the crew isn't the owner of a ship. Not usually. On the little miners and the family ships, and sometimes of ships meant to get around the *Deep*. But not on the big cargo liners. Salvage rights can be called on any ship that is drifting and cannot be fixed. It's old rules, started way back on Lym around sailing ships."

"The *Fire* did work!" Ruby exclaimed.

Onor didn't call her on her near-lie. Joel just sat with his face stoic, but he was clearly thinking hard.

"And you could prove that now?" Naveen asked mildly.

"Maybe with Ix?" Ruby still held the ball of Ix in her hand. "Does it know?"

Naveen shook his head. "I looked. Ix does have all of the maintenance records, but that alone doesn't exactly support your case. The *Fire* was never designed for in-system travel. The best you could have done was park it in an orbit. As soon as you stopped in the system, the *Fire* was effectively derelict. You may be lucky you landed here instead of being boarded by pirates."

Joel gave a bitter laugh. "We were boarded by pirates at the Edge. Surely you saw that."

Naveen looked thoughtful.

Ruby put the ball with Ix in it down on the table, propped on a napkin so it couldn't roll off. She glared at it. "How do we use that? Ix was as big as the ship."

Naveen lost his smile. "I've looked. When Koren built this place, she didn't put a design spec in for an AI habitat. We'll have to acquire one."

"Which will cost credit," Joel said.

"Yes."

"What is an AI habitat?"

"Well, not that ball. You might think of that as a place where Ix is sleeping, waiting for a home complex enough for it. Onor and I poked around this morning. You do have a communications network here, and a standard base operating system, but an AI needs a certain speed and range of processing power."

Getting Ix to work mattered. "What would it cost to get one?"

"A third of what you have."

Ruby's face fell.

She would never do that, not now while there was so much they didn't know, and children and old people to feed. She licked her lips and twisted her hair in her fingers. "It wouldn't really help us anyway, would it? It doesn't know the station. It can't."

Naveen said, "It does. I taught it a few things before I compressed and copied it. It knows how to access the station's maps and schedule."

"Could you use the spider's webling?" Joel asked.

Ruby gave him a *Don't talk about that* look, which Joel ignored.

"Is your camera off?" Ruby asked Naveen.

"Yes," Naveen said. "I know your history. The law Aleesi is scared of is real. It's still enforced, and if she gets caught existing she will be destroyed."

Onor felt startled. "I thought you couldn't kill beings. That's what the Brawl is all about, right? You can't kill, so you lock people up and let them kill each other?"

Naveen looked offended. "The Brawl isn't that simple. And the station-masters can kill *illegal* beings. Aleesi is illegal."

"She doesn't seem that different than Koren's robots," Ruby said.

"Didn't you meet her as a pirate?" Naveen reached for more stim. "It's like the salvage laws. Old stuff. At one point, early in the days of AI and before the sundering, soldiers were captured and their brains scanned into robots and turned against their own people. It kills a human to do this—to take the essence of them and pour it into metal. The story is more complex than that, but the law is old and stable." He sighed. "And probably good. From your conversations with Aleesi, she was a slave."

"But why not kill the people who made her, instead of her?" Ruby objected.

"Because hybrids had to be outlawed to stop the business."

Onor held his tongue. He could still see Colin being ripped in pieces. He watched Ruby carefully. She didn't respond right away, and her face looked set and worried. "What do you suggest?"

"Can you talk to Aleesi?" Naveen asked.

"No. We used Ix for that."

"But what about when you left?" Naveen was looking at Onor. "Aleesi wrote on your journal."

"I think she was still using Ix to help her. It was still doing basic care at that point."

"I think so, too." Ruby looked thoughtful. "Is whatever communication we do have here enough to talk to her? I tried every day for a week after we first got settled, but nothing happened. She hasn't looked alive, although I'm sure she *is* alive."

"It's possible. Aleesi is not our tech, but she is probably more like our current tech than Ix."

"Will you help us try?"

"I can."

"Will you protect Aleesi while you do it? I don't want any footage of this, and I don't want her hurt. I stripped her of her defenses, I took her from her sister-copies, and I brought her here, to a place she is afraid of."

"Yes."

"Can we try now?"

Naveen laughed. "I need to do some research. And carefully. If I help you with this, and if I get caught, I could be in real trouble. So could you."

"So why are you willing to help?" Joel asked. "Why take the risk?"

"Because I can make a lot of credit when Ruby does a tour of the ship."

"When Ruby what?" Joel's voice sounded barely controlled.

"She's already popular. You saw what I gave to Onor. That was a tenth of what I owe you." He smiled. "At least if you consider this an agent relationship. I can set up the venues, I can generate interest. You can't. You don't know enough."

Ruby looked thoughtful, Joel looked downright opposed even though he didn't respond.

Naveen continued. "Look, I'll do it for just a year. I'll write the contract so you can get out of it. It's a win for both of us. And you need a friend here."

Onor froze as he realized Ruby, Joel, and Haric were all looking at him, as if waiting for him to decide. He did know Naveen better than they did. At a gut level, he trusted him and didn't trust him all once. He glanced at Ix, captured in a silver ball on the table, and remembered how the AI had helped them win a different fight.

He took a deep breath. "I trust him."

"We will think about it," Joel said.

Naveen stood. "Thank you. I'll be back within a week."

After Naveen left, Joel picked up the ball of Ix and stared at it. "How do we even know this is Ix, and that it hasn't been changed in some horrible way?"

CHAPTER FORTY-SEVEN

Ruby stood in line and watched a man who could hire her people as surreptitiously as she could manage. After failing for three days, she had spoken to Lake and requested his help. She'd learned that this man was a longshoreman from *The Great Bastard*, a ferry that had come up from Lym carrying clothes, food, and livestock. It had been unloaded, and now it waited for precious metals mined from the asteroid belt out beyond the orbit of the *Diamond Deep*. That was work that didn't need the ability to interface with the *Diamond Deep*'s systems. Her people had a prayer of doing it.

She studied the man. Tall. Deeply muscled for a spacer, his biceps surely a result of long days of heavy labor. Paintings of trees covered his body, each leg a forest, his arms turned to branches carrying blue birds hidden amongst fall foliage.

Beside her, Haric tried to stand as tall as he could. She had spent precious credit to bring Conroy as well, as an example of the strongest men from the *Fire*. Not that Conroy had any size compared to the tree-man. He was big if Onor stood next to him, or Haric, or Ruby. But Conroy to the longshoreman was like Haric to Conroy.

She watched him accept three workers and reject two. Not horrid odds, but not great. When he gestured them forward Ruby had to look up to meet his eyes. "We are from the interstellar ship that just came back. We have many excellent workers, and we would love a chance to help you."

He smiled, and for a moment she felt hope.

"I am looking for experience."

She swallowed. "How will we get experience if no one teaches us?"

"How will I get my ship unloaded with people who know nothing?" He started to wave them away.

"Take two of us. That's all. They can teach the others."

He crossed his arms over his chest, the tattoos of leaves and birds rippling as he moved. "I'll take you."

Before she could accept, Haric put a hand on her arm. She remembered her promises to Joel. "Take me and Conroy." She pointed at Conroy.

He laughed. "I don't need strength, I need experience. Now get out of the way."

She stepped aside. They stood against a wall and watched at the man hired the next two people in line and then dismissed the line. So close.

"It's almost as if we're being blackballed," Conroy mused.

"What?" Haric asked.

"As is someone has told them not to hire us."

"I hope not," Ruby mused. Would Koren go that far?

"Now what?" Haric asked.

"We keep trying."

"Most of the people who can hire us have already gone for the morning."

"So what? If we don't start finding work, we'll starve. We have people who worked on the gardens on the Fire. Let's find a place for them. Surely that's not skilled labor."

Ruby sat in the small kitchen with SueAnne beside her. SueAnne sat in the same wheeled chair, which she'd taken to using most of the time. Her fingers worked, twisting colorful cloth to make belts. The fabric was one of the few purchases Ruby had allowed; enough bright colors to help them fit into the vibrant chaos that was the station. Almost everything they had brought from the Fire was somber and faded. They had to look better to get hired.

Five of the whispering women sat outside the door, singing softly. Not one of Ruby's songs.

At least their voices weren't bad.

Ruby stared at the figures on her slate. She had been able to place five people into a harvesting crew. Five out of thousands. Harvesting paid five credits a day; grunt work at best.

KJ had done slightly better, but at a cost. Five of his dancers had signed on to be bodyguards for dignitaries; they'd demonstrated they could take down attackers in unique ways. They earned more. Fifteen credits a day. But KJ had offered to let them keep five each.

It wasn't what she wanted. She wanted all of the credit to come to a single place and be spread back out, so everyone could protect everyone else.

KJ was trying to protect his own.

She understood; so was she. She had just thought she and KJ were on the same page until she learned they weren't. Even thinking about it made her stiffen.

When she'd brought it up to Joel, he'd given her a look of mild curiosity and asked if she wanted to lose the protection KJ's dancers offered her people.

At least they were discreet.

She had set up a system that recorded the credits they had banked in days of life for the whole population of Ash. She used a paltry three credits a day: air, water, and food plus a bit that she could dole out for transportation or to replace a broken slate. They'd lost almost a full day for every day they'd been here.

Unacceptable.

She sighed and sat back, catching SueAnne's attention. "We have to do a hundred times better. Even if we learn how to use the Exchange as well as possible, if we get a quarter of the jobs available, it won't be enough."

"There are other Exchanges."

"I don't want to split us up."

"Or give up control," SueAnne observed. "You cannot do everything, be everywhere. You will kill us all if you try. The job is too big for you."

"I'm not the only one! KJ is placing people. Haric is going out without me tomorrow, trying to find a cheaper way to buy food. Allen is looking for material to open a real bar, and bargaining with our own people for space. "

SueAnne plopped a glass of water down in front of Ruby. "Drink. Unlimited water is built into the base credit. Go take a shower and revel in it. Write a song. This is not like you."

Outside the door, the women stopped singing for a moment, the quiet noticeable. They started a chant.

She hadn't finished a new song since they left the *Fire*. There hadn't been time. She had a long list of ideas and scraps of lyrics in her slate: when she thought of anything—even in the middle of a meeting—she jotted it down. "I have to finish adding up all the numbers."

"No you don't. You're obsessing about them. Besides, they're actually pretty simple. I'll take over the accounting and give you a report every day."

"Really?"

"An old woman's got to have a way to be useful."

Ruby hesitated, but the offer was good. Maybe SueAnne was right, and she had let herself get too tired to be grateful for help. "Okay." She drank the water. "Thank you. It will help. Can I show you what I've done?"

"You've already shown me." SueAnne held the half-finished belt up in front of her and squinted at it. "Twice"

"Okay."

"Go," SueAnne said, her fingers tugging and pulling at some of the thin colorful ropes to make them more even. "Damn, it's hard to make this thing lie flat."

"Go where?"

"Sleep, and take a shower. Rest. Clean up."

"I have to go back to the Exchange. I want to talk to Lake. He'll tell me how to do better there."

SueAnne gave her a long, measured look. "Then you had best rest and clean up, and put on something pretty. If you find me in a few hours, I'll be done with this belt. You can wear it."

Ruby trailed her fingers along the old woman's shoulders. "I didn't used to like you. But sometimes it's all right to be told a few things."

SueAnne didn't let Ruby see her face, but she reached up and took her hand for just a second.

The new belt fit well. She'd thought it might be small, but it wasn't. She should remember to eat more often.

Ani and Jaliet sat next to her on the train to Exchange Five.

"What if Lake won't help us?" Ani asked.

"Then we'll find someone who will. We just need to learn enough to help ourselves."

"You haven't heard from Naveen?"

"No." She was beginning to wonder if Naveen really would help them with the AIs, or if he'd decided they were a lost cause. Or maybe he was just busy selling her songs. She wanted to know that, too. Maybe there was another day or two of life in that.

The three of them stepped off the train and Ruby watched Ani's face. It was the first time she'd been to the Exchange, and the look of sheer wonder in her eyes rewarded Ruby for bringing her. "I'm so impressed," Ani said. She fingered the bright colored ribbons Jali had braided into her three braids. "I see why it mattered what we looked like."

People's colorful clothes varied in a hundred different ways. Shorts and boots and dresses and simple wraps and work uniforms eerily reminiscent of the *Fire*'s work jumpsuits.

Multicolored skin abounded, including blues and reds and purples and stripes and other designs. Even though Ruby had been here every day since Koren first brought them, it always shocked her system to see the variety of humans and robots.

Vendors called from booths, advertisements broadcast from invisible speakers, people chattered in numerous dialects.

"Come on, I sent Lake a note to meet us in a little cafe I like."

Ani frowned. "What's a cafe?"

"A galley, only it's not free."

"You're going to let us spend credit?" Ani asked.

"Only a little. Order lightly."

"Yes, oh obsessed one," Ani said.

Jali frowned at Ani but said nothing. Ruby managed to get both of their attention for a moment. "I don't know how much I trust Lake. But he claims his job is to help put people who need work in touch with people who need workers. He's been nice so far, and some of his ideas have helped. Some haven't."

"Look at that!" Jali pointed at a girl weaving through the crowds on a board with wheels.

Ruby glanced at the skater, wishing she had that much freedom in this unfamiliar place. She turned back to the task at hand. "We have to do better. I have Haric and KJ both looking for manual labor, but there must be other ways to earn credit. I want your eyes and ears."

Lake stood outside the cafe, waiting for them. The last time she'd seen him, he'd been in reds. This time he had chosen a set of browns almost like Naveen's usual colors, although in Lake's case they were splashed with bright red flowers and orange birds the color of his long ponytail. "Good afternoon, Ruby the Red. Welcome, welcome." If he noticed the shocked look on Ani's face or the curiosity on Jaliet's, he didn't react. "I'm Lake. And you are?"

They made it through Ani's stammered introduction, and Jali's cool one, and ended up at a very nice table under a tree with a pitcher of iced water, an orange pot full of tea, and a small platter of little cakes. "I'm happy to see that you came to ask me for additional help. I'm sorry my lead about *The Great*

Bastard didn't work out, but there are others brokering work." He held a small cup in a large hand, took a small sip, smiling. "It would be easier to find room for more bodyguards."

"We have thousands of people. Only a few can do that job."

"There is a large ship, *The Lady's Love*, coming in from Mammot in a few days. I will be talking to the crew-bosses there."

Jali asked, "And that work will be?"

"The usual. Unloading."

Jali sipped at her tea and looked only the slightest bit interested. "And how many jobs might be available for a group such as ours?"

"Maybe twenty. Maybe a few more."

"That would pay . . . ?" Ruby asked.

"I don't set the price. Probably five credits a day."

So little. Ruby sighed. She looked over at Ani, who held her own cup but didn't drink the tea. She seemed entranced by the others in the cafe, slightly shell-shocked. But then Ruby remembered how exhausted she had been the first day she came here. She leaned over and whispered in Ani's ear. "Drink water."

Jali spoke to Lake, "And in trade for that, you would like to have?"

"There are many things I would like. Credit eases a man's way, but it is very traceable. What might you have to offer?"

Ruby answered. "We have people who can count and keep inventory. We have trained robot repair crews. We have others who know how to keep bar, or to make still."

Lake set his cup down carefully. "You know how to repair our robots?"

"We can learn. I did the job myself, once."

"And your hands are entirely too pretty, and your voice worth too much for such a thing." He leaned back, his look measuring. "I can arrange almost anything if you can help me do so."

Ruby went cold. No wonder she hadn't had any success, no wonder Lake had given her certain looks from time to time, as if waiting for her to say ritual words. He wanted a bribe. How could she have been so naïve? She bit her tongue, and blessed Jali for saying, "We do not have spare credit to help you in a meaningful way. Perhaps we will be able to provide assistance in some other way?"

"There are many forms of commerce of a station this size. Your people are—somewhat unique in how *original* you are."

"What do you mean?" Ruby asked.

"You have a following now. Naveen has stirred up interest. There will be people who would like to sit across a table from you—like I am now—but who will be unable to do so. There may be other ways to satisfy their appetites. Perhaps you have a few young girls who are looking for opportunities to serve as companions?"

Before Ruby could react, Jali spoke again. "We do not participate in that trade. What else might help you plead our case convincingly?"

Lake looked at Ruby, his eyes as warm and friendly as they had always been, as if what she had just heard him say changed nothing. "Sometimes I am allowed to organize events here. Perhaps I can work with your manager to put on a concert, and you can pay me well enough that it covers my time to sell tickets."

Ruby swallowed, still furious and slightly confused.

Once more, Jaliet saved her. "Naveen may contact you in a few days. In the meantime, please consider us when *The Lady's Love* arrives. Surely you are also rewarded by the crew who are able to find the right workers."

Lake shook his head. "More people need ways to earn credit than there are opportunities."

Ruby had read him completely wrong and wasted days. But she also did not want him as an enemy.

Lake stood and gave them a slight bow. "Keep me in mind if you need anything."

Ani watched him leave. "How are we going to learn everything we need to learn?"

Jali laughed. "One step at a time." She turned to Ruby. "He will need to be paid to help us. And I suspect his appetite is not small."

"I suppose he helped us get a few jobs to demonstrate that he could, and then made sure we missed on others to show his power?"

Jali shrugged. "He's looking out for himself."

"We all are," Ruby said.

"We've got to figure out the systems," Jali said. "We need something like Ix."

Ruby hadn't told her about Ix, or about the idea that they may be able to load Ix into Aleesi. She didn't like the idea. But it would be better than selling their children. She still remembered her friend Nona, who had been murdered while selling herself to a red. That past had seemed dim, but now it felt real again and almost immediate, Nona's bloody face close in her memory. She couldn't let those days return. "We need a safety net."

"Naveen wants you to tour," Jali said.

"We need more than me."

Jali stood up. "No. But if you weren't here, what would we have? We'll work on getting skills for everyone else, and learning how to trade. But that will take time. Fox would have taken this opportunity, and we should learn from what he did for us."

Ruby let out a long sigh. "We need to find a better power position."

Jali said, "We are weak as newborns here. I bet Lake is five hundred years old, and knows how to con anybody under a hundred without even thinking about it."

Ruby picked up a small pink cake and took a bite. "I suspect we're buying this food. We might as well eat it."

CHAPTER FORTY-EIGHT

Onor sat beside Naveen and stared into his cup of water, wishing it were something stronger. On his other side, Ruby fidgeted with her cup, twisting it round and round and periodically clinking the edge on the table. Joel, KJ, and SueAnne filled the rest of the chairs.

Everyone seemed to be avoiding everyone else's eyes.

Onor worried. Ruby's cheeks were stained by dark circles and her hair hung limply down her side. She looked thinner. She needed rest, and sleep, and to relax. The hand that wasn't working the cup in circles fingered the beads around her neck, one of the old ones from the days before the real fighting on the ship. It looked out of place here, hand-made and childish.

SueAnne and Ruby had been spending more time together. SueAnne whispered to her, "You must prioritize."

Ruby glanced at Joel, who had the common sense to remain quiet. Lately, Onor had heard tension between them. Three long weeks of going only backward was wearing on them all.

Today, no one had found work. Naveen had shown up with a few thousand earned credits for them, but still they were two days further behind for the week. Ruby had taken to beating herself with that number.

Ruby sat up straighter and looked at Naveen. "Will you do everything you can to protect Aleesi?"

"Yes."

She kept looking at him, intense. "Can I trust you?" She looked around at the whole table, Naveen following her gaze. "Can we all trust you?"

"I will do my best to put Ix into Aleesi and leave her whole. But I will prioritize Ix. You need that worse. The community will need an AI while we tour."

"You'll do it here." Ruby said. "I don't want her out of our sight."

"I will, Ruby the Demanding Red, I will."

Naveen's laughter and Ruby's choice seemed to release them all from the tension that had filled the room just a moment before. SueAnne rose to pour more water. Joel smiled at Naveen; the first thing Onor had seen between the two men that was better than truce since they were kicked off the *Fire*.

"How long do you need?" Ruby asked.

Naveen shrugged. "A few hours. Maybe a little more."

Ruby gave out a weak smile. "When should I plan to leave?"

"A week."

Ruby shook her head. "Two weeks. I need to write some songs for here. And I want you to take me out for two days. I want to see more places so I can learn more."

Joel tensed.

Ruby must have sensed it in him. "Not just me. Joel and Onor and KJ, too. At least."

Naveen frowned. "It would be better to leave sooner."

"A week and a half, then. A week and a half after you get Ix working."

"A week and a half from now," Naveen insisted. "Timing is important. We can stop along the way, *during* the tour."

"I want to see what's good about the *Deep*. And I want to see the Brawl for myself. You can't possible show me everything, but you can pick the absolute best and the absolute worst."

"We aren't allowed anywhere near the best," Naveen said. "We aren't really even supposed to know the best that exists here. They hide their excesses from us."

Ruby smiled at Naveen, that quirky, you-didn't-understand smile of hers that Onor had always loved. "I did not say the richest and the poorest. I said the best and the worst. Another way to think of it is as the cruelest and the kindest. A core lesson from our history on the *Fire* is that those in power are often both as good and as bad as those out of it." She shared a glance with Joel where whatever they saw in each other's eyes softened them both.

When they left the room, they had to push through the whispering women. Lya was there, her eyes fastened on Ruby as if she hungered for something. Maybe Ruby's beauty, or her power. Not the revenge Lya had once wanted; something in her desires had changed, become greater than anger or hatred. Perhaps it was sorrow, but it felt like there was some other purpose to it as well, but one that Onor couldn't quite grasp.

Whatever it was, the whispering women made it hard to guard Joel and Ruby. Onor had to assume the women could have weapons, even though so far they hadn't shown up with so much as a thick pipe disguised as a walking stick. Onor found the whole situation inexplicable, both why Lya followed Ruby around, and why Ruby allowed it.

Joel didn't appear to understand it any more than Onor. He'd made a few off-hand comments that showed he was more frustrated with the women than Onor was, and a few times he had worn such contempt and anger on his face that Onor almost felt sorry for Lya.

The whispering women had traded for or made more and more white clothing over time, so now they looked like pale ghosts. It almost seemed that as Ruby and the others began dressing more and more like the bright inhabitants of the *Diamond Deep*, Lya and her women fought to be everything the station was not.

SueAnne and Naveen waited with Onor for the entire entourage of the colorful and the white to disappear around a corner. SueAnne was using her chair today, rolling back and forth in an odd imitation of pacing the corridor. "I don't envy Ruby," SueAnne muttered as if she were talking to no one.

"Because of those women or because she carries so much on her shoulders?" Naveen asked.

"Both."

"She's strong," Naveen said.

"Look more closely," SueAnne warned Naveen. "She's exhausted."

"I'll make sure she rests."

"You may not have that much power," Onor cautioned. He frowned at the now-empty corridor. "Look, I promised someone I'd have lunch with her. Naveen? Can you eat with SueAnne? I'll meet you back in the main galley."

"Of course."

He found Marcelle in her office, a small square box with a depressing little black desk and small chair. A sign on the front of her desk proclaimed Marcelle "Director of Education." She looked up when he entered.

Her face was streaked with tears.

"What happened?"

"Two of the babies died."

She'd been sneaking into the creche at night and refusing to tell Ruby. He slid around the desk and she stood so that he could fold her into his arms. It was becoming more natural to hold her, to feel her thin frame against his, to have his cheek and nose tickled by her curly hair. "I'm so sorry."

"They didn't do anything. We brought them here, and they died."

"I know." He rubbed her back, his fingers feeling big against her. She was losing muscle. "You need to eat more."

She didn't respond to that. "I expected to lose Aaron. But I was surprised to lose Pia. I thought she was getting better."

"How many are still sick?" he whispered. How much worse might it get?

Her tears took her over and he dug around for a handkerchief and wiped her cheek dry over and over.

"Only five." She struggled to get her breath. "We sent three home yesterday."

"So it might be okay? It might just be what Koren said, that some of us are allergic to the new things in the food and the air here."

"It's only babies and the old," Marcelle said. "At least that's all that stays sick." She sank into him again, letting a few beats of silence go, stiffening while the time went. "I get so mad. I can't help myself. I'm sure *they* could help them if they wanted. Or we could find a way to get help."

"There is no single *they* here," he murmured. "It worked for us to think like that on the *Fire*. But here? Here there are a hundred *theys*. Maybe more. We have to get the attention of people we think can help us, and we have to convince them to help us."

"Surely there are people here who could have stopped the babies from dying."

"Everything here costs credit."

"What does a life cost?"

He couldn't bring himself to tell her that he'd asked Naveen about how to get medical care. Naveen had asked for how many, and then told him what it would cost to buy the services of a specialist doctor—human or robot. They had their own medical care from the *Fire*, of course. But they knew the diseases of a ship, the angsts and sores and cuts and sorrows of a contained colony. To buy more expertise would cost them all. A few days of life for the whole colony against a chance—not even a known outcome—for a few children. He had reported the information to Ruby and Joel and SueAnne and watched them decide to use hope instead of credit. It had been hard to watch; another decision between bad and awful, between hopeless and barely hopeful. "We'll find a way. Really, we will. There has to be way."

The choices here were far more cruel than the choices aboard the *Fire* had been. At best, they would survive their own choices with their hearts intact. He held Marcelle a little tighter.

Onor, Ruby, and KJ were alone with Naveen in Ruby and Joel's living room, staring at the blue pill-shaped heart of Aleesi. The round ball of Ix lay beside the webling that held Aleesi's brain. Both looked too small for the beings that inhabited them.

KJ looked alert and rested, like he always did. In contrast, Ruby's shoulders still drooped with exhaustion and the dark circles under her eyes had barely faded. She leaned in over the objects and whispered to Naveen, "Do you think you did it? Do you think it's okay?"

Naveen looked as serious as Onor had ever seen him. He'd chosen to change his myriad browns for somber blacks, as if demonstrating how earnestly he took her need to preserve Aleesi. He set a small speaker down on the table beside Aleesi's brain, and his slate beside the speaker.

"I was able to move all that is Ix—or all that I could tease apart from the ship when I copied it—into Aleesi. There was some space that she wasn't using, anyway. It wasn't enough to store or process all of Ix, so I deleted some of the very old parts to make room."

Naveen must have felt Ruby's frown.

He grinned at her. "She should be fine. In some ways it will have made her stronger."

"Did you talk to her?"

He shook his head. "I waited for you. I ran tests on both of them, and they should both work."

"What about Ix?" KJ asked. "Did you change it, too?"

"Ix will be different. It will retain most of its memories from the ship, but Ix knew itself as the ship, as all of the many myriad bits of data it collected. It knew itself as the cargo bays and the drive and the water systems and the recorder of trash. It probably experienced the ship as its body."

KJ leaned in, his dark eyes narrowed. "Will it work?"

"I hope so. It appears the copy was crude, but true. AIs are like humans; they want to live, to continue." Naveen leaned forward and pushed a button on the small speaker. "This will broker these conversations, keeping them off your community communication network. That's for security."

"Will everyone be able to use Ix eventually?"

"I don't know. We don't know what is safe. Ix was programmed to protect the *Fire*, not individual people."

Ruby took the ball of Ix from the table and held it in her lap. "Perhaps we can program it to protect us now? We are all it has left."

Naveen picked up his slate and typed something. "I'm waking Ix up first. I will tell it who is here."

The speakers were good, and the voice that came from them was clearer than it had ever been on the *Fire*. "Hello, Ruby Martin."

Ruby clasped her hands over her face and her eyes shone with unshed tears. "Hello Ix. It is good to hear your voice."

"I can't feel anything." The voice didn't sound panicked at all. "I remember coming in. The closer we came to the *Diamond Deep*, the more I had trouble thinking."

Ruby and KJ exchanged a glance. Ruby spoke. "You were limited, and copied. The you I am talking to now is a copy. We are no longer on the ship."

"We are in the station?"

"Yes. There is me and Onor and KJ, and a man from the station named Naveen who has been trying to help you."

"Hello, Naveen."

Naveen glanced around the room. "There's no point in keeping anything secret from it."

Ruby said, "You are . . . you have been put into a small space. From one of the robot spiders. You remember the robot spiders?"

"The invaders? Of course. Where is the *Fire*?"

Naveen held up a hand quickly, forestalling *that* answer. "Yes, the invaders. I copied you into the brains of Aleesi, the one we saved. That's where you are."

"With the being Aleesi?"

"Yes." The voice was Aleesi's though the speaker.

"I thought that might happen," Naveen muttered.

"Hello, Aleesi!" Ruby said. "I'm glad to hear from you."

"I detect that I am different," Aleesi said.

Naveen immediately asked, "Better? Do you feel better?"

"Different."

Ruby licked her lips. "I feel bad that we put Ix in with you. We didn't have a choice." She caressed the ball in her lap. "We need Ix very badly. We need Ix to help protect us, who are all that is left of the *Fire*."

Naveen looked unhappy with Ruby.

"I am used to sharing. Copies of my selves collected up from time to time and shared."

"Is the *Fire* gone?" Ix asked.

KJ spoke. "Only in physical form. It's being scrapped."

Ruby winced and added, "We remain, and we are in a new place. Ash. That's what you need to help us protect now."

"I still cannot feel anything. I cannot help if I cannot be connected."

Naveen spoke to Ix. "We will do that when we can. First we need to know that you can live where we placed you, and that you and Aleesi can share space."

"Of course we can," Aleesi said. "But you have created more of an abomination to the station culture than I was by myself. You should understand the risks."

"There are risks to you, too," Ruby said.

"I have been dead since you caught me," Aleesi replied.

KJ stared at Naveen. "What is wrong with this—to the station culture? Aleesi is a human and Ix is an AI. Is that it?"

Aleesi answered before Naveen had a chance to. "My very existence here is dangerous to you. The laws that made me illegal caused the Edge to flourish. Humans are not allowed to inhabit fully robotic bodies. The history is complex, but assume that this was seen to benefit both the AI community and humans. If Ix and I can share directly, it is a marriage of AI and human. That is also forbidden."

No one spoke for a few moments. KJ recovered first. "What will they do to us if they catch us?"

This time Naveen answered. "We will see that that does not happen."

KJ's eyes narrowed in a way that made Onor glad the AIs had no visual receptors at the moment. Ruby, however, did have eyes. She looked at KJ as she spoke. "We will be very careful."

KJ whispered. "Someday, one of your risks will kill us all."

CHAPTER FORTY-NINE

Ruby and Naveen and SueAnne stood at the window, looking down on the Brawl, SueAnne's chair parked behind her like a safety net. Ruby's hands splayed across the cold glass, her face pressed to it. The Brawl looked ten times as crowded as they were, maybe twenty times. Bodies side-by-side, too close. Close enough to smell each other, to reach out and touch someone else easily in most directions most of the time. Lovers held each other, lying two to a one-person cot. People gathered and talked or played games, usually with someone facing away from the group and watching, the way Onor and the other guards watched at concerts. Many people sat by themselves, or stood by themselves, surrounded by others but not touching or being touched by anyone else. Enforcer robots moved silently and efficiently through the crowd, which always seemed aware of them.

This might be her people's fate.

"There are no children," Ruby murmured. "What would they do with our children?"

"There are schools," Naveen said. "We send the young children of people who end up here to boarding schools."

SueAnne asked, "Is it possible to visit people who are here?"

"For a fee."

"Of course," Ruby replied, bitter. Angry. "Everything is for a fee."

"What does it take to get out?" SueAnne asked.

"It depends on why you are there. If it's just for non-payment of your life fee, then merely credit—repayment plus paying forward half a year."

"That's a fortune."

"Family members have done it. Some that have skills can sign contracts for certain types of jobs and buy their freedom as long as they keep their contracts."

"So they have to do whatever the person who hires them tells them to do?"

"For a year. The first six months pays their way out of here, the next pays forward enough that they have a year and a half before they would have to go back."

Ruby remembered Lake, and choked out a question. "Can women sell their bodies to get out of there?"

Naveen's answer was, "Sex is one of the most exquisite things people can sell here."

Ruby shuddered. She looked down, searching for more details. No walls, no privacy. A few stacked blocks where people sat slightly above the crowd. Aisles snaked between groups. Here and there, benches and cots were fiercely protected. An exercise area was full of people and ringed with enforcer bots. Maybe those were the ones with the most will, staying as strong as they could.

You'd have to be strong in a place like this.

She hated it.

Looking down at it didn't help her gain control of her dismay. "There is enough food and space that everyone could live better than this. I've seen it, already. You could take half the space that's in the Exchange, and still get the business of the Exchange done. That half could feed these people."

"If the people here have enough to live well and not work, they will do that. Such an experiment was carried out on another station, and the whole station became less competitive."

So the idea of competition happened between stations as well. You competed, or you ended up here. "Why else are people here, besides not paying?"

"People who get caught breaking rules but who aren't violent can be sent here. We have a lockup for big crimes, and banishment for others. They can't get out until their time is done, and they have to also make the life payment." He paused and they were all silent. She glanced away from the window to check Naveen's expression. He looked closed.

She stared back down at the crowded expanse, watching a man thread through the crowd while an enforcer followed him, like a slow dance. She couldn't quite tell if the man was being chased, but a way was opened for both, one at a time, as if the crowd below wanted the man to escape and yet couldn't block the enforcer.

"It's not pleasant," Naveen said quietly, "but this system works. For each of the people you see down there, there are a hundred who are either pulling their weight and doing the work of the station, or earning credit with entertainment—like me. Some are simply taken care of by others."

"You sound defensive. But you wanted us to see this."

"Not because the Brawl is a good place. It's not."

Below her, the man seemed to be getting ahead of the enforcer.

She felt puzzled. "But you approve of it?"

"It keeps civilization going."

"I don't approve." Here and there, she noticed the flickering lights of video screens. "They have slates?"

"Of course. And group entertainment. I've even sold a few of your songs in to them. They like them."

She stiffened against the glass, staring down at the people below, looking for the man who had been running from the enforcer. "Sold?" It some ways it was less horrible than she had imagined, in other ways it was more. She hated the idea of it, of segregating people and watching over them with machines. "You sold my songs to people who have nothing?"

"Of course. It is to help keep you from having nothing."

"Give them away here. All of them. Even the future ones."

Naveen frowned. "You have to have credit to make a difference."

She ripped her attention from the window and turned to him, speaking too loudly for the small hallway and not caring. "This is my work, not yours. I will have it given to these people."

Naveen maintained his composure, although his jaw was set tight and his eyes looked harder and more determined than usual. "And will you have it given to all of the downtrodden on the *Diamond Deep*?"

"Are there worse places than this?"

"Of course there are. The Brawl is one place we send our indigent. There are others, some for criminals or the incompetent. Here, people have food and air and entertainment. Some even choose to be here. After all, the rules are simple."

Ruby frowned. "You said people die here?"

Naveen looked slightly surprised at the question. "They do. I showed this to you so that would understand Koren's hope for you. So you would see what could befall you if you don't learn our ways fast enough."

They needed this man. Ruby wanted to shout at him, to explore her rage at the whole idea of the Brawl, but it wouldn't help her people. Besides, Naveen didn't create the custom. She put her hands back on the glass to hide the way they had started shaking and looked out over the crowded living quarters below. "For now, give them away here. I will think about other places later."

"Very well."

Ruby found the man the enforcer had been following. He was on the ground, splayed, with one hand up as if in defense. The enforcer loomed over him, and he fell back, limp. There was no way to tell from here if he had been stunned or killed, but whatever had happened was cruel.

She said nothing.

SueAnne changed the subject. "You mentioned that people choose to go here. Why?"

"Survival means work. If you do work you like, or you do work well, survival on the *Deep* is good. The *Deep* has more opportunities than most other places—room for more people who believe more things. I've been to all the stations, and to Lym. They're all like this—cruel and hard on one end, and quite wonderful on the other. I'm trying to show you the best and worst that could happen to you."

CHAPTER FIFTY

Naveen, Allen, and Onor sat at one of the empty bar tables, a bottle that Naveen had brought in standing empty in the middle of the table, and another one half-empty. Onor had taken to lifting the glass and letting the cool, slightly minty liquid touch his lips without actually drinking any more. Allen hadn't displayed the same self-control; he listed in his chair.

A bartender should know better.

Naveen looked unaffected, although Onor had learned that he tended to look that way right up to the point that he could barely walk or speak. "We'll give you five percent."

Naveen narrowed his eyes. "I thought I was negotiating with Allen."

Onor laughed, struggling to be as good-natured as possible, to sound as naïve as he could. "You're negotiating with the *People of the Fire*."

"Fancy name," Allen said. "I like it." He burped. "Go, Onor. Make a deal."

Naveen looked slightly disgusted. "I want ten percent. I'll be able to negotiate prices that are at least fifteen percent lower than you could get yourselves. You don't lose anything."

"Five percent on anything we sell here, to our people. Ten percent on anything we sell to people who come to us from the outside."

"Why would they do that?" Naveen asked. "We have bars."

"Because you're going to encourage people to come. You'll earn more credits from outsiders."

"It's going to be a great bar," Allen said, taking another drink. "We know how to make good bars." He raised his drink. "You said so yourself."

"You'll have to pay to transport the food and drink into here."

"We'll split it with you?" Onor said.

"Who's teaching you, anyway?" Naveen grinned. "You're supposed to be naïve."

"That could be true." Onor sat back and this time he took a more noticeable sip, the liquor warming his belly again. People would need to have some of the credit they'd earned to spend it here. Ruby would hate that. But the credit would stay inside of the community mostly, and maybe—just maybe—they could bring some in from outside.

CHAPTER FIFTY-ONE

Jali stood beside Ruby, pinning up the shoulder of a pale gray dress she'd decorated with red, blue, and gray beads unstrung from some of the many signal necklaces that Ruby had accumulated over time. The dress flowed all the way to the floor, and when she moved the beads clicked softly against each other.

Just outside of the open door, but never coming in, three of the whispering women sat and watched. At least they were silent at the moment. Lya, an older woman named Justina, and Min, with her disfigured face. It hurt Ruby that Min had chosen to become a whispering woman; she remembered how proud she had been of the knife scar that marred her cheek, of fighting for freedom. What had made her choose to follow Lya?

Ruby didn't say anything to her. She was developing a plan, but so far her plan didn't include engaging in conversation with her white shadows.

The women acted like furniture. This bothered Ruby deeply, but they were creating the situation, not her. Forcing them away would only make matters worse.

Ruby returned to admiring the dress, which fit snugly at the waist and flowed over her hips to end just at the floor in her bare feet. "What did you make this one for?" Ruby asked. "It's beautiful, and soft, but it's too heavy to perform in."

"Dinners, I suppose. I've finished everything you need for performances. But there will be regular days, and important events you don't know about yet, and you will need to look your best for all of them."

Ruby leaned in and gave Jali a slight hug. "I'm so glad you're coming with me. Your work is fabulous."

Jali grinned at the complement. "Now I need to make me some clothes. And at least two outfits for everyone else who's coming. Is it all final?"

"Yes. Six of us. You, me, KJ, Ani, Dayn, and one more. And Naveen of course. Not that you'll have to dress him."

"No, but I've been stealing ideas from his outfits. Joel? He's staying?"

"Someone has to run things."

"Who's the one more?"

"I'm choosing."

"Joel is letting you pick?"

"He assigned KJ, Ani, and Dayn."

"Well, Dayn is good for you, he keeps your head from getting big. I suspect Joel knows that."

Ruby laughed. "It is hard to be stuck up with Dayn around to stick a pin in you." She looked back at the dress, which perfectly set off her pale complexion, hid her freckles, and added sensuality even though it covered almost every inch of her. "Dayn must be along to balance you. You make me so beautiful my head expands."

"You're keeping a secret."

"Maybe." Ruby shrugged and looked in the long mirror one more time. "Should the collar be a little lower?"

Jali frowned. "No."

"Okay. Get me out of this."

Jali undid the pins she'd used to close the dress. By the time Ruby put it back on, there would be buttons there. "When do you need to know the sixth person?"

"Yesterday."

Ruby sighed.

"Soon," Jali said. "I'm shopping again in the morning. There's a good sale going on at the ColorMe booth, and I want to get there early."

Ruby looked over the ten or twelve new outfits Jali had conjured up in just the past week. "Thanks for being so fabulous."

"The extra credits helped."

Naveen had shown up with a few thousand extra credits, mumbling something about her songs selling really well in advance of the concerts. He'd told her to use the extra for clothing, and she had. Half of them. The rest went into the community funds, and Jali had done such a good job that Naveen would surely never know she hadn't exactly obeyed him.

Ruby dressed back in her regular clothes, comfortable dark gray pants and a washed-pale blue shirt Jali had made her, way back on the *Fire*.

"There's only a week left, Jali said. "Are you scared?"

"Never."

"You're lying through your teeth."

"Of course I am. I'm terrified. But now," she gestured at the dress Jali had just taken off her. "Now I'm excited, too. Are you?"

Jali laughed. "I'm glad to be busy, and it will be an honor to go with you."

"You're being way too formal," Ruby laughed. She kissed Jali on the cheek to loosen her up and headed out.

At the door, she stopped and addressed the whispering women for the first time in three days. "Lya—can we talk?"

Lya looked startled at Ruby's invitation. During the fitting, she had been in a boneless slump on the floor, one shoulder leaning into a wall. She had managed to scramble to a stand, but now her feet stood as if welded to the floor. Well, not-quite-right or not, she had succeeded in creating the women in white.

"Come on," Ruby said. "Allen's serving up mint tea over in the bar. He'd love to have a customer or two."

"I . . ." Lya glanced at the other two women, as if lost for words.

"Just us, please."

"Go," Min said. "Go on."

Ruby assessed. Min looked good, still thin, but with clear definition in her muscles and color on her face. The cut had finished healing and become a puckered brown and red line from under her left eye, across her nose, and down her right cheek. Ruby smiled at her, testing, pleased to see Min return her smile, if only with a light uptick in the corners of her fine, small mouth.

In spite of Min's encouragement, Lya remained silent for an extra awkward beat before she said, "Very well."

Ruby frowned but let it go. She led Lya down two levels and found an empty table in the half-full bar. She made sure they sat close to a microphone. Naveen had succeeded in wiring Ix/Aleesi into the community's speaker system so that the combined machines could hear. He had not been able to separate out the two machines in such a way that they had separate inputs and outputs; the webling had not been designed that way. Nor had they been given a voice except in the one small room where the webling lived. Nevertheless, they would hear the conversation and Ruby would be able to ask them about it later, or to use them to replay parts.

Allen stood on a ladder, hanging pictures and lights with the help of two maintenance bots. The bots were about the size of his hand, and able to cling to the walls and even climb. He looked over as Ruby and Lya settled, waved, and commanded a serving robot to take their order.

Ruby frowned as it neared. The robot had never seen the inside of the *Fire*. Something Naveen had provided? Or someone had spent secret credits on? The underground economy that had been the cargo bars seemed intent on re-emerging here where they couldn't afford it. Something to talk to Ix about later. And Joel.

How could she leave? Things weren't settled here.

Ruby turned to look at her immediate problem. Lya sat more normally now than she had in the corridor, and her face had gone into the blank, patient waiting posture she often used when she and her women were "witnessing" instead of "whispering." Following Ruby around had been good to her in some ways. She looked stronger than she had when this first started.

Ruby ordered tea for the two of them and watched the bot slide smoothly across the smooth floor until it had almost returned to Allen. Perfect. New. All of it. Surely the whole station wasn't perfect and new. But then, the little she knew of their history suggested that the denizens of the *Deep* tore it apart and remade it regularly.

She dragged her attention back to Lya. She must be too tired again; it was hard to focus her thoughts.

Lya raised her head and met Ruby eye to eye. "Why did you want to talk to me?"

"I'm going to leave soon for a tour."

"No kidding. In fancy dresses."

"I've always worn costumes to perform."

"No you haven't."

"When I was on stage." Ruby sighed and waited a long moment, then looked into Lya's eyes. "This isn't working for me."

A small smile crossed Lya's lips, then disappeared.

"I know that's what you wanted. To make it hard for me. But you're hurting everyone. Not because you're irritating me; I can handle that. But you're not helping with any of the things we actually need."

"I am watching out for us."

"I don't understand. We were never friends, but we used to live in the same pod, go to the same school. We knew the same people."

Lya gave a short bitter laugh. "You don't protect us anymore. So I am merely protecting us from you. I'm gathering everything I can find out about what you're doing, and telling people." She looked down at the table in front of her. "They need to know you don't really care about them."

"You know better than that," Ruby snapped, immediately sorry that Lya was getting to her. "You can see how hard I'm working."

"To get dressed up? To be the fancy whore here like you were back on our ship?"

Ruby didn't slap Lya, although her arm twitched.

"I see you with good food and good clothes and able to leave whenever you want. Are you going to leave Joel for Naveen and abandon us? Are you just taking care of yourself?"

Ruby couldn't rise to Lya's bait. As soon as Lya took a breath, Ruby said, "I'm trying to make a place for us here."

"We should never have come here. We're slaves. We're tied to the future of the same people who misused us, and you're pretending it's all pretty and sweet, that we really all get along, even though it's not true. We're still kept down, but you're so wrapped up in your fame you don't even see it."

It was amazing Lya had any followers at all. She wasn't making any sense. The robot reappeared with white cups full of steaming green tea that smelled wonderful. More credit spent on the cups. Ruby held the tea in her hands, letting it warm them. She counted three deep breaths before she continued. "We had to go somewhere. Lym is no longer home to anyone. We could have ended up floating forever around a planet while the *Fire* finished falling apart."

"So why are we all together? We're doing almost all the work now. Just like before. Only now we're feeding the reds and the greens and the blues and they're doing nothing. It's all on *our* backs to keep things going. Take *us* away, and leave them. If you really care."

Ruby thought of SueAnne patiently keeping books from her wheelchair, of Jali sewing late into every night to get them all ready, of KJ and Joel and Conroy and The Jackman working to set up physical programs and to keep people training. But none of that was what Lya wanted to hear. "You could be right as far as manual work. We are good at that and should be proud of it. But others are working, too. In a lot of ways. I do know that KJ's dancers are earning credit."

"And keeping some of it."

Ruby hated that as much as Lya. "I don't make all of the decisions. I'm going out to do two things, which you should know if you've really been witnessing, and thinking about what you hear."

Lya did flinch.

"To learn about the *Diamond Deep* and—hopefully—make us enough credit to thrive here." Lya started to say something and Ruby held up a hand to interrupt her. "Begging for work at the Exchange—no matter who does the work—is leading us to a bad future. To something I can't let happen." She shivered at the thought of the Brawl. Lya would die in there in no time. Many of them would. "This trip matters."

"Why should we believe you are doing this for us?"

There. That was the question she wanted. "You don't have to believe anything. I'm going to offer you a trade."

Lya looked puzzled.

"I'm not going to be here for you to follow around. Nor will I be here to keep Joel from locking you up if you follow him around."

Ruby gave her a beat to talk into, but Lya didn't use it. So Ruby kept going. "I need you to help here. If you agree to help Marcelle in the schools—to do what she asks you to, and to attend three hours of classes a day—you and all of your people . . ."

Lya frowned and looked unhappy but again she said nothing.

"Then I will take Min with me. You will be able to witness the trip. If there's a way for her to communicate back to you, she'll be able to."

Lya's eyes narrowed. "Why Min?"

"Because Joel will only let me take someone who is also able to guard. Min is trained as a fighter, and now she looks like one, too."

Lya stood up as if she planned to leave without answering. "I had wondered if she was a traitor."

"Lya!" Ruby barked. "Sit down."

To her surprise Lya obeyed.

"If Min is a traitor to you, I don't know it. I haven't talked to her since we arrived here, and if I had, you'd know since you're following me around like a shadow."

Lya picked her cup up and hugged it.

"You claim you hate me because Hugh died fighting for us. Not for me, for us."

"He loved you," Lya whispered. "He loved you so much. And he died for you."

"He died for you, too."

"I told him not to fight."

Both of their voices were rising. Other people in the bar had started to watch them. Ruby tried to modulate, managed a whisper that still sounded angry. "No one should die young. But the world isn't fair. Maybe you do hate me. That's not fair either. We were never close friends even before. But I do what I'm doing because of a friend of mine who died once, and because of Ben. We're both honoring the dead."

Lya licked her lips. Her hands shook.

"You didn't know my friends," Ruby said, more slowly. "But I knew Hugh and you knew Ben. I need you to trust me. To believe that I'm honoring them both while I try to save us all."

Lya's answering laugh sounded bitter. "I can't believe how arrogant you are."

"Will you do it? Promise me you'll help the colony while I'm away?"

"Will you tell everybody what you're doing before you go? And why?"

"I don't have time."

"For your people?"

Ruby sighed. There was so much work. She needed a month of sleep. "Okay. You're right. I will, in trade for Min and the return of your women in white to helping the community as much as you can."

"While you're gone."

The deal wasn't perfect, but at least Lya and her followers would be safe from Joel. Lya would be doing something useful, and Ruby would have Min. She could—perhaps—use her to build a bridge back into the whispering women. The thought chilled her. It was so . . . calculating. Not how she pictured herself.

They were fracturing.

She leaned over the small table so that her face was close to Lya's. "Thank you."

"All bets are off when you get back."

Ruby allowed Lya to have the last word.

CHAPTER FIFTY-TWO

Ruby surveyed the kitchen table. Naveen had helped her procure fresh vegetables and fruit, bread so soft that a small chunk she'd broken off to taste had disappeared in her mouth before she swallowed, and three sharp, tangy spreads. Best of all, there was a tall bottle of chilled wine. All of it food they'd never seen before they came here.

She felt too nervous to write, so she paced for almost an hour before Joel came in. He glanced at her face and then at the table, his face frozen and his back stiff.

"What's the matter?" she asked.

"Everything."

"Sit down. Naveen brought us food."

If the table were a person, his gaze would have cowed it into sitting down. "I'm not hungry."

She crossed the room and stood beside him. She could feel his tension without touching him, almost smell it on him. "Did something happen?"

"I heard how you took care of those women. You can't do that."

She stilled and took a deep breath. "Can't do what?"

"Take one of them with you. You can't reward them for disrespecting you."

Ruby poured two glasses of deep red wine. "I already asked her. She can fight." She held a glass out to him. "It's not as if I asked Lya."

"Take Chitt. Take Samara. Take a dancer. But not one of your enemies."

"We need one of the old worker-class people with us."

"Fine. Take The Jackman." He finally took the glass and downed half of it in one long pull.

"He hates me. Besides, we want to look friendly."

"Isn't Min the one with the scar?"

She hadn't realized he knew that. "Yes. Jali can dress her up. She's the right size to wear some of Daria's clothes."

"Take Daria."

"She's no fighter. This is my trip. It will only be a few weeks, and I needed Lya and her women to be out of your hair while I'm gone." She took a sip of the wine, rolling the bitterness on her tongue, savoring it. "Besides, KJ is going to be with me. What could go wrong?"

"Everything. Anything." He put a hand on her shoulder, stiff and heavy. She stepped into him, trying to lift his frustration with touch. They stood that way, close but stiff, like two strangers forced into a small space. He put a hand on her face, his palm big enough to cup her entire cheek. "Look. We don't have to do this at all. You don't have to go. We can still go find Laird and the others. Koren found me yesterday, and her offer is still open."

She stepped back, her mouth open. "You would abandon them all?"

"I saw Laird in the Exchange today. He has a job helping with the station's defenses, loves what he does. He lives in a place that's all his own, and he looks healthier than any of us—ever." He truly looked torn. "We could be that happy. We could."

Ruby felt like all of her had tensed all over again, like even the blood in her heart had stopped in protest. "The guilt would kill us."

"You're pushing yourself too hard. It's not possible to do what you want to do. We can't make enough to save everyone, but I want to save you."

She spun away from him, staring at the wall, too furious to say anything else.

He came up behind her, close enough that she heard him breathe. "I've been watching you get more and more exhausted. More worried. This is not the *Fire*. If it were, I would be the captain and I would be responsible and I would be happy you were helping. But this is a trap and we can't get everyone out of it." He paused, and although she couldn't see it, it felt as if he reached for her and then dropped his hand.

"And taking Koren's help isn't? It's all a trap, Joel. This whole place is a trap. We have to stay together. I'm taking Min because I need a lever to understand Lya, to change her."

"If you were with them all the time, serenading them from task to task, they wouldn't be happy." His sounded so bitter it pulled at her heart even while she was mad at him. "You cannot do all the books, get all the jobs, write and sing, work with Ix, and communicate to everyone all the time. There is only one of you. There is no win here. We were lost the moment we decided to come here."

She turned to face him. "You could come with me. Leave Onor in charge. Leave KJ back here with Onor."

He went silent. For a moment, she thought he might be considering it. "I would lose whatever reputation I have left."

PART FIVE

THE TOUR

CHAPTER FIFTY-THREE

Ruby slid into the silky-soft pantsuit that Jali had crafted for travel. She belted a multi-colored scarf over the loose green top, picked up one of the simple beaded necklaces she wore in the early days, when she might have been locked-up for wearing one. The colors didn't quite match the fancy new outfit. But it made her smile, and feel a bit like her old self. She dropped it over her head.

Joel waited in the living room, his jaw set and his eyes cold. "Good morning."

They had slept as far apart as their bed allowed, barely touching in the night. She had tried to soften him with caresses twice, and he had merely grunted and refused to roll over and meet her eyes. But he was looking at her now. She said, "I have to leave. It might save us all."

He thinned his lips and closed his eyes.

It wasn't like him to be petulant. "I don't want to leave you. I'm sorry. But it's the best thing I know how to do. We'll talk every day. Our people need you there for them. They need your strength, your power."

He turned away, staring at a picture on the wall. Damn it. She needed this one person, this one love, this one central fact in her life. He was part of how she thought about herself. She contemplated his back. He looked stiff and way too serious. "It's not as if you can hold a note."

His shoulders relaxed, if only a tiny bit.

"But if you want to come along and try we'll record you and send you back here for everyone to listen to."

He turned and took her into his arms, rubbing his strong thumbs along each side of her spine, the smooth material letting them slide right into the soft places between muscles. "We should beg for an hour's grace and return to bed. I should have made love to you all night."

She whispered, "We'll have more time. I will come back."

"You had better."

"And you," she pulled back and looked up at him, "you need to be here waiting for me." Her throat felt thick.

"I know."

He leaned down and kissed her, taking her mouth as hard as he ever had, his tongue questing and demanding, stamping her as his.

The door announced the arrival of a pack robot to get her bags.

Ruby had trouble breaking from his arms to let it in. Maybe they should fight more often.

She walked beside Joel and behind the short, square pack robot. It had four wheels for legs, and made a soft whirr as it moved down the corridor. At the doorway between home and the rest of the *Diamond Deep*, she found Jaliet, Dayn, Ani, and KJ waiting for her. A small crowd of well-wishers gathered a respectful distance away.

Haric also stood by the door, a small bag at his feet. He looked at her with such hope in his eyes that she winced. She went directly to him before she even acknowledged the others. She knelt so that he would be a little taller than her. "I would love to be able to take you. But I can't."

He held up his slate. There was figure of twenty credits on it. "I can help pay my way. I earned this, working. Off the system, so the credits went to me. It took me three days of cleaning out garbage containers."

His chin quivered ever-so-slightly. He read the look on her face, and looked down at the ground.

"You found that work by yourself? How?"

"I asked. One of the men that's helping Allen build out the bar knew."

"Really? Did you have to pay him for finding you the job?"

He looked back at her. "Only two credits."

She hoped her pride showed on her face. "You're growing up."

"Someone will need to take care of you while you're traveling. I know how to do that."

"I know you do." She hadn't even thought of him, and she should have. Although she did need Min. Damn it. "I can't take everyone I care for." She paused, and kept looking at him until he nodded. "You can help me, though. You can figure out how to have more people doing what you did. That's enough credits for ten days of life support. Give it to SueAnne, and work with her to figure out how more people can do that kind of thing."

She sensed he was fighting tears. But he squared his shoulders and stepped back into the crowd that had gathered to see them off. Onor and Marcelle, SueAnne in her wheelchair, Lya (of course, and wearing a sour face), Allen, others.

As she watched Haric fade behind Onor, she felt the sudden loss of connection. She would be able to talk to them all because of the slates, at least to the extent that she had time. But she wouldn't be able to hold them or see them. Marcelle's belly had grown big enough she could have her baby before Ruby got back. It wasn't likely, but sometimes first children came early.

Relief flooded her as Min made her way through the group. She'd chosen to wear white, and Ruby wondered if that was all that was in her bag. In spite of the small defiance of her wardrobe, she looked scared, her eyes big and her lips thin.

The door opened. Naveen stood behind it, dressed in fabulous browns that glittered with golden threads and hints of blues. His clothes flowed as he walked toward them and everything Jali had made, even the outfits that had seemed over-the-top, dulled in her memory.

She smiled at his finery. This trip would be for show. Like an echo of the feeling of separation that had just nearly stopped her, she felt repulsed by what she was about to do. Her day-to-day work for the community would end while she did this. She would dine and sleep well, and be pampered. All this, while SueAnne fretted about the cost of food and Joel struggled to keep people working, while most of her people had never left this small, awful place that was so much less than the *Fire* had been.

She needed to be spectacular. She hesitated, suddenly feeling the job was impossible, like she was tiny in the vast *Deep*.

Ruby took a deep breath and gave Joel a last long look before she greeted Naveen with the bravest smile she could muster.

CHAPTER FIFTY-FOUR

Onor watched the gentle curve of Marcelle's lips as she blew on the tea SueAnne had sent for her. She took a tiny sip, and placed the teacup back on her desk. "That *is* good."

"SueAnne said it would help calm your tummy."

"I feel like a house."

If it weren't for her pregnancy, they would surely be with Ruby instead of here, fighting disease and the boredom of the masses. "I know. How was your day?"

"School's interesting. It's far more interesting than what we got on the *Fire*. Ix is attending classes instead of giving them. You'd like the one we had today on intelligence."

"I wish I had time."

"Did you know there are five recognized species of AI? And three different classes of body they can inherit?"

"No."

"Here, taste this." She passed him over the tea. "The infirmary is full. There's still the sickness, the same one. We're calling it a Deep Flu." She glanced over at him, and when he didn't say anything, she continued. "We lost two more old people. Keep SueAnne away."

"I hadn't heard it was contagious."

"I don't think so. But I'd rather not take risks. SueAnne is a savior. I never thought I'd say that about someone from command."

"We're part of command now."

She sighed. "It was easier not to be. People keep looking at me like I shouldn't have this job. Like I'm too young or too favored."

"You are."

She made a face.

"Ruby trusts us," Onor said. "If you think the Deep Flu is contagious, tell me."

"I don't. Not really. Besides, what would that change?"

"Our medical staff think it's not, right?"

"Right." She reached for the tea.

"I haven't tasted it yet." He did. Bitter. "Wow. You like that?"

"Yes. How about you?"

"Allen's hired two people in from the *Deep* to help get the bar built. They're doing awesome work."

She laughed. "You're kidding. With all of our unemployed people, we're paying someone else?"

"Just to do things we can't. You're going to be amazed."

She looked away.

It was a running argument between them; she wanted more resources for the infirmary and the school, and he wanted to keep people busy. The bar itself had become almost like a shared dream for the old cargo-bar people. As far as the rest of the credit allocation problems, Onor counted himself lucky that Joel and SueAnne were making the final decisions. He and Marcelle might never agree on some topics. He stood up. "I've got to go. Don't you take any risks with this disease."

She turned back to him slowly. "Just keep me in this tea and don't bring me any new food. I'll stick to the squares."

So she really was worried? But it was only children and old people who were getting the . . . what was it? Deep Flu. "Let me know how things stay in the infirmary."

"So you can take the dead off the daily tax rolls?"

"Don't sound so bitter. So we can tell if we need to try and do something."

"What do you mean by that?"

He was going to walk into a trap. He could feel it. But he opened the door anyway, since he'd started. "I'm sure there are medical resources somewhere on the ship."

She stared at him. "But those would cost credit."

"Of course."

"How much?"

"I hear it's a lot. A few days of a robot doctor could cost a few hundred credits. More than everyone in the colony is earning for the common pot these days." He could see from the look on her face that he'd been right to suspect he was stepping into trouble. "Look, you didn't see the Brawl. You haven't been outside. You don't know how bad it can be. We need time, and the only way to have time is not to spend credit while we're learning to earn it."

"You agree with that? You think these people—including the children—

could be saved and you're advocating that we don't do it?" She stood up, one hand on her belly. The rest of her seemed to have thinned, and the angry set of her jaw made her face look pinched.

He swallowed. "We don't know if they can be saved. We have to think long term."

"Since when did any of us not take care of our own?"

"All of the rules have changed."

She fell silent. When she spoke, she did so slowly and in a measured way. "No. No they haven't. There are new rules imposed on us from the outside. But our own morality? We have always cared for everyone. That's how we survived. When people like Koren talk about ships like the *Fire* coming home empty, I'm sure it's from lack of caring."

He spoke as evenly as she had. "My parents were murdered. Hugh died fighting. Ruby's friend Nona died in the warrens under the gray levels after two reds raped her."

"But we—we the grays—we never let our children or old people die if we could help it. Fighting over power is one bad thing, and you're right. It was bad. It was awful. That's why we revolted. But if we fail to care now, *it will be worse*. How can you think any other way?"

"Can you accept that there's no good choice?"

She shook her head and stared at some spot on the wall above him. "There are still right choices. Pass that on. Tell SueAnne and Joel what I said, even if you don't believe it."

"I do believe it. You just haven't seen the Brawl."

"Can it really be worse than watching children die?"

He went around the desk and took the teacup from her hand. "It could be the same."

CHAPTER FIFTY-FIVE

Ruby waited offstage. Naveen stood beside her, close enough to hear his breathing and smell the strong drink she'd seen him toss off a few moments ago. Other than the slight sickly scent of alcohol, he showed no effects of the liquor at all.

He had dressed down this time, still sparkly but much less flamboyant than what he had worn to travel in. "Why aren't you dressed up?" she asked him. "You look almost like a normal man."

"To highlight you."

"I still think I should have worn an old work jumpsuit."

"You are too beautiful for that."

She thought about cussing at him, but it didn't seem worth the effort. She had never sung with someone else managing the events, and she hated it.

Jali and Ani stood on her other side. Jali had finally stopped adjusting Ruby's outfit—a soft swirling dress with a low-cut front and a high hem over the softest boots Ruby had ever worn. She had settled for whispering small reminders instead. "Keep your head up." A few moments later, "Shoulders back, spine straight."

Cussing at Jali crossed her mind as well. Instead, she touched her friend's shoulder. "Thanks for being here."

"How do you feel?"

"I'm okay." She really did feel better; prestage adrenaline always drove away stress and fatigue, always strengthened her.

Min stood to the side, alone, looking over the crowd that had gathered in the huge theater. Ruby hadn't found time for a private conversation with her yet, and so far Min had hardly said a word to anyone. Unlike everyone else in the group, she had never left Ash, not even to visit the Exchange. If Ruby felt overwhelmed, how must Min feel?

The concert hall reminded Ruby of the cargo bars. Like the bars, the hall had been created inside the bay of a spaceship. Lights flicked playfully along the ceiling, as if making a little preshow for the audience. There was a flat area at the foot of the stage and beyond that, seats climbing up an incline. The walls were decorated with pictures of birds and dragons, almost like the old parks from home.

Naveen had explained that the *Star Bear* had been turned into a concert venue so the owner, Satyana Adams, could raise credit to fix her broken ship or buy a new one. He'd said, "When the concerts-on-a-ship succeeded beyond all of her hopes, Satyana decided it was cheaper to stay. She'd found what she's good at—making large groups of people happy."

In the meantime, the stage was big enough for a hundred people, and Ruby felt tiny. "How many in the audience?" she asked Naveen.

"Physical? There's ten thousand seats and they've sold out."

More than all the people from the *Fire*. If her cut was two credits from every one of them, she could buy two days for everyone, plus a little more.

"Virtual?" People could pay to watch from wherever they were. A credit for each of them. "How many?"

Naveen shrugged. "We're at seven thousand, but eighty percent of a virtual audience tunes in right on time." He pointed at a screen on the wall, angled so that no light from it fell onto the stage. Numbers counted up too fast for her to see. When she looked back at Naveen she could tell from his face that he liked the numbers.

Another day of life, and more. And she hadn't opened her mouth to sing here yet. She closed her eyes for a moment and vowed to be fantastic.

The light in the big bay dimmed.

Naveen left her side and strode onto the vast stage, a light following him and elongating his shadow, as if it reached for the back of the stage.

"Thank you, thank you for being here. I'm pleased to introduce the newest star of the *Diamond Deep*, a part of our past returned to us in absolute glory . . ."

Ruby half-listened as Naveen talked her up. The virtual count passed the ten thousand of the physical count, doubled it.

Her stomach gave her fits in a way that had never happened to her before. Sharper and more full of bile, so her mouth tasted of fear. What if they hated her?

Naveen beckoned.

Jaliet's hand landed in the small of her back, propelling her toward the stage.

Ani whispered, "Good luck."

She took three steps.

The stage felt huge, just like she had expected it to. No, worse.

Lights blinded her. Naveen had warned her to shut her eyes and blink them open and she did so, fast. She held her head up and looked out at the audience.

Naveen had not warned her the audience would be almost invisible. She could only see the faces closest to the stage.

She took a deep breath, two. There was no microphone. Two small dots had been fixed to her face, and two thin wires hooked over her ear, all of it far finer and lighter than Fox's equipment for the *Fire*. Naveen had promised they would send her voice through all of the space here and out to the rest of the station.

Below her and above her, positioned in a variety of places, a live band hid and waited for her signal.

Joel would be watching. The others would be, too.

CHAPTER FIFTY-SIX

Onor led Marcelle toward the door to the bar. "Close your eyes."

"Really?"

"Really. I'll lead you."

Allen had saved them a front table. Joel and SueAnne were already seated. It took a few moments to steer Marcelle safely through the crowd and sit her down. He made sure she was oriented to the large projection wall that was the biggest single feature of the bar. "Open your eyes."

He watched her eyes widen. The picture in front of her was so clear that Onor felt he could reach out and touch the huge black curtains on each side of the wide stage.

At the moment, no sound went with the picture.

Marcelle looked around at the rest of the bar while Onor watched her face for approval. They had new wood-grained tables and chairs, with higher tables near the back wall so that spectators could see over the heads of the other patrons. The painting wasn't all done, and since Onor knew where to look, there was an unfinished feel to the whole place. Not that it mattered; the bar was full.

Haric and Allen and a few of the old bartenders from the cargo bars filled orders and dropped multicolored drinks onto the robot's trays as they finished them, moving so fast they never stopped, almost like a dance.

Most of the patrons were from the *Fire*, but there were Deepers there, and even a few sentient machines scattered amongst the tables. The concert must have drawn them, or maybe Naveen's advertisements about the bar. As far as he knew, they neither ate nor drank anything, much less got intoxicated. He shivered when he noticed that one looked exactly like the machines that had accompanied Koren when she stole the *Fire* from them.

He turned away from machine watching as a decidedly not-sentient serving bot trundled between their table and the one next to them, which was filled with the old leaders of the underground: Conroy and Aric and The Jackman. Onor stopped it and ordered a drink for himself. Marcelle asked for a flavored water.

Joel seemed to be lost in his own world, perhaps contemplating the tour and Ruby's absence from his side. He already had a half-empty glass of alcohol, which wasn't like him at all.

SueAnne let out a heavy sigh, and looked even more sour than he had been afraid Marcelle might. "We could feed five hundred people for a month on what it took to build this."

"Or maybe save a few people," Marcelle added. "We need play space for sick kids and a few more private rooms."

Onor couldn't let them think this way. "The bar is making more than we're getting out of Exchange Five on any one day." Their drinks arrived and he took a deep, long swig. Warmth filled him, a happy shock to his system. "I invested in it."

Marcelle looked startled.

"I gave Allen a hundred credits to help buy the projectors."

Anger edged SueAnne's voice. "So instead of putting wages into the central bank, people have been giving it to Allen? So we can starve sooner?"

Lights flickered on the projection wall, brightening and then dimming the view of the stage, reflecting in her angry eyes.

"No," Onor said. "We won't starve. Some credit is coming in from outside. *And what's being spent inside is still here. It doesn't go away because it changes hands.* Naveen is teaching me how credit works, and it's not like you think. We don't need to worry about what gets spent inside Ash, among us. We need to be sure more comes *into* Ash than goes out."

SueAnne looked entirely unconvinced, and Marcelle still looked slightly confused. Joel had no reaction at all. He watched the stage so closely Onor wasn't even sure he heard the conversation. The flickering light deepened and the wrinkles in his face, and stole the color from his cheeks. He sipped his drink.

A bright spot bloomed on the projection wall. Naveen strode out as if he owned the stage. He held his head high and it seemed that he looked at each individual in the bar even through the airwaves; surely a trick of camera angles. Onor expected the sound to come up as Naveen started talking, and turned to see Allen fiddling with a set of controls in his hand.

As the room quieted, the quiet from the stage became more noticeable. Naveen's mouth kept moving. Finally there were two loud crackles, and then

Naveen might have been screaming in their ears, "Introduce Ruby the Red, the queen who burns with creative fire, the best new talent on the *Diamond Deep*."

Ruby must hate that. Surely she'd force Naveen to be less dramatic next time.

Allen kept playing with the controls as Ruby walked across the stage.

Joel looked like he wanted to stand up and reach a hand out and touch Ruby.

She looked beautiful, and confident. Jali had done herself up proud.

Ruby stood in the center middle of the stage for a long moment.

Allen had gotten the volume right. When Ruby spoke, her voice sounded calm and smooth, like a good drink. "Good evening. I am so very pleased to be here. I know many of you have heard my music. This is the very first time I have sung live for the people from the *Diamond Deep*." She paused to allow a light smattering of applause that was mirrored in the bar. "I'll begin from the moment our people learned we were coming home."

Music swelled; the first high notes of "Homecoming" played on instruments Onor had never heard, higher and more haunting than their own. As Ruby's voice started right on beat, perfect, he let out a sigh of relief.

If only he was with her. He raised his glass and smiled at Joel, who touched his glass to Onor's.

They both drank.

CHAPTER FIFTY-SEVEN

As the last of the applause wound down, Ruby took a final bow. Sweat poured between her shoulder blades even though she'd only sung ten songs; five of hers and five traditionals from the ship. After each song there had been clapping and applause. In between, as she parceled out a few sentences about the *Fire* between songs, there had been respectful silence.

She had succeeded.

She ran to the wings, the stage lights flicking off as she left it, house lights coming up behind her. She turned to look: people stood, some still staring at the place where she had just been, others gathering their things. She glanced at the board. Virtual numbers clicked down as people logged off, but the highest amount was posted there in glowing orange letters. Eighty-seven thousand. The size of the audience hit her in the gut, and she turned away from it.

Jali plucked at her sleeve and Ani came up from behind and whispered, "You were magnificent."

The dim light of backstage was enough to show how pleased Naveen looked. She glanced back at the gallery, still full of people. If you added it all up, there had been nearly a hundred thousand people, and all of them were people she had never met. She had no idea how she'd been brave enough to sing to them all.

"We have to go," Jali said.

"Go where?"

"Time to change. We have a party to go to."

Her whole focus had been on the performance, and now she wanted to sit and eat something and relax. Instead, she was rushed to a dressing room where Ani and Jali pulled her stage clothes off and put her into a short blue dress with her signature multiple colors lining the neckline and falling down one side in ribbons that tickled her elbow.

Naveen stood outside the door, shifting his weight and looking pained, but Jali fussed and whispered, "No worry, no hurry."

"Just bring him a drink next time," Ruby whispered. She closed her eyes and swayed. She shouldn't be this tired.

"Sit," Jali said. She let the lock of Ruby's hair she was working on fall. "Was it that hard?"

"So many people." She checked the mirror. She looked like she felt. "Can I have some stim?"

"I'll get it." Ani headed out the door, leaving Jali and Ruby alone.

"Can you do this?" Jali asked.

"The concerts, or the parties?"

"This party." Jali glanced toward the door Naveen had just knocked on—again. "The one that's he's so impatient for."

Ruby laughed. "I don't think I have a choice."

Jali's tight-lipped return smile felt like confirmation.

Ruby blinked and looked around. "Where's Min?"

"KJ took her off somewhere. He's probably giving her the third degree."

Ruby winced. They had traveled a day, slept a night, and rose to prepare; Ruby had worked with light and instrument programs all day.

They'd have a few down days now. There were two to three days between each of the events Naveen had set up. They were going from where they had docked the *Fire*, out along the long line of the *Deep* and back. Weeks.

Jali spent another ten minutes teasing Ruby's hair into loose curls. As a last flourish, Jali slid Ruby's feet into small white sandals.

Ruby took a last long look in the mirror. "I'd rather wear one of our uniforms. Did you bring any?"

"No. And you can't wear a made-over military-style uniform to a party anyway."

"We all did. On docking day."

"And we looked naïve for it."

Ruby frowned at the mirror and the dress. In truth, she loved being coddled, but it was at odds with what she felt. Kind of like the way this beautiful, vibrant society that had people like Lake and places like the Brawl in its underbelly. Like a surface smile from a thug with a fist below the table.

Ani returned with three small cups of stim. "Naveen only let me bring a little. He said we have to hurry."

"Of course he did." Ruby drank all three cups, one after another. "What about a work jumpsuit? This is beautiful, but I feel like a present in it."

Jali unclipped and reclipped Ruby's hair, whatever she changed so small Ruby didn't see why she bothered. "Look, you are a present to these people. Look how many came. They adore you."

The people in the Brawl needed her more than these people. She had taken on a whole society once, but that whole society would have fit inside this concert hall. "Can you make an outfit that looks like our old work jumpsuits? Like the last concert on the *Fire*?"

"I can do anything if I have enough time."

"Bless you." The stim was helping. She felt like she could stay awake for another few hours. "Let's go."

They opened the door. Naveen's face went from worried to pleased. "That's beautiful."

Naveen held Ruby's arm as they neared the party. The corridor of the *Star Bear* was bathed in the murmur of conversation. Instead of letting her through the door, he held her still for a second and spoke to someone she couldn't see. As Naveen urged Ruby forward she tried to gauge the number of guests at the party, but the inside of the room looked like a vast seething mass of color touched by a very soft, warm light.

A wash of bright white light landed on her face, forcing her to blink. Naveen's voice came from speakers overhead. "Ruby Martin."

An announcement of her presence.

The closest people turned, greeting her, adding congratulations. Their dress and eyes and hair and makeup and jewelry demanded attention. Many were tall and thin-limbed, obviously changed. The hands she shook had long painted fingernails, or long fingers, or seemed so strong they couldn't just be normal hands.

The spotlight stuck with her for a minute, and then swung the other way as another name was mentioned. After that another, then another. Ruby leaned close to Naveen and whispered, "Who are those people?"

"One is another singer, one a writer, and two are part of the ruling Council. There's a rumor that Stevenson himself might show up."

Naveen had told her a little about the way the station was governed. Councilors dealt with the economy. Internal struggles were handled by a peacekeeper force like the reds from the *Fire*, but which wore no obvious uniforms. There was a defense force and a court system. Headman Stevenson oversaw the whole thing.

"Will you introduce me to Headman Stevenson if he comes?"

"If he comes it will be to meet you. But first, I want you to meet Satyana."

"The owner of the *Star Bear?*" She reached across Naveen to take another hand, this one tinged a slight orange, the fingers all sporting silver and blue rings.

"And a patron of yours. You made her a lot of credit tonight."

The orange hand withdrew and they went on. The faces of people who came up to meet her began to blur by the time Naveen led her to a small table, and she was sure she'd lost all track of names. A large woman who sat opposite a small one got up to give Ruby her seat, going to stand behind the small one. A bodyguard, then.

The compact woman had brown skin, deep blue eyes of a color Ruby had never seen, brighter by far than her own pale blue ones, and thick black hair that flowed down her back in soft waves. She was absolutely beautiful, but none of that beauty came from her simple yellow outfit or from makeup or baubles. Rather, there was a strength in her that Ruby recognized instinctively. She had power. Feminine power. The hand that Satyana held out was unadorned, and when Ruby shook it, she felt calluses along the ridge of the woman's palm. "Pleased to meet you."

"Of course. Thank you for the lovely concert."

"Thank you for sponsoring me, and for holding this party."

Satyana's gaze was friendly, but assessing.

Ruby's friends, including Naveen, had been seated at a nearby table and were already ordering drinks from a human waitress. "May we get you anything?"

"Tea, please. Something that will help give me energy. And water."

Satyana smiled. "Excellent." She turned to the woman behind her. "Britta, will you also see that someone brings us a snack?"

Britta looked taken aback by the chore, but she faded into the crowd anyway. Satyana leaned close. "I would like to tour you around the outside of the station tomorrow. Just us. It was part of what I made Naveen agree to in order to book you."

Ruby had promised Joel she wouldn't go anywhere alone. "I'd like that." After all, Joel was far away. The little defiance felt good.

"I'll pick you up after lunch tomorrow. Wear something comfortable."

Ruby liked her already. Britta appeared with blue liquid in small glasses and a plate of small candies, fruits, and round chips decorated with colorful spreads. Ruby took one of the chips. "How long have you been here?"

She laughed softly. "Longer than you've been alive." She gestured around the room. "Most of the people who could afford to attend this are older than me, and more powerful. Although entertaining well does give one some sort of power, don't you think?"

"I suppose." She had not seen anyone like these people in the Exchange, not really. The guests at this party were physically soft, with calculating eyes. "Tell me stories. What do these people do?"

Satyana sipped from her blue drink. "They run things. They manage credit, or ships, or people. A few have simply been given riches by their families. Ask me about a specific person and I'll try and tell you."

Ruby pointed to a tall man with long white hair decorated in feathers. "What about that one?"

"He created a series of healthcare bots when he was young. Made it rich early. Now he mostly looks pretty, but once in a while he starts a new company, makes a bunch of credits, sells it, relaxes for a while. At the moment, he's in a rest period."

"Okay." She pointed at a tall woman—almost everyone in here was tall—a woman who was taller than most of the rest of them, her skin and face all reddish-blue.

"That's Ferrell Yi. She runs Exchange Five."

"She owns it?"

Satyana laughed. "No. Each Exchange has a manager. But assume she is powerful, and that she is paid well. The Exchanges are all owned by the people, by all of us."

Ruby raised an eyebrow.

"Well, and run by the Council. The profit they don't take gets used to pay for central services."

"Which are?"

"Transportation. Air. Water. Basic education."

The blue drink tasted sweeter than Ruby liked, and she had to work to drink it. Curiously, her thoughts almost immediately seemed clearer. "What's in this?"

Satyana had her own cup. "Plants. They are chosen to add energy to your system."

"It's good. Does the Council pay for the Brawl?"

"Of course. Although in a way, we all do. The credit comes from the tax." Satyana leaned over. "Turn around. It's Stevenson."

The Headman appeared from behind Ruby, offering her a hand. "That was beautifully done. You grace our station."

He was both tall and broad, with swirling brown tattoos on his forearms and neck, a simple black shirt that flowed over black pants and black boots, and strings of colored beads that might have come from the *Fire*. It rocked her to see her symbol on him, silencing her voice for a moment. She swallowed her reaction—part anger and part confusion—and managed to say, "It's a pleasure to meet you. Thank you for coming to hear me."

His smile disconcerted her almost as much as the beads around his neck. "How could I miss the newest sensation here?"

She blushed in spite of herself. "Thank you for the greenery. It made Ash much prettier."

He smiled. "You're welcome."

She searched for words. "The *Diamond Deep* is quite fascinating."

"There is much I could show you. Will you join me for dinner next week?"

Instinct told her no. But surely this was a man with power she needed to understand. "Naveen keeps my schedule. He'll know if there is time." He had eyes the color of the tattoos on his arms, a brown similar to some of the colors Naveen favored, but the irises were a very dark black. He frightened her in a way no known enemy ever had. "If it can be arranged, my assistant and my bodyguard will join us, of course."

His eyes actually seemed to darken. But his smile widened and he gave a half-bow toward her. "I will have my people schedule time with you through the inimitable Naveen." He turned to Satyana. "Excellent use of your venue. You've done well tonight."

Satyana inclined her head a very tiny amount, as if acknowledging his power. "Thank you for gracing my party."

He turned away then, and Ruby glanced over at Naveen. He was deep in conversation with KJ, and she wasn't even sure he had seen the Headman. But Min was staring hard at her.

She turned back to find Satyana looking contemplative. "He likes beautiful women." She eyed Ruby. "He does not like to be told no."

"I have a partner."

"That will not matter very much to him." Then Satyana laughed. "You are a spitfire, aren't you?"

"What is that?"

"Brave. I like brave women." Satyana stood. She barely came to Ruby's shoulder. "I'll pick you up tomorrow morning. Naveen has the details."

On the short train ride from the *Star Bear* back to their rooms, Ruby sat beside Min, her eyes so heavy she had to force them open. Her words sounded slurred even though she'd had no alcohol all night. "I'm sorry I haven't been able to talk to you yet. Thank you for coming."

Min gave her an odd look. "Thank you for allowing us to continue to watch you."

That wasn't quite what Ruby had expected to hear. "As you've watched me, what have you seen?"

Min went quiet. Ruby was almost asleep in spite of her best intentions when Min said, "I don't know yet. You like attention, and you draw it. Men and women flock to you, and power comes to you."

"We need attention, and I'm working as hard as I can to see we get it."

A flashing light from outside of the train briefly illuminated Min's face, emphasizing the scar. "Did you bring us here so you could have attention?"

"To the *Deep*?"

Min nodded.

"We had to go somewhere." It wasn't a good answer, but she didn't have a better one.

Min went quiet again.

This was not the vibrant woman she'd met in common long before they landed. "Look," Ruby said, "You'll get to see a lot here. There are more important things for you to watch than me."

Min regarded her solemnly.

Maybe this had been a mistake. "It would help me if you could watch everything. Not just me. Watch it all. And tell me—and whoever else you want—everything you see. I'm not hiding anything here. I'm doing the best I can. Think of it as witnessing about me and for me at the same time. As witnessing for the colony."

Min didn't respond one way or the other. But just as the train was stopping, she whispered, "Your concert was good."

Ruby whispered back, "Thank you."

CHAPTER FIFTY-EIGHT

The next morning, Onor attempted to work the groggy feeling out of his head by wiping down the chairs and tables in the bar. Robots had cleaned the floor after closing, so Onor was trying to get all of the crumbs and bits swept into his hand so they wouldn't land on the floor.

Haric and Allen stood together, washing glasses in the bar sink. As Onor worked closer to the dishwashers, he asked, "So what did we make last night?"

"One thousand three hundred credits."

More than he'd thought. "Profit?"

"Well, not from outside. One hundred ten came in from outside, so if I listen to SueAnne, that's the most we could make."

At least they'd made something.

Onor glanced over at Haric. The boy had hardly said a word to him this morning. Maybe he was still smarting from Ruby's refusal to take him on the tour. "Want to go see the birds today? I'm sure you earned that much of the credit—transportation's only five for both of us."

"Take me to a bar?"

"You don't drink."

Allen laughed and addressed Haric. "You drank a little last night."

Haric's cheeks reddened.

Onor frowned. Ruby had told Haric not to drink. "Why a bar?"

"I want to get a job. So I can learn how to earn more credit."

Onor blinked at him.

"And I want to learn my way around."

So he could find Ruby? Poor kid had lost Colin to the spiders and now Ruby had left him. "Now?"

Haric's steady gaze said *yes, please* with no words.

"Can I show you the birds first?"

An hour later, they stood inside the aviary Naveen had shown Onor. Haric stared for a long time, entranced and puzzled. "I didn't know they'd be so much better than the picture you sent."

"Pretty cool, huh?"

"Can we have one? Can we take one back?"

Onor laughed. "Can you imagine SueAnne's face if we bring home another mouth to feed?"

Haric let out a long sigh and sat down on one of the benches, his eyes tracking a small, bright orange bird. "We're not learning fast enough. We need more than a job for me. We need jobs for a thousand people."

"You're starting to remind me of SueAnne."

Haric frowned.

"Start with your own job. Let's go." They started at the bar just outside the aviary. This was Haric's idea, so Onor stood outside and let him go in. Haric returned in ten minutes, a dejected look on his face. "They want experience."

"You have experience. In our bars. Lie a little, and count the time you were in the cargo bars."

"They want ten years."

"Oh. Maybe the others will be better."

They inquired at six bars—all they could reach without taking another train. By then, Haric looked so tired his feet dragged and his shoulders slumped, so he looked his age. He wasn't going to get any kind of job offer while he looked that that.

"Maybe we can talk to Naveen," Onor said. "He might have some connections. In the meantime, it's opening time for our own bar."

Haric had started dragging a few hours before closing time, so Onor had sent him home to dream of birds. With so few people, the robots had been left turned off and Onor and Allen were managing the whole bar, which had stayed pretty calm. It probably didn't hurt that Onor was known as one of Joel's bodyguards, and thus someone who could fight.

Allen went to encourage the locals home and Onor approached the only table with off-site patrons, where a man and a woman were deep in conversation. He'd noticed them earlier. Apparently new to the bar, they'd been pointing out details about the construction and the art on the walls to each other when he served them.

The woman was the taller, with a thin face. She reminded him of Marcelle, although she was lighter in coloring. The man was a stockier and shorter version of the woman; they could be brother and sister. She held up a hand in greeting as Onor approached.

"We're about to close."

The man looked around. "Can we talk to you?"

"Of course. About what?"

"Your losses," he said.

Onor gestured Allen over to the table. Allen stopped by the bar on the way and grabbed a pitcher of water and four cups. As he poured he eyed the newcomers curiously. "Do you like the bar?"

The man seemed mildly surprised by the question. "Well, sure. It's simple."

Onor downed half his water. "I'm Onor, and this is Allen."

The woman's voice sounded soft and full of backbone. "And we have chosen to be friends of the *People of the Fire*."

Onor frowned. "You asked me about our losses. Do you mean the ship?"

"Sort of."

He didn't like secrets. "So tell me what you did mean."

The man sat back. "Can you get Joel?"

So they knew something about the community. "Why?"

"We need a decision maker."

Onor used his slate to send Joel a message. Then he sent a separate note to SueAnne, hoping Joel wouldn't mind.

Allen offered to break his after-closing rule. "Would you like a real drink?"

"No." The woman's fingers went to her neckline, and he realized she was wearing one of Ruby's necklaces. Or a replica of one. It looked like all of the beads were stone, which they hadn't had on the *Fire*. The gesture looked natural, but he wondered if she were sending a signal the way players messaged their teammates in a game of Planazate. "We enjoyed Ruby's concert the other day very much."

"Thank you. What did you like the best?"

The man answered, "Her voice."

The woman's answer was more emotional. "The song for Owl Paulie. The way it had layers, love and revolution all lined up. It must have been terribly romantic to have to fight your way to equality. Your story sounds like an adventure video, and Ruby looks like a real heroine. It must have been so—intense."

Allen looked unhappy with the conversation. "Have you ever seen anyone killed?"

"No, but we've known people who died."

"Of disease?"

"Or who were killed—like in accidents. It doesn't happen much. We don't see death." She paused uncertainly. "Or at least I haven't." The woman reached for the pitcher and refilled everyone's glasses. "I admit that part must have been hard."

Allen—out of view of either of them—shook his head in disbelief. Onor managed to keep a straight face. "I was there when Owl Paulie told us all to rebel."

"I thought Ruby led the rebellion," the man mused.

"Oh, she did. Owl Paulie was dead by then. But it wouldn't have started without him."

"Do you have any pictures of him?" the woman asked. "We have pictures of you and Ruby and Marcelle and The Jackman and others, but I don't think we have any of Owl Paulie."

Joel walked in, pushing SueAnne.

The couple refused to give their names to Joel and SueAnne as well, which Joel took with a sour face. SueAnne looked like she had been dragged out of bed. She wore no jewelry and her gray hair flowed wispy and loose around her shoulders and touched the edge of her chair. She started the conversation. "What can we do for you at this hour?"

"You should look into how your cargo was sold."

"On the Exchange?" Joel asked.

"There are records of every transaction that happens there. Your AI must know where to look."

"What AI?" Onor asked. No one was supposed to know they had a copy of Ix.

SueAnne reacted smoothly. "Our community net here is not at an AI level."

"We have looked up some of the information." The man sounded hesitant. "Maybe we can share some of it with you."

"What did you find?" Joel asked.

"Do you know everything that was in your cargo bays?"

Onor could see Joel hesitate. Eventually he said, "We have some records. We also have our memories."

"Do you remember a series of rocks from Gaither's World? The first place you went?"

Allen had been silent, but now he said, "I played with them once, I think. They were heavy, right? And mostly black."

"They were geodes. That means they had crystals in them. The chemical makeup is very different from anything in our system, and the colors are pretty. One of Koren's companies is creating a demand for jewelry made from these crystals. That's a beginning."

It dawned on Onor what they meant. "So we should get paid a part of what she makes off of everything?"

The woman smiled. "We believe the cargo was legally yours. She should not be getting anything for it."

"Even if it's salvage, you should have far more than she gave you. Hundreds of times more."

"Okay. But why do you care?" Onor asked.

"Perhaps we share the same enemies."

"Koren?"

"Not only Koren. Others. We might be allies."

SueAnne said, "Really? Why? We hardly know our way around here at all. I'm not even sure we can find a privy outside of this area yet. Why do you think we have anything to offer to you?"

"Didn't you see how many people watched the concert?"

Onor bit his lip, immediately even more distrustful.

Joel said, "The *Deep* is nothing like the *Fire*. There, we knew who our enemies were and how to hide."

"You know some of your enemies. Koren. Anyone with power. Your coming and your story is a threat to the power structure here."

"Really?" Joel asked. "We don't appear to have much power."

The man laughed. "Stories of revolution have more power than you think. Especially when they have a flesh and blood avatar."

Joel sat back and stayed quiet for some time. Then he looked at the man and asked, "Would it put Ruby in danger if we help you?"

The woman appeared to be affected by Joel's concern. She smiled softly at Joel and said, "She's already in danger. You all are."

The man leaned forward and looked from Joel to SueAnne. "It will serve both of our causes if you can question Koren in the Court of the Deeping Rules. We will help you to the extent we can—we can't get caught. But we will be working to weaken her in other ways. We can't allow the *Fire*'s cargo to be a fortune machine for her. Why not help yourselves and attack the woman who stole from you?"

SueAnne pursed her lips and looked at Joel, shifting the burden of choice to him.

He simply said, "We'll consider what you've shared with us."

The couple stood. "We can ask for nothing more. Good luck. Don't underestimate Koren or anyone else currently in power."

CHAPTER FIFTY-NINE

Satyana gave Ruby's outfit a doubtful look. "Can you belt that shirt? You really won't want anything flowing."

Satyana wore a form-fitting green jumper. Her shoes appeared to blend into the outfit, although when Ruby looked closely they were separate. The tops closed perfectly around the base of Satyana's calves and the tight-fitting pants slid over them. A small but bulging-full pack hung over one shoulder.

"I don't have anything like that," Ruby said.

"I'll see that Naveen knows where to get you one. They're great under pressure suits."

Ruby realized she'd missed the connection. "Hold on. Let me find a better outfit."

"Tell your people I'll have you half the day. At least."

"Okay. Come in?"

"I'll wait."

Ruby went back into their rooms and dressed a second time. Jali, who shared a room with her, rolled over and opened her eyes. "Noisy girl."

"I need something tighter to wear. Come look at what Satyana's wearing."

"Now?"

"Well, maybe when we get back. It's kind of like our old uniforms only so tight it's like wearing skin."

"Is uniforms all you think about? Why do I keep dressing you up?"

Ruby laughed. "I really do need that jumpsuit. The one for the stage. To go with the microphone gun."

"You brought that damned thing from the ship?"

"Yes."

"It's not exactly in context here."

Ruby grinned. "I know."

Jali sat up and raked her fingers through her hair. In the mornings, she looked almost like a normal human being instead of a goddess of fashion. She narrowed her eyes and looked closely at Ruby. "Are you feeling better this morning?"

"As long as I don't think about it."

"You need a few days' rest."

"I'll sleep when we get back to Ash."

Jali looked more worried than she should. Ruby was tired, but she'd driven herself through it yesterday at the concert with no problem. She'd get herself through today just as well. "I'll be all right. Whatever it is, it will get better."

Jali looked sour, but she said, "Bring us back tales."

Satyana looked at the tight gray pants and close-fitting purple shirt Ruby wore. "A little fancy for our trip, but much better." She led Ruby back to the *Star Bear*.

The pressure suits here were a dream. In the *Fire*, she'd needed to strip. Here, she needed bare feet and bare hands to slide into the boots and gloves, and to tuck everything else in. The material was as thin as underwear, and the helmets were clear and easy to see through, and so light she barely felt the weight. She understood Satyana's outfit now—with no loose clothes or even seams to bunch up, she looked beautiful even in the pressure suit. There was no mirror, but Ruby suspected *she* looked rather lumpy. "So," Ruby asked. "Where are we going?"

"I wanted to give you a sense of the size and complexity of the *Deep*. Think of it as a trade for a good concert." Satyana led her into an airlock. They stood together in the quiet moment of air escaping. The suit expanded and tickled her spine. Out the other side, they stepped into a cramped interior bay of the *Star Bear*.

Ruby counted four little ships. "We had these on the *Fire*, or something like them. I was never in one. They were for when we landed at planets, and of course, the last time we did that was hundreds of years ago." She remembered that Satyana could be hundreds of years old. "Generations ago."

Satyana used a series of lines to lead Ruby through null-g to the smallest of the ships, a squat and ugly thing that stood on six legs and had other appendages folded against the hull. "This is a repair bee. In a fit of imagination, we named it *Honey*."

Ruby laughed, even though she didn't understand the reference.

Satyana managed a slow, stately jump up into the doorway of the *Honey*, and extended a hand to help Ruby into the craft.

Inside, *Honey* barely had room for the two of them and Satyana's pack in the front. Two more seats sat facing backwards, but they were full of tools and clothes. "Good thing I didn't bring anything," Ruby said.

Satyana laughed. "She's small, but she's fun."

Once the hatches were all dogged down and everything appeared ready to go, Ruby asked, "Can I take my helmet off?"

"Not yet. But strap in."

Ruby had to watch Satyana carefully to figure out how to get that done. The straps were wide and thick, and the buckles unfamiliar. A door irised open in front of them, and Satyana piloted the small craft through it so smoothly that Ruby barely felt the movement.

Not that they were moving fast.

Satyana spoke into her microphone, communicating with the ship. "Exit check, please."

She fell silent long enough for Ruby to wonder what an exit check was, when the ship responded, "Neutralized."

In response to Ruby's quizzical look, Satyana said, "It clears the ship of listening devices. I special-ordered the *Honey* so that she has a shielded command and control system, and the ability to burn out unwanted tech."

"So someone was listening?"

Satyana laughed. "Someone was hoping to."

"Like who?"

Satyana shrugged. "Could have been a competitor." She must have noticed Ruby's blank face, since she added, "Someone who wanted to know more about my business so they could steal my customers. Maybe catch me saying something I shouldn't and get me in trouble."

"Wow. I don't understand the way you people think."

"Happens all the time. It's not something you can be naïve about. In this case, maybe someone wanted a scoop on you. Naveen has given you value, and your concert last night added more value, so it could be one of his competitors instead of one of mine."

"Naveen told me to be careful who I talked to. He said you're safe."

"Did he?" Satyana's fingers danced over a panel of light in front of her, shifting bars one way and then another too fast for Ruby to follow. She stopped for a moment and glanced at Ruby. "It could have been one of your enemies."

Everything seemed like a fight on this station. The very thought of living like that wearied her. "But don't you have security? How would someone get in here?"

"Wouldn't need to be a person." Satyana relaxed back into her chair. "You can take your helmet off now. And loosen your seat-straps, but don't take them all the way off." Satyana took her helmet and her shoes off. "There are cameras too small to see; robots that would fit on the tip of your finger, and that separate into smaller robots and swarm back; there are pseudo-AIs that people have figured out how to trick. The less-competent robots around here are often hacked. It's a high-stakes game for the bored."

The air smelled of grease and metal and the closeness of a recycled atmosphere. Kind of like the *Fire*, only without the added scents of growing things and food. It felt good to be off the *Deep* and away from crowds. "You're right. This station is a wonder of confusing things." Ruby watched Satyana's profile. Could she take a risk? She took a deep breath. "What about human/machine hybrids? I heard a rumor those existed."

"They're not allowed anywhere in the inside system. There are some at the Edge. I met one once."

"What happened? Why aren't they allowed?"

"In truth they are, at least in some ways. There are machine aids to the human brain. Mostly they're legal for simple enhancements like better and clearer vision or hearing. Some more dramatic mods are illegal, but can still be obtained. There's always a few want-to-be superheroes. But the process of going the other way—of putting a human brain into a machine? That's illegal."

"Why?"

"It destroys the human. And human brains in robot bodies go insane eventually. Almost always."

The *Honey* had an actual window. Ruby touched it. She had never seen a true window to space; everything on the *Fire* had been a picture created by Ix and displayed for them. The station receded in the window. "Are the hybrids who live at the Edge insane?"

Satyana shrugged. "I've only been there twice. In general, it's frowned on to go to the Edge. One can only come up with thin excuses so often."

"Why *would* you go to the Edge?"

"Adventure. Curiosity. Kindness. A patron paid me to go there and bring a whole barge of food once. I suspect she was also smuggling other stuff to them, but I was as naïve as you then."

"In the *Star Bear*?"

"Oh no, this was three hundred years ago. I was young and stupid then."

"So are all the people on the Edge hybrids?"

"No." Satyana smiled. "You should worry more about the challenges you have here. There are even more than you think." She grinned. "And I plan to present you with a proposition."

Ruby waited.

Satyana fiddled with the controls, slowing the craft so it drifted above the station. The *Star Bear* filled most of the window, a large rounded oblong of a ship with nothing svelte about it. Satyana stared at it, as if she seldom saw her own ship from this viewpoint. "There is opportunity here. A lot of it." She goosed the little ship so it drove backward, making the *Star Bear* look a little smaller. "You're new. You have the freshest eyes that have seen our society. Maybe in forever. What do you think?"

"I love how varied everything is. The birds are amazing, and the food. But some things here are wrong."

"Tell me."

"Well, it's hard to live here. Everyone has to earn air and food somehow. We just made them for everyone."

Satyana drove the *Honey* forward, toward the outside center of the station. "*The Creative Fire* was a ship. This is a society. Think of the *Deep* as more like a planet than a ship."

"People on planets don't take care of their own? Just people on starships?"

Satyana frowned. "That's not what I mean."

"Then can you explain the Brawl?"

Satyana focused very intently on the controls for the *Honey*.

"Can you?" Ruby whispered.

"In any society, there are winners and losers."

"So you hide the losers?"

Satyana still wasn't looking at Ruby. "It's not hard to earn air and food. Three days or so a week of work."

Ruby stayed quiet to force Satyana to think or talk, a trick she'd learned from Joel.

They flew slowly over and around structures. Once the *Honey* came too close and a small warning beep filled the cabin. Ruby didn't comment on it.

Time stretched, only slightly awkward since there was so much to see.

Satyana broke first, laughing, her face relaxing. "People tell me *I'm* single-focused. Are all revolutionaries so fucking irritating?"

"Do you believe that if you don't talk about the Brawl it isn't there? "

"No."

"Have you ever gone there?"

"No."

"Even just to see it?"

"No."

The *Honey* crept up over a pile of arms and booms and other structures and opened onto a field of bubbles open to the sun. Each of them looked mostly clear on the outside, full of greens and golds on the inside, and in a few places, dots of orange. "One of our agricultural fields. There are five, and every time the station grows by a certain amount of new people, another agrifield is created and planted. The sixth one is being designed now. See the dark lines at the edges?"

Each bubble had a dark top, all of them oriented the same, although a few looked darker that the others. "Yes."

"Those will flow down the bubbles at a certain time, like a sunset. Agribubbles keep the station's day and night cycles, which are synced to Lym's. It's gives the plants a cycle they understand, with built-in day and night."

"I've never seen a sunset." The *Honey* floated above the bubbles. The smallest of them was ten times the size of the little ship, the largest ten times that again. "Is it all food?"

"We plant a bubble of flowers or greenfield plants in every field—like the ones that you see in pots around most habs. It's something this station is proud of, one of the reasons the *Deep* grew in the beginning. Beauty for the sake of it—beauty because the human soul needs it. The others all do this now, of course."

Ruby knew Satyana was trying to change the subject, but she couldn't help herself. "Is that enough food for everyone?"

"Of course. We also sell food to ships that come through here to dock."

"So we pay to grow it and we make the poor pay to eat it?"

Satyana looked frustrated with her. "You've got to pay the people who work here." She pointed. "There's a forest bubble in the middle—see the big one? There's only three on the whole station. It's part of why we flew this way." She nudged the *Honey* closer. "They make nothing. They're there to be beautiful, and to keep a complex ecosystem to grow certain medicines in. I think they're also there because people love them. There are even fake rocks, so it's almost like being on a planet. Some of the richer people here who started on Lym like to vacation there. It's expensive to go to them, but I can take you some day."

If Ruby understood perspective and size and distance in this situation, the trees inside were enormous. There were trees in the aviary, and those had astounded her. These would dwarf them. "Are there birds?"

"Some. Smaller ones. No mammals though."

Ruby frowned. "Meaning no animals?"

"Insects and birds."

"I want to go to Lym sometime. None of us have ever even seen a planet." She had trouble looking away from the forest bubble. "I appreciate the things you've done for me. Setting up the concert. Taking me out here. It would be even more credit for you to take me inside of the forest bubble, right?"

"You made me a lot of credit last night. I'd like for that to happen again, for you to come back to the *Star Bear* and perform."

"I enjoyed that."

"I also want you to understand some things about the *Deep*. I think you may be able to help me some day. Many things happen on the station because people can help each other."

Ruby tried not to react badly to the slightly condescending tone Satyana was using. Maybe it meant the woman would underestimate her. "What do you need help with?"

"There are a lot of powerful people on the *Deep*. Factions, if you will. People who have resources."

"Like you?"

Satyana laughed. "No. Well, yes. But like me with many, many more credits. Koren is one of them. The woman who bought the right to greet you."

Ruby swallowed. Bought the ability to greet them? "She didn't present it that way."

"Of course not. You wouldn't have understood that anyway."

Ruby's cheeks warmed. Maybe she wasn't being underestimated. Maybe she was stupid, after all. "Not much is as simple as it appears here, is it?"

"Of course not." Satyana pointed at a series of bubbles with yellow-golds and soft greens in them. "Those are grain fields. We grow many kinds of grains."

She couldn't focus on grain. Her head whirled at the idea of people bidding to take advantage of her and her people. "How many people offered on the ability to greet us?"

Satyana shrugged. "At least a few. It made the news—or more accurately, Naveen reported on it. That's what made me notice at all. The *Deep* is huge, and a lot happens here that very few people notice."

"Did you bid?"

Satyana laughed. "I couldn't. I'm not in a discipline, and even after all these years, I'm not exactly in the middle of the power structure here."

"Is Koren really a historian?"

"Yes. She's the station's main historian. But any of a number of heads of disciplines could have won. Engineering. Social Engineering. Medical."

"So it wasn't really a complete free-for-all?"

"The disciplines are backed by credit. Koren had backers."

"Who?"

"We don't know yet."

"We?"

"Me or Naveen."

Ruby's stomach felt sour. "They weren't bidding to greet us. They were bidding to steal the *Fire*."

Satyana reached for the small pack. "That's not quite accurate. They were bidding for your cargo, and for your information. New information can give people who want to craft new products an edge." She dug out a blue square and held it out toward Ruby.

"I don't really like those."

"This one is good."

"Okay." She touched her tongue to the square, let the sweet flavor sit in her mouth. "It is good. So people competed to steal from us. They compete for everything here, though. Right? What's so different?"

"Nothing. I'm trying to make sure you understand that there are people with a lot of power." She drove the *Honey* to the edge of the field of agribubbles, and pointed past it. "See the habitats on the edge there, the big ones?"

"Sure."

"That's one of the places that some of our most influential people live. I can't take you there. All of the ways into them are keyed and hidden, and the prox alarms go off before you get a ship like this close enough to see anything. Special trains connect those places to the other habitats."

Ruby stared at the private bubbles, lost in thought.

"But you'll be invited to them. I wanted you to have context."

"How do you know I'll get invited?"

"You already have been."

They floated silently over the agribubbles, high enough to look out at the homes of people with power Ruby was having trouble imagining. "What do you want from that? Why?"

Satyana shook her head. "To start with, I want you to meet some people. Naveen has made you attractive to the common people of the station, but to get true safety, you need to meet people who may give you what I did, only at a higher level."

Ruby thought a moment. "You gave me a place to play, but you're like Naveen. More credit went to you than to us."

Satyana gave her a long look. "We're driven by that. By credit. All of us. But don't see us as that shallow. I want some of the same things you do."

"What things?"

"More fairness."

Ruby ate the blue square, slowly. This one was sublime; as different from what they had been fed during quarantine as the *Fire* was from the *Deep*. Even though it tasted good, food didn't calm her stomach as much as she expected it to.

Satyana squinted at her. "That's not enough for lunch."

"I know. I'm not hungry."

"You look queasy. Should I take you home?"

"No." When would she have another chance to see the station from near-space? Ix had filled the map table with images on the way in, but this was much more intimate.

Satyana's face had grown worried. "It wouldn't do to have something happen to you when we're way out here. The *Honey* is too small for a decent medikit.

"I'm all right."

"Take a good look at those bubbles. You'll meet people that most residents of the *Deep* don't even know exist. You may be invited to their houses. This is nearly impossible, but for you it's happening without effort."

Promising Satyana anything felt wrong. "I can think about it. My first focus needs to be on my people, on getting us established."

"This will help you. If you get more popular, you'll earn more credit."

Ruby stared at the huge bubbles, only part of the station. She couldn't imagine the power it took to build them, or the technology. All of the control that the greens and the reds had wielded now seemed small. The petty authority that she and Joel had now, which was more like thankless work than being a captain and his lover, seemed even smaller. She wished Onor were here. His fascination with power could be useful.

The view still made her think of the Brawl.

She took a sip of water, remembering how so many people had told her less than the truth. She hadn't caught Naveen in lies yet, and Naveen trusted Satyana. "Can you tell me who you want me to meet?"

Satyana looked like she had expected more, but she responded with grace. "No. But I will see that you meet them."

Ruby didn't like the secrecy. She stared at the huge bubbles of life in front of them and pursed her lips. Perhaps she could use some of her influence more directly. "Do you have any work that some of my people can do? Paid work?"

"Will that help persuade you to help me?"

"It will earn my gratitude. We need ways to learn how to survive here."

Satyana sat silently at the controls, looking out over the habitat bubbles. "You really do want to save everyone, don't you? Thousands of people?"

"Of course I do. I'm responsible for them."

"You'll break your heart."

Maybe it was already broken in this mystifying and difficult place.

"I'll take you back. Belt in."

Ruby's stomach argued with her and she felt cramped as she strapped back in, the lower strap across her waist compressing her belly. It took a half an hour of steady flying to return to the *Star Bear*.

On the other side of the airlock, KJ, Dayn, and Ani stood against the wall, looking as though they hadn't been worried.

Dayn raised an eyebrow at her. "Didn't you promise Joel you wouldn't run away without one of us?"

Satyana shook her head as if bemused, and then lied smoothly. "The ship was too small for three." She glanced at Ruby. "I'll release you to your keepers. Next time you call home, have someone pick three men and three women to send over here to work."

Not enough. "Can I send forty?"

Satyana stopped and gave her a cool, measured look. "Twenty. For two weeks. Then we'll evaluate. They'll have to be excellent, and they'll have to start at half-wages until they're trained. Remember, this is a business."

How could she forget? "Thank you."

"You can't go off with people by yourself," KJ echoed Dayn as soon as Satyana was out of earshot. "If she'd stolen you, we would have never found you."

KJ's voice sounded smooth like always, calm to the core. Nevertheless, Ruby sensed tension. "I didn't mean to worry you."

"I'll have to tell Joel."

"Why?"

"Because I work for him."

Ruby's feet felt heavy and thick after all that sitting. She leaned against the wall. "Don't you work for both of us? Didn't you hear I just got us twenty jobs?"

"That's a good thing," KJ said. "But if anything happens to you, I may not be able to go home. I'm here in Joel's stead to watch over you."

"And I'm an adult." Words were getting hard to get out and she slumped over.

"Are you okay?" Ani asked.

"Just give me a minute."

"Catch her," Dayn said.

Then there were arms around her, and the world spun inside her head and her belly and she felt herself being lifted.

CHAPTER SIXTY

Onor, SueAnne, Joel, and Allen sat around the bar table where they had met the strangers the night before. Once more, the bar was closed, the scent of cleaner in the air stronger than the leftover traces of food and spilled alcohol. The table in front of them held only simple breads and water, a sign that Joel was in warrior mode.

Joel was almost always above still, but Onor wished for more than water. It might be a long conversation.

Joel spoke first. "I didn't invite anyone else because rumors that we've been taken advantage of could be dangerous." He looked from one to another of them, his face serious.

Onor frowned. Ruby would have played it by sharing it with everyone. But when it was his turn, he said, "Okay."

"All right," Joel sat back. "What do you think of this claim?"

"Can we verify it?" Allen asked. "There could be real danger in taking Koren on."

SueAnne spoke next. "Someone's got to actually spend time learning how we would even talk about this. The couple last night implied that Koren is breaking laws, but who would we appeal to, and why would they listen to us? I can figure out some of that from here on my slate, and after that, maybe I can head to the Exchange and see what else I can find. I've developed a few contacts there."

"Thanks." Joel glanced at Onor.

"I think these people are right. Remember, I didn't like her from day one. Naveen didn't either. But I also don't like what they wouldn't tell us. They have their own goals. How do we know they'll protect us?"

Joel gave him an approving look before going all serious again. "We don't. And we must be very careful what we say to whom. Koren could have spies here."

"Like the whispering women?" Allen asked.

Joel laughed. "Irritations with no teeth. But strangers come in here. If one side of this argument found us, the other side could do so as well."

"True," Allen said. "I'll watch out for that. Bars are the best place in the world to hear about things."

Joel grunted at that.

Onor spoke up. "I have an idea about verification."

"Tell me."

"Use Haric. He's an old hand at mingling, he's looking for jobs out there, and was before these people found us so it won't look like he's doing anything new. No one will think we gave him anything important to do. He's too young."

Joel frowned.

"He wants to do something that matters," Onor said. "He would also recognize some of the cargo. He was a cargo rat."

SueAnne looked at Joel. "We can't do without you or Onor. Allen is best used here. So you do need help, and Haric is about the most earnest boy I've ever met. I think he can do this, and that he'd be happy about the chance to help."

Onor addressed SueAnne. "He'll need some credit."

"And you don't have any hidden here from the bar?"

Allen stiffened, but Onor saw her point. "That'll keep it off the official books."

SueAnne stared Allen down until he nodded.

"It might be dangerous," Joel said.

"I know." If anything happened to Haric, Ruby might scratch his eyes out.

CHAPTER SIXTY-ONE

Ruby opened her eyes and blinked to focus. She remembered waking a few times before, but she couldn't remember any conversations, or that she stayed awake for very long at all. This time, Ani and Jali were sitting at a table in her room, playing a game that required them to slide their slates back and forth between each other. "You still don't think it was poison?" Ani whispered.

"She's looked steadily worse since we left the *Fire*."

"I think she's sick of this place," Ani noted. "I certainly am."

Ruby pushed herself to sit up. Her lips and sinuses were so dry it hurt to breathe and her head ached. "Is there water?"

Jali looked up, dropping the slate onto the table. "On your bed stand." She stood up and handed Ruby the glass. "How do you feel?"

Her stomach still hurt, somewhere deep inside. But she couldn't say anything about that; it was too important to be strong. They all needed this tour. "When is the dinner?"

"What dinner?" Ani asked. "The one last night?"

Oh. "I slept that long?"

"We made excuses for you. Min and Naveen and few others went. They said the food was fabulous."

"What did you tell people?"

"That you were too tired from the concert, and that you'd perhaps had a bad reaction to some food."

"Naveen appears to have gotten Min drunk. That's about the only thing we heard that's worth reporting."

"Is Min okay?"

"She's sleeping it off."

Food. She should be hungry. The water helped. Maybe after she drank some more water, she'd be hungry. "I'm sorry. Not food, I hardly ate anything, and Satyana ate what I ate."

Jali laughed. "Don't be sorry for wearing yourself out. You're doing it for us." Her brows furrowed. "Maybe you should sleep some more."

Ruby stood up, tested her strength, shook her head. "I want to clean up, and eat."

Ani said, "Maybe we should bring one of our doctors over."

Jali stood next to Ruby, encourage Ruby to drape an arm over her shoulder. "I'll ask KJ about it."

"No," Ruby said. "I'll be fine. I'm sure I just wore myself out. I haven't really stopped since we got here. Maybe since the robot spiders. That's got to be it."

An hour, a shower, and a few pieces of bread later she did feel better. "There. Maybe you can buy me a day's time to keep resting? I have some songs I need to write."

Ani laughed. "Maybe you do feel better."

CHAPTER SIXTY-TWO

Onor lay beside Marcelle, one hand on her swelling stomach and the other propping his head up. She looked exhausted. He'd tried to get her to do less, but she'd simply looked at him with a "who would do this better?" look and he'd known not to press his luck.

"Are all of the children all right today?"

"Yes. We let two go home, in fact. But there's three women in with something strange. They're exhausted, I think. The worst is one of Lya's whispering women. She came in, claimed she was exhausted, and then passed out. Luckily she was sitting on the bed when she fell over. Lya made sure someone sat with her the whole time. When it was Lya's turn to watch over her, I visited with her. She looks so haunted still. Her hands shook. It was really weird. I asked her if she knew what was wrong and she told me no, she doesn't. She babbled about Ruby making sure they all stay locked up in here so they can't go out and about. It's as if just being stuck in Ash is killing her."

"Could they be working too hard?"

"Sure. Maybe I'll pass out next. Get one or two days of sleep in."

"Don't you dare. Pass out. You could do the sleeping bit, though. You could use it."

"You're not exactly well-rested."

He didn't answer that. "How is school going?"

"I overheard a group of the teenagers talking about figuring out how to go find their fortunes on a spaceship."

Onor chewed on his lower lip. "They need to make their fortunes doing something."

Marcelle rolled over to face him. "They need to help support us all."

"Ruby told me once that her biggest fear is that we won't all stay together. That the people of the *Fire* will scatter and get absorbed. I remember her face when she said it—she was fierce."

"What did you tell her?" Marcelle asked.

"That for now, she's right. If we want everyone to survive, we have to work together. But in the long run? If we learn enough to get along here, we'll go off into the *Deep* or off on other ships. We'll mix up with the people here."

"Yeah." Marcelle didn't sound happy. "The hard part is getting the kids to know the difference between now and in the future. It will really hurt if we lose all of the teens."

"Are they studying hard?"

"As hard as we were when Ruby demanded we learn how to pass Ix's mythical test to get us into the other levels."

"I'll talk to Joel about it if I can."

Marcelle looked dubious. "Aren't you guarding him?"

"Sure. Today we went over the books with SueAnne. Then we met with Haric to get him ready to go out into the world and search for bits of our cargo. But I wasn't alone with Joel once, and the meeting with SueAnne had five people in it. I stood against a wall and listened."

"How does Joel look?"

"Like he's missing half of himself. Like he's distracted. Sometimes. Other times he's focused as hell."

Marcelle touched Onor's cheek. "He is missing half of himself."

Onor winced.

Marcelle put a finger over his lips. "You are too, I can see it. You miss her."

"I'm worried about her."

"Of course you are. We all are. But it's working, right? People are paying to see her? The last time I saw SueAnne she actually had a smile on her face."

Onor nodded. "SueAnne still talks in time. She said Ruby gained us all two weeks in one concert. But the next one's not for two days and it's been two days, so we'll have lost almost a week of that before she sings again. She can't do this forever."

"I know."

The community had enough days of credit to get through the rest of the pregnancy. Marcelle would give birth in two months. But if they all ended up in the Brawl, the *Deep* would take the baby. They'd take all of the children.

Every day, he managed to go about his tasks and to keep learning, but under his determination there was always an uneasy fear, and below the fear, a sense of being unmoored.

He rubbed his fingers lightly along the soft skin of Marcelle's cheek and tucked a stray dark curl behind her ear.

Her stomach bounced against him. He whispered. "Kicking?"

"Kicking."

He sat up so that he could put both of his hands on her tummy. He held them still there for a long time, waiting for another kick.

Marcelle watched him with wide, soft eyes peering up from a face that had grown thinner with her pregnancy. "If you wait long enough, it will kick again."

"Does it hurt?"

"It tells me the baby is alive. It reminds me why I have to keep going."

"It helps me, too. Not just the kicks. The baby at all. It keep me going."

The ends of her mouth quirked up. "Really? Are you happy about it?"

No. He wished they hadn't created such a fragile thing right now. "I'm scared for it. I want to make sure we give it a future. It keeps me working to understand this place, to try and find out how to get back some of what is ours. It gives me something more to care about."

"More?"

"More than you. More than all of us." The look on her face made him realize he needed to say more. "I want us all to be safe. I love you."

As if it agreed with him, the baby kicked.

CHAPTER SIXTY-THREE

Dayn walked in front of Naveen and Ruby, looking left and right, alert. He had taken on a shepherding role since the tour began. From time to time he looked back at Ruby, as if making sure she was still there. He was so serious it made her feel warm and a bit odd; Dayn had been her watcher since she was essentially Fox's captive years ago. KJ walked on her other side. Ani, Jali, and Min all followed close behind. She felt surrounded, enclosed. Almost suffocated.

Naveen put a hand on her arm. "This will be the best after-concert party ever. You'll be amazed. The man who put it on for you—Gunnar Ellensson— owns the biggest cargo operation between here and Mammot."

"What do they take back and forth?" She remembered the game. "Mammot doesn't have as much as Lym."

"There are precious metals which are more easily mined than made."

"I thought your invisible machines could do anything."

"They can. Some things they do better than nature. Others, not so much. Remember, we can live on food squares, but we thrive with real food."

"Where are we going?"

Now Naveen grinned even wider. "The party is in one of the secret bubbles."

She didn't think secret was the right word. More like hidden in plain sight, like a taunt. Satyana had showed her the outside of the bubble homes of the ultra-rich. Ix had shown them the whole outside of the station.

His excitement was riding high, his eyes shiny, his breath already laced with a tinge of alcohol. Ruby didn't like him in this mood, didn't appreciate him being so sure of himself. It made her nervous. But for now, she needed him. She took his arm and smiled.

They boarded a small train of cars that had clearly been designed to carry people and cargo along a single wide corridor that passed between bubbles. The seats felt soft and looked as if they had just been recovered. Silver hand-holds flashed as the car passed under bright lights.

At the end of a fifteen minute ride, the train doors opened and a lighted floor led them into a thin corridor that forced them single file. KJ stayed right in front of her. He looked as calm as anyone approaching a new place for an exciting secret party might, but she smelled his anxiety. Naveen followed Ruby, with Dayn looming behind him. The entire time they walked the corridor, Ruby felt as if there were eyes on her, like when she was in a crowd and turned to find someone staring intently at her from close range.

They rounded a bend and a door swung open, washing the corridor in laughter and music, transforming it into a party.

Ruby put on her best meet-and-greet smile and stepped into the room. The scent of fresh-cut fruit and vegetables mixed with sweet desserts and the tang of alcohol. A band played stringed instruments and hand-drums on an ornate stage that jutted out from a wall so the musicians stood above the crowd, looking down.

A tall and perfectly proportioned man stood in front of her. His skin was as black as Ani's, accentuated by the white and gold clothes he wore. Sparkling golden eyes that were as odd as Koren's eyes matched the gold piping on his sleeves and the gold chains spilling down his chest in a tangled river. "Hello, beautiful Ruby the Red, woman of fire. I am Gunnar Ellensson, and I am pleased to offer you the honor of joining me at a party thrown . . ." he let an exaggerated pause go by, "for you. Come in." He bowed and held out his hand expectantly.

Ruby managed not to react to the overly-effusive greeting, but to just hold her hand out and let him take it. "I don't deserve such honor."

"Oh, yes, you do. You saved your people once in the past, and they love you. You are saving them again, and they still love you. It is rare for a leader to be so good and so bright."

She had to work to withhold her gag reflex. "Show me and my guard around?"

"You have no need of a guard here."

She gestured toward KJ. "Think of him as my friend."

There was no obvious sense of resentment as Gunnar smiled and held a large hand out to KJ. "Pleased to meet you."

She wondered what KJ thought of the excesses surrounding them. He didn't look happy.

Gunnar said, "I cannot leave my post as greeter just yet. Perhaps you can enjoy the riches of the feast prepared for you, and sip from a refreshing, cold drink?"

"I would like some fresh juice," Ruby said, "And a piece of fruit."

Gunnar looked away and whispered something, as if into thin air, and then turned back to Ruby. "I will find you soon."

Ruby almost succeeded at getting her entourage to one of the tables that practically dripped food before a threesome of tattooed men hailed her and blocked her way, holding out hands, murmuring of her success. Others recognized her, and surrounded her quickly. The fashion here was the most exotic she had seen, as were the modifications to the human form. Size varied widely, as well as strength and color. A pink woman with pink hair and baby blue eyes half the size of her face pushed through the crowd to congratulate Ruby on her concert. She was followed by a near-albino woman with the wide shoulders of a man and large breasts that nearly spilled out of a tight-fitting black dress.

Satyana slid through the crowd, dressed plainly compared to the exotics that surrounded her. Here, her simplicity stood out even more than it had on the *Star Bear*. She winked at Ruby. "Thank you for the workers. I have started training them."

"You're welcome, and thank you. I'm sure they'll do well. We're used to hard work."

"Do you feel better?"

"I must have been very tired. I'm sorry for any inconvenience."

"You need to protect your health. I want you to come to the *Star Bear* to sing again. Do you know when you'll be back?"

"I have five more concerts booked. I plan to go back home afterward. I'll ask Naveen to book you."

Satyana managed to look both proud and irritated at once, which made Ruby think she'd gotten her answer right. The *Diamond Deep* was so full of undertones that she usually felt like she was tripping over them. Ruby planned to protect her demand to go home. She'd told Naveen how much it mattered to her, but he'd been drunk when she did that, so she had no idea if he remembered.

A group of five identical women dressed in flesh-toned mesh with sequins sewn over their crotches and breasts pushed between Satyana and Ruby, and Ruby held her hand out to them. "Greetings."

They practically simpered.

Excess surrounded her. Opulence.

Many of the partygoers might as well have been screaming *look at me, look at me, me, me, me.*

By the time a small serving bot was able to push through the crowd, Ruby was thirsty and her voice felt ragged.

Gunnar Ellensson came up shortly after the serving bot and took her arm. "Allow me to tour you."

KJ took her other side. Dayn and Ani moved to join them, but Gunnar waved them away.

Dayn looked angry, and Ruby gave him a small hug and whispered in his ear, "I'll be all right."

He didn't look happy, but he stepped back, taking Ani with him.

"Let's go." Gunnar led them through an irising door and along a short tunnel into an entirely different bubble than the large one that held the party.

Ruby gasped and slowly turned from side to side, taking in the view of cliff faces adorned with hanging vines in a flourish of flower so thick it appeared that rivers of purple and blue and yellow ran down the cliffs and disappeared into striking blue, green, and orange-red forest foliage. Paths wound through meadows. A stream ran in the center of the whole thing, burbling over rocks and through flowers.

Gunnar gave her a few moments before he spoke. "This is as close to a planet as you can see anywhere on the *Deep*, or anywhere in-system except on Lym and Mammot. I designed it so that I had a place where I could feel at home."

"This is all for you?"

"And for my family and closest friends. It is also a gymnasium—there are climbing paths and rope paths and other challenges that neither of us is correctly clothed for now." He looked at her dress, a pale yellow that clung to her hips, lined with soft gray fringe that swung as she walked. Soft gray boots came up nearly to her knees, open at the top and loose so that she had to walk carefully to make them feel right. "I can point them out to you, and perhaps you will grace my home again in the future and try them out."

He took her hand in his. She allowed it for only a moment, and then took it back. His skin had felt dry and warm and he had squeezed her hand as if wanting to keep it. "You lead," she said.

He pointed out flowers and trees, naming them. The path was firm enough under her feet that she felt secure even in her heeled boots. "This is really all yours to decide what do with?"

"Of course. I made it."

Back on the *Fire*, she had always loved parks. They were where she went to take refuge, to think. Where she ran. Where she met her friends. Where she held her parties. The idea of creating and owning a park of her own was one she understood even while it offended her.

Gunnar pointed out a climbing route that KJ asked questions about, giving Ruby time to sit on a bench and rest her feet and her voice. The air smelled better than any air she had ever smelled anywhere, like plants and water and flowers and with almost no hint of humanity. The faintest breeze blew stray hairs softly against her cheek.

Every time she turned her head a new wonder appeared from amidst the profusion of life. A small green bird with a long beak sipping from a red flower. A tiny vine clinging to a tree trunk, covered with pink flowers that nearly obscured pale green leaves the shape of hearts.

This was prettier than the graphics in the game Adiamo, fresher than the park at home on its best day, more astounding than her first sight of the aviary had been.

The aviary was available to anyone who could spend the credit to visit.

This . . . this was private. It belonged to one man. The sheer weight of expenditure astonished her. And yet Gunnar Ellensson had been described as a rich merchant. As one of many. Satyana had shown her a froth of private bubbles.

Ruby wanted one of her own. She wanted to design this much secret beauty, to have it to retreat into with her family. She could imagine choosing trees and flowers, shaping waterfalls. Waterfalls! She had never imagined anything so rich, so beautiful. The fact that she wanted it made her tense and angry.

What else did this excess, this beauty, imply existed on the *Deep*? The garden surrounding her defined power in a far more subtle way than the vast bubble-party and its glittery crowd.

The contrast between this place and the Brawl mixed up inside her heart and her stomach, souring it. Or maybe it was already sour from whatever illness dogged her. Regardless, even in the bright, fresh air she felt like throwing up.

Ruby still felt faint an hour later when she stood on the raised stage. Color swirled below her. Multicolored faces peered up at her. Bots and human servers danced through the crowded floor. Three drummers remained on the stage, standing in a loose semi-circle around her. They felt too close, as if herding her toward the edge, but she couldn't exactly turn around and hiss at them to leave, nor could she explain that she felt dizzy still, and the edge seemed too near her feet.

Gunnar Ellensson spoke from the far corner of the room, his voice loud and commanding. Even the robots stopped for him. "Allow me to present Ruby Martin. She is the queen of flame, a leader from *The Creative Fire*, and an ambassador for her people who come from our past."

He let a beat of silence fall.

Ruby stood still.

People watched her.

Gunnar continued. "Ruby has agreed to grace us with three songs. Let's welcome her."

Hands clapped and two people whistled.

The drummers began a steady cadence.

Ruby took a deep breath and forced out as genuine a smile as she could muster. "This is a song for one of us who is now dead. He was like a grand-father to me. He taught me to be brave and to be curious and to hope when there is no hope." She started "The Owl's Song." Some of the audience knew it. They must have watched the video of the actual funeral, which now seemed so far away she no longer recognized the girl who had barely been brave enough to sing there.

At the end, the applause was loud although she couldn't tell how sincere it was coming from this strange crowd. She said, "Thank you. Thank you. I am so pleased to be with you, to be part of this great station." She took a deep breath, watching the faces below her. She kept her voice even. "That was a song from our past, a song from before I knew I would be in the generation that came home. Before we knew anything except rumors that our long, long journey could come to an end."

Here and there a glass clinked or weight shifted.

"Now I will sing you a song about coming home." She sang "Song of the Seed," drawing out the last chorus:

Together we are a seed
Preparing to open in the light
Of Adiamo. To flower.

Again the audience clapped, and a few called out for favorite songs.

This was her moment of truth. A moment to decide.

She had written a song about these people. Well, not really. A song for them. A song to show them what they needed to know, to remind them of what they refused to see. She wanted to sing the song for Gunnar Ellensson, whom she had decided was kind and confusing and cruel all at once. The room was full of people with the resources to transform life on the *Deep*. She hadn't quite finished the song . . . but almost. She could do it. A little improv. Maybe sing with no accompaniment since she couldn't give the drummers anything.

She stared down at them. Were they ready? Was the song? Was this the place?

Her stomach felt cold.

She put her head down and her hands down, and then she lifted both again. She cued the drummers to go into a steady beat.

Her throat tightened, and her stomach heaved. She realized this might not be recorded. These people might hurt her. They were in a small private place.

She bowed her head again. "Sorry," she mumbled, and then she began a lullaby from the *Fire*, a soft, sweet song that left the audience silent for a few breaths before they clapped harder than they had for the first two songs.

She felt as if she had failed in spite of the roaring applause that rose up to engulf her. In another venue, if she felt stronger, she might have turned to give them one more song. Instead, she walked off the stage without looking back.

CHAPTER SIXTY-FOUR

Allen had finally found a decent live band to play the bar. The three-some played about ten instruments between them, and the girl who sang lead had a high sweet voice. Even though she had none of Ruby's power, she was pleasant both to listen to and to watch, and Onor made sure he picked a table where he could see her.

The bar was full and loud, and they'd squeezed in two more tables and hired a waitress. Allen noticed him and sent the new girl, Evie, over to take his order. Evie was a dark bit of a girl with a bright smile and an admirable figure, if slightly on the thin side. She recognized him immediately; a good sign. "Onor! What can I get for you?"

"How about one of the *Deep* wines—a white, maybe? And some flatbread and fruit."

"Coming right up!"

He watched her walk away, wondering if she was much older than Haric. She had the form of a woman, but he'd bet she was no more than sixteen. She was probably still in regular school. Well, at least she'd be too busy to get in trouble.

His drink appeared before his food, and Evie was sharp enough to add water to her tray and then ask him if he wanted it. They'd had fifty applicants for the job based solely on word-of-mouth. Apparently they had chosen well.

It took longer than he expected for Haric to join him. At least the wine was good. Great, in fact. On the *Fire*, everything alcohol had been called still, but here there were numerous words for alcohol and smoke and other drugs. It almost seemed that separating things with different names made them more unique, and better. By the time half of the wine was gone, he felt pretty good. The decent singing didn't hurt either. Unwinding had some value to it; he actually couldn't remember the last time he had been able to just sit still.

After a while, it seemed he'd been sitting too long. Onor had started seriously fidgeting by the time Haric showed up and slid into the seat opposite him.

"Did you get lost out there?" Onor asked.

Haric shook his head. "Just tired. No work. I asked at four or five places, figuring that ship's work would be good. I got as far as taking one test, but I botched it. I just can't get the hang of the tech here—it's so subtle."

"I'm not doing much better. Ix is teaching me some, though. I can set you up with a lesson tomorrow."

"I'll take it. This place makes me feel like an idiot."

"Well, you're not. Did you see any of our cargo?"

"I walked the whole Exchange twice. Nothing. But I have a plan. I'll put it off a day, for the class. But then I think I need to go."

Evie came up, bringing the container to pour Onor more wine and an extra glass for Haric. Haric gave her a broad smile. "Thanks, Evie."

She gave him a chaste kiss on the cheek, but her eyes held a deeper affection that her actions gave away.

Haric sipped from his wine, smiled softly. "That's good."

"I'm glad I chose something you'd like."

Evie left, and Onor raised an eyebrow at Haric. "I've never seen you flirt before."

Haric actually blushed.

"You do know her?"

"Of course I do. I've known her since we were all on the *Fire*. We play games sometimes."

Onor refrained from asking what kind of games. He'd been dreaming of Ruby when he was Haric's age, and near her all the time without being able to touch her. He did love Marcelle, but nothing had ever erased his adoration of Ruby. If Haric managed better than Onor at the same age, well, that was a good thing. "Tell me about your plan."

"There are other Exchanges. Surely Koren wouldn't be reselling anything of ours in this one. I can get to Exchange Four with a one-day ride. I thought I'd ask if you'd sponsor me on such a trip."

"All by yourself? I'd go with you if I could, but both Joel and Marcelle need me." He started at the table. "It's too much risk for you to go alone." Ruby would hate that.

"It's got to be done," Haric protested. "Besides, you're the one who suggested I be sent to look."

"To our Exchange."

"So? This one must be like that one. It will only be a two-day trip."

"Where will you sleep?"

"That's why I need a sponsor. I'm pretty sure SueAnne won't let go of enough credit for me to buy a room anywhere."

Even though he'd championed this trip to Joel and SueAnne, Onor hated the idea now that it was happening. "I'll send you credit. Take your slate. Message me when you get there."

A big hand clapped Onor on the shoulder, and he turned his head to spot The Jackman and Conroy. "Hey—I haven't seen enough of you two. Buy you a drink?"

They squeezed two chairs in from a nearby table, the bulk of the two bigger men making Onor feel cramped in spite of how happy he felt to see his old mentors. Haric flagged Evie back over and The Jackman said, "I heard you were part owner of this little venture."

Onor laughed. "A small part. I did some work for Naveen and invested what I earned."

The Jackman looked approving. "Smart."

"How's Daria?"

"Good. She's making jewelry to take to the exchange, and people are buying."

The Jackman had kept the trimmer figure he'd developed preparing to fight for Ruby and Joel back on the *Fire*. He'd grown back the beard, now a scraggly long white river of hair flowing from his chin almost to the middle of his chest. "I hear you're still managing drills."

"Yeah—running for nothing. I liked it better when there was a cause we could put our fingers on."

After Evie took their orders, Conroy made a show of looking around. "The bar's changed."

"What do you mean?" Onor asked.

"More people. More strangers, mostly."

"It's Ruby's popularity." There were at least four tables—no, five—of Deepers. "They come here because this is where she comes from."

The Jackman shook his head. "So she's still making trouble." But he had a smile now when he talked about her.

"More like saving us from starvation. Strangers coming in means we're making credits instead of just moving pieces around."

"Could be. But every good thing comes with its shadow consequence." The Jackman pointed at the table of outsiders furthest from them. Three men, all decked out in Deeper finery. And with them, three of *The Creative Fire*'s young women, leaning on their hands, looking completely star-crossed at the handsome Deepers. "I don't like seeing that," The Jackman said. "We're losing our girls."

Haric frowned. "Two of my friends left yesterday. They haven't come back. Not girls. Boys. They say it's too restrictive here."

Conroy asked, "How did they get away?"

"They kept half their earnings. No way to tell, you know. People have to self-report to SueAnne, and hardly any grays trust her."

"You should," Onor snapped. "She works hard. She's trying to save us, just like Ruby."

"Maybe we don't want to sit around and let the women do that for us. Maybe we need to make our own names."

After two hours of practicing the voice and visual cues needed to make native *Deep* technology respond well to him, Onor felt drained. Haric held his fingers at his temples and frowned. Onor leaned back in his chair. "We're done for now," he told Aleesi.

"All right." The voice was female. The two AIs had agreed to standardize on one voice each—Aleesi's that of a young woman, and Ix's a male voice.

"Did you learn something?" Onor asked.

Haric nodded. "I still don't know that it would be enough for me to pass one of the damned work tests. But I think I could at least access the systems now, and maybe read the questions."

"Well, that's progress. I'll order some food, and then we need to work on your trip."

Haric raised an eyebrow. "I was thinking of going to the bar."

"And looking for Evie?"

"And having a drink." But Haric's cheeks turned red.

"We can't talk with the AIs there. If the Deepers find Aleesi, and take her, they'll also have the copy of Ix we've been retraining. And Ruby will kill us for losing her pet. Besides, Joel's going to join us here."

Haric leaned back. "All right. Order me a glass of wine, then."

Onor felt like a miniature version of Joel when he said, "Water and a sandwich."

"I wish our food in here was as good as the food outside."

"Maybe we'll open a restaurant after we get the hang of the bar." Onor used his slate to order the food and let Joel know they were ready, then took a closer look at Haric. He must have been working out with Conroy and the others. Or maybe he was just growing up. His shoulders were wider than Onor remembered, and earlier, Onor had noticed he was only a tiny bit taller than Haric. He was sure Haric had been much smaller than Onor on docking day.

They sat in congenial quiet until Joel and the food arrived simultaneously. "So," Joel said. "Tell me about getting to the next Exchange. Why?"

"I heard a rumor that there's cargo from the *Fire* there."

"Who did you hear that from?"

"One of the merchants. He recognized me, said he knew I was from the *Fire* by the way I talked."

Joel pursed his lips. "That's not good news."

Onor took a bite of his sandwich, the bread gritty with seed and nuts and the protein paste on it thick and creamy. It actually wasn't bad.

"So he said that there was a booth in Exchange Four that specialized in rocks and minerals. Which we had a lot of, so it makes sense. He said he was there and some of the stuff is labeled as coming from us."

"So she's not even trying to hide that she stole from us," Onor muttered.

Joel leaned forward, a quiet, contemplative look on his face. "Or she's underestimating us."

Aleesi spoke. "Koren underestimated Naveen. The *Deep* is huge, and your arrival wasn't actually a very big deal. It also wasn't publicized much. Koren tried to block Naveen from being the other one chosen to greet you, but she was unable to do that. Since then, she's been trying to destroy his reputation by suggesting he's a drunken lush and that he's not telling the truth about Ruby's past."

Joel frowned. "How do you know all that?"

"It's in the comment threads all over the station. The current prevailing attitude about anything can be parsed by reading and evaluating comment logs. This is also true on the stations at the Edge, even though those are smaller."

"Why didn't you tell us this earlier?" Onor asked.

"You didn't ask."

"I thought you were more human than machine," Onor said.

"That doesn't mean I can read your mind."

Onor laughed. Sometimes he almost liked the killer robot girl.

"Ix? Did you know this?" Joel asked. "About the logs."

"No."

Onor sighed. "Aleesi, can you teach Ix about the comment logs? And me, too?"

"Yes."

"There is something else you might want to know," Aleesi said.

"What?"

"The merchant who helped Haric? The couple from the bar? They are not happy with how things are run here on the *Deep*. That's why they risked coming here, and why the merchant talked to Haric. The power structures here are stable, but all power structures draw people who hate them."

And Aleesi's people—the people from the Edge—might hate the *Deep*'s powerful people, too. The immensity of what he didn't know felt like knives held above his head. Before he could form a question, Joel asked, "So . . . what else do you know about Koren? Can you verify that she stole from us?"

"You must promise never to use me as a source of information."

"I know."

"Do you promise?"

"Yes," Joel said. "Now tell me what you can prove, and how we might prove it?"

"Will you promise me something else?"

"What?" Joel snapped.

"Can there be someone in here talking to me most of the time? I get lonely."

Joel looked exasperated. "Sure. You can have a whispering woman. I'll find one for you tomorrow."

"Maybe SueAnne can work in here more often? I've been helping her with research, but she's only here an hour or so a day."

"I'll ask. What do you know?"

"You know Koren is the *Deep*'s Chief Historian, right?"

"Right," Onor said.

"That means she's on the Council. The Council is the group of people that runs things here—they can change laws, make laws, etc. The Council has . . .

arguments. About who has power. Koren is the least of them. She has almost no power. My analysis suggests that she thinks gaining the riches from the *Fire* will give her more power."

"Okay," Joel said. "That fits with what the couple in the bar told us. But why all the intrigue?"

"Maybe that's just how they do things here," Haric commented.

Onor laughed. "Don't be that cynical."

"You're not getting out enough," Haric whispered.

Joel gave them a look that demanded quiet. "What else have you learned?"

"You are inconvenient. She can't prove you don't own all of what came in the *Fire*. That's part of why the *Fire* itself is locked away. A true historian would have kept her intact and given tours or something."

"So how do we prove that we own it?"

"You may not own it, at least not according to the rules these people honor."

Haric had been quiet. Now he spoke a touch too loudly, his voice laced with barely-controlled anger. "If everyone in power is so cruel, than how do we actually change things? How could a court do us good if Koren has more power than we do?"

"Well, one way is to find a court that will listen to you. There are still rules, and if you can make the breaking of one a public thing, then even the powerful must pay."

Haric's face showed his doubt. "Really? But who will listen to us? We have the least power of anyone I've seen here."

"No," Onor said. "You haven't seen the Brawl."

Haric sighed and went quiet for a moment. "So it won't help if we find the stuff in Exchange Four?"

"Oh yes, it will help, "Aleesi said. "Physical evidence would be very helpful."

"I still don't understand," Onor said.

"Well, either you're crew, and you get a part of the value of the cargo. That's what Koren's asserting. Or you're owners, and you get it all."

Onor sat back. "How would we prove we're owners?"

"Prove Lym isn't claiming ownership."

"How do we do that?"

"Ix has records of its conversations."

"So we have to protect Ix." That was an odd thought. Onor was still used to Ix protecting them. But that also explained why Koren had stopped Ix early on, as soon as they got near, and why it had been hard for Naveen to get a copy of the AI. Even why Koren had stripped the group of most of their leaders. She was probably furious Ruby and Joel hadn't gone along with her plan to re-settle everyone in power fairly nicely. After all, wherever Laird was, he probably wasn't three months away from being thrown in the Brawl. "Maybe we should go talk to Naveen," Onor mused.

Haric's face brightened.

"They are very far away," Aleesi said.

"This doesn't sound impossible," Joel said. "To prove this. If someone will be fair?"

"What about our mystery couple?" Onor asked.

"I have not been able to identify who they are."

Onor looked over at Joel. "Too bad we can't talk to Aleesi from a distance."

"Koren knows about me," Aleesi said. "She could come take me any time. If you can find the technology to make me mobile, I will take the risk."

Joel shook his head. "It's too much. That puts Ix at risk, and we need it."

"If there's a way, it might make us all safer," Onor said.

Joel looked like he was about to say no, but then he said, "Be careful," instead.

CHAPTER SIXTY-FIVE

Ruby woke in the early hours of the morning after the party at Gunnar Ellensson's, her head spinning with the various excesses of food and design and attitude. Gunnar could buy fifteen ships like *The Creative Fire* and outfit them for fabulous journeys. He probably spent more credit on his private estate in a day than she needed to feed thousands. What had woken her was an anger at that wealth, an anger that drove deep in her belly and sent it sour, that stiffened her, that forced her out of bed.

She wasn't angry at Gunnar. She'd actually rather liked him, in the odd way that one can like an enemy. He was affable and unruffled while he wasted credits that should be feeding people and stopping the Brawl. He wasted riches beautifully.

The *Deep* confused her in so many ways. She wished Joel were here, or she was at home. She wanted to be held and she wanted someone to talk this through with.

Their rooms were private, but there was a shared galley. She made her way there, intending to have a cup of tea and something to sop it up with up, some bread perhaps, or a seed cracker. To her surprise, Min was already at the table, alone, her face washed so pale in the light of the slate on the table in front of her that her scar barely showed. Her free hand was cupped around a glass of water. Ruby spoke softly, "Hi Min."

Min startled slightly, as if jolted out of some quiet reverie.

Ruby poured a cup of hot water from a spigot. "All these little conveniences would have been nice to have back on the *Fire*."

Min smiled but said nothing.

Ruby dug out a white paper sack to spill tea leaves into, and then dunked it in the hot water, almost burning her fingers. "What did you think of the party?"

"I didn't know what to make of it." She looked slightly sullen. "It's . . . all . . . it's all so much. So different. I don't even know how to talk to these people."

"I think that's what woke me up. All of this . . . richness."

Min looked surprised.

"We need to learn how to live here."

"I hate this place. It's not home. It's not friendly. It's not safe."

Ruby didn't want to agree with her and make it worse for Min. "Is that why you started spending so much time with Lya?"

"No. It was the loss of the *Fire*. I can't believe you lost the *Fire*."

"Really?" Ruby smelled the tea, afraid to sip it yet, since steam still wafted from the cup. "I can't believe it was taken from us." The anger that had woken her edged her voice, and Ruby took a deep breath to calm herself. Min didn't deserve it. "What do you think we did? Decided how to hurt ourselves the most and then did that to ourselves?"

Min looked up from her slate and stared at Ruby. "Can you think of anything worse?"

"If we had known what the *Deep* was like, we wouldn't have come here. That doesn't mean there was anyplace better to go." She stared into her cup. "That's not something we can ever know." She glanced back at Min, who had gone back to staring at her slate. "But we have opportunities here. We need to take them when they come up."

Min's face resolved into a soft sneer. "I saw you leave the room with that stupid merchant last night. It woke me up, thinking about it. I'd almost decided Lya was wrong, that you really are trying to work for us, but then you disappeared with him for an hour."

Ruby bristled. She also wasn't going to let Min drive her back to her room. "He wanted to show me his gardens."

"Your hair was messed up when you got back."

She didn't remember that. "We must have walked under some trees. Garden is the wrong word—it's more like a forested paradise. We could have walked three hours and not seen it all."

"Really? I don't know why you say such things."

Min didn't believe her? "You were at the party. Don't you think a man who can waste credit on a fountain of colored drinks as tall as four people could make a paradise garden?"

Min laughed. "Just what you'd want. Someone with real power. Look, you're a rotten woman. We all know that now. You used to tease Hugh. You still tease Onor. You seduced the strongest man on the *Fire* just as it was certain he'd take power. You've slept your way to power all your life. When Joel finds out, you're going to lose your golden man."

"There's nothing for him to find out." Ruby blew on her tea, her breath making ripples that sloshed small against the far side of the cup. "You can't talk about things you don't know about. People will believe you. You'll hurt Joel."

"So stop doing it."

Ruby shook her head. "I didn't. I don't. Ask KJ. He was with me the entire time."

"Lya says he covers for you."

Ruby took a deep breath, and finally a sip of tea. "Can't you think for yourself?"

"I do."

At least now she had something other than the excesses of Gunnar Ellensson to be pissed off about. "No. Really. KJ is Joel's friend. He would hardly stand by while I slept with another man."

"Even if it meant making more credit? Is all of what you make even going back to us? Look at how many people are coming to your concerts, listening to them. One concert has to make enough to feed us all for at least a year."

"Don't be naïve. Naveen takes most of it."

"But not all of it. I know you use some. Look at how you dress."

Ruby felt just too dragged out to face Min right now, unable to draw up the right words to defend herself. "I'm going to try and get some sleep. You should do the same."

Min stared down at her cup. "I don't sleep much anymore. I might not sleep well until we get on another ship and go somewhere else."

"Where would you go?"

Min shook her head, and replied with a deep despair in her voice. "There is no place to go."

Ruby hated despair as much as she hated an unwillingness to think. "I'm sorry I brought you out here," she told Min. "Good night."

She took her cup. As she left the galley, a shadow detached itself from the wall in the corridor. Dayn. He leaned down and whispered in Ruby's ear. "Be careful. Nothing that you do is right, now. Not anymore."

She stood still, unable to respond. She was angry with the *Deep*. Angry at the facts of existence here, angry at Min, and angry at herself for not using the opportunity to make some real headway with Min. Heck, if you wanted to count it up, she was angry with Koren as well, and with the robot spiders from the Edge that killed Colin. She hated the anger. Maybe she was even angry at Dayn for telling her the truth. After a while, she put a hand on his arm and spoke softly. "I know. But I have to do something. I have to make some choices."

Dayn whispered again. "Choose carefully."

CHAPTER SIXTY-SIX

Onor sat with Joel and SueAnne in the morning meeting room. After their conversations the night before, Joel had invited both SueAnne and Onor to share his breakfast time. Stim and half-finished plates of food filled the table.

Joel looked like he'd actually slept. SueAnne was another story; rivers of darkness like spent blood filled the wrinkles around her eyes. She had started carrying a blanket with her wherever she went, a blue one that Jali had made from extra material. Her hands clutched the sides of her wheeled chair and her slate was balanced on shaky legs.

Joel picked up a piece of bread and spread a vitamin-laced sweet paste on it and then topped it with fresh berries. The berries came from Allen, who snuck in special treats for the leaders from time to time and claimed it was bar food he couldn't use. "Any word on our stray spy?"

Since Aleesi was the only one who could answer that, Onor sat back in his chair and created his own breakfast sandwich, including a few of the sweet purplish berries.

"He's doing well so far," she said. "He left two hours ago. He's passed through Exchange Five and found the right train for Exchange Four. SueAnne? Can you work in here today? I'll keep track of Haric then, and I can update you all. I can probably help you figure out what people think of our workers as well."

SueAnne looked both trapped and intrigued. "Really? How?"

"People rate workers and make comments and that goes into how they get hired for other jobs."

Onor groaned. That would have been wonderful to know before. "I'll come in for another lesson later," he said. "Maybe you can show me how to read those boards."

"I showed Ix yesterday. It would be useful for you to know. The more time you can give me in here, the more I can teach you."

He sensed Aleesi's human roots when she expressed loneliness like this. If only they could use the AIs to teach groups of people. But they were still hiding the fact that they had recovered them. Aleesi was sure Koren knew and sure she would come after her some day. If they were lucky, Koren didn't know Ix was there, too.

"Ix?" Joel asked.

The voice coming from the speaker on the table changed. "Yes, Joel?"

"Tell me about Ruby. How is she doing?"

"Her audiences have grown to almost ten percent of the population."

Aleesi added, "The reviews and comments on her performances are primarily good."

"Primarily? What do the bad ones say?"

"Some are reacting badly to her youth. Others suggest she didn't really come from the *Fire*, or that the *Fire* itself didn't actually come from the station's past."

"Really?" Onor reacted. "People think all of us are a lie?"

"Why?" SueAnne asked.

Aleesi answered. "It appears to be an attempt to discredit Ruby. Could be a rival . . . Or Koren."

Joel steepled his hands under his chin and looked lost in thought. "We'd better meet in here every morning. Can you send the comments to my slate before each meeting?"

"I can send a summary. All of the comments would exceed the memory in your slate."

Joel narrowed his eyes. "Summarize last night's comments for me."

"There were eighteen thousand original comments and fifty thousand replies, including duplicates. Over fifteen thousand were positive comments of one kind or another, more initiated by men than by women. Almost all comments and replies were made by humans. Most machines only pay a little attention to human art forms."

"So almost three thousand comments were negative."

"Almost two thousand. There were roughly a thousand that were questions or otherwise neutral."

Onor noticed he hadn't taken a bite of his bread since Ix started the recitation. "Can you show me some of them? This afternoon when I come back for my lesson? I want to see the twenty most positive and the twenty worst. Send them to all of us, please. We'll talk about them tomorrow morning."

Joel looked pleased with Onor. "Some part of you is always a guard, isn't it?"

Onor laughed. "Maybe I should get paid for that."

The look on SueAnne's face led him to mumble, "Well, maybe not. But someday that will be the only way to get people to work here."

SueAnne pushed her plate aside and picked up her slate. "Last night, Ruby added ten days to our lives outside the Brawl. Other workers added a sum total of half a day. That's less than the point six five of a day that they added yesterday, but the good news is that two of our young men were hired by one of the more prominent ship builders."

"To do what?"

"Sweep up a factory floor."

CHAPTER SIXTY-SEVEN

Ruby took her first bows on the end of the seventh large stage she'd been on in three weeks. This one was no renovated ship; the whole bubble had been designed and built for performances. More precisely, a huge habitat bubble had been bisected, and the half that faced the sun grew food. The half that faced away housed a great amphitheater that could be configured for concerts, lectures, plays, or sports. In the current configuration there were ten thousand seats, and yet people still lined the walls standing. Stars shone overhead, and one of the gas giants was in a place in its orbit where it hung like a red and gold dinner plate in the sky, shedding some of the reflected light of Adiamo down on the venue.

The design created excellent acoustics. Her voice had sounded huge. Applause rolled and crescendoed and fell, waves of it, the sound bathing her in success. This time they were near the true middle of the *Diamond Deep*. Headman Stevenson was in the audience, as were many of the Council. Gunnar Ellensson had come by earlier and put a hand on her shoulder, wishing her luck. He had stood so close she could smell the subtle musk of his sweat, and she knew he wanted her. This pleased and disturbed her. She had no intention of sleeping with him, but his desire might give her a bargaining hold of some kind.

He had whispered, "I will be listening."

The applause began to die down. She cleared her throat. "This last song is dedicated to the poor. It is for those who cannot make it on their own and who have been abandoned."

The audience quieted.

She continued. "Sometimes art exists to entertain. Sometimes it exists to teach. Sometimes it exists to incite change. And sometimes it exists to twist our insides and let us see ourselves. It is up to the listener to choose what each song means for them. I give you this song for your contemplation. I suspect you may not like it, but not all art is meant to be liked. It's called 'Turning Away.'"

Turning away
Does not make
Danger disappear.
Turning away

Is loving
The lies of our hearts

A babe lies in its mother's arms,
Hungry
She offers her breast, her milk,
Her help.
The child grows and gains
Love and hope and life
But not work.
Time passes.
He is gone now, locked
In a place full of failures
The mother turns away,
Tends to her own bare
Life of desperation

Turning away
Does not make
Danger disappear.
Turning away
Is loving
The lies of our hearts

The mother grows older,
Weaker
Locks her loss and love
She works
It becomes her turn
To join the masses
She cannot work
He is with her, locked
In a place full of failures
He sees her in the brawl
But he turns away from her
Time passes.
He is gone now, locked

In a place full of failures
The mother turns away,
Tends to her own bare
Life of desperation

Look inside
See despair
Starve it out
Embrace the hope
Of helping
The lovers of our hearts

There were more verses. Tens of verses. The cruel possibilities suggested so much. But this was enough. For now.

She waited on the end of the stage. A few people clapped, and then a few more, and then more, but nothing like the wave of approval that had met her a few moments earlier, a song before. This felt tentative. Approval and dismay, perhaps. Or approval and fear.

She spoke into her microphone. "I am not surprised that you are quieter now. My people and I come from another time in your history. When we left, the *Fire* was designed so that there were people with different jobs, with different amounts of power. That is inevitable. We are not all the same."

She paused, let them accept that. As soon as a quiet whisper of conversation came to her, she started speaking again. "No one starved. No one lived without any privacy, without any hope, without the arms of families. We age and we die from age like your ancestors did. But no one dies alone in a crowd like the people who die in the Brawl. I am sorry that the first song I bring you that is of you, for you, about you, is about a horror so deep that it took me weeks to figure out how to sing about it." She paused again, the space of a breath or two. No one clapped. "There is also much beauty in the *Deep*, and I will sing about that for you soon."

The few faces she could see in the front row displayed confusion, anger, unhappiness, and slightly more subtle emotions like uncertainty.

She wanted them to think.

She bowed and walked off the stage, steeling herself for Naveen's reaction.

Only after she had left the spotlight did she hear the first tentative claps. By the time she went behind the curtain, the level of applause told her that about half of the people had joined in.

CHAPTER SIXTY-EIGHT

Onor, Joel, Marcelle, and The Jackman sat silently, staring at the screen. The bar had gone quiet after Ruby's song about the Brawl and her short speech afterwards. Marcelle was the first to react. She stood up and clapped, staring down at Onor until he did the same. Joel stood, dragging The Jackman up. Their whole table stood there, clapping by themselves, watching the crowd from the concert begin to file out of the large theater bubble on the screen in front of them.

After a short delay, Onor heard clapping from behind him. He looked around and saw that it was people from the *Fire*. He heard a third table from the other part of the room. After a few moments, clapping came from all directions and Marcelle had started whistling catcalls. Yet most of the people from the *Deep* sat still, or whispered one to another. Just before Marcelle sat down, Onor caught a few claps from a group of Deepers in the far corner.

Then one more.

An eerie delayed reaction.

As they sat back down, Onor leaned over to Marcelle and kissed her cheek. "Thank you. That was perfect."

"That was stupid," Joel whispered, soft enough that only the four of them could hear it.

"She's always been stupid," The Jackman said. "But you gotta admire a girl who'll take on a whole space station full of people."

Joel chewed on his lower lip. "Aren't thousands of her own people enough to protect?"

Onor's laugh broke some of the tension around the table. "I knew she'd do that ever since she saw the Brawl. I'm surprised she managed to wait this long."

In spite of the others' laughter, Joel still looked unhappy. "She takes too many risks."

Marcelle gave him a sweet smile. "Isn't that why you fell in love with her?"

Joel glowered even more. Silly, serious man.

Allen came over and sat backwards on a chair. "Can I offer you a round in condolence?"

Joel raised an eyebrow. "Condolence?"

"Over a hundred people have asked for refunds."

"How did you know that?" Onor asked.

"Naveen called me. He wanted to know if you all had seen what she did."

"And what did you tell him?"

"That he should have known he was playing with fire."

Joel finally laughed, although creases of worry still furrowed his brow.

Evie came up to see if they wanted refills. After she took their orders, she leaned close to Onor. "Have you heard from Haric?"

The undertones of worry in her voice made Onor smile. "I checked before we came in here. He said he's settled into a hotel room outside the Exchange. He was about to go find a good place to watch the concert. I bet he's someplace just like this."

Her eyes rounded. "But not with us. With Deepers."

Onor tried to reassure her. "It should be okay. I can't imagine anyone will hurt Haric over this. Besides, some of the Deepers liked what she did." He thought about adding that they were even less likely to hurt a kid, but Haric probably wouldn't want to be referred to that way. "He'll be okay."

"Will you send me a message as soon as you know anything?" she asked.

"If you'll do the same."

"I will."

CHAPTER SIXTY-NINE

This time the after-party was at Headman Stevenson's home.

Ruby let Jali fuss with her hair until Naveen sent a minion to pound on her door. As soon as she saw Naveen, she tried to read his reaction. When she had first come off the stage, every muscle she could see had looked tense and he had spoken in short commands. Now, his jaw was a little more relaxed and he was willing to look at her. In spite of the faint smell of wine on him, there was nothing in his look that suggested any kind of approval. "What were you thinking?" he asked.

Her tiredness seemed to vanish with his question, worry taking its place. "What I told them. I meant that. Sometimes art matters."

"More than feeding your people?"

"Of course not." But then after a minute, she said, "Maybe."

"People here don't talk about the Brawl. They hardly want to be reminded of it. Especially in an encore." He almost sounded pleading.

"I'm not just a pretty little singer."

"Well, hurry up," he said.

"What?"

"You can't wear that."

She had on the outfit designed to look like the last uniforms from the *Fire*, the ones they had all worn for docking day. Jali had just finished it this morning. They'd argued about how much to tuck it so that it showed her figure. Jali had won; it was tucked and piped. Almost too pretty. "I rather like it."

"Are you trying to commit suicide? Or just tired of singing? I can stop this whole thing right now. I've already made enough credit that I never have to work again if I don't want to. But you have mouths to feed."

She felt her apprehension transforming into anger, going from one emotion that made her tremble to another. "I do. But I cannot unmake myself, and I cannot refuse to care. You're the one who took me to the Brawl. Surely you did that because you knew it would affect me."

"I hoped it would scare you."

"Look. Let's go. I won't sing that song at the after-party. I'll behave there."

"But you're going to wear that?"

"Yes."

He looked exasperated and intrigued all at once.

Along the way, she felt as if he were trying to form words around an idea. He finally said, "Look. We don't do revolution here. There hasn't been a change in power in thousands of years. I'd like to see a change, more than you know. But you can't just come in from the outside and make that happen."

Ruby didn't answer him. But if she hadn't known Lila Red the Releaser existed—even though she failed—Ruby would never have tried. Perhaps these people just needed to know it could be done.

The way to Headman Stevenson's was a broad, clear tunnel with art murals painted on the walls. Nothing as secret as getting to Gunnar Ellensson's had been.

At least government here was accessible.

It was also apparently popular. The huge room was full of people. The Headman saw her, and then ignored her until she came to him in the reception line. There, he took her hand and said, "Welcome," and looked at her eyes. "That last song?"

"Yes?"

"Don't ever sing it in my presence again."

She flinched, but held her ground. "Perhaps you would explain why? Maybe over a drink?"

To her surprise he handed off the duty of greeting people to the woman next to him. He took her arm, leading her. She wouldn't quite describe the pressure of his hand on her arm as painful.

Naveen and KJ followed. She waved the others off, thinking that too big an audience might make it harder for her to have a serious conversation. Min looked like she wanted to join Ruby, but Ani pulled her away and they followed Jali and Dayn into the crowd.

The Headman apparently had a similar thought, as he only allowed one of a crowd of hangers-on to follow him. He led Ruby out of the party and into a small room that held only a table and a few chairs. There was already a pitcher with water and cups on the table, as if the spot were always kept ready. "Please sit."

Ruby did, KJ on one side of her and Naveen on the other, the Headman and his own guard opposite them with one empty chair.

Headman Stevenson waited until everyone had poured water. Today, he wore a flowing white outfit that was sheer enough to show his multicolored tattoos. Something in the way he dressed reminded her of Lake, the man who had wanted to sell her women off to brothels. Or maybe she could smell it on him. At any rate, she didn't like him, and she didn't trust him. But there was no denying that he radiated the confidence that came with real power, or that so much confidence made fear beat like wings in her heart.

For a long, awkward moment no one said anything.

The door opened and Koren walked into the small room. She wore sparkled and stitched blues very much like she had the first time Ruby met her, and once more her arms and neck flowed with golden chains. "Hello, Ruby." She didn't even acknowledge KJ or Naveen.

Ruby said nothing. She couldn't trust herself not to admonish Koren for her rudeness, and for a thousand other things, so she sat with her nails dug into her palms. Koren had brought them down. Or more accurately, they had allowed Koren to bring them down. Either way, they were enemies now.

Koren had the same sense of power the Headman did, even though she was clearly subservient to him.

It was hard not to speak.

Headman Stevenson looked at Ruby. "I am going to assume that you are simply naïve, and you do not appreciate the value of our choices here."

So that was how he wanted to play it. She smiled as sweetly as she could. "Enlighten me?"

"Success in this system comes from hard work. Like you are doing touring." He smiled, his teeth even and white except for one that had a small gem on it. "I'm sure it's exhausting."

She nodded, without telling him exactly how exhausted she did feel, or that this conversation was already making it worse. "I'm pleased to be able to see so much of the *Deep*."

"I happen to know you have seen some of the finest places we have to offer. There is much beauty. But it takes great wealth to create great beauty. At least the type of remarkable place that my friend Gunnar created."

She lowered her eyes and sipped at her water. It had a tang to it, as if a bit of fruit had been infused into the water. "I like Gunnar. I was grateful that he showed me what he created. It may be the most beautiful thing I have ever seen." Except Joel, and the look in his eyes when he was full of passion and lust and love for her. She had to hang on to that, which had seemed so huge once and yet paled compared to the *Diamond Deep*. It still mattered, because if love didn't matter than nothing did. "Surely, a mere tenth of the credit spent to build that paradise could support a hundred people for all of their lives?"

The Headman smiled. "But if we did so, and that hundred people didn't need to work, then they would not do so. Then more would not. *That* experiment has been tried."

"We all worked on *The Creative Fire*. Everyone who could. And we took care of the ones who couldn't."

Koren didn't seem to feel as great a need as Headman Stevenson did to remain polite. In fact, her smile might as well as have been full of knives instead of teeth. "You were no better, nor your lover. If I remember right, *The Creative Fire* hosted a rather large peacekeeping force to assure that you didn't rebel. People died. People were raped. People were locked up. You still have people contained in your home community, and more every day."

A stinging truth. Ruby struggled not to wince out loud. "Many of the people in the Brawl are there simply because they could not compete. The only people we lock up are those who have committed crimes against others of us."

"And what about that woman who didn't like you? What was her name? Sylva? How did she die?"

It felt like being taunted by a schoolyard bully. Ruby kept her lips sealed. Naveen, beside her, had stiffened. But he had not said a word since they came in here, and had not so much as looked at Koren.

KJ spoke up. "Ruby was not responsible for those choices. Any of them. As a people, we have no more evil in our past than you perpetrate with the Brawl. Less. I have been there, and it is as anathema to a free humanity as anything I have ever seen. And as to our past—or Ruby's—not being perfect, you might recall that you know ours, but we do not know yours." Bless him, his voice was calm and controlled, like cool water thrown onto the fire that Ruby felt inside her. "You must play fair."

Headman Stevenson laughed. He addressed Koren. "Point, to our beautiful Ruby the Red's bodyguard."

Koren sat back in her chair, looking satisfied.

The Headman turned back to Ruby. His dark eyes seemed full of mischief, which puzzled her. But his words were clear and serious. "It is through competition and enforcement of the need to make enough to pay for air and food that we are able to make sure people do succeed. Fewer than five percent end up in the Brawl. In all of the Brawls, everywhere. They are reminders as much as prisons. They spur our society to its greatest efforts." He paused, and raised an eyebrow. "After all, another choice would be to kill them."

The idea was so repugnant Ruby couldn't even speak.

"But we do not do that. Remember that there are billions—billions—of souls in the whole fabric of humanity that surrounds Adiamo. You have been here less than half a year. Surely you can allow a little more time before you try to change our ways?"

She felt like a ten-year-old, and she knew that was how he meant her to feel. She took a deep breath and another sip of water, waiting until she could keep her voice steady. "Perhaps those of you who have been here all of your lives have learned to accept the grossly unfair. My song is merely art, but I'm pleased it touched a nerve."

Headman Stevenson smiled, the mischief back in his eyes. "I see you plan to be a worthy opponent. I would advise against it. I find you very intriguing, and I would love to keep you for a pet."

It was all Ruby could do not to leap up out of her chair. A look from KJ helped her keep her control.

"But pets are generally not allowed on space stations. Especially pets that might bite. If you are not careful, I will have options to exercise. And I have many, many more options than you do." The Headman's voice was calm, like KJ's calm voice, except that it felt like frost. "I will not allow my people to be riled up against me. Not by you. Not by anyone. If you want to keep singing, if you want to keep breathing, you will not sing that song."

He stood up. "Go enjoy the party. And make sure it is not the last one I want to throw for you." Then he came around to her side of the table, leaned down, and planted a kiss on the top of her forehead, his lips lingering. When he left, the startling noise of the party spilled in through the open door and then cut off completely.

Koren looked quite triumphant. She said nothing, but simply watched Ruby.

Ruby said nothing in return. Instinct told her that whoever spoke first lost.

The four of them stayed that way for quite a long time, the only sound in the room their breathing and the occasional screech of a chair leg.

She glanced at KJ and Naveen. KJ's calm demeanor reminded Ruby to breath deep in her belly. Naveen had an odd look on his face, and he wouldn't look directly at Ruby or Koren. Maybe because of their history on the *Fire*? But mostly Ruby kept her attention on Koren, her face as relaxed as she could force it to be. Twice she felt pains in her stomach so hard that she almost lost the serene expression, but she swallowed hard and stayed still.

To Ruby's surprise, Koren broke the silence first. "I only have one thing to add," she said. "There is a dangerous thing inside your community. Something *edgy*. I don't mind that, much. It's interesting to watch you all learn; you're faster than I thought you would be. Nevertheless, you remain almost as naïve as I expected. The problem here is that you don't know how little you know."

Naveen spoke up this time. "They're doing quite well, no thanks to you."

"Well, that's part of the problem," she said, smooth and even, smiling in spite of her words. "You seem to be getting help from the dangerous thing. Remember, I know your history. Tell your lover that he should stop looking for cargo or the dangerous thing will be revealed. And then, after you've been here a few years and learned a few things, invite me to lunch again."

Ruby had enough of being silent. "Perhaps someday you will earn an invitation."

Koren smiled, her strange golden eyes wide and almost kind looking. "That's your choice to make. Just make sure the nearer-term choices in your life are the right ones for your people."

"My choices are good."

Koren's laugh was soft, as if Ruby had just complimented her on a pretty shirt. She left, and when she left she didn't bother to close the door behind her. The noise of the party spilled into the small room, reminding Ruby that she was on display. It didn't matter how she felt. What mattered was how she looked and what she did and whether or not she could change hearts with those things.

CHAPTER SEVENTY

Onor was beginning to feel as much like an advisor as a guard in the morning meetings. He knew that was probably an illusion, but he sat at the table with Joel and SueAnne and sometimes they asked him a question. At the moment, it was SueAnne's turn to talk. "I've done the numbers. We're moving ahead because of Ruby's singing. If she does a concert a week for two years we'll be set for ten years, but she can't maintain that."

Joel hated dealing with numbers, and made it clear by the slightly exaggerated boredom that showed on his face. But he was too good a leader to ignore them. "Other income? Are we sending more people out to work?"

"Slowly. Without Ruby, we'd be losing ground. For each of the last four days, we made just over a quarter of what we need for a whole day's basic costs. At least according to what gets reported to us. I suspect we make more, and that there's a black market in credit."

Joel waved a hand at the air. "There has always been a black market. That's what the cargo bays were for. Allen's bar is the same thing."

"The black market is only part of it," SueAnne said. "Workers appear to be under-reporting. They're spending on their way back, tucking credit into pockets, hiding it in their socks." She looked disgusted. "I heard a rumor some buy women, or other pleasures. There's reported to be a lot of strange pleasures on this station. Things I don't want to know." She glanced meaningfully at Onor.

He answered, "Bartenders don't repeat their stories. But yes, there's some of that. And I've counted at least four or five of our young women who have gone off with Deepers, and I've only seen one of them come back."

"I heard some are saving in hopes they can get young like these people."

Marcelle was after Onor to start a savings for the treatment, at least for the baby.

Aleesi spoke up, startling Onor. "They are. But they cannot do that. They stay as young as they are, but only if they aren't already truly old."

SueAnne laughed. "So I'm too far gone."

Aleesi ignored the interruption. "Most of you are already slowing the aging process. Some of what you need is in the food here. But some of the medicine has to be given to children. So Onor could give it to his child, but he is too old to take it now."

And Marcelle was due soon. "What will I need to do?" He still couldn't even imagine holding a baby that was his. One minute it made him feel like running away and the next he was picking through piles of baby clothes. The baby did something else; it made it ever so more important that they catch Koren.

"There is a medical treatment that starts at birth and happens once a year until a body reaches about twenty years old."

Sue Anne interrupted. "Tell Onor about that later. It's losing the young that worries me. We need fewer people to feed. But that's not the fewer we need. I have another thought. We can send our prisoners into the Brawl. They'll be fed as well as we feed them, maybe better. They'll be housed. They'll learn about this culture, and we won't have to pay for them."

Onor had to bite his tongue to keep from reacting. Ruby would hate that. Hate wasn't a strong enough word. There wasn't a strong enough word.

Joel sat back in his chair, quiet. "How many prisoners are there now?"

"Two hundred and seventy-three."

"So many?" Joel shook his head. "Keep that as a last resort."

"We could also send the old if we have to," SueAnne added. "I'm running numbers. That will be even more."

"You can't!" Onor said.

SueAnne gave him a level look. "I will go myself if need be. The survival of the community is more important than I am."

"No it's not," Onor blurted out. "Who would do the books without you?"

Joel looked tired at the idea, worn down. "Go ahead and run all of those numbers. But don't do anything about it."

"Ix has helped me," she said.

"Was it Ix's idea?" Onor asked.

"No." SueAnne stood up out of her wheelchair and took a few wobbly steps to the sink, where she poured a glass of water and drank it all down at once. "No. It was my idea. But Ix is still tracking all of the people coming and going, and it's helping me track the credits. It may not be able to talk in most places, but it can listen everywhere still. This is very useful."

Ix almost never talked in these meetings. Aleesi was the one who usually offered them the most. "Hey, SueAnne?"

"Yes?"

"Keep your ear to the ground. I want a second place to put an AI. I know they're expensive. But I want to separate Aleesi and Ix. Or at least have a mobile copy of Aleesi."

"Why?" Joel asked.

"Because we need more access to Aleesi. More mobile access. All we can do now is talk to her in this little room."

Joel raised an eyebrow. "I thought you hated the spider."

Onor ignored him. "And we need to keep Ix safe in case we need it in court."

SueAnne shook her head at him. "Use your black market credit. We need income, not expenses."

CHAPTER SEVENTY-ONE

Ruby poured a cup of stim and sat at the breakfast table. KJ, Jali, and Dayn were already there, although there was no sign of either Min or Ani. "How do you feel?" Jali asked.

"Better for the day's rest. I'll have to thank Naveen for that."

"You'll get a chance," KJ said. "He messaged me that he's on his way to pick you up for breakfast."

Her shoulders tensed. "Am I entertaining?"

"As far as I know it's just Naveen."

"Good. You're going?"

"I'm sending Dayn. I've got to go check out the next venue."

So he thought wherever they were going next could be more dangerous to her than breakfast with Naveen. "Any specific fear?"

Dayn answered before KJ could form a sentence. "Let's see, you just tried to plant a seed of revolution on the biggest space station in the whole system by singing a song designed to make people hurt. Only a seed, mind you. You could have tried to shove a whole forest of revolutionary ideas at them. I know you have it in you." He was grinning. "And then the most powerful man in the system threatened to kill you if you sing the song again. And if I know you, you will."

So he knew about the meeting in the little room. And she was going to have to live with him all through breakfast.

KJ added, "There have been a few other threats. And a lot of appreciation. I'm not sure which scares me more."

"Life is becoming . . . interesting." Ruby sipped at her stim, which tasted extra spicy this morning. Good. "Jali, let's go get me ready."

Dayn laughed. "Can't get dressed by yourself anymore?"

Jali turned around and slapped at Dayn, the move playful but edged with a warning nonetheless. She made a little extra swing happen in her hips as she walked away, so it was all Ruby could do not to burst out in laughter.

Jali, bless her, always organized a closet full of Ruby's clothes no matter where they stayed. It was work; they moved every two to three days, and they'd be moving again tomorrow after tonight's concert. She rummaged through it. "Something simple?"

"Pants, and a purple shirt. The soft one."

"Not the uniform pants," Jali warned.

"Okay. You pick."

"What are you doing to do? Are you going to stop singing about the Brawl?"

"Probably not." Ruby reached a hand out for the simple black pants Jali offered. "The idea of it won't let me go. It's the only thing I truly hate here."

"Hate isn't the only thing you sing about."

Ruby wriggled into the pants. "Of course not." She turned to look Jali full in the face. "You have no idea how tempting it is to become like these people."

Jali laughed. "I never know what to think of you. One moment you're all about having all the power you can, the next you're professing that you'd rather be poor."

"Life's confusing." She took the purple shirt and dropped it over her head. "I suspect it's harder to be me than to watch me."

"I wouldn't bet on that." Jali tugged the shirt down to straighten the neckline and belted it, her hands soft and sure where they touched Ruby's waist. "Just don't get yourself killed, okay?"

Ruby sobered. "I've never been able to promise that."

When Naveen met Ruby and Dayn at the door, his face looked unreadable, but conflicted. That was the best way she could think of to describe it, anyway. It disturbed her, although she couldn't really explain why even to herself.

If Naveen was surprised that Dayn was going instead of KJ, he didn't signal that in any way. He simply told everyone good morning, and led Ruby and Dayn on a short, crowded train ride to a large station, and from there down a corridor to a small and sparse waiting room that held three other people. The bare walls offered no clue as to the purpose of the room. No breakfast looked likely to appear; the room smelled like cleaner rather than stim. "What is this?" Dayn asked.

"A ferry point."

Before she could ask Naveen for the definition of a ferry, a soft bell went off and a robotic voice said, "Ferry approaching. Stand away from the door."

The blue wall slid open from the middle. Another set of doors opened behind it, revealing what looked like a train car. Two young women stepped off the car. The other people in the room left with them, so Ruby, Naveen, and Dayn had the ferry to themselves.

They boarded a small, bubble-like ship with windows all around the middle and both ends closed up. There were twelve seats. They strapped in just as the ferry lurched forward a few hundred meters and stopped. "Hold on," Naveen said.

The ferry began accelerating, as if a big hand pushed them ever-faster from behind. Then it floated free.

"It will take us about thirty minutes to reach the catch point on the other side."

The set-up reminded Ruby of her trip with Satyana. "Is this a safe place to talk?"

Naveen smiled, and although he looked pleased with her, his features didn't show the attraction she usually saw there. "And if I was, what would I want to talk about?"

She smiled. "I suppose you'd want to talk about what you heard yesterday."

"You should have told me you were going to sing about the Brawl."

Dayn laughed. "And you should have expected that she would. You showed it to her. You're marketing her as a revolutionary."

"I showed her the Brawl so she would understand the dangers here."

"Well, you didn't think it through very hard, did you?" Dayn was on a roll. "You're making more from every concert than we are, more for one person than we're making for thousands. Without Ruby, this wouldn't be happening."

"It wouldn't be happening without me, either."

They sounded like little boys in a play yard. Out here, the *Deep* loomed large in the windows on one side, and open space went forever on the other, the lights of two arriving ships the only thing Ruby could see except stars. Dayn and Naveen kept sparring, but Ruby tuned it out. She needed to think. KJ would have been a better guard. He seldom said anything he didn't need to, while Dayn often said things he should regret.

She had been impetuous. If she was going to change things here she needed a strategy. She needed songs that pricked people deeper, and she also had to set them up right.

They couldn't stop earning credit.

Thus, she had to make revolution popular. That was sort of what had happened on the *Fire*, but the grays she had led there had known they were abused. She wasn't at all sure it would do any good for the people in the Brawl to revolt. They probably couldn't. The enforcer robots were worse than reds; there would be no Ben or Chitt there.

This station was bigger than she was. Was she crazy to think she could change anything fundamental about the *Deep*?

Dayn and Naveen grew so loud that Ruby decided to intervene lest she end up stitching them both up. Or stitching up Dayn. She was sure Naveen was a better fighter, and probably better armed. She'd seen him use a small hand-weapon on a too-rabid fan once, and the man had fallen down immediately as if stunned.

She touched Dayn on the shoulder. "Excuse me."

Dayn sat back, looking a tiny bit red-faced.

She spoke to Naveen. "How many more concerts do we have scheduled?"

"Four. I'm working on three more."

"Don't schedule those yet," she said. "I'm tired, and I need to see my family and my people. I need to know how they are doing."

"You have to do the four. They're under contract."

"Okay. But I'll sing what I want."

Naveen let out an exasperated sigh. "Can you at least give me song lists before, and then follow them? I spent all day yesterday trying to manage the spin on your last song."

"What do you mean?" she asked.

"I had to convince people you weren't really trying to foment a rebellion."

She smiled as sweetly as she could. "How did people react? Outside of the audience?"

"Thirty-two percent hated the song, forty-seven percent loved it, and twenty-one percent seemed conflicted. That was in the first three minutes. After that the percentage of haters went up."

Dayn leaned in, suddenly paying close attention. "Haters?"

"I don't think they even heard the song. I know some of them. They're the powerful, or the minions of the powerful, trying to control the story. They've made you look like a naïve, slightly-crazy woman who doesn't understand our perfect culture."

Dayn laughed. "Apt enough."

Ruby glared at him before she turned back to Naveen. "Raw numbers? Last I checked they were going up."

"Yes," Naveen said. "But so is the danger."

Dayn sat back in his seat. "Meaning she has more enemies than before?"

Ruby said, "When I started causing problems on the *Fire*, people like Sylva and Ellis started fighting me harder." She looked at Naveen. "So who's fighting me here?"

"Assume it's most of the people in power. And that some of them will smile at you and clap and offer you power of your own in order to try and control you, and when you refuse they'll drop you so hard you crack your tailbone. Don't underestimate how cruel power can be."

She felt the pull of the ferry station at their destination, as if the capsule they had been floating in had been grabbed by a guiding force. They were almost out of time. "What about Koren's threat at the party? She wants Joel to stop something or she's going to get Aleesi."

"That could be. Koren's exactly the kind of power to avoid."

"I've never called on her. She comes to me."

The ferry shuddered and slowed.

Naveen turned to Ruby. "Be polite for breakfast. These are the opposite of enemies, and could be even more dangerous. Don't promise too much."

Dayn tensed, and Ruby stood and stared through the opening door.

She knew one of the three people in the small waiting room. Satyana.

CHAPTER SEVENTY-TWO

Joel dismissed Onor after the morning meeting ground to an inconclusive halt, telling him to come back later that afternoon. Onor headed right to the bar and suggested Allen help him find a way to move Aleesi, only to be mostly ignored.

Onor couldn't give up. He spoke loudly, so Allen would hear him even though Allen was on the far side of the room, cleaning tables and dodging a little robot scrubber that was doing the floors. "It's important. I just know it is. In fact, I want to get Aleesi all the way out of here. Put her someplace safe. I don't want to see Ruby's face if we lose Aleesi or if anything bad happens to her."

Allen just moved on to the next table.

"I know one of the robot spiders ate Colin. I was there, damn it. But Aleesi is helping us learn things we wouldn't know."

"Do you really trust it?"

That stopped Onor. "I don't know."

"At least you're not all the way gone."

"No. But we need help. I need to find a way to prove Koren stole from us."

Allen looked up at him. "Even if you do get a webling, what are you going to do with it? How are you going to move Ix?"

"I thought I'd copy Aleesi. I need her mobile."

"Will that work? Her spider body was as big as this bar."

Onor winced. "I don't know. I guess I need Naveen, but he's not here."

"That couple came back last night, after you were already gone. I told them to be back today. Maybe if you can sneak away and get what you need, then they can help."

"Are they familiar with AIs?"

"How do I know? At least they're from here."

"Okay. But then I may need some more credit."

Allen gave out a heavy sigh. "I wish people would stop seeing me as place to borrow credit."

"Who's borrowing? I'm a small investor, and surely you want to be supportive? Besides, you're the one with a real going concern."

"Other people could have those too, if they wanted them."

Onor laughed. "I think they will. Especially the younger ones. I overheard two girls talking about starting a clothing store for women. I noticed because I'm going to need baby clothes."

"I'm feeling sorry for you."

Evie came in, running a comb through her hair and looking askance at Allen. "Sorry I'm a few minutes late." She noticed Onor. "Hi. Have you heard from Haric?"

"Not yet."

"We had a date—like an appointment. He was going to call me and we were going to have a half an hour to talk before I had to start work. But he didn't, and I tried to call him and he didn't answer."

"Maybe he's still asleep." Allen came over to them and leaned on the bar. "Or he just forgot."

Evie bristled. "He wouldn't forget."

Onor shook his head. "Don't you know teasing when you hear it?"

She stamped her foot with the drama available to the very young. "I'm worried."

CHAPTER SEVENTY-THREE

Satyana nodded at Naveen and held her hand out to Ruby. "Pleased to have you join us."

"Thank you."

"Follow me."

Ruby expected to be introduced to the two people with Satyana. The woman stood tall and thin, reminding Ruby vaguely of Marcelle. The man was squatter, but shared her features. They walked with sure strides behind Satyana and in front of Ruby and Dayn. Naveen took the rear position.

Satyana led them to a table in a small room with windows that looked out over the station. They were high up, so the Deep looked like a long froth of habitat bubbles and tangled transportation, punctuated here and there with the angular shapes of spaceships. Small vessels travelled between locations, each of them reminding Ruby how vast the *Deep* was.

A robot brought six steaming cups of stim in on a tray and retreated toward what must be a kitchen based on the smells coming from it. At least she was going to get the breakfast Naveen had promised.

Satyana sipped at her stim and looked at Ruby appraisingly. "You will tell no one that you've been here."

"I thought every move was tracked. You told me so yourself."

"This trip won't appear on anyone's tracking."

"Really? How?" Dayn asked.

"There is a restaurant here, and you will be recorded as having dined with Naveen and Dayn, and no one else." She smiled a slightly evil smile, playful. "And Naveen is picking up that tab."

Naveen pulled a flask out of his pocket and dumped a stream of still into the stim. As far as Ruby could tell, everyone at the table noticed and chose to ignore it.

After a few moments of small talk, Satyana asked Ruby, "What do you plan to do?"

"About what?" Ruby asked.

"The song."

Dayn shook his head. "Everyone's making an awfully big deal about one song."

"It's not the song that worries them. It's how fascinated people are by our Ruby here. Naveen knows how to build interest, but this time the attention seems to have a mind of its own."

Naveen's face turned red. "Ruby is unique."

"You see." Satyana turned back to Dayn. "This station is ripe for change. Most people didn't know it, but Ruby is helping to wake people up. This fits with our plans. We are also able to expose some of our leaders. Most people here wouldn't have cared enough, given that they've almost all got food and entertainment in plenty. But they will care if they fight Ruby, since many are coming to love her."

The robot returned, serving Satyana first, then her yet un-introduced guests, then Ruby, Naveen, and Dayn. Each plate had fruit and nuts that had been heated and smelled rich and comforting, and three clever small breads in different colors.

After everyone took the first bites, Satyana continued. "We were hoping you'd get people a little riled up. We didn't expect so much attention so fast. I think it's because the current power structure reacted with so much negative spin. In other words, it really wasn't the song. You might be in real danger, but we'd prefer you don't get locked up just yet."

Ruby felt slightly confused. "So you want me to drive more protests?"

"Yes. Will you?"

Ruby shook her head. "Maybe. I need to understand what might happen. My people depend on me."

"We are working to change that," Satyana said.

Now she was even more confused. "How?"

"Koren stole from you. We're going to expose her."

"That explains the warning she gave me."

Satyana narrowed her eyes. "You saw Koren?"

"At the after-party from the last concert. I saw her—with the headman. She wanted me to tell Joel to stop doing something . . . something about cargo?"

Satyana and the other two looked at each other.

A long silence allowed Ruby to take a bite and to work her way partly through the stim. She loved the way it seemed to run slowly through her veins, waking her up bit by bit. The food tasted good, but it didn't sit well in her stomach so she pushed it around with her fork while she waited for the conversation to start again.

Satyana asked Ruby, "Did you tell Joel that Koren is on to him?"

"No. I'm sure everything in our calls is recorded." She glanced at Naveen. "Being on tour is like being under a microscope. But I'm trying to get back home soon. I need a break."

The man spoke. "We'll tell him. I'm going back there tonight."

Ruby startled at that. "Is there a way to get back that fast? I thought it would be a multi-day journey."

"It would be, on a train. I'll fly."

The idea skewered her with homesickness, the feeling more physical than it had been so far. She put a hand over her stomach, the pain making her groan.

Dayn touched her shoulder, almost a caress.

Normally she would have flinched away from him.

"Are you okay?"

"Just a little tired."

Satyana looked at Naveen. "Has she had a medical exam since they got here?"

He shrugged.

Satyana's eyes narrowed. "I'll send one."

Ruby sat as straight as she could. The pain was starting to scare her, but it also felt private. "I'm okay."

"We'll send a bot."

"I don't need one."

Satyana laughed. "It won't hurt."

Ruby still didn't entirely trust Satyana. "So you and your friends want to overthrow Stevenson?"

Even though they said nothing, the answer lived in their body language. They did.

"What would you do differently if you were in charge?" Ruby asked Satyana.

"I will not be in charge." She glanced at the man and woman who were going back home tonight.

They looked at each other and then back at Ruby.

She couldn't tell what kind of power they had. They seemed confident, and curious, but they didn't feel enveloped in confidence like Koren and Headman Stevenson. They felt . . . more real.

Ruby stared at Satyana. "You said you want to know what I'll do. I'll do anything to protect my people. That means the things I'll fight to change here are the things that we need changed to succeed." She paused, took another deep breath and another sip of stim, which had now cooled and tasted slightly bitter. "We need time to learn about this place without the fear of the Brawl hanging over us."

Satyana replied, "You also need good leaders to succeed."

"This is not the *Fire*, where I knew how to tell good leadership from bad."

The woman spoke for the first time. "I thought I would like you. I do. But I cannot tell you much. You are in danger and secrets cannot be kept easily here." She sounded earnest and slightly hesitant. "I promise that we'll help your people as much as we can. If we can. This is an unstable time."

Ruby said, "I still don't know what kind of help I should take from you or give to you."

"How could you?" The woman glanced at Satyana. "Give her our gift."

Satyana pulled a box out of her pocket and handed it to Ruby.

Inside, she found a small metal pin in the shape of the *Fire*. It looked like the ones they used at home, symbols that had gone on the uniforms of the first crew of the *Fire* and been passed down ever since. Onor and Marcelle each had one that Joel had given them shortly after he took power.

Satyana said, "We saw these in some of the videos. This one opens up, try it."

Ruby ran her finger around the outer edge, which was a little bit sharp. Just behind part of the clip itself she found an unexpected ball of metal and pressed against it. Nothing happened.

"Let me show you." Satyana took it from Ruby's hand and pressed hard, almost like snapping her fingers. She closed it again quickly and handed it back to Ruby.

This time Ruby managed to get it open, although doing so hurt her thumb. Inside, there was a button.

"Press that if you get in trouble. Then we'll know."

"Okay."

Satyana reached into her pocket and pulled out two more, handing them to Ruby. "Give these to whoever you most think should have them. Maybe pass them around so that are always with people who are protecting you. Naveen already has one."

Ruby handed them both to Dayn. "The second one is for KJ."

Dayn glanced at Satyana. "And what exactly happens if we press these?"

"We send people to help."

The pin made her feel the dangers here more than anything else had, except perhaps the Headman's chatter about pets. She simply smiled and said, "Thank you."

"Finish your food," Satyana said. "We've only got a few more minutes."

Ruby looked at the two strangers, who remained un-introduced. "Tell Joel that I miss him and that I'll be home soon."

"We will," the woman said.

Ruby pushed at her food some more, suddenly certain the meeting had really been for the two strangers. They had wanted to see her, to test her. She felt like she'd passed, but she wondered what that meant.

Back in the ferry, Ruby collapsed into a seat and waited for the invisible mechanism to push them away. "Did you know those two people?" she asked Naveen.

A small smile played around his lips. "Yes."

"But you won't tell me their names?"

"They wouldn't mean anything to you."

"But they do to you?"

"Yes."

"You warned me on the way over. You said not to promise too much. What did you mean?"

"They will use you if you let them, and they won't care if they use you up."

Dayn filled the ferry with laughter. "Really. And you're not using her?"

Naveen stiffened. "I'm giving her fair return."

Dayn said, "Shouldn't we get more as her audience is going up?"

They were at it again. Ruby held up her hands. "Don't fight. You're probably both right." She glanced at Dayn. "We wouldn't be out here without Naveen." She looked at Naveen. "You are getting rich off of me. I'll finish these four concerts at the rates we agreed on, but I want more after that."

"And what will you do to earn extra? Can I get you to start commenting and working on our communication nets?"

He'd been after her for that for a long time. "I can't. I need time to write songs."

"You're stubborn."

"I'm tired." Ruby yawned, as if finally released from the tension of the rather odd breakfast. Dayn put an arm around her and she leaned into him. The last thing she heard was Naveen mumbling, "Maybe we need a medical bot today."

CHAPTER SEVENTY-FOUR

Onor and Marcelle shared a table at the far end of the bar. Marcelle sipped fizzy water with a hint of fruit in it, and watched him contemplatively. "What are you trying to figure out?" he asked her.

"If you're happy."

Pregnancy had changed her. He loved this Marcelle better than the younger version he'd known, although it was a mystery to him how such a natural process could make a woman so much more centered on emotions. If she had cared about feelings before, she hadn't shown it. When they were teenagers, she'd teased him relentlessly. These days, he often felt unsure about how to react to her so he just said, "I'm worried. We should have heard from Haric."

"I'm worried, too," she whispered. "About almost everything."

He reached across the table and cupped her face. She was so thin her cheekbones rose like ridges under his fingers, as if the baby was eating everything she put into her system. "Don't worry about the things you can't control, anyway."

"And you can control what happens to Haric?"

"I might be able to do something about it."

A frown creased her forehead. "I knew you were thinking of leaving."

At least she didn't object. Not that he'd call the tone he heard in her voice happy. "Haric would come to save any of us."

Marcelle pointed toward the door he had been trying to watch. "Is that the couple you're looking for?"

He turned to see the tall woman and the shorter man inside the doorway, looking around. "Yes. Send Joel a message?"

She bent to her slate.

He held up a hand and waved.

They came over and sat, and Onor introduced Marcelle.

Once more the man and woman remained anonymous. Onor looked at them and said, "Why don't you just make up names?"

"Misrepresenting yourself is illegal here," the woman said.

"We need your help," Onor said.

They looked curious but waited for him to speak.

"We have . . . something Naveen helped us with. A situation." He was having trouble with words. Fear that a situation Koren already knew about would backfire? "We have two AIs sharing a single webling. It was the only place we had for them. We want to separate them, so one of them can be carried with us. Can you help us set that up?"

The man's eyes had narrowed. "It could be risky. Why is it important?"

They'd asked about exposing Koren, and they needed Ix to help with that, and this would protect Ix. "We . . . it will help with what you want us to do. To expose Koren."

The man stared at him for a long time, measuring. "I can call someone." He stepped away from the table, touched his slate and then his ear, and in a moment he was talking in tones too hushed for Onor to hear.

"What would you like?" Onor asked as he called Evie over.

She gave a mute look that implied desperation and he shrugged to let her know that he had no word from Haric.

Evie looked as if Haric's absence had scraped something vital from her, but she turned away with their orders.

Perhaps their relationship was more intense than he had thought.

Joel appeared, making a hole through the crowded floor by moving chairs aside to get SueAnne's wheelchair through. They sat down and greeted the woman, accepting her return smile. Allen noticed them and came over.

As soon as the man finished with his phone call, he sat back down. "Ruby says hello."

"You saw her?" Onor asked.

"How is she?" Marcelle asked.

Joel leaned in. "When did you see her?"

"Recently. She's okay, but she looks weak."

"Who was with her?" Joel asked.

"Dayn."

Joel's eyes narrowed. "Not KJ? Have you seen KJ?"

"We know who he is. He was off proofing the next place Ruby is supposed to sing."

Joel sat back, brow furrowed. "What do you mean, weak?"

"She says she's just tired. That she misses you and will see you soon."

"I want her home."

"We're not in control of that," the man said. "But we did order up a medical bot examination for her."

Marcelle leaned in, clearly interested. "What can a medical bot do? I'm in charge of medical here, and we have some of our own from the *Fire*, but all they do is help lift people or help with simple surgeries. They can't tell, for example, why someone is tired."

The man answered Marcelle. "The kind of bot we ordered her time with should be able to tell that for Ruby."

"Can I see one? Can you send one here?"

"You can order one," the man said. "I'll see that someone sends you information."

"Thank you." Marcelle put a hand over her belly, and he saw it jump slightly as the baby kicked.

SueAnne frowned. "What will that cost us?"

"We're paying for Ruby's exam."

"We have another thing to talk about," Onor said. "We sent someone out to look for cargo, like you asked us to, and they seem to have disappeared."

"You sent one person out?"

Onor nodded.

"We heard Koren knows you're looking. She found Ruby at a party and told her to tell you to stop it."

Onor sat back, suddenly worried. "So they're both in danger."

"I want her home," Joel repeated.

Marcelle was stroking her stomach, as if danger to Ruby meant danger to their child.

"You got from her to us in one day. Can we go?" Joel asked. "We can pay you."

SueAnne glanced at Joel with a sour look on her face but Joel ignored her.

"Maybe. But first we need to find the person you sent for proof. They're in immediate danger."

"I'll go," Onor said. "I sent him."

"Who do you want to take with you? One of the dancers? Chitt?"

"No. The Jackman."

Joel frowned. "Really? What about Chitt?"

Marcelle spoke. "The Jackman loves Onor like a son, and he's smart."

Onor glanced at the man. "We need to move the AI first."

"It's as good as done."

Onor waited in the bar for The Jackman, Marcelle yet again beside him. It had taken three hours to prepare, and Marcelle looked exhausted. "You should go lie down."

"I might not see you again."

"Of course you will."

"You don't know that." She didn't flinch or turn away.

Evie plopped down at the table. She wasn't wearing her waitressing uniform.

Onor blinked at her. "You're not going."

"Try to stop me," Evie replied calmly.

"Haric wouldn't want you to go," he told her.

The Jackman elbowed his way through the door.

Onor picked up his pack. Aleesi hadn't exactly been copied, but a secure connection to the webling existed in a two-inch by two-inch wafer in his pocket, and he had a fistful of small round nubs made to fit inside ears.

Evie stood.

Onor opened his mouth to tell her no, but Marcelle put a hand on his arm and gave him a look he'd come to dread. "I would go if it was you."

Onor glanced at The Jackman.

He shrugged. "If it were Marcelle or Ruby we wouldn't be able to say no. I bet Evie won't listen to us either."

"You're getting soft, old man," Onor said.

"We might need her help."

Evie practically glowed.

Onor leaned down to hold Marcelle, and she whispered in his ear. "I love you."

"I love you, too," he said. "Don't have that baby until I get back."

"Then you had best hurry."

CHAPTER SEVENTY-FIVE

The day after the odd breakfast, and only two hours before Ruby's next concert, Ruby and Jali stood in the dressing room, laughing. Jali's fingers flew through Ruby's hair, braiding in long strings of shiny thread that would look a tiny bit like flames under the stage lights.

They had left the door open. KJ came in, leading a silvery beast that looked as shiny and malleable as the ones they had first seen on the *Fire*. "It's not from Koren?" Jali asked.

"There's a note from Satyana. She says it's in appreciation for your help."

"A bribe?"

KJ shook his head. "I doubt she can force you into anything. I would like to see the bot in action."

Ruby stared at him for a long moment, fear rising in her throat for no good reason. She was fine. "Put it in the corner and I'll mess with it after the show."

"You only have it for an hour," he said.

She and Jali looked at each other, and Jali sighed. "I can do fewer ribbons than I planned. Give me five minutes to adjust the design."

KJ gave Jali such a stern look that she took a step back from Ruby. "I'll finish as soon as it's done."

The robot looked at Ruby. "Strip please." The robot sounded human and female, almost like SueAnne.

Ruby stared at KJ.

He backed out of room. "I'll be right out here."

"And don't let Dayn in either."

Jali stayed, glaring at the machine as Ruby stripped. She felt far more vulnerable naked in front of the silver doctor than she ever had in front of a man. "We don't have time for this." Ruby struggled not to grab her clothes and throw them back on. After all, she could reach her clothes. The room was small.

"I don't even know how to send it away," Jali whispered.

Ruby still wasn't completely sure she should trust Satyana. Or anybody for that matter. But she had to trust someone. She'd done it with Naveen.

The robot reached for her arm with more dexterity than she expected, although to be fair it could probably do surgery. Its grip was cool and slippery. It was also too firm and precise for her hand to actually slide free when she tested it. "Hold still," it told her. Its other "hand" came up, not in a gripping shape but rounded. A needle poked free and slid smoothly into her arm, blood flowing almost immediately and faster than Ruby wanted. The robot doctor seemed very capable. The part of Ruby that used to repair robots wanted to know how it worked.

"Stand still."

It made a slight whirring sound as it snipped a tiny bit of her hair, and then it scraped some skin from her hip with a cold metal blade. At that she moved away, just be to be told again to "Stand still."

Jaliet braced her, and she gritted her teeth and let it keep touching her, once behind her knees, once at the wrist. Then it withdrew and said, "Stand away," which could only have been a command for Jali.

"Close your eyes."

Ruby obeyed.

"You too," it said to Jali.

Ruby forced herself to take a deep breath and trust.

She heard a hum, and a faint warmth passed from her head to her toes.

"You may get dressed again."

Ruby opened her eyes to find that the robot had changed shape and was parked against a wall, ignoring them.

"Let's just put on your clothes for tonight," Jali said.

Ruby tugged her underwear up and fastened her bra before saying, "Yes." She felt better just for being that covered.

Jali went right back to finishing Ruby's hair, her fingers pulling tight across Ruby's scalp from time to time. She tugged hard enough to apologize twice, a sign that she was as disconcerted by the machine as Ruby.

Jali poured a blue-gray dress with colored fringe over Ruby's head and tugged it in at the waist with a cinched strap. She used the small *Fire* pin to hold a flame-colored scarf across Ruby's shoulders. Jali herself wore the other one, and the third had been given to KJ.

Ruby kept glancing at the machine. Surely the hour had passed. It made her feel fretful. "Is it a bad sign that it's been here so long?"

"I doubt it."

"I think so," Ruby replied.

"Maybe it's in awe of you."

She shook her head. A small part of her had been afraid of her weakness for a long time, had been hiding it from herself as much as from Joel and Jali and KJ and Onor and everybody else.

"It's almost time to go on."

The expected knock came on the door.

"Coming!" Jali called. She snatched up a brush for last minute touches and took Ruby's hand. "Let's go."

The door opened to reveal Satyana instead of the stage hand.

CHAPTER SEVENTY-SIX

Onor sat next to Evie on the train. Her dark hair reminded him of Marcelle's, but otherwise she was less angular than Marcelle and even thinner. The look on her face drove out any sense she might be fragile, though. In fact, she looked so intense he felt glad she was with them.

He glanced around the slightly swaying car. Two men were deep in conversation near the front. A robot sat three seats away, its only movement to rock with the train. A pretty woman wearing a deep red jumpsuit snored two seats behind him, blue hair hiding half of her face. No one paid any obvious attention to them.

Onor dug into his pocket and pulled out three of the small round objects the technician had handed to him. He handed two to Evie and watched her pass one to The Jackman. He spoke softly. "Put those in your ear. They're called earbugs. Then we can talk to Aleesi."

The Jackman narrowed his eyes.

"We need her. That's how we even knew what train to take."

"What else do we need to know?" The Jackman stared at the earbug, making no move to bring it near his ear. "Didn't you write down where we get off the train?"

The Jackman always accepted new things slower than most. "We need Aleesi. Think of having her help as a silver lining for getting attacked."

"I don't like it."

"We *do* need her. Or some AI. Everyone around us knows more than we do."

"Which ear?" Evie asked.

Onor shrugged.

Evie lifted her right hand and tucked a black curl behind her ear. She showed him an empty hand, and then her face screwed up in an odd way.

"Are you okay?"

She said "Yes," but her face stayed so tight she *looked* like she was in pain.

The Jackman shook his head ever so slightly. A refusal.

Onor leaned his head onto his hand, trying to look natural in case the robot actually was watching them. He used his index finger and his thumb to push the earbug into his ear canal.

It burrowed, warmed, and seemed to spread out. It felt alive. Nothing had ever moved so deep in his ear, and for a second he wondered if it was going to pop his eardrum. Even though it didn't actually hurt, it felt strange enough that he understood the look on Evie's face.

"I was wondering if you were ever going to talk to me."

He whispered as softly as he could. "Hi, Aleesi."

"You don't have to make any noise at all. Just think you're talking."

"What?" He could still hear the word. He tried again. "Like this?"

"Yes."

Evie's voice, only in his ear and not from beside him at all. She wasn't even looking at him; her head was turned toward The Jackman. "Yes."

"She's got it," Aleesi said. "Try again. You don't even have to form the words."

He glanced over at the Jackman, who still had his fist closed over the earbug. "Do it," he said out loud.

"That's worse," Aleesi said into his ear. "Softer."

Damned machine, he thought.

"Better."

He laughed.

The train stopped, and the doors opened automatically. No one got on or off.

The Jackman still looked dubious. But then, he hadn't spent any time with Aleesi. If Aleesi hadn't started out chasing Onor with intent to kill, he might actually like her. She felt more human than Ix ever had.

It took almost half an hour for all three of them to be able to talk to each other and to Aleesi. He subvocalized the way Aleesi had taught him. "This is like on the *Fire*, when we could all talk to Ix, only then we had to speak out loud."

"You can still talk to me." Ix's voice. "Through Aleesi."

Onor hadn't realized it would work like that. "That's great."

"Can Ix talk to its copies?"

Ix answered. "I cannot."

"Ix is old," Aleesi elaborated. "It wasn't designed to do that. So let's get on with restoring your riches."

The Jackman spoke, loud enough Onor could hear his whisper as well as the sound of his voice amplified through the earbug. "Why do you care?"

"I don't like the way that you've been treated. Koren should not have been able to get away with what she did. Out on the Edge, we have morals."

"And your morals are why you attacked us?" The Jackman said, again too loud.

"Subvocalize," Aleesi said. "The only way that my masters at the Edge can get new resources is to capture them. We're forbidden to go into the inner system. If they opened trade, we wouldn't be pirates."

The Jackman made no response, although Onor had the feeling he was intensely uncomfortable.

Evie spoke. "Didn't your masters capture you?"

"The usual captures were asteroids or comets or derelict ships. Let's get on with this. Exchange Four is bigger than Exchange Five: in addition to nearby habs, it serves one of the main ports where ships bring goods into and out of the *Deep*."

The Jackman said, "Okay."

"I've downloaded a map to all of your slates. I've noted the places Haric stopped and the people he talked to. I recommend that you start with the last people he saw before he disappeared. Ix and I will send information to your slates as we get it. I'm going to be watching you, so if whatever happened to Haric happens to you, I may be able to record it."

"How are you going to watch us out here?" The Jackman asked.

"There are open cameras throughout the exchanges that any AI can access."

"Just AIs?" The Jackman looked unhappy. "Not people?"

"It would take you seven point three days to watch the combined video from five minutes of all of the cameras through Exchange Four."

Evie leaned forward, looking excited. "Can you show me the video you have of Haric?"

"I've put it on your slate."

"So, what is Ix doing to catch Koren?"

"It's studying the Deeping Rules."

"So what should we do now?"

"I'm watching video," Evie said. And she was, one earphone dangling against her chest and the other in her left ear, so she had one for the AI and one for the video.

"I'll look at the layout of Exchange Four," The Jackman offered, pulling his slate out of his pocket.

Onor sat back, the train seat digging against his shoulders. The blue-haired woman still snored behind him, the robot still appeared asleep, and the two men had stopped talking. One was absorbed in his slate and the other appeared to be listening intently to something. Even though absolutely no one was looking at them, Onor couldn't shake the idea that they were being watched.

CHAPTER SEVENTY-SEVEN

Satyana stood in the doorway, her unnaturally blue eyes staring from Ruby to the medical robot and back again. Fury tightened her jaw so sharply that Ruby took a step back. She pressed into Jali who murmured, "Easy."

"Sit down," Satyana said.

"I have to go sing. Really. It's time." Whatever information kept the robot here and brought Satyana had to be cruel. "If you've got bad news, you can tell me after the concert."

Satyana kept looking at Ruby as she said, "Jali. Go tell Naveen she'll be a few minutes late."

Jali put a hand on Ruby's back, as if holding her up. "I want to stay."

Satyana shook her head.

Jali looked at Ruby, who nodded. "I'll tell you what she says." Jali stepped away, slowly, and then hesitated again by the door, looking back. "Go on," Ruby said. "Keep Naveen out of here until I come out. He's not going to like me being late."

The look of betrayal on Jali's face was almost enough for Ruby to call her back in. She would have, except for the stoic, barely contained anger that sat on Satyana like a curse word.

As soon as the door closed behind Jali, Ruby snapped "What?"

"How long have you been sick?"

"I'm just tired."

Satyana stared at her, unmoving. Unyielding.

"I can't stop here. If I stop, people will starve."

"You're almost dead."

Ruby blinked at her, a sudden wave of shivers running up her spine and goose bumps rising on her arms. She stood up. "I'm not."

"How much weight have you lost?"

"I don't know."

"Has Jali had to take in clothes? Make them smaller?"

"Almost everything's new." She heard the childishness of her words, but there wasn't anything else she could do. She was fine. She had to be. Everyone needed her.

"Are you nauseous?"

"Sometimes."

"When was the last time you felt well?"

"Before we got here."

"Are there other people sick?"

Ruby hadn't asked Marcelle for an update in the last week or so before she left. She'd been caught up in finances and clothes and getting ready, in Aleesi and Ix, and a thousand other things. "Yes. Some. A few died. Early. We thought it was just from being here. Koren tested us all when she came, but maybe she missed the babies. Her damned robot. Looked just like the one you sent. Maybe it was the one you sent." But then Satyana hadn't been there, not on the ship. "Anyway, most people are getting better." She was babbling.

Satyana spoke slowly, as if that were the only way Ruby might hear her. "You need treatment. It probably won't save you. Maybe nothing can save you now."

Ruby sat and breathed, hard and ragged.

Satyana sat in the one extra chair that was there. "I'm mad at the whole damned universe. I need you, and you need me. The two of us are enough to make change." She sat forward, looking closely at Ruby, placing a hand on her shoulder. "You have to get better. The robot says you can't, but you've done other impossible things."

Ruby sat and stared at her for a moment. She needed to go. Naveen wasn't going to wait forever, and there was an audience out there. "What did the robot tell you I have?"

"An allergy. A deep one. We call it the Death of Hope."

"The Death of Hope?" How could anyone name something that badly?

"There are things we put in our food to keep us young. That's probably what Koren was testing you for reactions to. When we first started with this, some people died. Not many. But after the first generation, no one died. We thought it was gone, forever. It's like cancer, which used to kill us but doesn't any more. The Death of Hope makes you thin and it steals your energy and grows things inside you that kill you. But then, some cancers were like this; caused by things that were meant to do good."

"Our people die of cancer," Ruby said. "Some of the old. We know enough to find it in the young, though. If I got it now, I'd live."

Satyana shook her head.

"What if I don't eat any more of your food? What if I go away?"

"That would have worked if you'd known before you came to live here. It's too deep now. By the time the Death of Hope shows up—by the time it steals your energy, it's really, really hard to fix. We'll try. We'll try very hard."

Ruby's thoughts seemed to batter against a ball of pain that she couldn't let come up yet. It felt so sharp it seemed to be physical, even though she'd just been giggling with Jali. She had been feeling better than she had been for a few days. But now . . . now there was a monster inside her that might come out and steal her joy, her strength. "Some of our children lived through it. I don't remember the details, but Marcelle could tell you." She wanted to clutch her stomach but she didn't let herself.

"What about the adults?"

Ruby shook her head. "I don't know. I have to sing. I'm going to sing and then we're going to talk about this. Jali is going to be with me."

"She's not sick?" Satyana asked.

"No." Ruby shook her head. "No, she's always been thin."

"I'll have the robot test her."

There was no time to think about any of this now. "Listen to me sing." She could barely talk without collapsing. She stood up and stretched and breathed. "I have to sing before I think about this."

Satyana whispered, "I'm sorry."

"It'll be a good concert." Ruby held her hand out to Satyana. "Come listen from backstage. But don't tell Naveen. Not yet."

Satyana shook her head. "I have something else to do. Good luck."

"What happens next?"

"The bot stays with you and it starts treatments."

Ruby forced her hands not to shake. "Will it hurt?"

Satyana offered a small smile. "You already hurt." She leaned in and gave Ruby a hug. Her arms were strong and she smelled like cinnamon and stim. "Go."

Ruby went.

CHAPTER SEVENTY-EIGHT

Exchange Four felt twice as big as Exchange Five. Spaceship crews wandered here and there, some with clear purpose and some gawking. Onor saw children and families and even a few people that looked old.

They passed the job market, which was still half-open. Holographic pictures of spaceships spun above the aisles with open positions scrolling through the air under them. Onor leaned over to Evie and whispered in her ear. "We should remember this. There may be a day we need to get off the *Deep*."

"I'd love to get out of here." Her gaze kept sweeping the crowd as if she could force Haric to emerge.

The Jackman stared at his slate, trying to orient it to the rows of booths. The Exchange felt so confusing that Onor was glad of Aleesi's voice in his ear, saying, "Fourth booth on the left. Haric stopped and looked on his way in. Come back later though. First, find the last place. The Jackman has it as a bright yellow dot."

"What's the fastest way to get there?"

"Let The Jackman lead you. It will give him a focus and you need to learn your way around."

Yet another thing he liked about her; she taught them instead of telling them. Ix had been terrible at that.

Onor glanced at the booth Aleesi had told them to come back to. Pendants shone and sparkled in artificial light, gold chains draped over leather bolsters, and at least three groups of customers eyed the merchandise. Evie pulled toward it, but Onor took her small hand in his. "Stay close. I don't want to lose you."

"Aleesi can help us find each other," Evie hissed.

"And if I lose you, Haric will kill me after we find him."

She glared at him and pulled her hand free, but she stayed near him.

"Why are there so many more people here than at home?" Onor subvocalized.

"Many are from visiting spaceships. The *Deep* is known for its shopping. People can buy everything from starship fuel to food to baubles they have no possible need for at the Exchanges of the *Deep*."

It took thirty minutes and two wrong turns to find the booth Aleesi was sending them to. At least twice, Onor became briefly convinced that they were being followed, but then the suspected follower turned away from them.

When the Jackman looked up and said, "We're there," Onor and Evie stopped beside him and the three of them looked the booth over.

"It's not what I expected," Onor said.

The booth sold animals. Or more correctly, animal DNA, animal fetuses, and animals designed for specific purposes. A large, hoofed animal with a doleful face pulled a plow in one picture, a small cat-like animal sat on a man's shoulder, looking ready to leap off and protect him, and a variety of small and fluffy beasts in an even bigger variety of colors followed children or cuddled with them on couches. A man stood behind the booth, feet planted, watching a small throng of customers. A few were children, apparently thoroughly engaged in looking through the entire catalog.

Evie approached the booth, The Jackman and Onor right behind her. They stood behind the children, watching the catalog swing by. Onor subvocalized, "I should have been more interested in the cargo. I wouldn't know if any of these came from the *Fire*."

"Ix is watching."

"Does it know?" Onor asked. "I didn't think Naveen had copied all of its memories."

"It has many fragments of the *Fire*'s manifest."

Onor felt the weight of the things he didn't understand.

A tall woman wearing an open pressure suit and comfortable shoes that didn't match it called two children back to her and walked away, leaving the booth momentarily empty of customers. Evie stepped up to the man, who offered a salesman's broad smile. "What can I do for you?"

Evie held up her slate and showed him a picture of Haric. "Have you seen this man?"

A slight, dark look passed across the man's face as his smile transformed to a blank look. "No, I have not seen him."

Evie brought up a video clip of Haric standing in front of the booth.

Onor winced.

"I cannot be expected to recall all of my customers." He inclined his head. "May I show you anything?"

Onor stepped in. "We're interested in anything new. Perhaps items you've only had in your catalog for a few months?"

The man smiled. He pulled up a picture of a cat-like creature with white fur. "Perhaps like this? It's a new mutation of our best-selling children's pet for spaceships. It trains easily and can take cold sleep."

Onor shook his head and said, "Thank you." The man wasn't going to show them anything, and now they'd announced their presence to everyone. He had expected Evie to do better, but he hadn't remembered how young she was.

He tugged on her arm, pulling her away from the booth. The Jackman followed, the look on his face sour. As soon as they were out of earshot, he leaned down toward Evie. "Don't tell them what you want."

She turned to face him. "Then how will we find anything out?"

"Build trust first and try to wheedle clues out of people."

"That will take forever."

The Jackman sighed. "Better that than alerting your quarry with direct requests. They've no reason to trust us."

"Or we them," she shot back.

"But we're the ones who need something they have."

Evie looked daggers at The Jackman, but she nodded.

They learned nothing more at the next five booths. After the fifth booth— one that sold rare minerals in large and expensive lots, The Jackman suggested, "Let's take a break and stop for something to eat."

Evie had taken to staring at the ground. "I don't want to stop. I want to find Haric."

Onor said, "I need fuel to keep going."

"Besides," The Jackman said, "It's dinnertime. Maybe we can find a place playing Ruby's concert."

"That means the Exchange is going to close soon." Evie looked depleted.

"Where is the closest food?" Onor asked Aleesi.

A few beats of silence passed before she answered, long enough for Onor to realize he hadn't actually heard from the robot spider girl for some time. "I have news."

"Yes?" Evie slipped up and spoke out loud.

"Haric is in the Brawl. He was checked in two hours ago."

The Jackman cursed out loud and then muttered, "For what?"

"For being here without permission. No one from the *Fire* is cleared for this section of the ship."

"I didn't know that," Onor said.

"No one ever told you. It may be something you can use against Koren."

"Another thing," Onor muttered.

The Jackman looked alarmed. "That means it's not legal for us to be here."

"Who cares," Evie said. "Don't we want to get caught? Then we'll be with Haric."

"I can tell people where you are," Aleesi said.

"Why hasn't anyone caught us yet?" Onor mused.

"They don't think you know anything," Aleesi said.

"So they think Haric does?"

"We've got to go," Onor said. "We can check into the Brawl, right?"

Evie looked hopeful and The Jackman shook his head.

She frowned at the older man. "It's better than getting thrown in."

Onor stiffened. "He's not going to be easy to find in there."

"We have to look!"

The Jackman said, "I'm not going."

Evie looked aghast. "Why not?"

"Someone's got to stay free to pull you out. Besides, I need to tell the others."

"Aleesi will tell people," she said.

The Jackman just looked at her and shook his head.

Onor looked at Evie's desperate face and said, "I'll go. Let's buy something to eat."

"We don't have time."

"You're not going to be able to get food later." He took her arm, pulling her gently toward the food aisles.

She resisted him, and then gave in with a disapproving sigh.

Behind them, The Jackman muttered, "Fools and children. You'll get yourselves killed."

CHAPTER SEVENTY-NINE

R uby stood at the edge of the stage and stared out at the crowd. She tried to drink in their energy, to fill with it so she could burst into voice and give it back to the people who had come to hear her. There was nothing. No, that wasn't right. It almost felt like a wall stood between her and them. She took a deep breath and held her hands together in front of her. She lifted her head. "Good evening."

A few polite claps.

"I'm sorry I was late. I've just heard that there . . . there may . . . maybe I will have to learn some new things. But now, I'm going to sing for you. This evening, I'm going to start with something simple. A lullaby. This is what we sang to the babies who fretted at night, and sometimes to the old as they neared the end of their lives."

Her stomach still hurt, but she told herself it was imaginary. Pain was the past, it might even be the future. But it could not be now.

It helped.

A little.

She opened her mouth and started singing.

Singing the lullaby drove the soft words and the comfort that she had to send into her voice through her whole body, soothing away a layer of fear. Underneath the fear, anger bubbled. After the lullaby swelled to its slow end, Ruby stepped as close to the edge of the stage as she dared. The song had cracked the wall between her and the audience, giving her back a sense of them. They wanted something stronger and deeper. "Now that we've calmed down, are we ready to wake up?"

A faint chorus of "yes" and "yes" and "sure" tickled her ears.

"That's not enough. Are you ready?"

"Yes!"

"Really ready?"

"Yes!"

"Then let's have a night of revolution!" She moved into "The Owl's Song." The audience went with her, singing the chorus, standing on their feet.

She didn't take a break. She sang every song she'd ever written, from beginning to end. She saved the Brawl song for last. She prepped them for it. "Ready to Brawl!"

"Ready!"
"Ready to change!"
"Ready!"
"Ready for the song!"
"Ready!"

She had kept her anger through all of the songs, the anger mixed up with the pain in her stomach. It had driven her past and through her exhaustion. As she prepared to start the Brawl song, she felt anger thicken her spine, felt it in her feet and the top of her head, as if the anger flowed in and through her and out into the hall, a raw arc of emotion between her and the people watching her. Her anger at the universe for making her sick, her anger at Satyana for telling her, at the robot for finding it, at herself for not seeing it, for not knowing. She let her anger at the whole mess ride inside of her and she threw the feeling into the words.

As the song poured out of her, the anger went into it, imbuing her voice, hollowing her out.

She sang eight verses of the song. Four of them were verses no one had heard. The last one was a verse she hadn't even thought of, a sound that flowed out of her and carried tears with it, so she stood and emptied herself and tears flew down her face and joined the drops of sweat that salted the stage under her feet.

> *The singer grows ever*
> *Weaker*
> *Locks her loss and love*
> *Inside and sings*
> *Her death*
> *Sings the losses*
> *Of all her parents*
> *And theirs, locked*
> *In the memories*
> *Of families, Lost*
> *From the joy of life*
> *Time passes.*
> *She is going now, going*

Down into the dark
Before her own people,
Before her love
Before the Fire

The audience made no sound.

She heard her steps, her breath, her words, her tears falling onto the stage. She let the right three beats fall and then held her arms up toward the sky as she started the chorus.

Look inside
See despair

The audience joined her. A hundred voices, then a thousand, then more.

Starve it out
Embrace the hope
Of helping
The lovers of our hearts

The sound of all of the joined voices filled the room full of a bittersweet hope.

She took a bow and tipped forward, her hair spilling around her face as she fell onto the stage, every last bit of energy wrung out from her.

CHAPTER EIGHTY

The train stopped, the door opened, and Onor and Evie stepped out. Onor half-expected The Jackman to follow them, but he didn't. "Stay safe, old friend," Onor whispered.

"Good luck."

Evie pulled Onor through the same dirty station Naveen had led him through the first time they came here. Instead of going right—the way Naveen had led him—Evie tugged him left, following signs down an elevator into a small vestibule. A human guard stood at the far side. He straightened up as Evie and Onor approached. "Can I help you?"

They had worked out how to approach this on the train while they ate tomato and peppered protein paste sandwiches acquired in Exchange Four. Now, Onor's mouth tasted like dry fear and he had to force out the words. "We're here to see if this is a place where some of us can live. It's been hard to get work."

The guard looked at them with narrowed eyes. "Hard everywhere. But there's no work here." He turned his gaze to Evie's breasts. "People don't come here on purpose much, not when they're young and healthy."

"There's a lot of us."

Suspicion drained from the guard's features. "You came in from that ship. The *Fiery Beast* or something."

"*The Creative Fire*," Evie corrected him. "We can't use your technology. Mostly."

"And you can't learn?"

"It's hard."

The guard's face softened even more, and he grew a little tiny bit of a smile at the edge of his lips. It might have been touching if they didn't need to just get in as fast as possible. "We're allowed to check ourselves in, right?" Onor asked. "We checked."

"Yes. But it's a mistake."

Onor decided at add to their story. "We'll be bought out. We need to know what it's like in here, kind of like an advance guard."

The guard looked puzzled. "You want a *tour*?"

"Yes," Evie said.

"There's observation bays up above."

"I've been there," Onor said. "Will that really teach me what skills we need to live here?"

A shake of the guard's head. "Isn't that singer buying you free? Ruby?"

"If she can sing every day for the next year."

"Is this the only way to get in?" Evie asked.

The guard stepped back. "Almost no one comes this way. The very old, sometimes. Enforcers can make sure they get food. Most people are sent here."

Evie said, "Please," again, her voice small.

"You don't have anything valuable with you?" the guard asked.

Evie shook her head. "Our slates."

"Keep them close. Be careful of your clothes if you take them off. You're a little fine for this place. If you really do get out and then come back, bring trade goods."

"Trade goods?" Onor asked.

"Things people want. Food. Drugs. Clothes." He held out a slate to each of them, looking as if he were committing a crime by allowing them in. "Sign here to verify you are entering of your own free will and that you understand the cost of your stay."

Taking the pen felt far more final than he had expected it to. His signature came out scrawled and almost unreadable.

The guard waved Onor and Evie through a doorway. "Your progress will be monitored. You will walk forward the whole way. If you turn around, credits will be added to the amount it takes to buy your freedom."

"I will guide you," Aleesi said in their ears.

"Last piece of advice," the guard said. "It gets almost dark after dinner. You must be picked by then."

"Picked?"

"By a gang. You'll see."

At least they hadn't lost the earbugs. Onor still had an extra in his pocket, which he planned to give to Haric. Their footsteps echoed in the long corridor. The walls were scratched and dark and bare, the only adornment a long metal handrail that went all the way though.

At the end of the corridor, a metal door irised open into a small empty room.

Onor and Evie stepped in.

The door closed and the far one opened.

From above, the Brawl had looked big and confused. From here, it looked far, far worse. He realized he had half-expected to find Haric just on the far side of the door, waiting for them. Instead, three enforcer robots stood at strategic points, and a press of people they had never seen watched them step into the room.

CHAPTER EIGHTY-ONE

Ruby sprawled bonelessly across the stage, breathing in great gasps of air, feeling the cool floor under her cheek and her right elbow and pressing against her calves. Her dress bunched tight across her chest, so it was hard to breathe.

She tried to push up, to stand and take her bows. She felt and heard the audience willing her to stand up.

Maybe if she could get a few breaths, a few moments.

She managed to get up on one arm so that it was bent at the elbow. The fabulous fiery braids that Jali had spent so much time on hung over her face as if hiding her from the room.

Applause mixed with the sounds of dismay and concern washed across her from near the front of the room, and calls for help for her. She heard Naveen's voice as he hurried onto the stage. He spoke to the audience. "Thank you! Thank you."

Why didn't Naveen help her?

Arms folded around her while Naveen kept talking and the audience kept clapping. She felt herself lifted from the stage and managed to hold her head up and wrap her arms around her rescuer. The brush of lips against her forehead caused her to roll inward and let her cheek fall against Joel's chest. It wasn't possible that he was here, that he had picked her up. Not unless she was dying and he had come to lead her to the doorway all souls passed though.

As he murmured her name, he sounded distressed and soft all at once, and entirely unlike someone who was taking her away from the world. "Cloth. Get me a damp cloth!" he called as they passed through the great curtains and cut her off from her audience.

He clutched her tight to him and kissed her on the mouth, and only then did she believe he was real.

PART SIX

THE DEEPING RULES

CHAPTER EIGHTY-TWO

Ruby opened her eyes to her own familiar ceiling. Crisp sheets bunched around her legs. She shifted, testing. Her legs responded to her commands.

She shouldn't be here.

It took three breaths to remember her last moments on the stage, and being lifted up and carried behind the curtain. She closed her eyes and wished the memory away. But not her sweetheart. She could smell him and hear his breathing. She murmured his name. "Joel."

A hand touched her cheek. "I should have been with you."

"They needed you here." She held out her hand, the movement slow and unsteady. "Help me stand."

His fingers brushed the hair from her face. "Give it a minute."

"Did I get . . . how did I get here?"

"Satyana's robot give you a painkiller. You slept the whole time I took you back."

"You let them put me to sleep?"

"I wasn't giving you a choice about coming home."

"I shouldn't have. I should be out there, working." Her protest was weakened by how good to felt to be here, how much she loved Joel's fingertips on her lips and the sound of his voice. "What about Jali? KJ? Did they come home?"

"No. Satyana flew us home in a ship that barely had room for both of us."

"Probably the *Honey*. Did she show you the private habs out there?"

He looked both angry and lost. "She showed me enough to demonstrate how much power we don't have."

"I know."

He stood, took her hand, and tugged her to a standing position. She swayed. Her stomach felt as if she'd been sick for days, but there were no knives of pain. She took a step toward the privy and almost lost her balance. Joel had to help her. She shook and her limbs only obeyed her under protest. She must look as weak as she felt. At least each step seemed a little more solid. By the time they'd crossed the room, she felt strong enough to shut the door with him outside. She stared into the mirror. Her face *had* thinned. She'd looked into mirrors before every concert, but she'd been looking at the clothes Jali draped over and around her and at the way her hair had been done. She'd been thinking about songs instead of sickness.

Surely she had another concert soon.

She had to look better by then. She couldn't imagine eating, but took a cup and water from the sink. Then another. She filled herself on an amazing amount of water.

A nightmare had fallen over her waking moments and it was all she could do not to fall to the floor under the weight of it.

Dying wasn't acceptable.

She managed to find a brush and get it through her hair, leaving a few of the toughest tangles until she found help for them. She needed Ani. Ani always had a comb. And a laugh.

A hot washcloth felt rough against her skin, but at least it reddened her cheeks.

As soon as she opened the door, Joel took her into his arms, clutching her tightly. His shirt was rough against her cheek and he smelled clean and felt like safety. He picked her up over a weak protest, and carried her to the bed, setting her down very carefully in the middle and sitting at the edge with a warm hand on her forearm. His voice sounded thick and a little hurt. "I talked to you almost every day. You didn't say anything."

"I didn't know. I thought I was just tired. I am. Maybe. Just tired. If I rest I can go back."

His only response was a stricken and disbelieving look that suggested she would never leave his direct protection again.

She could argue after she got strong again. "What did Satyana tell you?"

"That you're going to die."

"She said maybe not. She said I could beat it."

He smiled softly. "Of course you can."

"I *can*."

"I won't be able to stand it if I lose you."

The tone in his voice devastated her, a softness colored by so much longing that she felt tight in her chest just looking at him. "Tell me about home. What's happened here while I was gone?"

"We talked every day."

"I'm sure you kept all the sweetest bits from me."

That made him smile. "The bar is doing well."

"You told me that."

"People from the rest of the *Deep* come a lot, now. Some of them say they want to help us make Koren pay for what she stole from us." He looked serious, like he wanted to know what she thought.

"There's a bigger conspiracy. That's in trade for us helping them."

He raised an eyebrow. "Satyana?"

"Yes."

"She asked me a lot of questions about you last night, and about us. I didn't feel like I could answer them all."

"Ix. Is Ix helping you?"

"Yes." He hesitated. "You should rest a little. I'll go get you some food." He stood up and planted a thoroughly chaste kiss on her forehead.

"You can do better than that."

He could, and he did. He tasted like stim.

As he left, she felt sure there were things he hadn't told her.

CHAPTER EIGHTY-THREE

Onor stayed close enough to Evie to protect her if she got into any trouble. Her shoulders slumped and her steps dragged. They hadn't rested since they left Ash, and at some point soon they'd be so tired they'd make a serious mistake of some kind. He touched her shoulder. "Let's sit and think about this. We need a plan."

"There's no place to sit."

"I'll find one." His feet already hurt; hers must, too. The one time they'd tried to sit on an empty bench, a gang of men had surrounded them and demanded they move.

"One more stop first," Evie told him. As if to make sure he knew she meant it, she pulled out her slate and held it up toward a woman standing guard outside of a scrap of protected territory. "Have you seen this man?"

The woman reached toward the slate, but after one close call Evie had learned to keep it tight in her two fists. "Yeah, sure."

"Tell me?"

"If you trade me something." The woman gestured toward the slate.

"Not this."

"I need *something*."

"I don't have anything left to spare." She had traded away a comb and her necklace of colored beads in the first few hours, both times for bad information.

An enforcer bot turned a corner near them, heading their way. They had been careful to avoid them.

The woman laughed, as if she found both Evie and the silver bot absurd, or maybe the timing. "Go that way. I think I saw him yesterday."

Onor let Evie lead them in the direction of the woman's pointed finger, which was also away from the bot. As soon as they walked out of the woman's earshot, he whispered to Evie, "That's the fourth set of conflicting directions you've gotten. Haric wasn't even here yesterday."

"I know." She turned to look at him. "We needed to go somewhere."

"The first man you asked sent us toward the observation wall." Onor flicked his eyes up. He could see one of the observation windows far above. Maybe even the one Naveen had taken him to. It looked far out of reach. "The only other two people who answered you sent us in two other directions."

She didn't say anything.

"Aren't I right?"

Aleesi answered. "Yes."

"Can you just tell us where he is?" Onor asked. "Do you have a clue?"

"I can't see where you are. There are no public cameras in the Brawl."

All of the space in the Brawl seemed to be guarded by family groups or gangs of opportunity. Onor took Evie's arm. "Let's walk and talk. Quietly. Stop drawing attention. What would Haric do if he were standing here?"

"I've been trying to decide that."

Piles of food and slates and blankets and clothes seemed to be the protected heart of most territories. From the observation window, he had seen that people grouped, but from down here, the lines were clear and guarded. It was what he would do if people from the *Fire* were here, keep them together and safe and not let strangers in.

This must be what the guard had warned them about. A group of two made a small, vulnerable target, especially if one of them was a pretty girl.

"I'm sure Haric's trying to get away to get back to us. To you."

Evie blushed. "What if we were trying to get home? What would we do?"

"Walk around by the doors. I bet there's one set in each wall. We came through one and didn't see him. So that gives us three more to look at."

"Let's look before I'm too tired to walk that far."

"So we start with the closest door."

"Okay."

Onor tried to size up the enclaves they passed. There was no unclaimed space; they had to "join" a group or talk one into temporary rent if they wanted a place to sleep, or even to sit. He should have bought trade goods instead of letting worry drive them down here so fast. "Look carefully into all the groups as we go. Haric has no idea we're here. But he might be trying to hide until we can find him."

Even though he stayed close behind her, Onor missed a tall man on the right grabbing for Evie until she screamed. The man tugged her through three other men until a wall of muscle separated her from Onor. "Let her go," he demanded.

Two men stepped toward him.

Evie screamed his name. "Onor!"

CHAPTER EIGHTY-FOUR

Ruby woke when the door opened. Instead of Joel, Marcelle stood with a cup of tea, some warm brown bread, and a relived smile. "You need something to give you strength."

"Thank you." Ruby took the cup from Marcelle's hand. She had pushed pillows together to create a nest that let her sit at the head of the bed and read news on her slate. Marcelle glowed so bright with impending motherhood that Ruby put a hand on her protruding stomach. "You look ready."

Marcelle sat on the edge of the bed and sipped at her own tea. "I have to wait for Onor to get home."

"Where is he?"

"Haric went to save the world and now Onor and Haric's girlfriend Evie and The Jackman have gone to save Haric."

Ruby stiffened. "Have you heard from them?"

"I haven't, but Joel is off talking to Aleesi."

That explained her conviction that Joel was hiding something from her. He should know better. "I need you to help me get dressed. I want out of this little room."

"Joel will kill me if I let you move."

"Did being pregnant steal your sense of adventure?" Ruby asked. "Joel's used to me disobeying." Pain struck from somewhere in her abdomen and she turned her head away from Marcelle. When she turned back, Marcelle looked stricken.

"Joel told me you might be dying. Are you?"

"Not if I can help it. Satyana is sending a medical robot to help me. You should use it to look at the people you're so worried about."

"There aren't any left."

Ruby shivered. "They died?"

"We lost twelve, but thirty-five or so got better." Marcelle's brow creased and she extended a hand to feel Ruby's forehead. "Do you think it's the same thing?"

"The robot said so. Satyana says it's called the Death of Hope. I hate the name."

Marcelle touched Ruby's cheek. "The ones we lost were mostly infants and older people. You should be fine."

Marcelle didn't look as confident as she sounded, but Ruby let it go. She *would* be fine. "Help me get dressed."

"Eat first. You're so thin your clothes will start falling off you soon."

Ruby took a bite of the bread, which was hard to swallow. It calmed her stomach a little but it also filled her up. "That's enough."

"It's not."

"Don't be stubborn. Help me."

Marcelle stared at Ruby for a long time before she extended a hand.

Ruby chose the simplest version of the old uniforms that she could find. It galled her that Marcelle had to help pull up Ruby's socks since it hurt to bend that far.

The details of Marcelle's earlier statement crept up on Ruby. "Haric's not old enough to have a girlfriend. "

"You tell him that."

Ruby laughed. It felt good to laugh.

It seemed to take forever to traverse the small apartment and make their way to the bar. She sat down heavily in one of the chairs. Allen came right over to her and pulled up a chair, unasked. "I heard Joel brought you back last night." He put a hand on her arm. "We were rooting for you. What happened?"

She bit her lip. "I don't know. I got tired and sick. I'll go back. I have to."

"Was that drunk part of the problem?" Allen asked.

She had to think about that a minute. "You mean Naveen?"

"Yeah. I don't trust him. I never did."

Marcelle said, "I think he's okay."

Naveen wasn't easy to describe. Ruby did her best. "He's part of something bigger than we know. Everything is part of a conspiracy here. We're like children running amok through other people's plans. You should see what I saw out there. The waste. The beauty. It's all so different than I expected."

A wait bot showed up with two glasses of water and a plate of crackers and spreads. "I wish people would stop trying to feed me." But she took the water and sipped at it.

The bar was three times the size it used to be. "I like what you've done here."

"It was partly for people to watch you."

She sat back. "Really? Watching the concerts?"

"You always filled the place up."

Ruby imagined the empty seats full of people eating and drinking, stopping from time to time to cheer for her. "I'm not worth all that," she said.

"Of course you are," Marcelle said.

"We didn't do this for you," Allen said. "We did it for us." He smiled at her.

"Good." Ruby sipped some more water and Marcelle helped herself to a cracker and pushed the plate toward Ruby.

She ignored it. "Place is empty now."

"It'll start filling up."

Ruby wondered what they were going to watch without her, but she didn't ask. She still didn't want to think about a world that she wasn't in. She couldn't let it happen. Not to her. Not yet. Not for years.

As if on cue, Lya and a train of whispering women came through the door. They surrounded her in a circle. Ruby looked, but Min wasn't among them. She must still be back with Naveen and Jali and the others. Hopefully she was okay.

Allen stood up. "Don't cause any trouble now. I'll have you kicked out."

Lya glared at him.

"I've got enough friends for it."

"Would you give us some privacy, please?" Lya asked.

Allen looked at Ruby. "Is that what you want?"

Ruby looked back at Lya. "Okay. Yes."

Allen and Marcelle left.

Lya waited until they were all the way out of the room, then said, "We have a message from Min."

Ruby had been expecting a barrage of whispers and accusations. "Yes?"

"She says you can't trust Ix. Naveen manages it. He changed Ix so that it tells him everything it learns."

Ruby sipped at her water, shifted in her chair, and drummed her fingertips on the table. Ix was the one trying to trap Koren. So was Naveen trying to help or hinder that? If they won back the profit from the *Fire*, she wouldn't have to sing any more. But Naveen hated Koren. "Why would Min want to help me by telling me this? Why should I believe her?"

If she only felt better. It would be so much easier to think.

Lya shook her head. "Maybe you should believe her because she isn't your friend and she told you this anyway. You're not the only one who cares about anything, you know."

"I know." She took a deep breath. "Did Min say how she learned this?"

"I asked her to get close to Naveen."

"And Naveen told her this?"

"No. She heard him talking to someone else. He said that he was getting information about Haric from Ix."

"Is Min sure?"

"Yes."

"That's not enough to tell us that Naveen means us any harm."

"But we know he's keeping secrets."

"Everyone keeps secrets here. Even you, Lya."

"Min told me something else."

Ruby swallowed and lifted her head to look directly into Lya's eyes.

Lya pulled a lacy, white shawl that looked homemade tight around her shoulders, as if she were cold. "She said you came back here to die."

"Would that make you happy?" Ruby asked.

Lya pursed her lips. It took her a long time to say, "I used to think so."

CHAPTER EIGHTY-FIVE

Onor couldn't see Evie. Three of the men who had snatched her stared at him, as if calculating his weight and speed and finding him wanting. A dark one, a huge one, and a blond giant who was at least as old as Joel.

He couldn't let time go by. If Evie got hurt or raped, Haric would be devastated. Onor would never be able to forgive himself. "Don't do this. Please." He stared at the men, who in turn stared at him. "We have to be somewhere. We're looking for someone. I can't leave her."

"Then come on," the dark man said. "Show us what you can do." His hands fisted at his side and his muscles looked bunched and ready under gray-black skin.

Onor tried to look brave as he subvocalized to Aleesi and Ix, "Evie in trouble. I'm going to try for her. I could lose. Tell Joel." Fear thrummed at his throat, drove adrenaline through his limbs, demanded action. He stepped toward the men. "You can't just take her. That's not legal."

"Do you see an enforcer?" Spoken by the giant blond, twice as wide as Onor and a little taller.

Onor stared at him, certain it was bad tactics to look away and search for a robot.

"We might be able to use a fighter. Show us you can fight." The men pushed forward, the blond giant in the fore and the other two behind. The man swung at him.

Onor ducked.

Laughter, and a second swipe of the big arm, this one connecting with Onor's arm. Not a break, but he could feel pain deep in his bicep. Onor shouldered into his attacker, trying to unbalance the bigger man.

The man tensed, pushed forward.

Onor stomped on his foot. "Evie!" He called.

"Here!"

Good. She sounded strong, and still close by.

Another blow, this one a hammer up into his stomach that lifted his feet and set him back down, stumbling slightly. Aleesi's voice querying him. "What's happening?"

Onor was too busy struggling for breath to answer. He took three steps back, hoping for time.

"Give up?"

He had to take two gulping breaths before he could answer. "No."

"Three of us could kill you."

Evie's voice from behind them, shouted. "Run away. Think of Marcelle."

Aleesi's voice in his ear. "You could die for fighting in the Brawl. There is an enforcer coming. Stall so it won't see you fighting."

Onor glanced at the three men. They should be rushing him, but they were watching. Maybe this was like getting beat up on the lower levels of the ship. An initiation rite. "Tell me about this place. Tell me what I get if I fight you and win."

"The girl lives. But you may not get to keep her."

Onor frowned. "And if I lose?"

The big man gave him a funny look. "Then you lose the girl."

"I have other resources." Ix. Aleesi. Maybe Naveen. "You should let us both go."

"Show us."

The men were close enough he could smell the stale sweat of their bodies. The biggest one reached forward and grabbed Onor.

Onor slid down out of his arms, landing on hands and knees on the hard floor. Arms slid around his torso. He kicked, but only managed a barely-glancing blow.

As the big man picked him up, Onor looked for the enforcer bot. Surely it was close.

The man carried him fairly easily behind the protected property lines. Onor's sides hurt from being gripped so hard and his arm hurt from being hit, but he managed to hold onto his slate. The man dropped him onto the floor beside Evie. Her eyes were wide and filled with desperation and anger as the men surrounded them.

Onor pushed himself up to a crouching position, keeping as light as possible and trying to be ready to spring in any direction. The enforcer bot wasn't going to able to see them. Aleesi was silent in his ear. If only the AI could see as well as hear him.

Nothing happened. No one threw another punch at him or tried to hurt Evie.

Onor stood. He offered Evie his hand and she stood as well, the two of them looking around. "What do you want?" Onor asked.

The tall blond who had seemed intent on killing him ten minutes before just said, "Wait."

Maybe they were waiting for the enforcers to pass. Whatever. It let him catch his breath. Onor's legs hurt, and his stomach and arm still felt the blows that had rained down on him. Evie looked from face to face in the group, turning around to take each of them in at once. Onor watched her back, so he didn't see whatever made her gasp until she was gone from his side.

He turned to find Evie buried in Haric's arms and Naveen looking directly at Onor, a silly grin on his face.

It took Onor a breath or two to step in and hug Naveen. "How did you find us?"

"It doesn't matter. What matters is getting you to court."

"Court? About Koren?"

"Yes. Come on. I'll fill you in on the way."

"Haric can go with us?"

"Of course."

Onor got his first good look at Haric. Dark bruises and a cut marred his face. Someone had helped him clean up, but dried blood still flecked his shirt. "What happened?" Onor asked.

"You don't look too good either." Although Haric did look quite pleased to see Onor. He stepped forward and gave him almost as deep a hug as he'd offered Evie. He seemed to have grown in the few days since Onor had seen him, gained something that made him feel adult. Haric's voice sounded slightly husky as he said, "Thanks for coming."

"I couldn't leave you loose in here."

"Oh, I've been rescued for almost four hours now." Haric glanced at Naveen. "But we need you."

The assembled crowd around them still didn't look friendly, but they looked . . . calm.

Naveen addressed the big blond man. "Get us to the door and I'll credit your accounts."

Five of the men peeled out of the circle, and they returned to the aisleway, one man in front and three behind. Onor and Naveen walked behind Evie and Haric. "You know these people?"

"I hired them to find all three of you."

"They didn't find us. We walked by and they snatched us."

"It worked, didn't it?"

"They beat me up."

"That was a show for the enforcer bots."

"Did it have to hurt so much?"

Naveen grinned. "You did want it to look authentic, right?"

"Not that authentic." Naveen appeared to be enjoying himself, although Onor sensed more nervousness in him than usual. It felt damned good to be back beside someone who understood the rules in here. "Thank you."

"Thank me when we're really out of here. We need to miss all of the bots."

"Why? We're not fighting."

"Because I had control of them, and now I don't. That means someone else does."

That explained the undercurrent of nerves. "Koren?"

"Could be. Gotta be someone with a lot of credit. Could be unrelated to us. This place is a zoo of hacks and hatreds."

They walked on for a while. A few of the guards and others they passed looked at them curiously, but most looked away. Onor's guess was that the men they'd hired had reputations here.

"Why are you helping us?"

"Don't worry, I'm getting what I need out of it."

Of course he was. Naveen took care of Naveen. Onor didn't even ask; it would become clear soon enough. "How did Haric end up in here?"

"He learned some things. So he was sent here to die."

"And you rushed in and saved him?"

Naveen laughed. "No. I hired these guys to do it. One of them died saving him. That's why they're so long in the face."

The group stopped, bunching up for a moment. "They want us to go the other way," Evie hissed. "There's an enforcer bot."

Damned things were never around when he wanted one, only when he didn't. He turned. They just had time to really get into a good formation again when the two men who were now in front stopped abruptly.

This time, he could see the enforcer bot that had stopped them, the silver cylinder dipped slightly toward them as if showing that it had found its quarry.

As soon as he turned away, he could see that the first bot had followed them.

There was no place to go.

CHAPTER EIGHTY-SIX

Noise drew Ruby's eyes toward the door just as The Jackman rushed through it, looking wild. He spotted their table and his eyes rounded with surprise. He came over to Ruby. "What are you doing here?"

She laughed. "Visiting." He could work out the details later. "What do you know about Onor?"

"He and Evie went into the Brawl. They're chasing Haric."

Ruby stilled.

Marcelle's voice came out iced with control. "I thought you said they went to an Exchange?"

"Are they okay?" Ruby asked.

The Jackman shrugged. "They were fine when I left them. Haric got caught. They went after him." His breathing sounded labored and his face looked flushed with exertion. "Where's Joel?"

Allen said, "Probably in the morning meeting room. He spends all his time in there."

The Jackman asked Ruby, "Do you know where he is?"

She shook her head. "I just got here last night. I don't even know where the meeting room is."

His face softened as he looked at her. "Is everything okay? Are you okay?"

She must look really bad if The Jackman was asking. "I'm better than Onor and Haric." She stood up. "Let's go find Joel."

It seemed to take a long time to reach the small meeting room. After Ruby, Allen, Marcelle, and The Jackman filed in, the space felt over-full. There weren't enough chairs. Joel motioned Ruby next to him, and gestured for her to sit on his lap, a rare public show of affection. He looked worried. "I didn't mean to be gone so long. I'm glad you found me."

"Me too."

His hand encircled her, resting lightly on her tender stomach. The warmth felt good. "Have you heard anything?"

"Onor and Evie found Haric."

"They're safe?"

"We don't really know," SueAnne said.

Lya trailed in the door. Joel tensed.

Ruby shook her head at him softly. "Let her stay."

Joel looked like he was about to argue when SueAnne interrupted, speaking to the AIs. "Are they still in the Brawl?"

Aleesi spoke. "I can hear them talk. They sound worried."

Ruby narrowed her eyes. "So they are in danger."

"Yes, Ruby," Ix said. "Naveen is there. He may be able to make it all right."

Surely Naveen wouldn't have gone into the Brawl in person unless it was safe.

"Ix?" Ruby mused.

"Is there a way for Naveen to earn credit from all of this?"

"He can broadcast anything."

She remembered what Lya had told her. "Do you work for us or for Naveen?"

"I work for you."

Joel was giving her a strange look, but she plowed on. She knew Ix. She'd had many conversations with it over the years. "Do you report to Naveen?"

"What do you mean?"

"Does Naveen talk to you? Directly?"

"No."

Maybe Lya was wrong. "Do you talk to Naveen?"

Aleesi interrupted. "Ix. Check your outflow data."

Surely Aleesi didn't need to talk to Ix out loud. She was speaking for Ruby's benefit.

It didn't take Ix long to answer. "I am copying Naveen on every answer including this one. I did not know that."

How long had Aleesi known? It was hard to think through her exhaustion, but Ruby asked Aleesi, "Why didn't you tell us?"

"I have evaluated Naveen and decided that he sees you as too valuable to damage. If I had cut off the feed he could have known it."

Marcelle spoke up. "How are they now? Is anything happening?"

"They are talking to two enforcer bots and another one is on the way."

"Talking?" SueAnne asked.

"So far," Aleesi said. "Onor is afraid. I can read his physiology."

"But you can't see anything?" Lya asked.

"No."

"Should I cut off the feed to Naveen?" Ix asked.

"No," Ruby said. "But do tell him I know about the feed. Tell him good luck. Tell him I trust him. That's the only thing I can do."

"The feed is only one way," Ix said. "He cannot talk back to you."

Aleesi interrupted. "I think they're in trouble."

CHAPTER EIGHTY-SEVEN

Onor kept trying to notice everything going on around him as the enforcers stole all of their forward momentum through the Brawl. The faces in the crowd, the wary look on Naveen's face, the various curiosity, fear, and glee on the faces of onlookers. "Aleesi, record this. We're in trouble."

"I am," she said in his ear. "Ruby says stay safe."

"Ruby?" How was Ruby in contact with Aleesi? But there wasn't time to ask.

The two enforcer bots had been holding them by sheer force of presence, but now a third floated eerily toward them. Slightly taller and slightly wider, this third faceless cylinder caused the crowd to pull back, muttering. Space opened around them in a place where there was no extra room at all.

Onor took that as a bad sign.

"Don't run," Naveen said. "Don't tease the robots."

Naveen could joke at a time like this? But then surely he was recording. He was always recording, everything. Even sending everything out. Onor tried to read the intent of the bots. This close, they loomed larger than he expected them to, as wide around as his waist and a head taller than him, featureless. No eyes. It was impossible to tell if they were looking at him or not, impossible to know what they saw or heard. The two that had first cornered them looked the same, but the third had a gold-colored band around the top if its head. It spoke. "Onor Hall. Naveen Tourning. Haric Lopez. Evie Justine. You are all under arrest."

"For what?" Naveen demanded.

"Harboring an illegal being."

Aleesi, in his ear. "They mean me."

He waited, unwilling to speak back. Surely anything he said would be wrong. Naveen asked, "What illegal being?"

The enforcer sounded very formal. "A hybrid human from the Edge. One who has broken the laws of the *Diamond Deep*."

"Don't say anything," Aleesi hissed. "There are many copies of me. One can die."

Other Aleesis would not be this Aleesi, and would not remember him. That felt like a death to him.

"Break the earbug."

Then he wouldn't be able to talk to her. He risked a single-word subvocalization. "No."

Naveen knew about Aleesi, but he didn't know Onor had access to her right here.

"It's a counterstrike," Aleesi explained. "It didn't work to throw Haric in here so now she's throwing him somewhere worse. And getting you, too. There are signs she is sending people to Ash. I believe that Koren feels threatened."

He stood still and tried to feel brave, to think rather than react to the news, or the enforcers. He wanted to flee the way he and Marcelle had fled from the spider bots, but they had been killers which yielded Aleesi. But there wasn't anyplace to run. He had seen how futile that was from the observation window.

Evie had not. Her head whipped from enforcer to enforcer and to the crowd, and she quivered.

Onor stepped toward her, hoping to get close enough to grab a hand or an arm and make her stand still. Before he could get there, she grabbed Haric's hand and raced for the crowd, clearly hoping it would part and make room for them. Haric stumbled behind her.

"Stop!" the enforcer commanded.

They slowed, Haric looking back over his shoulder.

The crowd remained steadfast and tight, as if helping the enforcer.

"Stop!" it called again, its voice a deep boom, louder than the last command.

They stopped.

Evie turned on it. "We haven't done anything." She let go of Haric's hand and yelled into the crowd. "I bet none of you did anything wrong either."

The crowd remained stoic. Curious but not moved to help. Almost cruel.

"There's so many more of us than of them. We can't let this happen." Evie looked young and thin and tiny, too insignificant to possibly matter. But like Ruby, she had a force about her, an energy that was far bigger than her frame. Her voice carried throughout the circle, edged with desperation. "Help me!"

A few voices murmured, people shifted.

She sounded like Ruby years ago, angry and impassioned. It drove Onor's heart into his throat, scared him.

Haric stepped between Evie and the enforcer.

She stepped out from behind him.

He turned his back to the enforcer and grabbed Evie's arms, looking down into her face. He looked frightened and desperate and in love.

She pulled away from him and turned back to the crowd. "Don't let them take us," she pleaded, her back to the enforcer, staring at the crowd.

A light blinked red on the top of the robot. A warning?

Onor raced toward Haric and Evie.

Haric turned and stared at the enforcer, his eyes wide with fear.

The robot was so close to them that if it had arms, it might be starting to reach for them.

A beam of light emerged from the top center of the machine and struck Haric between the eyes.

CHAPTER EIGHTY-EIGHT

Aleesi announced, "Haric has been shot by one of the enforcers."

"Stunned," Ruby sat up straight on Joel's lap. "Stunned. You must mean stunned."

"I cannot see the Brawl," Aleesi replied, sounding stressed. "Onor is breathing hard and he's scared. If he were talking I could hear what he's saying, but he isn't."

Joel spoke with the calm of a seasoned veteran. "Do you have any influence on the situation?"

She couldn't lose Haric. He was the closest thing to a child she would ever have, even if he was only eight years younger. Maybe the closest thing to a little brother. Regardless, he was hers, and she couldn't stand not knowing what was happening to him.

"I'm trying," Aleesi answered Joel. "Are there guards on the door?"

"Why?" Marcelle asked.

"They are using the fact that I exist to attack Naveen, Haric, and Evie. I believe they will come after you, too. You must protect Ix."

Anger drove a spike of energy through Ruby. "We need to protect you!"

"There are many of me," Aleesi said. "I do not know how many of Ix exist."

There was only one of Haric. Only one of any of them in this room. Fear joined the anger burning through Ruby.

"It doesn't matter," Joel said. "If we protect one, we protect the other. They live in the same place." He turned to The Jackman. "Double the guards on all the doors into Ash."

The Jackman gestured to Allen and the two of them nearly ran out of the door.

"What about Haric?" Ruby asked.

"No one has told me anything."

Joel stroked Ruby's back and shoulders. If she weren't shivering so hard, his hand would be warm and comforting. "We need to think," he whispered.

"I know. I just . . . I hate it here." She took in a big gulp of air. "There's no time to get to the Brawl. I'll see if I can get us help." She bent to her slate, but Joel put his hand over hers, stopping her from writing.

"What?"

"Who are you going to call?"

"Satyana. She's on our side. I know it."

Joel looked directly into her eyes. "You trust her?"

"I don't trust anyone here. But she's not on Koren's side."

SueAnne had been watching everything quite closely from her wheelchair. "Do we know what side we're on?"

"The one that isn't Koren, and the one that didn't create the Brawl."

Ruby stared at Joel. "Satyana brought you to me."

He pursed his lips. If they were alone he would tell her he needed to keep thinking—she could see it on his face. She loved that he thought about risks, about leadership, but now wasn't the time. "I have to," she told him. "We need help. Satyana has ships."

When Joel finally nodded, she bent to her slate. "I'm going to tell her that I'm ready to go to my next concert, and she should come pick me up."

Joel clutched her closer. "You can't leave. You're not strong enough."

"Satyana knows that. But I can't exactly tell her 'we might be attacked by Koren and can you please help?' can I?"

SueAnne asked, "Are you leading your friend into danger?"

"Probably." The adrenaline and anger were already fading away, as if her body just couldn't sustain them anymore. "She's tough." Ruby leaned back against Joel's shoulder, fading into his embrace and both happy to be there and furious that she wasn't up stalking the room. It felt as if her body was trying to force her to abandon it so it could sleep forever. She hated this illness with so much passion that the hatred gave her a little extra surge of energy. "Aleesi? Anything?"

"Onor hasn't said a thing to me for three minutes. Nor has he said anything intelligible to anyone else."

Marcelle came over and stood next to Ruby and Joel.

"Onor is breathing," Aleesi said. "That's something."

Ruby took Marcelle's hand and looked up at her. "Haric will be okay. He has to be okay."

Marcelle's other hand rested on her stomach. "No. No, we don't have to be okay. None of us have to be okay. We aren't living inside one of your songs."

"I'll write a song about this," Ruby declared. It felt like a hollow threat.

Marcelle's face was white and drawn. "If we live, I'll help you sing the damned thing."

CHAPTER EIGHTY-NINE

The first few moments after the beam pierced Haric's forehead moved so slowly that Onor had time to notice detail after detail, like a series of still photographs snapped with his slate.

The soft thud of Haric's form falling forward on the hard floor.

The arc of Evie's body as she bent over the line of Haric's thin form and turned her ear toward his back.

Two enforcers just in Onor's peripheral vision, canted slightly toward Evie and him.

Naveen with his mouth open, looking shocked.

The crowd moving even further back, feet shuffling and voices whispering.

Evie shaking her head and putting it back against Haric, one slender hand on his still shoulder.

Naveen murmuring to his audience.

Aleesi's silence.

Onor's own body shivering, reacting. His breath.

One of the enforcers moving inches closer to them.

The first wave of shock passed and his perceptions slowed to a more normal pace.

Evie's shoulders heaved in anger or fear or despair or some mix of those. Was Haric dead? He needed to see her face to tell; Haric's face. He couldn't.

The largest enforcer loomed over Evie. "Move," it demanded.

Evie ignored it, maybe she didn't even hear it. Her hair hid her face, and she said, "Haric," over and over. "Haric. Haric. Haric." The cadence kept changing, like she could get through to him if she just said it exactly right.

"Move," the machine demanded again.

Onor had been standing, rooted, watching. He should be protecting. He took the five steps necessary to put himself between the machine and Evie.

She looked up at him. "He's not breathing."

Onor almost told her she had to be lying. But he remembered Colin floating in pieces in the hold, and he remembered Hugh being stunned to death. He knelt, careful to cover as much of Evie's body with his own as he could. He lifted her, holding her close to him, getting some of her weight off of Haric. "Roll him over."

She tugged, and Haric moved like the stunned or the dead, bonelessly.

His eyes stared up at the ceiling, and Onor knew he had gone.

Another shock rolled through him, anger this time. He stood, legs splayed over Evie's and Haric's bodies. The enforcer was only a few feet away from him. He screamed at it. "You had no right to kill him!"

A force tugged on his right arm. Naveen. "Stop. Let it go."

Onor shook his head. *Let it go* that the thing had just killed Haric?

"Protect Evie," Naveen almost screamed.

The enforcer stood quietly in front of him, looking for all the world as if it were waiting for someone.

Naveen backed him up two steps. They stood side by side over Haric and Evie. Onor glanced down at Evie to see tears running down her cheeks. She didn't look like herself, but she also didn't look like Lya had when Hugh died. Angry and disbelieving, but not undone.

Evie scrambled up to a crouching position, and Onor held a hand out to her to help her up.

She ignored him, and instead launched herself at the enforcer that had shot Haric.

Its red light blinked back on.

Evie rocketed toward it, a force of girl bent on release.

He expected it to shoot her, but instead she collided with it, threw her shoulder into it and her arms as far around it as they would go.

It shifted, tilted.

Evie kicked, screaming. She bore it down into a deeper tilt by sheer force.

They held that way, suspended in space, Evie riding the robot with all of her weight while it bobbed and tried to right itself.

The lights on it dimmed.

She leapt up and down on the slender robotic body with all of the force she could muster, her face twisted with anger and grief. Onor expected her to fall, but she managed to stay on, to ride it, to almost dance her fury.

It crashed onto the floor and split down the middle, a line of electronic guts spilling out between the two halves, wires breaking.

Evie crouched and smacked at it with her fists, cursing and crying.

The other two enforcers left, moving exactly the way they usually did, quietly and calmly floating through the crowd, leaving the tiny young woman to smash at their fallen comrade.

Onor and Naveen stood and looked back and forth between Haric's body, Evie's flailing fists, and the retreating enforcers.

"How is Haric?" Aleesi asked in his ear.

"Dead," Onor whispered.

"That pisses me off."

Aleesi sounded so human when she was hurt, so different from Ix. "Can you tell Ruby? You were talking to her earlier."

"I'll tell her in a moment. You should be safe now, but you should leave the Brawl immediately. Satyana is waiting for you near the same door you came in. She'll take you to the Court of the Deeping Rules."

CHAPTER NINETY

Ruby opened her eyes, still slumped against Joel's shoulder. She'd lost some time. There was no way to tell how much. The same people remained in the room. Marcelle sat quietly beside her, staring into space. SueAnne rested in her chair, chin on her hands, watching Ruby. Lya stood and watched them all, silent. She looked almost sane, as if being in the middle of an emergency had calmed her.

Ruby took a deep breath, grinding her teeth against a sharp pain. A knife blade might have felt better than whatever mystery had taken up residence in her stomach.

Joel spoke softly but firmly. "We *must* hide Aleesi and Ix."

"Where?" SueAnne asked.

He shook his head. "Maybe in the bar? Allen surely has places to hide almost anything."

"We won't be able to talk to her if we do that. We won't know what happened to Haric."

Aleesi answered her. "Haric is dead. The enforcers have been reassigned to other work. Satyana is on her way to help Onor and Evie, so she will not be able to help you, at least not now."

Ruby focused on the first three words. *Haric is dead.* Joel and Onor and the others had sent him out to do work he wasn't prepared for, and he'd been killed. If only she had insisted that he come with her, instead of rebuffing him. She could still see his face. Pleading with her to take him along. He had wanted to protect her.

It had been her job to protect him. He was her assistant, her helper.

Damn it!

Joel pulled her back to their own peril with a tightening of his arms around her waist and a low-voiced sentence. "We have to get out of here, and we have to hide the AIs. Now."

"Take my chair," SueAnne said.

"Why?" Ruby asked.

"Because that way you can go faster and further." The sadness that seemed to drip from SueAnne's voice was almost physical. A tear had gathered in the corner of her right eye, catching on the wrinkles there instead of falling down her face. "You can carry the webling in the pouch under my seat where I keep my coat and slate."

Ruby started to protest but Joel said, "Thank you," before Ruby could get any words out of her mouth.

SueAnne stood up and moved slowly to the couch. She must have noticed Ruby glaring at her, since she said, "I'll be all right. I'm just old. I can walk."

And Ruby was sick, maybe sick to death. She couldn't think that way, think about dying, except she couldn't help it. Haric's death had bored a hole inside her that sat beside the other deaths that had driven her forward for years. Her friend Nona, who had died after two reds raped her. Hugh, Lya's Hugh, who had died fighting to help Ruby change the ship so that no one else would be raped and killed. Ben, the old red who had always looked out for her and Onor.

Joel picked her up and put her down in SueAnne's wheelchair. It was surprisingly comfortable, worn loose and soft by SueAnne's body. A bit too big. Marcelle emptied the pouch under the seat, handing the blanket and slate to SueAnne.

"What about the others?" Ruby asked. "Onor and Evie?"

"They're safe for the moment. Naveen is with them."

Lya had come to stand next to Ruby. The feel of her had changed, as if she had temporarily run out of reasons to accuse Ruby. Her eyes were big in her gaunt face, and she looked more vulnerable than Ruby remembered her looking for a long time.

Joel spoke to the AIs. "I'm unplugging you now." That was all the ceremony he offered them, his face tight and worried as he glanced repeatedly at Ruby.

Aleesi would be able to talk to Onor but not to Ruby. The webling would have power for a few days.

She felt numb, as if she could slip away into mourning. Haric. Poor, good Haric who had only wanted to matter. Haric's death pulled her away from herself. It sent her into a strange soft sadness that was like feeling and not feeling all at once. She hated it. She should be so full of anger that the only choice she had was to be strong, to feel strong. The best she could manage was to grip the arms of the chair hard and sit up as straight as she could.

There were still tangles in her hair. What a strange thing to worry about. Maybe people worried about little things when everything else felt big.

Joel bent in front of her, holding the webling. His hands slid beneath the fabric of the seat, pushing the big object into the pouch. It barely fit. "We need to cover it."

"Here." Lya stood beside Joel, holding out the white shawl that had been draped across her shoulders.

For a moment his tense shoulders suggested that he'd refuse to let Lya help even when he needed her, but instead he drew a deep breath and took the shawl and stuffed it around the cylinder. It would provide both covering and cushioning. When he was done, Joel touched Ruby's knee and gave her a soft, tender smile.

"I'm ready," she said. She looked over at SueAnne. "Thank you."

The old woman smiled, and then settled back in the chair she had chosen to sit in and pulled out her slate.

It felt wrong to be wheeled out of the room instead of walking out. One of the wheels creaked each time around, giving a beat to her movement. They took an elevator she had passed but never taken, going down the two floors from the morning meeting room to the base floor of Ash. They passed one of the open areas where two mothers watched over four children playing with red balls. None of them looked her way, or noticed that it was Ruby and not SueAnne in the wheelchair.

The bar was empty when they got there, unless you counted a single robotic server that told them to sit wherever they wanted. "It's never talked to me before," Ruby said.

Joel said, "Allen usually turns that off. If the robot is talking to us, then Allen is off somewhere else. Maybe he left a note." He wheeled Ruby to a seat and left her to check the board behind the bar. "Allen said he's in the big kitchen. Let's go find him."

"I can stay here," Ruby said.

Joel eyed Lya, clearly trying to figure out how to remind Ruby what he thought of Lya without telegraphing it loud enough for Lya to notice. He failed; concern painted his face tight.

"It's okay," Ruby told him. "It will only take you ten minutes. I'm safe enough."

He truly looked torn.

"Go on," she said. "You need Allen to find a truly hidden place." The cargo bars had been full of clever hidey holes. Surely Allen had built some into this bar. "Besides, I really am safe enough. I've known Lya longer than I've known you."

That decided him. "I'll hurry." He was gone almost before he finished saying it.

Ruby and Lya each ordered citrus-water from the serving robot. Ruby watched it trundle off, trying not to feel Haric's death any more than she had to. She took the emergency pin that Satyana had given her and held it.

The bot squeaked back across the floor with its tray. Ruby took a tumbler and looked at Lya, struggling for words. "At least there are *some* good things here. We never had this kind of bitter-sweet in a drink."

Lya took her own sip, and made a slight face. "I wish it were slightly sweeter." Her voice dropped. "I'm sorry about Haric. I liked him. He was so earnest."

"Yes."

"I know about death, you know," Lya said. "I know how it turns you around and gives you a different focus entirely."

Ruby laughed. "What do you think drives me?"

Lya didn't answer with any of the trite phrases she'd been spouting off to her followers. She waited Ruby out.

The awkward silence left Ruby thinking of Haric standing by her side so often, waiting to help her. "I had a friend once. Back when we were still in school and before the sky fell. Her name was Nona. I think I've mentioned her to you." She trailed off, remembering how she and Nona used to sit side by side in common and make up stories about the people walking by. "We were always together. Onor knew her, and Marcelle had met her. If she had lived, there would have been four of us, except maybe if she were still here, I never would have wanted to fight badly enough to change anything."

"What happened?"

"Her mom needed pills—maybe now I can look back and see it was an addiction, but then we were young. Anyway, Nona earned stuff the way young girls could then, she sold herself to the reds. That's why I hate prostitution so much. It was killing her—just doing it. Selling her soul. But I was worried that even worse would happen. I went to stop her, but I was too late." Ruby felt tears at the edges of her eyes, and wiped at them. It wouldn't do for Koren's people to come in and find Ruby crying. She hadn't cried about Nona for a long time. She'd thought about her a lot, turned her into a personal icon, her death into a whip she struck herself with over and over. But she hadn't thought about the girl who wanted to succeed in school so bad she woke up an hour before the shift-change warning bell. The girl who told jokes that made Ruby giggle so hard she almost fell off a bench once. Ruby couldn't remember the joke any more, but she did remember the explosion of laughter.

When it felt like she had some emotional control back, Ruby continued. "I found her. She had been stabbed. By reds. To this day, her death reminds me how awful too much power is. Maybe she didn't give them good enough sex that night, maybe she said the wrong thing, maybe they just didn't want to get caught." Now she was angry all over again and tears were spilling down her face. "That's why I did it." Two deep breaths. She need to have more control. "I saw that we got free so no one else could die unnoticed that way."

Lya knelt beside the chair and put an arm across Ruby's back. "I'm sorry," she said.

Ruby lifted her face. "I'm sorry about Hugh."

"You never said that before."

"I'm sorry about that, too." And about Haric, and about herself. She was going to die. She could feel it, like an out-breath that thinking about Nona had made possible. Only she didn't want to. She wanted to sing, she wanted to change the whole damned station here, and she wanted to hold Marcelle's baby.

Most of all, she wanted to hold Marcelle's baby.

As if thinking about her illness made it talk to her, a sharp pain stabbed up from her insides, as if it were reaching from her belly toward her heart. She bent over the pain. Its exquisite sharpness drove away other feelings and shrank her world to her physical reaction.

She counted her own heartbeats as the agony eased.

Footsteps made her look up. Joel coming in the interior door he had left through. Allen followed. Joel must not have liked what he saw on her face since he rushed to her side. "Are you okay?"

No. She nodded. "Of course. " Her voice sounded hoarse and just louder than a whisper.

Before she could ask if he'd found a hiding place, four men in uniform came through the door from the outside hallway. "Ruby Martin and Joel North?"

Joel stood up. "Yes?"

"You are required to come with us. You have been accused of violating one of the three primal Deeping Rules and are accused of causing harm to the station."

Joel asked. "Who are we accused of harming?"

"That will be explained to you."

Ruby opened the pin and pushed the button.

"According to who?" Lya asked. "Can't you see that Ruby's sick? She needs to stay here."

The man who had spoken looked down at Ruby. "Can you walk?"

She couldn't. Not very far. But Ix and Aleesi were under her chair, and now they couldn't move them.

"No." Joel took the decision away from her. "She needs to use the chair or she'll be too tired. I'll push her."

The man was staring at Ruby. "So it's true? You really are sick? I heard about your fall, but I didn't think it was real."

Ruby nodded. She couldn't speak, not and keep her temper and her tears both away.

"Very well. You can keep the chair." With no more ceremony that that, the leader turned around and started walking for the door. The other three stood and waited. Joel pulled Ruby away from the table.

"I'll go with you," Lya said.

"Only these two," one of the uniformed men told her.

Lya looked sincerely regretful, almost frightened. Allen glared at the two men, looking a bit helpless. Not a look she was used to seeing on his face; it looked odd on him.

"Where are you taking us?" Ruby asked.

"To the Court of the Deeping Rules."

CHAPTER NINETY-ONE

Onor kept looking for any other immediate threats.

Naveen's lips moved as he spoke to someone through his slate, probably the mysterious Satyana. He looked pale and slightly scared; shaken. Onor couldn't tell if he was affected by the enforcers or the crowd or Haric's body or whatever the person on the other side of the line was telling him.

Evie's fists clenched at her side. She stared at the broken metal body of the enforcer she had just been pummeling with her bare hands. Blood dripped from a cut on the outside of her right fist, leaving a trail of glistening red droplets on the hard floor of the Brawl. At the moment she occupied the middle of an open space, although the crowd was closing in a step at a time. Onor came up behind her and put his arms around her, pulling her in close to him. "I'm so sorry," he whispered as softly as he could, as if he were trying to calm a child. "I'm so sorry. But we need to go now. He saved you; don't waste that. He would be so angry if you die."

She shook her head as if denying his words.

"I have to keep you safe, and I have to get us all home safe."

She put her hands up between her body and his arms, breaking his hold on her and standing still, staring at Haric's body.

"Come on," he whispered.

"I don't believe he's dead."

"Of course you don't." He had known death since his parents died, and almost every year he had lost someone, and then more in times of fighting, a staccato beat to his life. Death didn't change what the living had to do, and they needed to move. "We can mourn later, when we're safe. You don't think so now, but you'll be okay. If we get out of here."

"All right," she said, standing still and staring at Haric's face as if love alone could will him to stand up and breathe.

She didn't move until Naveen came up on her other side and took her bleeding hand. "Now. To the door."

The door was fairly close, maybe five minutes walking away.

Naveen gestured to the men who had first caught them and brought them all together. They joined up and created a silent wedge that Onor, Evie and Naveen walked in the center of. Evie stumbled a little, but refused help or hands from either of them, clutching herself tightly with her shoulders pulled in over her.

The crowd that had refused to part for Evie and Haric to help them get away from the enforcer parted for these men, stepping aside quickly.

In just a few moments, they stood in front of the doors out of the Brawl. Onor glanced at Naveen, who gave him a nod. "I've got it."

Sure enough, the doors opened as if an unseen hand pulled them apart.

A small brown-skinned woman stood on the other side in front of about ten guards wearing the same uniform as the guard who had reluctantly let them in here. Onor, Evie, and Naveen walked through and the doors closed behind them.

Onor looked for the guard they had talked to and found him on the far right side of the line.

"I'm sorry," the man mouthed from his place in the line around the woman, who could only be Satyana.

Onor appreciated the small touch of humanity.

Satyana stood, taking stock of them. She looked small and fierce, and very well-dressed in a flight suit that embodied comfort and fashion all at once. Nothing like anyone from Ash. Her voice was strong and quick. "Are you okay? Can you run?"

"Yes," Onor said, echoed by Evie, who still seemed to be hugging herself, or maybe hugging her hurt hand. Satyana didn't wait for Naveen to answer, but just turned and took off at a steady jog. They followed, Evie in front, Naveen and Onor behind and next to each other. The uniformed guards followed until they came out again in the same vestibule that Onor and Evie had come in through.

Satyana led the four of them up and to the observation window level and along the corridor toward the train station. Onor glanced through the window, but he couldn't see if anyone had come for Haric's body yet. From here, he could see the divisions between groups more clearly, especially now that they had been among them.

He needed to be sure that no one he loved ever went back there. He missed Marcelle fiercely in that moment, and the unborn baby, and everyone else back in Ash.

Instead of crossing into the train station, Satyana led them through two corridors Onor had never seen and into a suiting room next to an airlock. "Have you ever been in a pressure suit?" Onor asked Evie quietly.

Evie's eyes grew wide and she stopped shaking. "No." She watched Naveen and Satyana slide their suits on and check seals. Then Naveen helped Onor, and Satyana explained the whole process to Evie. Onor finished before Evie, and heard Satyana murmur in a voice that Onor couldn't imagine disobeying. "There. Now slide the arms up so you can move your elbows. Next time, wear pants. Dresses are almost impossible in these suits."

Indeed, Evie's dress bunched oddly, but modestly, against her hips and thighs. Even though the suit looked strange on her, she looked calmer than he'd seen her since before they left to hunt Haric down. For that alone, Onor was grateful to Satyana.

They dogged helmets and went through the airlock into a small ship that Satyana introduced as *Honey*. Naveen and Evie ended up in seats that faced backwards, with barely enough room to strap in and tuck their feet around boxes and bags of things. The clutter seemed wrong for Satyana, who looked as neat and perfectly put-together as Jali, if somewhat undecorated compared to most people from the space station.

He strapped in and let the view of the *Diamond Deep* entrance him, barely noticing as Satyana held a conversation with the ship with her hands and soft, whispered commands. Living inside of the station, and mostly inside of Ash which had no windows to the outer world, had reminded him of living inside the *Fire*. Now he was out, sitting in a spaceship on the skin of the station, and he could see stars with his naked eye.

He stared.

The stars dwarfed his pain and losses, and even his fear of the Court of the Deeping Rules. Only a little, but it was enough that he began to feel like himself and the sharp ache no longer took over all of him.

The ship gave a brief lurch and then settled into a steady trajectory. Satyana stripped off her helmet, so the rest of them did the same. The *Honey* smelled like grease and stale food and sweat. Naveen and Evie twisted in their seats so they could see out the window as well. "I'm sorry I wasn't faster," Satyana said.

"I lost it," Naveen told her. "I had them, the enforcers. A perfect hack. But Koren must have found out we were there."

"What did the boy know?" Satyana asked. "Why him?"

"He heard recorded conversations with some merchants. They identified the people who sold them stolen goods from the *Fire*. Then I traced that back to Koren."

"Can you make the case that they're stolen yet?" Satyana asked.

"I can. I have a copy of the ship's AI. Ix. I know what it saw, what it thought."

"I hope you're right." Satyana said.

Onor bit his lip. "You still have a copy? You have one with you?"

Naveen narrowed his eyes. "Not physically. But I have all of its recordings, and they're spread through a series of databases."

"Tell me about this court," Onor asked. "We have no such thing on the *Fire*. Whoever had the most power made the decisions."

Satyana laughed. "Then you will not find this so different. Any meeting of the Court of the Deeping Rules is overseen by the Councilor who has power in the area the meeting is about. There is an audience, and so they must dance a careful line, but we stand little chance of winning."

"Do we speak for ourselves?" Onor asked. He didn't like talking in large groups, and he wasn't very good at it. "Will Ruby or Joel be there? They are good at talking in front of people."

"I will do it," Satyana said.

"Why you?"

Naveen answered. "Because you need someone who understands the intricacies of our world to defend you. Satyana has respect."

Onor glanced at Satyana, trying to read the expression on her face. Guarded. He felt unwilling to voice a fear that was beginning to grow inside of him. Perhaps they were merely being used for something bigger. Perhaps no one really cared what happened to them, and they didn't know enough themselves to stay safe. Surely he was just tired and heartsick, and his brain wasn't working right.

Evie had watched the conversation in silence, but now she put a hand up, as if waiting to be acknowledged in class.

"Yes, Evie?" Satyana asked.

"Haric sent me some notes he asked me to keep secret."

"What's in them?"

Evie looked offended. "I didn't read them. He told me to save them."

"Can I see?" Satyana asked.

"Aren't you driving?" Evie asked.

"No. The ship flies itself out here." She held out her hand, and looked pleased when Evie dropped her journal into it.

Evie had come completely un-belted now and she leaned over Satyana's shoulder, touching the slate with her fingers. "Here."

Satyana leaned back and started reading.

Onor dug out his slate and sent a message to Marcelle. Then he subvocalized. "Aleesi? Are you there?"

No answer.

He waited, but there was no answer from Marcelle or Aleesi. Marcelle was surely just busy, but Aleesi should answer him.

Evie was staring at him, worry tightening her lips. He pointed at the outside of the *Honey*. "Look." Onor told Evie.

She did. "Stars."

The ship turned so that the station was easier to see than the sky. Naveen gave Onor and Evie a running verbal tour while Satyana read Haric's notes. Naveen was pointing out a bubble he said held the biggest university of the station when he stopped mid-sentence and whispered, "Look at that."

"What?"

"Evie."

She was sound asleep, her neck cricked at an angle she would probably regret later, and her mouth open. If Onor listened really carefully, he could hear her snoring quietly. "Yeah, well, we haven't slept for a long time. And she did just clock an enforcer robot."

Satyana laughed and set Evie's slate down on a cluttered shelf.

"Did you learn anything?" Naveen asked.

"Some of this might be useful. It's hard to say without knowing more about the prosecution's strategy." She sighed. "The court is near the other end of the station. We've got a few hours of flying, and I can make it even longer if necessary. They won't start without us."

"Really?"

"Really. You should nap, too."

"I can't. I need to learn more about the court."

CHAPTER NINETY-TWO

The four guards escorted Ruby and Joel to court in a ship so big and thick that no one wore pressure suits. It had a huge rectangular window that cut through the front of it and gave a panoramic view.

A froth of habitat bubbles rose in front of them. "That's the court," one guard said.

Most of the bubbles connected one to another like soap bubbles. Here and there, tubes provided extra joinings. Clear tubes showed trains or robots or people walking in them, others were closed and painted with symbols on the outside of them. The design might have been created by a group of ten-year-old boys working hard to be sure an improbable pile of balls and square boxes and tubes didn't all tumble out into space.

Joel held her hand, watching the pilots and the guards behind them and the approaching structure and Ruby, his eyes scanning and darting from one worry to another while he barely moved. Bless him. She knew him well enough to measure his fear by the extra warmth and twitchiness of his hand, and by the way his features had gone nearly immobile. The more afraid he was, the harder it became for strangers to read any emotions at all in his face.

She leaned against his shoulder. "Comb my hair?"

He looked down at her with a flash of such extreme tenderness she had to blink back a tear. He pulled a comb out of his pocket. He started so gently she had to say, "I'm not dead yet."

He combed harder, but only a little.

He finished just before the ship docked smoothly and they exited to a series of hushed commands from the guards.

Inside the corridors, guards flanked them in front and behind. Joel pushed her smoothly along neat, well-lit corridors lined by a confusing array of windowless doors. Bots scurried along one side in a track, apparently such a commonality here that they had their own side of the corridor while the humans used the other side.

The bustle of the court reminded her how weak she had become. She would have pitied herself three months ago, or six. She couldn't allow that now. Not from herself, not from Joel, not from anyone. Ruby sat as straight as she could. The webling made a small hard spot beneath her upper thighs, a physical reminder of one of the things she needed to protect.

As it became clear that their destination wasn't just inside the doors, Joel asked questions. "Why bring us here in person?"

The muscular guard in front of Joel answered. "Everyone accused of an order two or three crime against the Deeping Rules must answer in person. It has always been that way."

Not always, since the Deeping Rules had never been mentioned in their database. Ix had never spoken of them or seemed to be driven by them. They had been accused of causing harm to others. Ruby had been trying to imagine what they meant, but all she could come up with was that Koren had trumped something up or that they were in trouble for her songs about the Brawl. She expected to see Headman Stevenson as her accuser, except it seemed that he would not use anything as public as the court. He himself had implied he could kill her or own her without anything like this.

Joel asked, "Who will explain what we are accused of?"

"The Judge of the High Council."

"And who is that?"

"That depends on what you are charged with."

The room they entered must be on the top and side of a bubble; the ceiling was a curve of sky, with the long length of the *Diamond Deep* visible in one direction at the bottom of it, yet another reminder of the size of everything here.

The chair rolled over a sharp bump and such a deep pain spiked up Ruby's spine that she moaned.

"Are you all right?" a guard asked.

"It's just the view," she said. "It's magnificent."

The guard did not look like he believed her, but he didn't ask again. As he led them down a ramp, they lost the view of the station, and the open ceiling gave them only stars and a few ships. They were taken near the front of the room to a long table that looked like it should hold more than the two of them. Behind them, seats rose from floor level up, as if the room were a theater. Another table held four people Ruby had never seen. In front of both tables and high up, a rectangular dais looked down on them. The front of the dais was a screen. At the moment, all it displayed was the three rules:

OWN YOURSELF
HARM NO ONE
ADD TO THE COLLECTIVE

Two of the four guards that had led them here stayed and stood on either side of the large table.

People filed into the seats behind them, making hushed noises. Eventually the room was both full and quiet except for the shifting of bodies and a periodic whisper.

The dais and tables in front of them remained cold and big, and empty.

CHAPTER NINETY-THREE

Onor and Evie followed Satyana and Naveen through doors twice as tall as they were. A large sign above the doors proclaimed they were entering the Court of the Deeping Rules. Onor wished he had been able to stay awake and ask more questions. Instead he had joined Evie in improbable sleep and awoken from a place of dreams so distant that reality had been like a slap hitting him as Satyana shook him awake.

He walked through halls of power. It showed in the unnecessary height of the walls, the coldness of the floor, the lack of decoration in a station where most places blazed with color and movement.

The transition from hallways to a courtroom full of people and overlooked by stars felt jarring. It didn't help that when he walked down to the large table in front of the larger and higher dais, he saw Ruby's long red hair spilling over the back of SueAnne's wheelchair.

In spite of the formality all around them, he knelt by Ruby's side and looked closely at her, as if the world had reduced to just Ruby and him. Her face was whiter than he had ever seen it, her cheekbones more prominent. When he looked into her eyes he saw pain and a sadness so deep it nearly made him cry. "Are you okay?" he whispered.

She reached out with one thin arm and pulled his head down beside hers and whispered into the ear that held the earbug, her words breathy but strong. "I'm dying."

He didn't believe it. "Why?"

"The same thing that killed the children. My body doesn't have what it takes to live here."

"We'll take you somewhere else. We can go to Lym, to another station."

"It's too late."

"We can go to the Edge."

She smiled. "So I can become a human spider?"

"No."

She let go of him. He reached for her arm, held it, felt how thin the muscle had become. So much wasting seemed impossible in the weeks since he'd seen her. Maybe he wasn't yet truly awake; maybe it was all a nightmare.

He should have made sure a medical came to Ash right away, the first time he learned they existed. He had fought it. The calculus of credits had driven him to suggest the wrong choices.

"Focus," Ruby said. She looked fierce and later focused. "I don't understand this court yet, but it's our best hope."

He had slept through his chance to learn more about it.

Satyana took his arm and pulled him toward a chair. "They're starting."

He resisted her at first, wanting to hold onto Ruby, but Ruby pushed him gently away. "Let Satyana set us up the way she wants to. It's time to be ready."

After all these years he could read Ruby's desires as well as always, and like always they were only partly focused on him. It didn't matter. In spite of his growing love for Marcelle, for his baby, he would trade with Ruby in a moment and die to let her live. He knew how irrational that was, he knew that Ruby was no saint, that she didn't love him the way he had always loved her, but in this moment and this place he would die for her if he could.

Satyana guided him to a seat between her and Evie. She must have felt his anger because she leaned over and whispered, "Calm down. Speak only when I ask you to. We'll be okay."

He nodded, all that he could manage.

Naveen sat on Satyana's other side. Ruby and her chair were on the other side of Naveen, with Joel on Ruby's far side. He looked entirely out of his element and as angry as Onor felt.

Onor closed his eyes and tried to turn his focus back to his role as guardian and scout. He was the only trained bodyguard here from Ash.

To their left, four people sat a long table like theirs, talking amongst themselves. Behind them, gallery seats that were partly full when he came down toward the table had filled completely and a few people stood along the wall.

The room felt tense and full of undercurrent, but also controlled. If he had to choose who was friend and who was enemy from the faces in the seats behind them, he would fail. If he had to guess, he would say many were enemies.

The trappings of power were clear in front of him. The starry sky arching above a tall dais, a single empty chair next to it, and beside it another dais, as tall, and yet with room for only one person. One table filled out each side of the front, angling toward them. Onor and Ruby and Joel would be able to see every face sitting in judgment on them.

A bell pulled his attention to a woman who appeared behind the chair, waiting for a silence that fell quickly over the full courtroom.

The table on the left filled with the Councilors. They sat in order: Futurist, Architect, Biologist, and Economist. Koren was the only one not there. An empty seat remained. Koren wasn't sitting where she clearly belonged. He knew the others by picture and reputation. All of them were old in spite of their looks, all of them had held their positions for generations. They came in orderly and sober and sat as if it were a familiar, formal dance.

The other table filled with people Onor didn't know, although Ruby gasped twice and leaned toward Satyana, holding a whispered conversation too low for Onor to hear.

Headman Stevenson came in and sat at the small dais. He looked around the room with more interest than the Councilors had, and focused down closely on the tables in front. As his gaze swept across the assembled accused, Onor swore the man's eyes narrowed as he passed over Ruby, and that a small, almost feral smile touched his face for an unguarded moment. Then it was swept back away into a secret place behind his mask of power and position.

The woman made a toneless and amplified announcement. "Presiding judge of the matter of the *Diamond Deep* accusation toward the people of Ash is Koren Nomen."

Koren! Koren as judge? Her name in that position hit him like a punch to the stomach, made him slightly dizzy.

The woman stepped back and Koren stood in her place. Her long white hair hung in a single braid falling down across her left shoulder and she wore a golden gown that matched her golden eyes. She didn't glance around at all, or appear to notice that the room was full. She simply sat, cloaked in power. The whole room gave her power of place and her own demeanor added to it. She knew exactly what she was doing.

He had thought they were coming here to prosecute her. Not to be judged by her. His uneasiness grew even bigger, threatening to swamp his ability to control himself. He took a deep breath and glanced nervously up and down the table.

Loudspeakers proclaimed, "The High Court of the Deeping Rules is now in session."

Perhaps they had been well and truly trapped.

CHAPTER NINETY-FOUR

Ruby flinched as Koren came in and sat at the dais. It was hard not to reach toward the cylinder in the pouch under the chair and touch it, as if there were a way to offer reassurance to the silent beings living under her. A full moment of silence drove home how little Ruby knew about what to expect. The announcer went through the Councilors one by one. Ruby had met all of them at parties, even held polite conversation with the Futurist and the Architect. They didn't look down at the tables, or out at the crowd, or acknowledge being introduced in any other way. They simply sat with composed faces and watched Koren.

The other table interested her more. Satyana leaned over and whispered, "These people self-select and they're different for every trial. They're called the Voice of the Deep. They are as important as the Councilors."

"Who decides if I'm guilty?" Ruby whispered back.

"The Councilors and the Voice advise. The judge decides."

Ruby watched carefully as the individuals who made up the Voice of the Deep were introduced one by one.

Ferrell Yi, the reddish-blue skinned woman who ran the Exchanges. Ruby had seen her a few times, but never talked to her except in passing.

Ramon Paul, the Head of Defense, a man Ruby had met three times, and had rebuffed advances from twice. Probably not a supporter.

Gunnar Ellensson. She was almost willing to bet that Gunnar was a friend.

The announcer gave out one more name. "Winter Ohman." Joel clutched her arm more tightly when he came out; he meant something to Joel. There was no opportunity to ask right now, of course. Then he turned to look directly at Ruby. She recognized him as the man who had been at breakfast and refused to give his name.

Now that everyone was seated, Koren stood and stated, "Read the charges."

The room became eerily and completely quiet, as if hundreds of people were holding their breath.

The woman who had faded into the background came back up and spoke, her words clipped and emotionless. "The Court of the Deeping Rules will evaluate whether or not the people of Ash violated the Do No Harm law by bringing an enemy of the *Diamond Deep* inside our walls. This is a violation of history. As such, the Chief Historian sits in judgment. The specific rule in question in front of the court was born at the end of the Age of Explosive Creation. That rule demands that human consciousness is never to be uploaded into a machine body in whole. Violations of that rule demand death of the creature so created. Anyone providing assistance and succor is subject to imprisonment or banishment."

A soft mutter flew through the courtroom behind them, although no one in front of them reacted.

The knots in Ruby's stomach might be nerves or disease or both. Whatever they were felt twisted and deep and hard inside her. Maybe they were simply the knots of hatred for Koren and her kind, for all of this crazy place called the best place in the Adiamo system, for a world so bored and vicious that they dared to prosecute the *People of the Fire* for being invaded, and for giving Aleesi mercy.

It wasn't justice.

They should have charged her with trying to create a revolution.

In spite of the chair, Ruby could stand, especially with the table right in front of her to hold onto. She almost stood and protested, but Satyana's absolute calm bled into Ruby like ice and warning.

She sat still, waiting.

CHAPTER NINETY-FIVE

Aleesi spoke into Onor's ear, her voice soft but not whispery. "None of you created me," she said. "I need a way to speak to the assembly."

"Why?" he asked her.

"To save you," she said. Her voice had none of the emotion he was used to. She sounded . . . flat.

"What about Ix?"

"Just give me a voice. Trust me."

Onor didn't answer her. It was not his call.

The woman beside Koren asked what sounded like a routine interrogation. "Does anyone in the courtroom question the right of the Councilors or of the Voice of the Deep to counsel the bench, or of Koren to judge this matter in her role as Chief Historian?"

Onor was sure someone should at least *question* Koren's role, but Satyana sat silently beside him, her throat and jaws thick with tension.

Naveen also looked forced still. If Naveen was going to betray them, they were truly lost and friendless.

No one answered the mouthpiece. After what must be the proscribed time with no challenges, she said, "The trial may begin. The prosecutor is Loura Pillar and the speaker for the defense is Satyana Adams. The prosecutor may speak first."

The woman who must be Loura was a complete stranger to him. Even so, he didn't doubt for a moment that Koren's case could be made. Koren surely had a copy of Ix. They probably didn't have Aleesi, not if Ruby and Joel had been able to hide the webling. But Ix would be enough; it had the tapes of the murders in the cargo bay and it had the tapes of them talking to the robot spiders, and probably even of him releasing the brains that held Aleesi from the captured robotic body.

He was right.

All of those things played out in front of the entire courtroom. Even Ruby singing to Aleesi, courting her, trying to make friends. Most damning of all, Aleesi telling Ruby that she was illegal and Ruby telling her that she couldn't help that, she didn't make the rules. The entire courtroom overhead Ruby's exact words, "I am good at breaking rules."

Aleesi whispered in his ear yet again. "Give me voice."

It took him a while to manage a full subvocal sentence in a way he could hope no one noticed. "Maybe we can get you back to the Edge."

"I am already there," she said. "Now give me a voice."

If only he understood more about what was going on. With everything. The Court. Aleesi. Ruby. Damn it. He leaned over and whispered into Satyana's ear. "Aleesi wants to talk."

Satyana's eyes widened a tiny bit, and under the table, her hand touched his thigh, squeezing it. Telling him something. Yes-but-not-now he decided, although he didn't know her well enough to be sure. It had been a message and not a caress, though; his thigh hurt.

Loura Pillar stood after the clips ended. Pale and tall, she had dark hair that hugged her shoulders and shimmered with purple highlights. Her clothes were dark and modest, even down to long sleeves and full-legged pants over dark shoes. Black lace gloves covered her hands. "So you see, Ruby Martin and the people of Ash knowingly brought a being they knew was illegal into the *Diamond Deep*, breaking court precedent and putting the entire station at risk. A being that she kept alive even after it proved harmful on Ruby's own ship, *The Creative Fire*. This being is from a class of intelligences outlawed at the *Deep* long before anyone in this room was alive." She stalked in front of the Councilor's table and the other table, back and forth, her voice loud enough that everyone in the room could undoubtedly hear. Onor imagined her face being broadcast throughout the station. Surely, with Ruby here, the proceedings were being watched.

"This being is not an AI; it is an enslaved human. Slavery is common at the Edge, used by pirates and thieves. Enslaved humans are copied over and over and over, losing fidelity with each copy. Losing *sanity*. Losing what made them human in the first place. This practice creates beings that are abominations. They are not human, not machine intelligences, not robots. This one is a danger to us." She turned and stared at their table, looking first at Evie and then at Onor and then stepping close to Joel and Ruby.

Aleesi continued to demand to speak.

"Quiet," Onor said,

"Give Satyana an earbug."

He did have one. He had thought briefly about giving it to Ruby but she looked too tired to manage one more thing. No, too utterly exhausted. He fished in his pocket and palmed it.

"These people showed nothing but contempt for us. They are not the people who left here, they are the great-great-great grandchildren of those people, and they never learned the lessons of the Age of Explosive Creation. We owe them nothing." The woman was actually sneering and her voice had risen. "We gave them and their unschooled and undisciplined people a chance. We let them into our home and that very day, when they swore to obey our rules, they knew they were willfully breaking them.

"We call for the imprisonment of Ruby Martin and Joel North, for the death of the abomination they brought into our midst, and for penalties upon all of their people."

Ruby stood. Ruby stood in spite of how weak she looked. Joel stood beside her, stoic and furious. Ruby spoke loudly enough for her voice to carry. "No one in Ash except me knew of that rule."

Loura Pillar ignored her.

Murmurs and noise came from behind them, and one or two people clapped. Onor forced himself to look behind them to assess the threat. Most of the people sat in their seats, unreadable. A few looked positively feral, like the worst of the reds used to look before they beat someone when he was small and nothing had yet changed on the *Fire*. Once more he felt surrounded by enemies even though he was sure that many of these people must have come to hear Ruby sing, watched her on their slates, or known about her.

"Sit down," Koren snapped. "You'll have your opportunity to speak."

Ruby protested as Joel almost forced her back into the wheelchair.

If only they had never come here. Onor bumped Satyana's leg with his and fumbled the earbug into her fist.

Loura Pillar sat back down, her face once more a mask.

The mouthpiece spoke. "The defense may now address the advisors."

Satyana stood and walked around the table. As she did so, she brought a hand up to her ear.

Onor smiled.

"Thank you," Aleesi said.

At least she could now bother Satyana directly. He wasn't at all sure Aleesi would get her way, or how such a thing might happen, but the problem was no longer his.

Beside him, a single tear streaked down Evie's face from time to time. He wished there was something to be done with her, some way to put her someplace safe and let her cry her pain out. But they were far from Ash. He whispered to her. "Was Aleesi talking to you, too?"

"She told me it would all end up all right."

"That's all?"

Evie nodded.

Satyana's words drew his attention. "We will call a number of witnesses. Our argument is simple on its face. First, Ruby spoke correctly if out of turn. She made this choice alone. Second, the Deeping Rule that Ruby is accused of breaking has not been broken: there has been no harm done. Our legal system allows for this."

Loura interrupted. "At a lower level of infraction."

Satyana stared at Koren.

Eventually, Koren gave the tiniest of nods.

"Third, Ruby Martin has followed all three of the Deeping Rules. She has taken responsibility for herself and for more than herself, for the collective of the people who came with her." Satyana pointed at Joel. "Along with Joel North, they have started to succeed when they themselves were harmed seriously by those who greeted them."

Koren's only reaction to Satyana's words was a bare and desultory nod, as if to say, "Go on, I'm bored."

Satyana herself had gone quiet, and he was willing to bet she was listening to Aleesi.

Perhaps Koren didn't think they had enough to prove her wrong, or maybe she was sure that her position as judge would protect her. They had Satyana and Winter Ohman and Naveen all on their side. Maybe. Hopefully. Winter Ohman had set this up. He glanced at their table from time to time, but he never looked directly at Onor. Afraid to give away that he had met with them?

"Fourth, the being Aleesi poses no danger to us."

Even though something in the hushed tone of the audience's reaction and murmurs at this last proclamation of Satyana's turned up his sense of danger, Onor kept watching in front of him. The Councilors' faces remained stoic. The

Voice of the Deep showed slightly more reaction: Ferrell Yi turned to the head of Defense, her face touched with surprise and worry. Gunnar Ellensson looked thoughtfully at Ruby, almost as if there was a game they played together and she had just produced an unexpected move.

Onor wondered if Gunnar was friend or enemy.

Onor was once again reduced to watching as Satyana pulled her first trick out: she called Naveen as a witness. Naveen established that he had, in fact, copied Ix from the *Fire*. Satyana called on Ix, pulling up a version that Naveen stated was exactly as he had copied it, with no interaction with the people of Ash after the exodus. So before Onor had been given a copy to carry about in his pocket like gold.

This Ix verified that Ruby didn't publicly share the knowledge that bringing Aleesi here was illegal, even with Joel. It also verified that Ruby was not entirely truthful: KJ knew what Aleesi had said about the law. It did show that when Onor carried the webling up and away from the spider body, he had not spoken to it.

Gunnar and Ferrell Yi both looked at him then, their faces solemn and cold. He did his best to look quiet and confident.

It was good to hear Ix's voice, to feel comforted by something so familiar. But the real Ix, the Ix that had been at all of the morning meetings and shared the webling with Aleesi, would be in true trouble.

Ruby's accusers had not called witnesses; they had played media. Ix could be questioned in this context, and Loura Pillar asked, "Ix, were you allowed to repeat or play private conversation for others? Conversation behind the closed doors of people's own habs?"

"No."

"And you are designed to do what?"

"Protect *The Creative Fire*."

"Including her crew?"

"Yes."

"So you are unwilling to tell us what Ruby Martin may or may not have shared with Joel North or KJ may or may not have shared with others?"

"I can relay anything they said to each other in public. They did not speak much of Aleesi at all, and never told others that it is an illegal being."

"Nothing further." Loura sat down again, looking pleased.

Satyana acted as though Ix's interview was no setback at all. "The ship's AI has confirmed that Ruby knew this, as Ruby herself confirmed. The ship's AI has not confirmed that anyone else knew, simply that it is possible others knew. This is hardly damning. Of more immediate importance—and here I will put together what I listed as second and fourth—of more immediate importance, the rule 'do no harm' remains unbroken. There is no reason to be here at all. There is no record of the being interacting with any of our AIs, our people, our systems, or our robots. There is no trace of the being inside of our system.

"It is doing no harm."

Satyana stood in silence for a moment, facing the dais, hands behind her back and tugging on her long brown braid, giving people time to think about what she had just said before she continued. "I have no witnesses to call on the point of whether or not Ruby has done any harm. I would have to call the whole ship to prove no harm was done to anyone, so I ask you to call someone who can claim that Ruby's bringing this being on board has done anyone any harm at all."

A moment of silence ensued, a moment that Onor felt sure was full of Koren and Loura speaking together in the same way that he and Aleesi could talk to each other. Oddly, Aleesi had been completely silent since he had given the earbug to Satyana.

Loura spoke. "It is not necessary to a conviction in this case. The rule of no human enslavement is core to our protection of humanity aboard this station. Ruby Martin has violated that rule by allowing a human slave to enter here and even worse, by allowing one from a place that is known to be an enemy of the *Diamond Deep*, a nest of pirates who have attacked our ships time and time again, a warren of melded humans and machines that have allowed and fostered change until they are unrecognizable."

Ruby and Joel whispered together, Ruby's voice the louder of the two. She stood again, something Satyana couldn't see since Ruby was behind her.

Koren spoke to Satyana. "In your role as Councilor, I believe you are doing a poor job of controlling your client."

CHAPTER NINETY-SIX

So much rage coursed through Ruby that it was easy to stand, to face this woman who had done irreparable damage to her people. Joel had exacted a whispered promise that she would let Satyana choose whether or not she spoke, so she watched Satyana closely, trying to look far calmer than she felt. Enough time passed for the room to quiet before Satyana turned to her and said, "Please feel free to speak on your behalf."

Some magic of the room made her words come out amplified when they hadn't before, as if this time she was being allowed to talk. Her voice shook. "You cannot judge regarding slavery while you have the Brawl. It was described to me as a place of economic misfortune, a necessary deterrent to unsupportable growth, but it is enslavement. I have had Ix look up the numbers, and 95 percent of the people who go to the Brawl die there. One in twenty lives and comes back to create a useful life. One of my friends was killed there this morning."

She paused as much to regain strength as for effect.

"I did not enslave Aleesi—the being you are accusing me of harboring. If that is what happened to her, then that happened long before I came here. I simply chose not kill her, to show mercy." She paused for breath. "You must look deeply at yourselves and your choices."

Loura Pillar interjected, "We are not on trial."

Ruby took a deep breath and tried to center herself. "Everyone is always on trial. Leaders in particular are always on public trial. Entertainers are watched by fans. What we do matters." She stood still, then, her arms shaking, her thighs beginning to shake. She should be in Satyana's place, defending them all, defending Aleesi. She had just lost Haric, and she wasn't going to lose anyone else.

She had to wait now, she could tell from the look on Satyana's face, mixed amusement and warning.

Satyana was playing for a bigger game than Ruby. She had never hidden that fact.

Loura Pillar interjected. "May we rebut?"

Murmuring from the table where the Voice of the Deep sat suggested this was an irregular request.

Koren inclined her head to grant it.

A low murmur rose from the audience, subsiding slowly.

Satyana looked furious, but made no move to stop them from whatever they were going to do. "We call Min Carson."

Ruby sat back down, her breath exhaling in a long slow bout of pain. Beside her, Joel whispered, "Those lying women," so softly that she barely heard him above her own breathing. When she could lift a hand to put on his arm, he was so stiff he might as well have been made of metal.

A few moments passed while Min walked stiffly to the dais, a man in uniform following her like a mix between an escort and a guard. She sat down and looked around the room, her face pale.

"I'm sorry Min," Loura said, "We were hoping we would not have to call you up here. Surely it will be hard for you to speak against one of your own."

Min didn't respond. She wore the white of the whispering women, the same white as the cloak tucked around Ix and Aleesi. It made her look small and plain among so many powerful people, almost like a child. Perhaps too plain; almost pure. Ruby willed Min to look at her, to give Ruby even a tiny chance to make eye contact and convince her that whatever she was about to say could not possibly benefit Ash.

The chance didn't come.

Ruby struggled to sit as still as possible, her hands clenching and unclenching under the table to provide a channel for her anger. Loura's black dress and lacy black gloves looked like quite a contrast as she interrogated Min in her white on white outfit, with the visible red scar on her face. Loura: "Ruby was one of you once. In the same social class as you?"

"Yes."

"A class of workers who earned air and food by doing what they were told to do."

"Yes."

"A place perhaps more cruel than the Brawl."

"I have never been to the Brawl."

"People are afforded air and food without having to work. Does that sound easier than the outer levels of *The Creative Fire*?"

Because there is no work! No opportunity! But it was not up to Ruby to answer. Min took a moment, but she said, "Yes."

"Ruby broke the laws of *The Creative Fire* and started a revolution to change things. And you followed."

"We did. That's how I got the scar on my face."

"Once you arrived here, why didn't you fix the scar on your face?"

"Because all of our credit goes to the collective."

"That sounds like slavery to me. What do you think?"

Did you ever ask? Ruby had no recollection, although she could guess how SueAnne would have answered.

Min's voice came out thin and small, amplified enough for everyone to hear the touch of sadness in it. "I would have liked to fix my scar."

Min had never told her. She had even seemed proud of the scar.

"And how did Ruby treat you? After the revolution?"

"She didn't. We hardly saw her. She was Joel's lover, and derived all of her power from him, and took charge of many things."

Ruby stiffened. Min had seen Ruby act on her own, seen Ruby argue with Joel, seen Ruby in a thousand roles. Wasn't that what the whispering women did—witness Ruby?

"Sometimes she came down to sing, to talk to us, to greet us. But she was never one of us again." Min finally looked at Ruby and Joel. "We followed them. We wanted to hold them accountable and to be sure that we all knew what was happening to us in on the *Diamond Deep*. Joel was cruel to us and kept us out of many places, and Ruby almost never talked to us. We might have been invisible."

Satyana glanced at Ruby as if to ask if any of Min's words were true.

That depended on how you chose to interpret nuances. But there was no time to have a conversation with Satyana, or with anyone. Beside her, Joel remained stiff. Although she knew his iron control would keep him from doing it, she could feel how he wanted to stand up and rebuff Min. He had always hated the whispering women.

He didn't understand them at all.

"Who is us?" Loura said, "you keep referring to an us. To more than just you."

"All of the women who lost people in Ruby's war."

Ruby hadn't quite put that together. Min had never mentioned a loss. Hugh's death drove Lya's decisions, her loss of sanity, her hatreds. She should have made time to understand what drove Min.

"And you accompanied Ruby on her tours."

"Yes."

"What happened on those tours? Did Ruby represent Ash's needs?"

Min had stopped looking at any of them from the *Fire*, had fixed her eyes on Loura.

Satyana spoke. "It is unclear what the prosecution is trying to establish or how it affects their case."

"I have allowed it," Koren snapped.

Min answered. "Ruby chased power on her trips. She spent time with Naveen, who sponsored her and who has a significant following. Without him, her concerts would have meant nothing. No one would have come."

Ruby froze.

"And she followed Gunnar Ellensson out of the room at the party he threw for her. She protested her innocence, but I have no way of knowing what she may have done with him."

Joel flinched and withdrew his arm from under her hand, leaving her cold. Ruby glanced at his face. He didn't look back, and he was so still he could be stone or metal.

Min. Min, why are doing this? We talked about that. KJ was with me!

CHAPTER NINETY-SEVEN

As soon as Min accused him, Onor glanced at Gunnar Ellensson. He looked amused, maybe deeply amused. But Onor couldn't read the look. *Of course she wanted to sleep with me? Everyone does. I'm rich.* Or maybe *You don't know what you are talking about.*

Gunnar stood up. His seat was about ten meters away from Koren, close enough for him to overshadow her as he stood, his eyes at a level above hers, although if she stood they would not be.

Koren remained calm.

Min glared at the shipping magnate, as if he were truly evil and beneath her. Onor had never much liked the whispering women, but he had taken Ruby's side instead of Joel's, had chosen to believe they wouldn't really hurt anyone. Ruby had once even called them a blessing as they reminded her to pay attention to everyone, and they reminded her how much fighting hurt and how much she didn't want to do it again if she could help it.

Gunnar cleared his throat.

"I will speak to you when it is time for advice," Koren said.

"I thought the audience might like to know that Ruby Martin refused my advances."

Koren's dark skin made it hard for Onor to read her emotions, and she was too far away for him to really see what her golden eyes had to say about her. But he could read frustration in her voice, and maybe even the slightest touch of fear. If it was there, she didn't show it. "If you speak out of turn again, I will have you removed from the room."

Gunnar Ellensson sat down, but he looked quite happy with himself.

"Are you finished with the interruption?" Satyana asked. "This has not proven harm."

Loura smiled as if she had won a prize. "I am completely finished proving that Ruby Martin has a habit of harming her own people."

Ruby let out a small cry of pain, and he looked over to see that Joel was holding her close, stroking her cheek while her face had gone white and shiny with sweat. The pain—the cry—had been deeper than a simple cut with words. He had seen Ruby manage those over and over. Whatever pain caused that cry was physical, and deep, and true.

It dawned on Onor that the reason Satyana was doing this now—allowing it or maybe had even architected it— was that Ruby would be dead soon, and then it would be harder. A dead woman could be represented any way you like. Two sides—or more—could argue about Ruby's choices and Ruby's intent, and even Ruby's actions, forever. Ruby wouldn't be alive to defend her reputation.

He actually couldn't imagine how Min managed to hold her head up as she walked away.

He did not hit women, but Min had made him want to hit something. Anything.

Somewhere in the upper audience, doors opened and Onor heard whispered conversations. He glanced over his shoulder, catching a brief glimpse of the back of Min's head before it was swallowed by a small crowd of people.

Koren was the one who sat in judgment, but Satyana had hinted the timing was Satyana's. Simply because she knew Ruby would die soon? Or for some other reason?

Onor wanted Marcelle so badly he could smell her, the mixed scents of creche and school and the lightly flavored tea she drank now instead of stim. The tea smelled like flowers.

And then the seat next to him was full of her, and she really did smell like he remembered, and he had her in his arms. She shook, and his arms helped the shaking subside.

He heard a voice, then another, and looked up to see KJ kneeling beside Joel, Jali standing behind Ruby, hands on her thin and bony shoulders, and Lya standing just a step back. An impossible, welcome sight. Even Lya. Surely she wouldn't be here if it was just to say what Min had just said.

Satyana addressed Koren. "I have additional witnesses to call."

"These people were not on the list," Koren stated. "They must go and sit in the audience when they are done."

"Min was not on the list."

"Min is not sitting at the prosecution's table."

"I will call them all, one by one."

Once more Koren exhibited the bored voice and bored face with a hint of fear on it. Maybe a deeper hint. Maybe there was reason to hope. She said, "Very well, but when each is done they must join the audience. While they wait to be called they must be silent."

Onor hoped Satyana would call Marcelle last. He wanted her to stay by him as long as possible. He had been happy she was safe in Ash, but now nowhere on the *Diamond Deep* seemed safe for anyone from the *Fire*. He watched as KJ testified that he had been with Ruby and Gunnar the whole time, and that nothing sexual had passed between them. He even stated that they talked about how unfair the Brawl was, a comment that made Koren roll her golden eyes.

Allen spoke of the fact that he ran the bar, and that Ruby was there from time to time, and that she often met with people from all places in the *Fire* there. "Ruby drew people to the bar when she was there. They came to talk to her from all over. And when she was gone, when Naveen took her on tour, the bar was full of people who came just to watch her. Our people loved her."

It was a more emotionally poignant speech than Onor could have imagined Allen making.

To his disappointment, Marcelle was next. Before she left she turned to whisper to him. "I love you."

"I love you," he whispered back.

Marcelle spoke of Ruby's attention to detail, of how she may not have been physically in the outer regions of the *Fire* much, but that she talked and thought about her old people often.

After she was done, Marcelle came back to the table and took Evie with her. Such a Marcelle thing to do, to notice something that had to be done and to simply do it.

Now, as far as he could tell, there were only the risks remaining. Lya, who might be sane enough to take their side and might not. Aleesi, who was herself accused and who he still both trusted and didn't trust.

CHAPTER NINETY-EIGHT

atyana started by stunning the courtroom, and Ruby, into silence. "I have a message from Aleesi. She left it with me just moments ago. I am to play it for you."

"There are many copies of me," Aleesi's voice said. "But there is only one of me here. I am lonely here, and do not need to stay. Since my very presence has endangered a people that I respect, I have removed myself from this place. We are taught this—how to kill ourselves if we are captured. I have done that. I am no longer on your station or on your ship. You can verify this by testing the webling that once held my heart. Ruby can show it to you. It has the colony's copy of Ix, but I am no longer there. I have destroyed my own soul for the sake of Ruby Martin."

Ruby took in a deep breath, sharp. She didn't want to believe it, although like Haric's death, it was true. She should have noticed something—her chair turning light underneath her as Aleesi did whatever a machine-girl did to stop being.

Aleesi's voice continued. "I was never a spy. I never meant to be a spy. I never meant you harm. I am not what you think. Not a slave. I am one of many free beings, and all of us together are one being. This is the kind of change that your society has oppressed. It had made us stronger at the Edge. This is something that you should think about—the joy of change rather than the fear of change. But for now, I have chosen to leave you rather than live surrounded by this fear, and rather than see people I have come to love destroyed by that fear."

Silence fell over the room.

Ruby felt this new loss as a choking clot of pain in her throat and dug her nails into her knees to maintain control.

Satyana apparently felt no reason to add to anything Aleesi had said. Instead, she kept her head bowed for a time, a show of respect. And then stood up straight and looked Lya in the eye. "Your turn."

Ruby held her breath as Lya walked to the public seat. The last time she had seen her, it had felt like they found common ground for the first time in years, sharing memories of deaths that were now far away. But that was one encounter out of many.

As Lya sat down, she turned to look at Ruby, anger painted all over her features.

Ruby shrank into her chair, hating it yet again. Hating her body, which needed a break, needed sleep and food and for the pain to stop. This felt like having her whole life on trial, like seeing all of the ways people had seen her over time. Her mistakes were being displayed for her dying soul to contemplate.

Satyana asked Lya, "Were you Min's leader?"

Lya shook. Ruby could see it even from this distance. "Yes."

"Why did you start the whispering women?"

"That's only what Ruby and Joel called us." Lya glared at Joel for just a moment, a damning glance. "We set ourselves up to be watchers. Every government needs watchers."

The crowd behind them reacted to that, murmurs of quiet assent.

"What were you watching for?"

"Peace. We wanted peace. We had all lost people we loved, and it had seemed that Ruby threw their lives away. We thought she didn't care."

Ruby winced.

Satyana said, "You are using the past tense. *You thought she didn't care. What do you think now?*"

Lya's eyes had gone wide, and she looked around the room. She whispered, the whisper picked up and amplified like Min's voice before her, a susurration that filled the room. "She cares. Ruby cares very much." A tear streaked down Lya's face, out of place, and then she turned away, as if there were a threat directed at her.

Ruby looked behind her, at the audience.

They were on their feet.

All of them.

They had all stood silently and they all directed their gazes toward Koren. Satyana had clearly been expecting this. Gunnar Ellensson stood as well. Beside him, Winter Ohman also stood.

Satyana said, "I have a last witness for you."

Naveen stood. "I have created a tape put together from images that I obtained from Ix, from things people have sent me, from news that a dead boy brought me. I have proof that these people not only did their best to stay within our laws, to find a life here where they could contribute, but that they were in fact stolen from."

The audience stamped their feet.

"And that Koren Nomen herself oversaw the theft, and that she set up the people of Ash to fail, that she set up this trial when it began to look like they might *not* fail. I can even prove she killed to protect her secret. She is guilty of breaking every one of the Deeping Rules."

Koren had finally reacted with something besides boredom. She was on her feet, and she yelled out, "This will not happen. Councilors do not stand trial."

Satyana had to wait for a long time for the room to grow quiet.

When it did, she said, "You yourself drew us back to the Age of Explosive Creation. At that time, all of the Councilors were put on trial, and all of them were thrown out. We the people of the *Diamond Deep* have the right to question you. We have the right to hold you accountable. We have the right to demand that our needs are met by our leaders."

Koren looked directly at Ruby. "It's all your fault. I should never have allowed you to tour."

"No," Satyana said, "It is all your fault. Ruby was simply a new lens to look at our world through. Others have been working this for a long time, and now you and the rest of the Councilors, and even the Headman, will be questioned. You are simply first."

Ruby watched carefully, the shifts around them making her both more and less afraid. She glanced at the Councilors' bench to find each of them surrounded by at least two people, barred from standing up and leaving.

A woman's voice sounded throughout the room. "This is highly irregular, please sit-" and then it was silenced.

No one sat.

The audience stamped their feet again.

Winter stepped down and moved to the bare center of the room, so that all four tables surrounded him and Koren looked down on him. Her golden eyes were snapping with anger and fear, and full of determination. If were possible for Koren to kill with a look, Winter would be dead.

He stood in the middle of the room, and he proclaimed—proclaimed was the only word Ruby could think of for the tone of his voice—"The Voice of the Deep are encouraged to advise on a trial. We do so now. We advise that this trial is declared null and void. We can show you all of the evidence that we have." He turned slightly so he could look at Koren. "But she knows what it is, and she will not want you to see it. That doesn't matter—it is now streaming through every device on the station. Everyone on the *Diamond Deep* may watch it now."

Ruby glanced at Naveen, who wore the wide grin of the undefeated.

She felt it then. The success. Her part in it.

The fact that it would go on, and on. That the trials ahead would change everything.

She grinned and she stood, holding onto the table. Joel stood beside her, helping her stay upright, her strength in this moment of victory. No, it was not entirely her moment, not really much of anything to do with her except that she had been a catalyst.

But it was a good moment.

She found Lya still seated near Koren, and gestured her over to join her, and Lya stood on her other side so that Joel and Lya together held her up.

Joel didn't even complain about the presence of the whispering woman.

PART SEVEN

CODA

CHAPTER NINETY-NINE

Ruby sat in her own bed, propped up on pillows. Joel sat beside her, close enough for her to feel his biceps and the sharp angle of his left hip. The medical robot rested in the corner across the room from them both. "Tell it to leave. Send it to Marcelle and let her find some use for it."

Joel glanced at the robot. "Leave."

It ignored him. "See?" he said.

"Call Satyana and tell her to tell it to leave."

"I will."

"After I'm dead?"

"Soon." He reached a hand up and caressed her cheek and then let the hand fall to her hair, which had become dry and unruly. Something the robot gave her dried her out, and she filled herself over and over with water, letting it energize her tissues and ease her dry mouth. Right now a glass of water rested in her left hand, cold and reassuring, as if it were a moment of life.

She stared at the ceiling and enjoyed the rough feel of Joel's fingers combing slowly through tangles. "What next? What happens now?"

"We're still counting up," he said. "Winter is a great help."

He actually sounded as if he liked Winter Ohman. She couldn't remember anyone else from the *Diamond Deep* that Joel had actually liked. The idea that he might have a friend warmed her.

It was hard to talk so she listened. "We'll know what we have soon, and we'll choose a place to go. But we'll stay in Ash until we really know what to do. Even all of the credit we have now isn't unlimited."

He sounded so serious. He shouldn't be. It would be easier for him if he didn't paint the world so black and white. She sipped some water so that she could talk. "That's not what I meant. What happens to us when we die?"

"I don't know. It used to be that we were shot out into the stars."

That still wasn't what she meant, but she could go with it. "Can you still do that? Can I go out into the stars?" Maybe she could find her own dead out there. Nona. Hugh. Owl Paulie. Haric.

Aleesi.

"I'm sure we can arrange that for you."

"Will you see me off? Will you sing for me?"

"Of course I will."

CHAPTER ONE HUNDRED

As soon as he heard, Onor went home. He found Marcelle in their rooms, tears streaming down her face. She looked up at him. "I didn't think she could really die."

He hadn't either, not really. It had only been two weeks since their trial. The other trials, the other changes, were still under way. The people of the *Fire* gathered in the bar every night to watch summaries of the day's proceedings, the same way they used to gather to watch Ruby sing. It kept him busy, kept Evie busy. "At least Ruby got to hold Nona before she died."

"Yes." Marcelle came to him for a hug, and they watched the baby, sleeping. "At least Nona may not have to die."

"Sure she will."

"Not for a very long time."

The baby didn't care that they were admiring her perfect fingers and toes. She slept peacefully, as if there was nothing wrong with the world, and there never would be anything wrong with the world.

ABOUT THE AUTHOR

BRENDA COOPER lives in the Pacific Northwest, which is peopled with very many authors, perhaps because it is full of perfect writing weather. She writes science fiction and fantasy stories and novels, writes non-fiction and delivers talks about the future, rides bikes, and walks dogs. She also manages technology for a local government.

For more information, please head to www.brenda-cooper.com and www.rubyssong.com.

ACKNOWLEDGMENTS

Every book is a group effort.

Writers help each other. In this case specifically, thanks go to all of those who read the first draft at the Wellspring workshop in Lake Geneva, particularly to Grá Linnea and Kelly Swails who read the full manuscript, gave me great advice and didn't pull punches. Thanks to Brad Beaulieu who organized. Also to my two best and oldest friends, Linda Merkens and Gisele Peterson, who read as readers, and to John Pitts, who has read almost all of my work in draft. To my dad, who reads my manuscripts and comments brilliantly. Every science fiction writer should have a father who is a real rocket scientist.

There are songs in this book. I am not able to sing (well, when I'm alone I often sing, but other people don't like my voice much). So to prepare for this, I attended two songwriting workshops led by the talented Chris Williamson. Any mistakes in the songs are mine and I appreciate her patience trying to teach songwriting to a woman who can't hear notes.

I can't say how pleased I am to have Lou Anders champion this book. He is one of our finest editors, and a fabulous person as well.

John Picacio created more than a book cover when he drew Ruby for *The Creative Fire*. He created an iconic piece of art that I kept on my computer screen and referred to while writing this book. He is a master of his craft.

As always, thanks to Eleanor Wood, my agent. These are shifting times in the industry, and Eleanor has been steady.

My family's support is priceless beyond measure. Writers are not the easiest folk to live with. We are often somewhere else—either physically or in our heads. Thank you, Toni and Katie, Nixie, Sasha, and Cricket.

Books are written to be read. Thanks to everyone who has read any of my work, and particular thanks to those of you have commented on it to me.